A BROKEN
CIRCLE

A BROKEN CIRCLE

Contact Information:
www.cliveparkinsonauthor.com
cliveparkinson1@gmail.com

Cover design, typography, photography and typesetting by Clive Parkinson.

Main body text set in Adobe Garamond Pro. Headers, footers and pagination set in Good Times; also incorporated within the cover title design. LTC Remington Typewriter Pro used for setting typewriter text.

ISBN: 9798326565259

First published, independently, in 2024
10 9 8 7 6 5 4 3 2 1

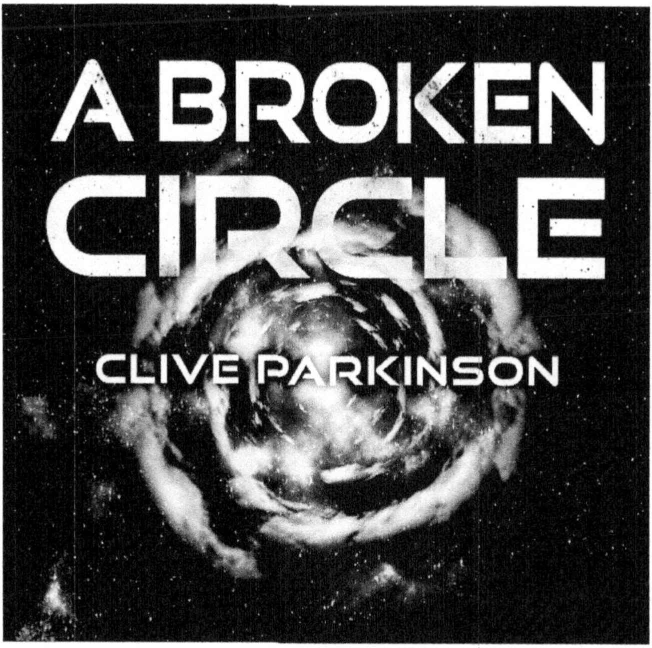
A BROKEN CIRCLE
CLIVE PARKINSON

For those who engage in forward motion,
allowing their minds to travel in any direction

CONTENTS

ACKNOWLEDGEMENTS

My eternal thanks to family, friends and all those who inspired me, *both human and non-human,* to begin, to joyfully surrender to and complete this journey.

01

Dawning

One step in front of the other; both rock face and new challenges met with fear, adrenaline and sheer determination pumping from mind and muscle. Letting go of the old and accepting the new. Family and friends; lost and found.

Peaty soil gave way between my fingers as I tried in vain to pull myself up; crumbling from my grasp, paralleling the loss of loved ones I would endeavour to hold onto in the weeks, months and years ahead. Often, we are oblivious to what can take a long time to form; such things possess the potential to disintegrate in seconds before our very eyes. How did I end up here? What contribution had I made to a series of events which ultimately led me to this predicament, this forty-foot fall? How did I survive this? Will I survive this?

I need some rest, my arms are burning but I'm afraid to let go, one more pull upwards and I can reach the next ledge. What a view... pity I ache too much to enjoy it.

The mangled mess that is, once was, my top of the line Swiss made mountain bike does not add anything of beauty to the vista below. Neither does the trickle of warm crimson metallic collecting over my eye and dripping onto my t-shirt as I gently take off my bike helmet. I've got to sit down; my head is pounding now. It's starting to get dark, I'll have to stay here for the night... too tired... too dangerous to make any more progress in the fading light. I'm not cold because of the unusual heat wave of extremely high temperatures we've been having for the past four months. That coupled with what seems like non-stop rain, our climate feels more subtropical than temperate oceanic.

From this ledge you would swear you were looking down upon a pocket rainforest in the Blue Mountains near Sydney, Australia - not the glacially eroded valleys surrounded by the granite mountains of Eastern Hibernia. I'm fighting sleep now but with the darkening of the day and of my mind I can no longer focus on a way out of here, or an escape from thoughts predicated by fear of what's to come, loyalty to my friends and love for my wife and young children, Kyle's thoughts dominated and held him ransom.

A loud shrill cry and the pungent aroma of what smells like a combination of aniseed and roasting meat suddenly awakens him. Feeling faint he lurches forward to start running again until the realisation of where he is pulls him back from the precipice and either certain death from falling or from meeting one of *"them"*. The noise dissipates, they've gone and he is sort of safe again... for now. His watch broke in the fall and since they came there has only been a poor phone signal at best and dwindling power sources to charge anything.

I don't know what time it is; feels like dawn is not too far off but you can never quite tell these days, climate change was the excuse they gave us for decades. We all believed the forecasts the government meteorological office had supplied to us via the TV weatherman with a friendly smile and a wink. The poor fools we elected thought they were protecting us from them, that we were better off not knowing. We either just accepted their explanations with vitriol or shrugged our shoulders with apathetic neglect. Why should we believe anything said by the powers that be, the age-old apathy we all express towards governments who are just in it for themselves? The elected leaders didn't know what was going on, they really had no more a clue than you or I, thought Kyle mockingly, internally.

***

Four months previously...

I've got to get these posts buffered for the week. Next, I need to collect Saoirse from school and Ellen from kindergarten, make their lunch, some website maintenance, occupy the kids - jigsaw for Ellen and bead craft for Saoirse, email designs to the printer and then... and then... why is it so damn hot? thought Kyle.

Later that afternoon... Kyle turns off his computer and goes to the kitchen for a drink of water. As he opens the kitchen door he is confronted by an enormous black mass covering the patio door, almost blocking out all sunlight.

"Saoirse... Ellen! Are you alright?" asks Kyle.

"Yesss Dad-dy! Turn on the light... it's getting dark...

it's nearly night time!" answers Saoirse with a tired almost southern drawl; in a trance focussing on threading a pink sparkly bead and completely oblivious to the pulsating dark mass on the patio door window.

It's only three in the afternoon. As I edge forward, the black mass seems alive and is now emitting a clicking, whistling sound. Where have I heard this repetitive sound before? Cicada... when I was travelling across Australia - that's it! There are hundreds if not thousands of these insects blocking out the daylight. I first heard of these fifteen years ago while on a year "finding myself".

This is not the right climate nor the right part of the world for these "noisy little blighters", Kyle's mind rebuked.

Kyle drags the patio door open hard and half of the heaving mass falls off the window onto the step. In doing so, the kitchen is simultaneously filled with sunlight, protests from his daughters that *"it's too bright!"* and a muffled howl from their pet beagle, Mister Waggles.

Kyle steps out into the garden, tip-toeing as he crunches past the fallen cicada to read the garden thermometer and taps the reading in disbelief.

That can't be right... forty-five Celsius? This isn't Australia. I better turn on the TV to check the weather forecast, double check the weather app on my phone and look back at the garden thermometer. There's news footage of crowds flocking to the beach, all of them smiling and eating ice creams.

Here we go, the news reporter spilling out the usual rhetoric of how she wished she hadn't already booked her summer holiday abroad this year, how she should have had a "staycation".

Enough of that, turn it off... too late, she still has the opportunity to impart one final note of wisdom:

"Sure, isn't this the best country in the world... where else would you want to be going? If only we could have great weather all the time, if only we could put a roof over it!", mimicked Kyle, inside his skull.

***

Three months previously...

"Honey!... Are you ready yet? The kids are in the car and I've got the cooler box in the boot with cold chicken sandwiches, lemonade and a few beers for you, I can drive back," said Kyle's wife Crystal, wilfully.

Every day it seems to get hotter and hotter. This is not just a heat wave, things are different... something has changed. Last week while mowing the lawn I started to feel light headed, resulting from... I thought... spending too much time in front of the computer, lack of sleep and this damn heat.

I lay down on the grass to rest for a few minutes when I feel something slither across my foot. In the corner of my eye I see an orange brown ring around a large dark eye, a snake was flicking its forked tongue out smelling the air near my left ankle.

Instinct told me no sudden movements, hold my breath and reach slowly for the garden rake to my right side. Silently yet expeditiously I swing the rake almost 180 degrees and pin the snake to the ground. Neither the Eastern Brown Snake nor myself were hurt; although what with the violent thrashing of the snake as if someone was cracking it like a whip - I was not going to let go for fear of being bitten. Memories return of years ago whilst hiking through long dry grass in the Blue Mountains near Sydney; I saw snake skin that had been shed and caught on the long grass. It was blowing gently in the evening breeze, calming and hypnotic yet this natural flag was a warning for me to be very careful of where I tread, thought Kyle.

"Crystal! Crystal, come quick!" shouts Kyle.

Without panic, this woman whose strength he never doubted, is a determined business woman and never backs down from anyone, has also been known to shriek at the sight of a mere house spider; upon said occasions would summon Kyle to dispose of the eight-legged fiend. She walks calmly and quietly over and decapitates the snake. Silence fills the air. There are no birds calling, there is no wind blowing, there is definitely no serpent hissing.

Crystal sits down beside Kyle, takes the rake from his hand and replaces it with a bottle of cool pale ale.

"I can't stand this heat," said Crystal in a long drawn-out, tired voice.

Kyle remained silent; enjoying the calm that the weighty feel of the ice-cold beer bottle rolling in the palm of his hand imbued upon him.

"Let's head to the mountains next weekend... it's gotta be cooler up there, right?" she asked, raising a right brow.

"Yep, let's do that," replied Kyle when his momentary meditation was fractured and he was summoned back to the present.

Crystal, without another word, picked herself up and tossed the snake into the garden waste bin.

***

Two months previously...

Every weekend for the past month we've been trying to go up to the mountains to escape this heat but something always crops up. First, it was Saoirse's sixth birthday party with obligatory bouncy castle, indoor adventure play hire and party loot bags. What is it with kids these days, more specifically - their parents? Are they all preparing their little darlings for movie award ceremonies? Today it's jellies and chocolate eggs, tomorrow it'll be caviar and eggs of the diamond encrusted variety. Two weeks ago we all got hit pretty hard with yet another "Flu". It has only just cleared and I swear I've got to get out of the house and go somewhere cooler this weekend, thought Kyle.

The following morning Kyle reluctantly woke at a few minutes past six. Stretching his legs out from under the duvet onto the wooden bedroom floor, he tip-toed past the baby monitor (a parental survival tool still used for peace of mind even though Ellen and Saoirse are now four and six) and his still sleeping wife to hopefully have an undisturbed cup of coffee before packing the car for their mountain trip.

Two hours later they were in the car heading up past Silver Mountain reservoir near Glenrock. Windows open, cool breeze in his face, volume turned right up to eleven allowing one of Kyle's favourite band's tracks to echo through the valley below; finally they were on their way.

There are very few moments in Kyle's life nowadays when he can think clearly, or at least be able to have the space and time to think, without distraction. Driving was one of them, cycling was another. *There's something about forward motion that allows the mind to travel in any direction,* he often thought.

Apart from the stifling heat, they were experiencing other strange natural phenomena, locally strange that is. In the sense that here on the fringes of western Europe there have been tropical storms on and off for the past two months coupled with heat patterns usually associated with Australia while the antipodes were under a metre, and counting, of snow. The latest natural phenomenon, occurring almost daily now - are sinkholes. First making news and in the general public's consciousness after the tragic death of a Florida man when a one hundred foot deep sinkhole appeared beneath his house and swallowed him alive while still in his bed. People were led to believe that sinkholes are essentially holes created by water drainage and erosion. These phenomena whether natural or not, can sometimes be the result of human activity. What if they were the result of non-human activity?

Car parked and with food hamper hand in hand, Kyle and Crystal walked across the gravel path with their two little ones hop skipping to a small grassy clearing that looked eastwards out towards the sea. Crystal spread out a large rectangular piece of soft woollen tartan so they could all dine alfresco in comfort. That picnic blanket was a gift for Crystal, a long time ago. Long before children, long before this heat, long before the arrival of unwanted neighbours; an eager stroll past the snow dusted Molly Malone statue and around the corner along Suffolk Street for a last minute Christmas Eve purchase.

"Daddy! Daddy! Look!" a young voice trailed away.

I turned with horror to see golden curls and a pink hair bobbin disappear from my horizon. I jumped up and ran over to the edge to see Saoirse just metres below me, sitting frozen in her gaze, out across the valley towards the sea. From where I had been lying on the picnic blanket, what had looked like my Saoirse vanishing off the edge of a cliff turned out to be a gentle decline of soft boggy peat.

I say turned out to be, as if we would let our kids wander off in danger; we never did, it's just that now more than ever you protect what you hold close to your heart. None of us uttered a single syllable for what seemed like forever; apart from Ellen, being only four years of age, uttering several as she emptied a packet of ginger-nut biscuits onto the ground. I broke my silence with the usual four lettered wisdom.

Something shiny, half-hidden in the undergrowth, catches my eye but I forget it's there when my focus is drawn elsewhere. I could not believe my eyes, out beyond the tree line of emerald conifers, dark elliptical shapes formed one by one, not dissimilar to a giant child's dot-to-dot picture.

Where once there were road intersections, shopping malls, houses, schools and ultimately hundreds if not thousands of innocents, now there were ten, twenty, no - thirty or more sinkholes which appeared and from below swallowed everyone and everything above. The emerging sound was strange, yet familiar to my ears.

The repetitive industrial BOOM... BOOM... BOOM... did not correlate with a natural phenomenon. This occurrence was more reminiscent of an opal mining operation. It seemed as if explosives were being detonated in an engineered fashion to carve up Mother Earth.

It felt as if the planet's inner beauty was being cruelly torn up for some otherworldly gain.

We stood up... We got into our car... We drove home, recounted Kyle, to himself.

***

One month previously...

Waking on the morning of his forty fourth birthday, he did what he had been doing on the morning of every birthday since his fortieth - getting out of bed a lot slower than he did on previous birthdays. Walking into the bathroom and after flushing the toilet and washing his hands he looks in the shaving mirror capturing his face from nose to chin; definitely more grey in his beard these days and upon tilting the mirror upwards, more lines around tired eyes emerge, adding character to an increasingly follicle-challenged head.

I never really minded losing my hair at the age of twenty five, what I do mind is the expectation of me to laugh in a self-deprecating way at other people's "bald" jokes. If you ever go bald at a young age, the best advice I can give you is to shave it all off. The freedom from stupid hair styles is highly recommended. Also, do refrain from punching the face of "bald joke" comedians; as they tell their hilarious little quip it is more effective to direct your eyes up and down their hairline. If they question why your gaze is fixated upon their also declining tresses, just reply "Nothing, nothing, please continue, you are just the funniest person I know". This will have a longer lasting result than a smack upside the head as they will proceed to raise their hand to feel if their own forehead is getting taller. They will no doubt be in front of a mirror before the day is out, thought Kyle.

As described, Kyle has a shaved head and greying beard. Back in the 80's he was one of the tallest in first year of secondary school, five foot eight and a half inches tall at twelve years of age.

Growing quite tall at a young age involved a lot of growing pains. Visits to the family doctor were often accompanied with the comment that *"this boy is going to be a six footer!"*... liar. Unfortunately, he is the same height some thirty years later.

While never an athlete he always kept himself at a reasonable level of fitness. Cycling up and down mountains in his teens and early twenties kept the weight off. However, after college and spending years at desks in front of computers, not to mention the fondness of a pint or two of the black stuff followed by battered sausage and chips at weekends - the pounds had accumulated. It was only after becoming a father in recent years that opportunities to sit on a bar stool were somewhat curtailed. The decision to get back in shape was a recent one. Kyle was contemplating buying a new mountain bike. Money was tight; freelance work could only be part-time while minding his two girls at home.

Kyle's mirrored trance was broken by the sound of the doorbell. Pulling on a pair of jeans he ran downstairs to open the front door just in time.

"Are you Kyle Parsons?" the courier, chewing gum at seven in the morning, neutrally asks.

"Yeah, what's this?" Kyle replied.

"Looks like a pretty expensive bike to me, must be someone's birthday, can you sign here?" asked the courier nonchalantly, still chewing gum.

Crystal had left early for work and the two girls were asleep upstairs. He lifted the bike, still encased in cardboard, through the kitchen and out into the garage. It was his birthday but he hadn't ordered a new bike; he was thinking about it but had said nothing to Crystal. Carefully, he transferred a pile of bubble wrap to the floor and beheld a fantastic black, red and white hardtail mountain bike.

This wasn't from Crystal, but who? What's this GPS device and envelope doing taped to the underside of the saddle, thought Kyle, curiously.

Kyle opened it and read the instructions which were crudely typed on a sheet of old cream vellum. The words were all uppercase and the paper had slight impressions from the old typewriter used to type the ominous note:

I BELIEVE YOU'RE IN BETTER SHAPE THAN YOU HAVE BEEN IN SOME YEARS. GIANT HOLES, UNUSUALLY HOT WEATHER HERE AND SNOWING FOR THE FIRST TIME IN OTHER PARTS OF THE WORLD HAS NOTHING TO DO WITH MOTHER NATURE. HOLD OFF PLANS FOR BIRTHDAY CELEBRATIONS THIS WEEKEND. DON'T USE YOUR CAR, TAKE THIS BIKE AND CYCLE ALONE. YOU'LL RECOGNISE SOME OF THE ROUTE FROM BACK WHEN WE WERE KIDS.

I WILL EXPLAIN WHEN/IF YOU ARRIVE. DON'T GO THE TOURIST ROUTE. GO VIA THE RESERVOIR. AT SOME POINT YOU'LL HAVE TO DITCH THE BIKE AND GO ON FOOT. THE COORDINATES PROVIDED ARE NOT YOUR END DESTINATION. YOU WILL FIND ME ON HOLLOW GROUND SHORTLY BEFORE. IF I DON'T SEE THAT BIG BALD HEAD OF YOURS COMING THROUGH THE TREES BY SUNDAY MORNING, I'LL ASSUME YOU HAVE EITHER BEEN TAKEN OR ARE DEAD.

53° 15′ 6.7″ N, 6° 19′ 49.24″ W

The phone rings. It's 10am. It's Crystal.

"Hi hon, Happy Birthday! You were still snoring when I got up this morning. How were Saoirse and Ellen?" asks Crystal.

"Fine, both skipped into school with smiles on their faces," I reply, still on edge from the delivery earlier.

"I'll be home around six this evening, would you like to do something special for your birthday?" asks Crystal.

"Dunno, not sure... something has come up... I can't explain yet, let's talk later," Kyle said, staring at the letter.

Whoever sent this seems to know me from a long time ago and might be watching me right now? Why would someone buy me an expensive bike that I'm supposed to ditch after a short time? I'm thinking that a cyclist in the mountains on such a serious bike would look more fitting, attract less attention and also a bike would be a lot easier to conceal than a car. Internet connection and mobile signal have been intermittent at best recently. After our experience of the "dot-to-dot" sinkholes I wouldn't want to get trapped somewhere in a car anyway. The weird weather, the snake incident and one conspiracy theory after another has everyone spooked.

I don't feel comfortable leaving Crystal and the kids alone, not now, but I can't bring them with me. Okay, I've got to do this, thought Kyle.

Kyle turned on his computer and luckily was able to get online long enough to download and print off a map of the coordinates. It was near the Hellfire Club up on Silver Mountain.

"...YOU'LL RECOGNISE SOME OF THE ROUTE FROM BACK WHEN WE WERE KIDS..."

"...DON'T GO THE TOURIST ROUTE. GO VIA THE RESERVOIR..."

When I was a kid I had gone to the Hellfire Club several times with school or with Mum and Dad. Never had I cycled up Silver Mountain with friends. I had often ridden through the Silver Mountain Reservoir grounds and on out to Red Lake; sometimes just to the other side of the reservoir where you could escape suburban life and feel closer to nature.

Many hours spent during teenage years sitting on the surrounding wall with a friend could unlock the secrets of the Universe or, more often than not, lead to heated differences of opinion about who should be included in the ultimate rock band, Kyle reminisced to himself.

While he loved the cycle tracks around the reservoir, he was never fond of the neighbouring Silver Mountain. Maybe because the Sun always seemed to shine on the reservoir in Glenrock valley or maybe because of the sinister associations with the Hellfire Club on Silver Mountain which always left him feeling cold to the bone.

If his memory served him correctly, small narrow roads at the back of the reservoir should wind eastwards towards Silver Mountain. These roads would eventually turn north and he would indeed have to ditch the bike if he were to try and travel as the crow flies. Most tourists would approach the Hellfire Club travelling south.

The Hellfire Club was not a disco devoted to devilish dancing, it was and possibly still is a club devoted to the worship of the devil. It was originally a passage tomb, a cairn, constructed thousands of years ago.

A speaker in Parliament, built the club house on the site in 1725 and used it as a hunting lodge. In the process the cairn was destroyed and the stone used as some of the building materials. This was said to have cursed it from the start. The speaker died in 1729 and the building then came to be in the hands of the Hellfire Club. Many similarly named clubs existed and were associated with all kinds of debauchery.

One infamous incident occurred on a stormy night when a travel weary stranger called in to escape the tempest raging outside. Keeping his long coat on, he sat down with a whiskey in hand accepting an invitation to join all present in a card game. When one of the other players bends down to pick up his fallen card, he notices that beneath the stranger's long coat where you would expect to see a boot, there was instead - a cloven hoof! Screams ensued and with a loud bang the stranger disappeared leaving only a smell of sulphur and the pale faces of others still seated.

Many versions of this tale and others exist about the Hellfire Club including the sacrifice of a dwarf. Strangely putting some credence to this, the skeleton of a dwarf was unearthed by workers nearby on the grounds of a large Victorian house. Demons and stormy nights aside, Kyle's own present reality was becoming stranger by the day.

***

One day ago...

Crystal arrives home exhausted from a long day at work but always with a chuckle and a smile as she is greeted with big squeezy hugs from our two little chickens. After a late dinner and kids all tucked up for the night, I show her the mountain bike and the note, possibly from a long time ago friend.

At first, she disagrees, because of all the recent events, that I should go alone on a mysterious and potentially dangerous adventure. However, after I emphasised that it may be from a friend in trouble, she suggests I go tomorrow morning, early so as to avoid an inquisition from a four and a six-year-old, remembered Kyle, smiling to himself.

***

Sixteen hours ago...

5.30am - after pedalling over the Foreshore Bridge, Kyle turns right and recognises a familiar stretch of road leading past Lodge Road Cemetery. As he passes by he glances over the wall and can see in the wakening light, rows upon rows of crooked stone billboards pointing angrily towards the dawn, advertising that those who lie beneath are indeed not awake anymore.

He takes another right turn down a lane way, overgrown with blackberry bushes and nettles; as kids they used this lane for a short cut down to the parallel road. This leads him on and across Castle Bridge.

As he starts to round the next bend he hears some sort of commotion - a cacophony of voices shouting in an unknown language, a harsh screeching cry followed by pulsating "*zzzit, zzzit*" sounds and then silence. As Kyle peers around the corner he sees a trail of light travelling at fantastic speed up the hill and ascending into the amber daybreak sky.

The entrance gates into the reservoir are firmly locked. He cycles a hundred metres or so further along the road and is able to scramble over a partly fallen down dry-stone wall, pulling his bike up and over using his jacket tied to the crossbar. After dragging himself and his bike through some brambles and nettles, he emerges onto the gravel path pulling twigs out of the chain wheel and thorns from his stinging legs. Standing silently in the gradual brightening listening for any further disruption, there is nothing, no sound at all; no dawn chorus, no wind moving across the top of the rye grass. A nearby river does not bubble, gurgle or splash. All sound has been sucked into a vacuum by whoever or whatever was responsible for the previous dissonance and phosphorescent traces, trailing towards the skyline.

As he cycles on through the growing stillness, times of past silence enters his mind...

***

Five years of age waiting in line to enter for my first day of school; amid all the chaos and tears of parents and children alike, the squeeze of my mother's hand and our exchange of a lingering half-smile reassures her and I for the briefest of moments, for eternity, cancelling out the surrounding din.

***

Ten years of age waiting in line to enter the boxing ring for the trainer to assess my natural fighting ability; after failing to conceal yet more episodes of being bullied, my father squeezed my hand and we exchanged a lingering half-smile as he left me to the door of the boxing club. Ironically, as I waited to learn self-defence, a kid who stood head and shoulders over me decided I would be his next victim.

We entered under the ropes and after listening to a few words regarding the rules we began our sparring shimmy. Amidst the encompassing taunts and cheers from the now spinning audience, I felt my heart race and my face redden with anticipation. Everything fell silent apart from inside my head I could hear my Dad say "Now! Now!".

Out of complete fear or perhaps natural talent, I popped my opponent one right on the nose. I just managed to see his eyes water and a trickle of blood before being ushered out of the ring to a chorus of congratulatory colloquialisms.

***

Fifteen years of age waiting in line to enter the school hall for final exams. Squeezing my hands together I exchange a lingering half-smile with my classmates. Sitting in the exam hall there is complete and utter silence apart from the frantic scribbling of some who endeavour to divulge several years of education in ninety minutes.

Meanwhile, I sit in a trance, gazing out the window, listening to the distant cries of joy as other kids peel out of the school doors to a summer full of sunshine and promise.

***

Twenty years of age waiting in line at the bus queue squeezing my last fiver tightly in my hand as it is the last I have to get me home from college for the weekend. I sit across from a girl that would be the perfect girlfriend for me if only I had the courage to ask her out. I take off my headphones and stop listening to my mix tape for a moment because I think she is smiling at me.

Upon my realisation that she is looking past me out of the finger-smeared window, very happy to see her six-foot-two, blond-haired, blue-eyed boyfriend catching the college bus just in time and her realisation that I thought she was smiling at me... we exchange a lingering half-smile. I put my headphones back on but now the batteries have died and I spend the remainder of the homeward journey in silence.

***

Twenty-five years of age waiting in reception for a job interview as a graphic designer. I squeeze the handle of my portfolio so tightly that it leaves an impression on the palm of my hand for two days. I also left an impression, a good one apparently, on my prospective employer because just as I arrive home my mother tells me there was a phone call for me with a request to ring back as soon as possible.

Dropping my portfolio to the floor I phone immediately. I am offered the job (on my birthday as it happened) and asked to come in to discuss salary and conditions.

When I called back into the studio, the following day, there was an exchange of a lingering half-smile upon hearing the respectable sum which left me sitting in complete silence... I stayed there for ten years.

***

Thirty years of age waiting in line to do my driving test for the second time. I squeeze the steering wheel in anticipation of having to reverse around the corner while staying perfectly parallel to the kerb. The instructor and I exchange a lingering half-smile as I wait in silence for his verdict, which turned out to be that I passed. I then proceeded to rip off the Learner Plates and drive home with a smile from ear to ear.

***

Thirty-five years of age waiting at the door of a church on the top side of a valley in Bavaria, Germany, standing with my eyes in line with the corner of the car park watching for the wedding car to arrive. As is the tradition in Germany, we enter the church together. Walking down the aisle we squeeze each other's hand and our exchange of a lingering half-smile reassures her and I for the briefest of moments, for eternity, of our love for each other.

***

Forty years of age waiting in line outside the maternity ward all dressed in surgery cap, gown and clogs. There is silence as I am led through the double doors and am seated near my wife's head. I squeeze her hand and there is an exchange of a lingering half-smile as we reassure each other in anticipation of our new-born's arrival.

***

Phut!... BOOM!!! All of a sudden Kyle is brought back to the present as all sound returns. He is knocked off his bike from what can only be a shock wave from, he guesses, the recent propulsion of lights over the horizon. Dazed and confused, he climbs back onto his bike and meanders alongside the now babbling river. As he trundles on, the wakening Sun scans Glenrock Valley, welcoming him to the new day and he is reminded of the beauty of this place. Silently in the distance a grey heron travels the waters-edge with wingspan outstretched to the fullest; reminiscent of a much larger creature that possibly flew across these valleys and cliffs many aeons ago.

It's about seven in the morning as Kyle rises out of the saddle to peddle up a short steep incline, at the top of which he is presented with the upper reservoir. Normally, there is a green metal frame bridge leading out to a small stone outlet tower. Strangely, the bridge is missing and although there is a stiff breeze starting to pick up, the water is completely calm. Dismounting and leaning his bike against the perimeter wall, Kyle walks over to the waters-edge. Even though the temperature must be reaching into the mid-nineties, as he bends down and reaches out to touch the surface - it freezes solid! A light suddenly goes on in the tower and a pulsating alarm deafens him to the point of near collapse.

Pulling a tissue out of his pocket, he rips it in two and hastily inserts each half into his ears, bringing somewhat of a relief. He jumps back onto his bike and looks over his left shoulder, peddling frantically along the gravel track, to see concentric circles of blinding light emerging from deep within the centre of the reservoir.

One of these rings of light reaches him and somehow pushes him hard to the right. He doesn't fall off but ends up careering down a slipway which thankfully has been reduced to only a trickle. Speeding along towards some tunnel pipework for a place to hide, he is soaked in the process. The tunnel is not big enough to pull his bike in. He opens the quick release lever and manages to drag the bike, minus the front wheel, in onto his lap. Just then a second ring of light passes through the tunnel.

As the pearly fluorescence reaches him there is a brief pause and he can just about make out some obscure writing and number-like configurations on its surface. It passes through him and the readings change. As it leaves him he can barely move, he is momentarily frozen and as he thaws, the icicles forming at his fingertips fall away but he can still feel frost on his eyebrows and beard.

A further three rings pass and then silence. As he crawls out, the frozen extensions to his fingers splinter and tinkle to the ground. Slowly retrieving the front wheel he continues along the sandy trail in half shock and suspicion of what might be around the next bend. Eventually he makes it to the end gate which luckily has been left ajar. Turning left he slows down after a few hundred metres; feeling a little warmer having defrosted quickly in the heat and safer now that he has nothing pursuing him... nothing that he is aware of anyway.

Travelling eastwards now he passes over another small bridge and meets a fork in the road. In an act of hopeful reassurance, Kyle talks himself through the unnerving journey ahead, in his mind...

If I go left it will bring me back north around the other side of the reservoir and I don't fancy being scanned by those rings of light again. If I decide to take the road to the right, southbound, it will bring me further up into the mountains.

Ideally, I need to travel east as the crow flies but it is nigh on impossible. The fields ahead rise up sharply; that in itself is not the problem. The brambles are too dense and the ground too boggy in parts, it would be like navigating through a mine field trying to avoid hidden bog holes. Instead, I will start cycling south with the hope that the winding country lane will rise up eastwards after a short while. Something's not quite right. I've been cycling for a few hours and can't help feeling I'm not alone. Light will start to fade soon and I don't want to be stuck out here overnight.

The note said I would be expected to make it by tomorrow morning at the latest or the assumption would be that I had "EITHER BEEN TAKEN OR WAS DEAD." - To be completely honest, neither would suit me. Ever since I had scrambled out of the pipework, after being scanned by some unearthly technology, there has been a dark presence; quietly following close behind me.

Hustle and bustle, the thrust of all leaves blown up in front of me from all sides; rising up to form an autumnal curtain blocking my path. Then, speedily yet methodically, my bike and I are enveloped in a leafy shroud. It pulls tight around me and for a moment I cannot breathe.

Through the shadows I can make out a hooded figure, wearing some sort of goggles or breathing apparatus, moving long bony fingers through the air in a dance hither and tither. Icy luminescence emanating from its fingertips, reminiscent of Halloween sparklers and yet again there is complete silence.

A hand is raised summoning from above, a craft covered in a mirror-like substance that oozes and drips from its extremities. Concentric circles of light, similar to those which scanned me earlier, pulse outwards from the base of the craft and once again I am surrounded by a blinding light. I cannot see the hooded figure as ice crystals form all around me.

My bike and I are lifted about five metres off the ground and hover just beneath the base of the craft. Then dragged at speed through the air we head south towards the mountains.

Through a small parting in my enclosure I can just about make out the giant "dot-to-dot", "sinkholes". As I struggle I am able to lift my chin up a little and my eyes focus on obscure writing and number-like symbols, I recognise seeing before when I was scanned in the tunnel earlier. I can see them a little more clearly this time. They look like some sort of numerical and letter based graphic iconography. The image consists of three triangles with either a letter or numeral above each one and there are five ovals beneath.

I wonder if the image has any significance, any relation to where I am being taken. There are more than sixty peaks within the Dublin and Wicklow mountains, perhaps the three triangles refer to the three highest or maybe it just signifies that there is a base or entry point or a passage near the mountains? Then it would be plausible to think that the five ovals represented either lakes, tunnels or even landing pads for alien craft.

The first icon above the triangles looks like the letter "I" or number "1", the second looks like an abstract letter "D" or "P" or maybe an abstract number "4". The last icon could be a letter "C" or "E".

What do they stand for? Maybe the "1" stands for "1st", the middle icon might mean "Doorway", "Portal", "Passage" or even "4th". My best guess for the third icon is that it is simply "E", for "Earth".

Kyle's focus leaves the image and lettering and returns to his present predicament. He fears for his life and cannot break free. Out of frustration at what seems like a futile situation he spits with a derisory laugh in contempt at the graphic above him. In doing so he unwittingly reverses the power hierarchy of the situation.

Upon his saliva making contact with the symbols and the wet mirror-like surface, the craft halts suddenly and starts to vibrate violently. Concentric circular ripples appear all over the surface of the craft; similar to tossing a stone into a lake and rings flow outward from the point of contact.

The bright rings of light disappear shortly after and all he can hear is the wind rushing up around him as the craft seems to limp towards one of the sink holes. Kyle is left free falling... still entangled in the web of leaves.

Seconds pass and his fall is halted when he finds himself suspended on a rocky outcrop. His belief that he is now safe is only temporary; following a squeaking sound not dissimilar to that of a twisting balloon, his leaf constructed net dissipates. He falls crashing to the ledge below. Everything fades to black.

In throbbing pain, Kyle's thoughts race as nausea ebbs and flows...

I struggle to look up and can only see red from my right eye; a trickle of blood swims from a cut on the side of my head to add to a globule of already congealed blood, collecting as a result of my helmet strap tearing through the edge of my left ear on completion of my fall.

The light seems the same but it is hard to say if I have been unconscious for minutes, hours or days. Looking up and despite the forty-foot distance I can see that my fall was broken several times by now bent pine tree saplings; deciding that it was probably only minutes I take the only way out of here... up.

He begins to climb and after a short excruciating slog Kyle sits on a ledge, too tired to enjoy subtropical views.

He sees the mess that once was his shiny new bike, twisted and broken on the scattered scree below. After falling into a deep sleep, a loud shrill cry, that pungent aroma of aniseed and meat awakens him to the terrible dawning of a new day... Sunday.

The supplier of the bike had told him that at some stage he would have to ditch the bike and continue ahead on foot. Little did Kyle know that it would be an involuntary ditching.

Jumping up and running forward, he stops himself just in time from falling to his death. Kyle about turns and pauses to find the GPS and printed coordinates still secure in his pocket.

He continues on foot, with careful urgency, towards his appointed destination.

After, he guesses, an hour or so he arrives at a forest clearing, thinking to himself, *I must be close now as I remember the note saying...*

"THE COORDINATES PROVIDED ARE NOT YOUR END DESTINATION. YOU WILL FIND ME ON HOLLOW GROUND SHORTLY BEFORE."

I walk silently on a carpet of fallen pine needles and traverse the forest floor. It is indeed morning after all as I can see the Sun blossoming through the dappled canopy above.

I start to feel a combination of safety and anxiety as I am happy to have the endurance of the previous day behind me and yet nervous to discover whoever typed this note and had it delivered along with the bike to my door.

Will it be a long time ago friend or someone pretending to be? I walk on and gradually under foot feels different; gone is the cushioned pathway provided by the pine needle carpet and it's replaced with a vacant sound.

I find myself on hollow ground as the creak of an opening trap door and the dawning of a new day presents the barrel of a shotgun pointing directly towards my face!

02

The Bike Supplier

Recycle or revolt? Whiskey or water? Leather or linen?
Friend or foe? Truth or tale? Love or loathe?
Kindle or kill?

Without so much as a whisper, the trigger is pulled, no bullet hits him but once again he is enveloped in a net. Kyle falls to the ground, before he can struggle he feels a sharp pinch in his left buttock and as he is dragged downwards, everything goes dark. Upon waking, Kyles thoughts comment on the scene before him...

Fluttering my eyes open I am presented with a glass of Bushmaster whiskey; twelve-year single malt printed on the label. The bottle rests on an oak side-table next to the rather grand, albeit cold, tufted brown leather chair I now find myself sitting in. I move my arm from the warm, snugly wrapped blanket to retrieve the enticing liquor. The room is warmly lit by a gently flickering turf fire which caresses the edge of the grate and small candles are dotted throughout the room; each placed in little alcoves and shelves hand carved out of the stone walls of this subterranean dwelling.

"Two ice cubes I seem to remember," said a gruff but cheerful voice from the shadows; bluntly stepping out into the light and dropping the ice into Kyle's glass with a bandaged hand.

"What the hell..." said Kyle.

"Don't try to speak, the drug is still wearing off, drink your whiskey and gather your thoughts, we have much work to do," interrupts the stranger.

Kyle reaches for the glass and lets out a grunt; in pain he rubs his backside with the heel of his hand.

"What the hell did you stick me with?" said Kyle.

"Eszopiclone or lunesta... normally used by dentists, not my drug of choice, chloroform is so hard to come by these days. Although the acquisition of lunesta is not without risk for the purveyor either. Standing on a street corner pretending to be a user does nothing for my hyper anxiety," explained the red bearded gargantuan towering over him.

"Most people when in a dangerous or tense situation will have a normal fight-or-flight response; which is to either fight or flee. I however, despite my size, have a tendency to flight... or flight," he continues in a rather matter of fact tone.

"Why did you drug me? Why did you have to stick the needle in my goddamn ass of all places!" spat Kyle with a raised anger in his voice.

"I couldn't risk a struggle, I didn't want to alert the Polar Neridians to the location of this hideout or to your presence and our plan," said the ginger giant.

This guy is enormous. I now recognise him as the gargantuan bar tender who often served me a pint of stout and a shot of Bushmaster whiskey, with two ice cubes, in Shaney's Bar; every Friday evening after college, before I headed home, I'd have a few to end the week and ease myself into the weekend, thought Kyle.

That was twenty years ago now and Kyle thinks this man seems not to have aged a single day.

"Polar Neridians?" quizzed Kyle.

"Never mind for now, I'll explain all and more in the morning. What you need now is a good night's sleep," Mick recommended.

"But I arrived as the Sun was starting to come up?" proffered Kyle cautiously.

"True, the lunesta had you out for only minutes but I administered another anaesthetic while I checked your body over for any implants, evidence of abduction or experimentation, it's past midnight now," colossal hands assured, with a firm pat of Kyle's shoulders.

"You're Mick, Mick Flannery! You pull pints, at least you did twenty years ago! You don't drug people or hide from Polar Neridians or type instructions and send expensive mountain bikes as presents!" agitated Kyle before sinking back into his chair and confusion.

"Mr Michael Flannery, present and correct sir!" released rather loudly and almost subserviently.

"Yes, I do all that, I have been for more than twenty years now. The barman job was only a cover while I identified possible candidates for our mission.

"A complicated operation that we have been planning for the past two decades. However, as a result of recent events we've had to speed the process up quite rapidly," explained Mr Flannery.

"Come with me, I want you to meet someone," about-turning heavily yet almost elegantly, for a robust and rotund man, towards the other side of the room.

They walked past the fireplace and upon opening a small wooden door, which all six foot eight of Mr Flannery had to stoop under, Kyle sees another turf fire-lit room. In the corner is a man sitting with his back to them, typing on an old Crandall typewriter.

"As I said to you just now, I did do all that you say, all except the note and the bike. I've never cycled anywhere around here with you, but this man sitting across from us most certainly has," pointed Mr Flannery.

The man in front of the typewriter pushed his chair back slowly, it made a screeching sound that did not conceal its age; he stood up and turned to face them.

"I see you got the bike and the note then, where is the bike? Did you have to leave it somewhere? Kyle, it was me, Jim... Jim Kelly." began Kyle's old friend.

"You, you sent the bike? Why all the secrecy? Why did you not tell me when we last spoke on the phone... a few weeks ago?" Kyle said to Jim.

"And you! Mr Flannery, why the hell the twenty-year quest? Why haven't you aged?" blurted Kyle.

"Time," answered Mr Flannery.

"Time?! That's what you would shout in Shaney's Bar when I tried to order another pint all those years ago! Let me tell you something about time! I haven't the time nor the inclination to deal with all this! I'm going back to Crystal and the kids right now!" roared Kyle.

With that Kyle made a run for the door but the whole room started to spin and he collapsed to the floor.

Mick and Jim lifted him into a camp bed where he fell into a deep sleep.

***

Dreams brought him back to visit an earlier time…

Climbing out of his saddle as the hill rose up before him, it was just about all Kyle could do to keep up with his friend Jim who disappeared over the top and turned left down a narrow tree lined country lane towards the back of the reservoir.

It was summer-time and college had finished for the penultimate year; the last few months of freedom before a year of exams and then entry into the real world.

Kyle freewheeled down the hill known, only to them, as *"Long Tall Sally"*. They had nick names for different routes they cycled around these foothills; another was *"Sweaty Betty"*. Upon reaching the bottom of *"Long Tall Sally"*, Jim Kelly was nowhere to be seen but Kyle recognised the familiar sound of his friend playing a heavy blues tune about a levee, on harmonica.

Leaning his bike against the reservoir's solid granite wall he climbed over the old steel gate, walked through then around right and under the bridge to find his friend hunkered down, eyes closed, enjoying the acoustics that this two-hundred-year-old bridge surrendered.

"There's gold in them thar hills!" Jim announced, pausing to take a drink of water from his back-pack; putting on a rather bad American accent in the process.

"Huh?" breathed Kyle.

"There was a mini gold rush in these mountains and valleys around 1795. Most of the gold found was from panning the river gravel. They never found the mother lode," relayed Jim.

"Funnily enough, a bar tender who works in my local near college mentioned something about that!" a smile beginning to appear on Kyle's face.

"How is Mick these days?" asked Jim.

"Mick? How do you know Mick the bar tender? You've never been to Shaney's Bar... have you?" challenged Kyle.

"Ah sure I stopped off for some lunch on my way to Galway last summer," revealed Jim.

"But why ask after him if you only stopped to have lunch?" a puzzled look upon his face.

"No reason, hey do you reckon the mother lode is still up there somewhere waiting to be discovered?" Jim tried to change the subject rather quickly.

"Mother lode?" pondered Kyle.

"Yeah, you know, what I was sayin', the mother lode of gold," replied Jim.

"Oh yeah... gold, gold... gold," Kyle and his thoughts drifted off.

***

Waking back to the present...

"Gold... gold... gold," said Kyle in a repeated mantra as Mick Flannery and Jim Kelly tried to rouse him from a restless sleep.

Eventually Kyle woke up completely soaked through with sweat. Jim helped Kyle sit up and gave him a big mug of strong black coffee and went to fetch him some breakfast. As Jim left the room Kyle eyed him up and down thinking that, along with Mr Flannery, Jim had hardly aged in the years since leaving college. He thought Jim looked almost similar in age to what he had done in his erratic dream.

Jim Kelly who received PhDs in geography, biology and astrophysics never really looked the stereotypical studious type; similar in height and build to Kyle but had skull tattoos covering most of his back, chest and arms - stopping short from his neck and hands. He always wore black jeans and a white t-shirt - never with a brand name or design; never wanting to use his clothing to advertise for a multinational company, display his taste in music or impart anything of a sense of humour.

As Kyle had observed, Jim seemed pretty much, in appearance at least, the same age as they were twenty odd years ago when they were cycling around these foothills in anticipation of their final year at college; apart from one thing that caught Kyle's eye just before Jim disappeared from view past the fireplace and through the little wooden door. He still had long black hair without a trace of grey. However, being tied back in a ponytail, what seemed to be a small concentric circular tattoo or mark was revealed; almost exactly like the concentric circles which had scanned him while hiding in the reservoir tunnel. This particular circular tattoo was not familiar to Kyle and perhaps might have been a more recent addition.

Kyle wiped fried egg from the corner of his mouth and pushing the breakfast tray to one side before he stood up and walked over to the corner desk, where Jim had been working, to take a look at some notes and charts left scattered. Tidy transcriptions of concentric circles and iconography similar to what he had experienced were repeated over and over again across the sheets of paper in what seemed like an attempt to decipher them. Just then, Jim walked back into the room.

"Interesting... aren't they?" suggested Jim.

"I'll say and then some!" enthused Kyle.

Standing side by side, Kyle could now see that the concentric circular tattoo on the back of Jim's neck was not a tattoo but looked more like a burn or a branding mark or even a puncture wound? Jim noticed Kyle's stare and decided it was time for a little more information, after all that had happened and considering their friendship, it was only right that Kyle was prepared for what was soon to come.

"Sit down Kyle, it's time I put you in the picture, I'm sure you want to know what this is all about," Jim's warm smile migrating to a serious look across his face.

"I have more than a few questions, but where to begin..." Kyle's heart rate increased as he began thinking more about recent events.

"Well, firstly, the heat, the changing weather, snakes and sinkholes... *I saw thousands of people disappear...* and then on my way here as I cycled through the reservoir - the lake freezing upon touching it and then being scanned by those concentric circles of light which left icicles falling from my fingertips.

"Plus you and Mick seem to have not aged! I mean, I have seen you regularly over the years and come to think of it you look younger now than you did three months ago!" said Kyle hardly pausing for breath.

Jim ushered Kyle back into the front room to sit by the turf fire and poured two large whiskeys.

"Something that is of no use to them... Irish whiskey or any whiskey for that matter, alcohol is poison to them. Perhaps if I tell you what I know, then at least some of your questions will be answered and the others, well, we'll try to figure them out together," assured Jim as he turned, raising a toast.

With a momentary pause taken, a deep inhale and a long, tired exhale... Jim began his story.

"Twenty years ago when we were returning to college after the summer to begin our final year, I gave you a lift back to your college as I wasn't starting for another few days. After dropping you off I stopped by Shaney's Bar for lunch before making the return trip. I got talking to our mutual friend, Mick Flannery, he seemed an affable guy and because of the partial solar eclipse that morning our conversation turned to all things space related. The bar wasn't particularly busy and Mick seemed to relish in having a conversation with someone who shared his interest of interstellar travel, wormholes, the possibility of other Earth like planets that support life and so on.

"I went to use the bathroom and upon my return Mick was motionless, staring at me from across the bar. Everyone else was moving rapidly in a silent blur leaving light trails as they went from one side of the bar to the other or even when they lifted their drinks to their lips. The light trails were reminiscent of photographs of car lights taken with slow shutter speeds. In essence, they looked like they were moving at the speed of light!

"Rather cautiously I sat back down on my bar stool afraid of bumping into one of the light speed patrons. While this blurred motion continued all around us, Mick continued our conversation," said Jim, feeling troubled, as he remembered that afternoon; when nothing would ever seem the same again.

Jim continued to recall what he knew and describe to Kyle his strange first meeting with Mick Flannery.

"What do you make of this Jim?" asked Mick.

"Is there something wrong with my eyesight, why do these people seem to be oblivious to our presence and why are they moving in streaks of light? demanded Jim.

"They are not moving Jim, we are," corrected Mick.

"You've heard or read about the theory of light years?" Mick leaned forward.

"Yes, of course, the measurement of travelling vast distances in light years meaning, for example, travelling at the speed of light for 500 years would be required to try and reach a planet deemed to be 500 light years away," expounded Jim, still glancing from left to right at the faded neon contrails surrounding him.

"That's correct but this would still take far too long for most people; the majority would find it difficult to leave loved ones behind. Imagine a crew would have to breed several generations, educating each generation about the mission before burying the passing one aboard a craft capable of travelling at light speed just to reach a planet nearest to the closest star after our own Sun!" shouted Mick, although unnecessary amid the silent, colourful blur.

"Putting the space traveller into a deep sleep - because of people and their attachment to each other, I can't imagine an amount more than seventy or eighty years being emotionally practical, anything nearing the average human life-span. Space would need to be folded somehow, a wormhole or we would need to discover a means of travelling faster than the speed of light, perhaps a system that manipulates space time using gravity; akin to time travel," explained Mick.

When the blurred motion ceased, both Jim and Mick were standing still in the same positions. Mick was still finishing pulling a pint of stout and Jim drained the last of his coffee before replacing his cup onto its saucer. However, the patrons of this fine establishment were now different people altogether! The people sitting all around seemed, as usual, mostly art students and older locals with some noticeable exceptions - their style of dress was more modern and smart phones had holographic keyboards projected onto the same old tables made from beer barrels. One regular who had been sitting at the opposite end of the bar was still there only he was about twenty years older!

Mick produced onto the bar counter what at first looked like a pint of blue beer. On closer inspection Jim could see that this was no beverage, it looked like a thin hour glass and within it a tornado of blue liquid stretching between both ends of the hour glass had a black light pulsating in the middle. Mick, holding the device and connected to Jim by handing him a cup of coffee, had transported them both forward in time.

Just then as Kyle's silent gaze was fixated on this bizarre recounting of Jim's first encounter with the gigantic Mick Flannery, that same gargantuan walked back into the room. He sat down between the two of them and poured himself another rather large whiskey.

"Perhaps I should continue the story from here on, about the time travel mechanism and our first meeting in Shaney's Bar?" proposed Mick.

"Sure, knock yourself out, some of the details are sketchy at the best of times. All that travelling backwards and forwards plays havoc with my long-term memory anyway," relinquished Jim.

"Well then, to cut a long story short, I will try my best to answer all your questions in a moment but just so you realise the gravity of all of this... we are dealing with an alien race called the Polar Neridians who, we think, want to turn planet Earth into a long-haul space craft and fly it to a destination I'm not quite sure of where or why yet!" Mick's hand was trembling as he put his glass down.

"The change in climate is due to the Earth's axis being artificially tilted by them. They need to alter the angle in preparation for launch. I read in a recent scientific magazine, an article about how the Inuit elders had warned the PNSE that the Earth had tilted to the north. They say that the Sun doesn't rise where it normally use to and that daylight hours are longer. Temperatures and wind directions have changed making it very difficult to predict the weather.

"They fear that global warming isn't the only cause of our extremely weird weather. With this change in the axis angle, we are experiencing what I like to call the antipodal shift; snowing in Australia and baking hot here plus dangerous snakes turning up in our back gardens to boot! Some sink holes are indeed just the result of natural soil erosion, others are the Polar Neridians' original entry points or hiding places, opening again in preparation for *'The Journey'*.

"They first arrived here perhaps thousands of years ago but notably return every twenty years, of our time. We reckon that wherever they come from may or may not be the same place they want to take the Earth but it might be a twenty-year journey. I can't tell if that would be ten years each way or a single trip of two decades," said Mick, pausing to take another sip of whiskey.

"They had waited hoping that through war, famine and pestilence we would eventually wipe ourselves out and make their task of turning Earth into some sort of intergalactic cruise ship a little easier with the human species not around to interfere," continued Mick.

"The problem for them is that everything on Earth, everything to do with life on Earth is cyclical. You are born, you grow and learn, you procreate, you die, your offspring repeat the process. Thus we go to war, we then have peace and then we go to war again and then we have peace again. Every generation repeats the mistakes of their forebears, yet the human race lives on; life always finds a way. Any hope the Polar Neridians had of creating a spaceship from this planet without bringing along a few billion unwilling stowaways was long lost.

"They have actually tried to infiltrate or advance human intelligence, directly at our core DNA; this was another hope of theirs that if they could not eradicate us or wait for us to eradicate ourselves then why not try to advance our technologies to their level more quickly by introducing higher brain capacity to more of us. History is littered with very intelligent people born and then acquiring enhanced cognitive function as a result of the Polar Neridians, through a science which is beyond me at the moment, secretly administering drugs of their own creation to human new-borns via a branding type injection at the base of the neck; Da Vinci, Einstein and Hawking – all have or had a concentric circular marking on the base of the back of their necks.

"You may have noticed what seems to be a tattoo on Jim who currently holds several PhDs in geography, physics, biology and astrophysics to name but a few. No offence Kyle but if it were not for the Polar Neridians, Jim would've probably sat next to you in Art college," finished Mick, almost regrettably bursting out loud into a fit of uncontrollable laughter.

"None taken Mick, while the scientific world's loss of me to the design one is no real loss to the scientific, the same is true of Jim and the art world. How come they didn't just eradicate us anyway?" quizzed Kyle.

Mick regained control of himself before continuing.

"Several reasons; not really a matter of too much time I suppose but more one of supplies. With the Earth they have a ready-made cruise ship and the animals provide a ready-made larder! However, a Polar Neridian stands, on average, seven-foot-high and some can reach over nine feet tall! They are technologically advanced, but because of their size, so is their appetite! I have seen evidence of experiments in trying to breed animals from their home planet here; several large species which seem dinosaur-like. There are some called terratons and they are bigger than our elephants but not quite like the brutes from our Jurassic period. Sometimes their experiments fail and the animal goes rogue, upon which it is usually euthanised before we humans discover it. A result of the euthanising method is a pungent smell similar to liquorice and cooked meat," Mick screwed up his nostrils in memory of the unpleasant odour.

"I think I may have experienced this as I entered the reservoir on my way here yesterday," remembered Kyle.

"We, myself and Mick, think that the smaller seven and a half foot tall Polar Neridians must have enslaved the taller, hairier ones at some stage in their history," offered Jim Kelly.

"The name *'Polar Neridia'* derives from the fact that the two species of Polar Neridians lived in the north and south poles where they adapted to a cold climate; the rest of their planet had been destroyed by war and irreversible climate change," continued Jim.

"The *'Neridia'* part of the name is derived from Greek mythology. The Nereides nymphs or goddesses of the sea; patrons of sailors and fishermen, who came to their aid when in distress and goddesses who had in their care the sea's rich bounty. They also represented various facets of the sea such as salt, foam, sand, rocky shores, waves and currents, in addition to seafaring skills. They lived with their father Nereus in a silvery cavern at the bottom of the Aegean Sea. The Polar Neridians live in cave systems below the north and south glacial landscapes surrounded by water; we ascertained this from one of the big ones we made contact with. There are also theories that the South Polar Neridians are responsible for the *'Bigfoot'* sightings across remote, heavily forested, areas of our planet. We came up with the name *'Polar Neridians'*," elucidated Jim, feeling rather pleased with himself.

"Although, the actual name of their planet is not as of yet known to us yet," interjected Mick.

"Hold on a second, you made contact with one of them?" inquired Kyle with a worried look on his face.

"Yes! Come meet our new friend!" replied Jim.

Jim and Mick led Kyle through a trap door, down small narrow steps into an abandoned mining shaft to a large steel door the width of a house. They took a few moments to punch in a code and turn numerous flywheels before the door opened with a hiss and a release of refrigerated air. They are greeted by an icy fog and sounds of approaching heavy footsteps.

"Oh, before I forget, we had better put these on!" indicated Jim, handing Mick and Kyle winter coats, hats and gloves.

As Kyle finishes pulling on his hat he looks up to see two large arms reach out through the icy fog and proceed to pick him up a metre off the ground. He lets out a muffled squeal as he is given the biggest hug he has ever received in his life.

"Ok Amatheia, put him down. Kyle, I would like you to meet our new friend, Amatheia," said Mick, without concern or a change of tone in his heavy, deep voice.

"Come in, close the door, you're letting all the cold air out," whispered Amatheia in a soft voice with almost perfect English. Each word sounded difficult to get out in a kind of wheezy struggle. It was comparable to a human, uncomfortable in a high-altitude environment.

As the door is closed behind them the frosty mist settles and they are presented with a rather utilitarian room. Stainless steel walls, table and sink. It looks like a laboratory apart from a large sofa bed which is now occupied solely by Amatheia's enormous frame. Amatheia stands up and although the room is four metres high she bumps her head off a hanging light bulb.

"I must apologise for my enthusiastic greeting. You are one of only a few humans I have met before," atoned Amatheia with a demure, humble stance.

"Apology accepted, I suppose." said Kyle, feeling a little more than slightly bewildered.

"Please bear with me, my speech is a little difficult as I am still acclimatising to Earth's atmosphere. Jim and Mick have been so kind to create this room which feels a little more like home for me on Polar Neridia. You must understand that this is a name Jim has come up with based on my description of home.

"We do not have any name for where we live other than *'Oikia'* which means *'home'* in my language. I must emphasise that not all Polar Neridians want to take over Earth! I come from Neridia's South Pole, where food was more plentiful and we lived in relative peace for almost 10,000 years. Just over a few centuries ago we were invaded and many were either killed or enslaved by the North Polar Neridians. We call ourselves *'Oikians'* from the south pole and the *'Kolassians'* come from the north pole of Neridia; a bad place we call Kolassi," explained Amatheia regretfully.

"The North Polar Neridians, the 'Kolassians', are slightly smaller at seven and a half foot tall, hairless and have superior technology. They are the ones who have come here to hijack Earth. Amatheia belongs to the South Polar Neridians, while less technologically advanced, are still streets ahead of us. Plus as you can see, despite their size, are a gentle race," described Mick.

"The Kolassians, the North Polar Neridians, are quite feeble and rely on their advanced technology to survive. They get out of breath quite easily and must wear a sort of breathing booster apparatus," added Jim.

"I saw one of these when it enveloped me in a kind of net and tried to transport me while I hovered beneath some sort of 'UFO'. When I spat at the base of the craft it vibrated and dropped me?!" recalled Kyle.

"Another reason they wear those masks is that they are very susceptible to disease," divulged Amatheia, sitting back down.

"So, is there some grand plan, am I now part of this team? I will agree to help but I'm not sure why you chose me! I'm not seven-foot-tall and I don't hold several degrees and I don't have a concentric circular tattoo on the back of my neck!

"All I want now, is to make sure my family are safe. So, why choose me?" demanded Kyle, desperation building within his core and spilling out for all gathered to witness.

"Friends," said Jim.

"Because of our friendship, because you are someone I can trust with my life!" continued Jim in a stoic but slightly raised tone of voice.

"The plan is to head towards Iceland; a large cave system in the west of the country. Vidgelmir is a large lava tube cave, probably the largest in Iceland. It is situated at the Hallmundarhraun lava field about one hundred and thirty kilometres north east of Reykjavik. The roof of the lava tube has collapsed creating two known entrances.

"One end is blocked by an iron gate but this is the entrance you must try to penetrate because halfway along this leads to an unknown, to the public anyway, large underground cavern. This happens to be the Kolassians', the *'North Polar Neridians'*, headquarters. We think the large sinkholes that have been appearing at various locations all across the planet lead to a whole network of tunnels. One in particular, in the Wicklow mountains, leads under the sea and opens up via another sinkhole in the Hallmundarhraun lava field," added Jim.

"Why don't I just fly to Reykjavik and make my way from there?" asks Kyle.

"It's not safe now. There are eyes everywhere! Even though they are using the sinkholes and lava tubes as subterranean highways, you will be much safer travelling right under their noses, beneath the cover of darkness," said Jim.

"What about my wife and kids?!" asks Kyle.

"You will travel towards Vidgelmir and the Kolassian headquarters with Mick using the Wicklow mountain sinkhole. You must try to somehow disrupt or destroy the mechanisms they have in place for launch.

"You leave in the morning. Amatheia will go to your house and stand guard over Crystal, Ellen and Saoirse. I will remain here for the time being trying to figure out how they are arriving here. Maybe there's an entry point located somewhere in our solar system.

"We'll need to know what to do next after you both complete the mission, or more importantly, what the hell we do if you don't," directed Jim.

"But how do you think Crystal and the kids are going to react when they are greeted at the front door, no offense Amatheia, by what looks like a nine-foot-tall ginger-brown ape with a speech impediment!" shouts Kyle with his face first turning red and then purple as he proceeds to hyperventilate.

Amatheia calmly picks Kyle up. Sitting him on her lap she cups her hand gently over his mouth; allowing him to breathe his own exhaled air, in an attempt to counteract his hyperventilating.

"Thank you Amatheia, I'm sorry... it's just that I fear and long for my family's safety," laments Kyle.

"Apology accepted, I also long for the safety of my family... something we have in common, but that is a story for another day," gazing past him with a distant look upon her face; thinking of loved ones far away.

"Have you got something I can show your family, to prove we have met and are friends?" asks Amatheia.

"Here, take this graphic t-shirt I designed, Saoirse will know it's mine," offered Kyle as he peeled the garment off over his long sleeve vest.

"Ask Saoirse when did I come up with the logo design. Before Saoirse answers, tell her you know that it was while we were drawing together... doodling and sketching. She will then know that we are friends and this is something I shared with you," replied Kyle regaining his composure.

"Very well Kyle, it will be done," said Amatheia.

The four friends bedded down for the night falling asleep to thoughts of what tomorrow might bring.

03

A Child Leads

An asteroid skips along the surface of a distant galaxy; journey halts at the edge by the gravity of a blue planet. It pauses for a moment and is released into a black hole continuing its path to somewhere else.

We all skip along the fields of our lives until something momentarily stops our progress as we prepare to enter the next phase, dimension or new life.

Saoirse's dreams struggled to hold her mind captive...

I woke up calling out for my Dada but he didn't answer. Usually when I wake in the morning I call across the landing for my daddy to lift me down from my top bunk and carry me downstairs for breakfast. He always jokes pretending that his back hurts saying I am getting too big for this coz I'm a big six but I think that he secretly enjoys this as much as I do; snuggling into his neck as we go weeeeeee... down the stairs. I call out for my mum, she's getting brekkie ready but the kitchen clock says twelve; I've slept till lunchtime!

After I finish my yogurt I slide down off my chair and I think I will go out to play in the back garden while Mum cooks pasta. She says that because of the very hot weather my school is closed for the rest of the week and that I should only stay out for a few minutes and to wear my floppy hat and bring a bottle of water with me.

I know Mum said I should only stay out for ten minutes but looking at the warm breeze blowing along the top of the wheat in the field behind our house makes me want to squeeze through the gap in the hedge and explore!

Hands stretched out wide, I run. I love the way the wheat tickles my hands when I run through it! Golden yellows become a blur as I spin round and round over and over again and again until I fall over dizzy looking up at the big blue sky! As I lie down looking up at the blue the only sound I can hear is a gentle breeze as it rolls along the top of the wheat field. My head has stopped spinning now and I guess it is time for me to go back home to my mum.

But wait, where is my floppy hat? It must have fallen off when I was running and spinning around. I stand up just in time to see a speck of white flying along the top of the corn and catching on one of the blackberry bushes at the edge of the field. I'd better go fetch it before going home or Mum won't be happy. I am six and a half and very tall for my age but I can't reach my hat. I don't want to scratch myself and as I try to reach out one more time I nearly fall into the thorns; but a strong brown furry arm holds me up and allows me to reach my hat.

"Now you can reach your hat," explained a calm but strange voice coming from high and behind; interrupting Saoirse's thoughts for a moment.

I say thank you without thinking and look around. A huge monster, bigger than a big bear smiles at me as it gently places me on the ground. Still holding my hat, my head starts spinning again and everything goes all dark. I wake up to find this hairy, scary but kind faced monster smiling down at me, Saoirse thought quietly to herself.

"Who? What are you? Leave me alone! I'll tell my dad!" cries Saoirse, in what she thought was her loudest voice but barely a whisper left her quivering lips.

"I know your father Kyle, he is my friend. He asked me to come here to mind you, Ellen and your mum. Some naughty people who come from Space - where I come from but look a little different than me, are trying to take your planet Earth and use it as a big spaceship. Your daddy and I, plus some other friends, are going to try and stop them!" said Amatheia in a strong but still friendly voice; not wanting to scare the little child.

"Mum and Dad said never to talk to strangers and you are a strange stranger! You are the *strangest* stranger ever! How do I know if you are tricking me?!" shouted Saoirse.

This time her lips were steady and Amatheia found it necessary to wipe spittle from both their chins after the child's outburst.

Amatheia produced a t-shirt from her leather satchel and showed it to Saoirse. She recognised it as one of Daddy's graphic t-shirts he had designed.

"Where did you get that?! Did you hurt my daddy?! Did you take it from him?!" asked Saoirse impatiently.

"When did your father design this logo?" softly asks Amatheia, patiently pointing towards the abstract image printed on the front of the t-shirt.

Before Saoirse could answer, Amatheia tells Saoirse that she knows it was while they were drawing together... doodling and sketching. This brings a calming smile to the little freckle-nosed face. Saoirse pulls the t-shirt close, breathing in her daddy's scent before reluctantly handing it back to Amatheia who returns it to her satchel.

Saoirse stands up and puts on her floppy hat. As the Sun starts to get lower in the sky a glint of orange highlights the two contrasting figures walking hand in hand as Saoirse leads Amatheia across the wheat field back towards her house. Approaching the back garden, Saoirse senses that something is not quite right. The patio furniture is strewn about the place and large muddy footprints lead up the steps to smashed glass and doors hanging off their hinges. On hearing movement inside the house Amatheia picks Saoirse up in a motherly fashion shielding her from any potential harm and her eyes from possibly anything that a child should not see.

The interior walls of the house are covered in scorch marks from weapon fire. After a quick search it is apparent that the intruders had left only recently. It was also evident that Crystal and Ellen had been taken unwillingly. On the stove was a pot of pasta sauce still bubbling away, waiting to be poured over the three bowls of pasta sitting on the breakfast bar. Just above the hob on the stainless-steel splash-back, desperately hand written in smeared pasta sauce, were the words 'ALIEN' and 'MASKS'.

Amatheia turns to sit down gently onto the sofa with Saoirse on her lap. With a gentle stroke of the child's cheek, she tries to comfort her.

"Now listen to me child. The naughty people have taken your mother and sister but I doubt they will harm them. They must have somehow found out what your father and my other friends are up to. The best thing we can do is carry on as your dad instructed me; to protect you all and because your mum and Ellen are not here, we must find them.

"Listen to me Saoirse, I promise you I will mind you, I will take you to your father. I will not let any harm come to you. Now, we must pack a few things for the journey," explained Amatheia in a reassuring tone.

"Where are we going? Where is Daddy?" asked Saoirse rather tentatively.

"He's heading to Iceland and therefore so shall we, have you heard of this place child?" asked Amatheia.

"Yes! There are volcanoes and it is very cold there so we must, *or I must*, bring warm clothes... you don't need any with your big furry coat!" outlined Saoirse, now a little more relaxed, starting to trust Amatheia.

"What is your name?" asks Saoirse.

"Amatheia!" replied the towering Oikian.

"Amafiaf?" attempted Saoirse.

"No child, sorry, words sound funny the way I speak your language. You say my name like this, AM-ATH-EA," demonstrated Amatheia.

"AM-ATH- EAF!" repeated Saoirse with great effort.

"Close enough child!" Amatheia smiled.

Just as they were finished packing and while Amatheia was helping Saoirse put on her little pink rucksack, in bounded a beagle dog knocking over Saoirse as it tried to greet her with licks from ear to ear!

"Mister Waggles! Where did you go?" shouted Saoirse as she laughed recovering her footing.

Mister Waggles turned abruptly and started to growl at Amatheia; afraid he might attack, Saoirse threw her arms around her pet dog preventing him from lunging forward towards Amatheia.

"No Mister Waggles, no! This is Amatheia, she is nice, she is going to take us to Dad... and find Mum and Ellen... I hope?" wished Saoirse, now feeling upset at the thought of not knowing if her mum and sister were safe or not.

Amatheia knelt down and held out her hand to the now subdued pet. Mister Waggles approached slowly and sniffed. Amatheia and the beagle stared into each other's eyes for a moment, then the silence was broken when Mister Waggles proceeded to cover Amatheia's face in dog licks too!

"Can Mister Waggles come with us?" asked Saoirse, filled with anticipation.

"Of course, I wouldn't have it any other way and he may indeed prove to be very useful to us on the journey ahead!" replied Amatheia joyfully.

Hand in hand, and one wagging tail, they set off. It was mid-morning and they had about two days journey to the north-west coast; from there a means of travelling across the ocean would need to be decided upon.

Sitting on Amatheia's shoulders with Mister Waggles trotting alongside they started to cover ground very quickly indeed. Standing over nine feet tall, Amatheia's stride took them through the wheat field at a pace that could match any 400 metre hurdles champion.

To reduce the chances of being seen by the invading North Polar Neridians and humans alike, Amatheia kept her course parallel to the roads but hidden by hedgerows of dense blackberry bushes intermittently disturbed by sycamore and mighty oak trees.

They were about halfway to the coast when the Sun started to set. It was time to make camp for the night. After crossing a snaking fresh water stream they chanced upon an abandoned fox's den. Taking several three metre arced swipes, Amatheia soon transformed the den into a night shelter big enough for the two of them and a dog. A fire was not needed as Amatheia preferred the cold and her huge size cradled Saoirse quite snugly as they all fell into a cosy slumber.

Ooh, it's morning time, I must get up out of bed and get dressed. I want to be first downstairs to say hello to my cheeky Mister Waggles! thought Saoirse.

Saoirse turned her head, frowning upon remembering she wasn't in her own bed. At first feeling afraid, then secure as she patted Amatheia's arm; dually keeping her warm and protected from unwanted visitors. Just then a little red chested robin settled on a pine branch hopping and hoping for a free breakfast.

Even though yesterday was extremely hot, this morning brought little flurries of snow; tickling Saoirse's nose and collecting upon Amatheia's fur. All was silent apart from the robin's gentle chirping and the slumping to the ground of snow that had become too heavy for a nearby sapling to hold any longer.

However, just as Saoirse stretched out her hand to offer the little creature a few biscuit crumbs, the ground and tree branches started to tremble and shake violently. Simultaneously, Amatheia grabbed the little bird and Saoirse, leaping up and proceeding at full speed in the opposite direction; away from rapidly approaching chaos.

Rumble, tumble, fumbling as she crashed through the forest knocking down small trees with her elbows and half-dropping Saoirse, regaining her grip; Amatheia sweated profusely, panting for more air to relieve her burning lungs as she continued at full speed to try and elude whatever was gaining fast behind them!

No time to look back, must keep moving. My arms ache, feeling warm and wet at the elbows. Saoirse is still smiling at me oblivious to the danger hunting us. I feel a fluttering in my right hand; something feathery and ticklish. Can't stop, won't stop - I wish I could stop! Amatheia thought, as she rapidly gasped for air.

Then sudden silence and a feeling of weightlessness. Surrounded by a white sky and a flurry of flakes - they started to fall. Amatheia realising that in trying so desperately hard to escape the pursuing threat she had mistakenly brought them off the edge of a cliff. They were now free-falling towards a deep dark blue lake one hundred metres below.

She released the little bird from her hand and it flew off into the white leaving them plummeting to their fate. As she looked beyond her outstretched arm she also noticed a Kolassian surveillance drone hovering above, calculating its next move.

She could not know how deep the approaching water was, if it would cushion their descent or kill them instantly; curling up into a ball with Saoirse enclosed was all Amatheia could do to protect the child and herself. The water was approaching rather swiftly as they gathered more and more speed. At the last second Amatheia pointed her feet downwards and the rush of wind was replaced with a hard splash; then nothing but the sound of the drone retreating and a beagle yapping as it frantically paced along the stony lake shore.

***

A few hundred kilometres back and a day before...

"Okay guys, safe journey and remember only contact me with these devices once a day to report your progress unless there is an emergency," directed Jim Kelly, in whispered tones to Kyle Parsons and Mick Flannery. It was early morning and still dark, Amatheia had left a few hours earlier and was making her way towards Kyle's house to protect his family.

"What are these devices?" inquired Kyle.

"I re-engineered parts from one of the Kolassian drones I captured some time ago. I was able to create a communications device with a power cell that seems to never drain, plus I adapted the signal so that its frequency alternates after each use and should keep you both undetectable," said Jim smugly.

"Let's go now, the sooner we start, the sooner we finish!" said Mick, feeling very eager to get the expedition under way.

Then with backpacks on, containing a few essentials, Kyle and Mick crawled out from the pine needle covered trap door to begin their trek towards the mountain sinkhole. The plan was to follow the tunnel which would lead westward and out under the sea. It would connect with lava tubes opening out from another sinkhole in the Hallmundarhraun lava field in Iceland.

The distance would be too far to cover on foot but while Jim was dissecting his captured drone he was able to view recorded footage from inside the tunnels. Floating on magnetically suspended carriages, the Kolassians traversed great distances across our planet. These carriages ran coupled in groups of ten.

The tenth one always had blackened windows. Jim did not know their usage but told Kyle and Mick that they more than likely contained cargo or maybe were a power source for the coupled carriages. Either way, these end carriages with blackened windows would hopefully be their best option to travel fast while remaining hidden.

As they travelled across the forest floor the silence was intermittently broken by Mick's voluminous exhaling and the cracking of a twig underfoot now and then even though they tried to move stealthily.

Looking up over Mick's gigantic frame, Kyle gazed upon the full Moon and the Milky Way stretching out beyond into the distance. It was so beautiful to ponder but that was short lived. Exciting thoughts that there was indeed other intelligent life out there were replaced with ones of fear and dread, plus the realisation that not all of our new neighbours were as kind and affable as Amatheia.

Looking back at Mick, Kyle wondered if he had told him the truth, or even knew himself, of his origins. In this contrasting light, silhouetted by the Moon, at this angle

Mick looked like a distant relation of Amatheia. He froze, eyes glazed black as he began reciting strange poetry.

"Midnight I rise welcomed by that blue/white guise
Are you my friend twelve hours dead?
Your colour has changed, your face rearranged
as I stare at you from my cold grey bed.

What poisons did you take?
Why am I present at my yellow star's wake?
No songs of woe do I hear,
only those below singing songs of cheer
What cheer? The writer's name? Why it's, beer!

Blanketed by watery pillows,
your head seems strangely mellow
Yet all around darkness aside
I rest upon your earthly bride

Your complexion changing, colours rearranging
Is this an old friend I see?
Warms my face, brightens this cold grey place
Time for me to re-join my own race

Another time Mr Moon, your half-brother
is strongest at twelve noon
Opposite ends of the day,
Brothers in the Universe going their separate ways"

Feeling bewildered and a little scared, Kyle took hold of Mick's huge wrist.

"Come on big fella, we need to hurry onwards," comforted Kyle.

No sooner than he had touched Mick's wrist, he let go again... it was ice cold as Mick remained motionless with a blank stare.

After a minute or so Mick regained his composure and they continued on their journey.

"What was all that about?" implored Kyle.

"What do you mean?" replied Mick, puzzled.

"You just recited a poem in a scary monotone voice. Something about the Sun and Moon and re-joining your own race?" stated Kyle rather cautiously.

"Ah, oh, I'm really sorry if I startled you. Jim has a recording of me reciting that poem several times in my sleep. It seems to happen on clear nights when the Moon is visible. Lately it's not only happening in my sleep but more regularly on cloud free nights like this; while I'm awake I can momentarily go into a trance and start reciting the poem. I don't know where it comes from but it has been in my head ever since my biological mother left me at an orphanage at the age of five; well, just fragments of it, I started to remember more as I got older.

"They told me she just couldn't cope anymore, that she suffered from terrible nightmares and her health was deteriorating. I only know her name was Rosemary," Mick recalled with a longing, distant look in his eyes.

The two men, finding their way by moonlight, trekked onwards around a ridge and then down towards the valley floor surrounded by the smell of tree resin as they were brushed by low slung branches. As they left the tree line they were faced with a meadow of shoulder high ferns which they had to move across in order to reach the entrance of the sinkhole positioned at the base of the mountain. The gentle breeze flowing across the top of the ferns increased in strength and in doing so took Kyle's Australian bush hat tumbling across the field. He went off in pursuit with Mick striding steadily behind.

They stopped in the middle of the fern meadow when Kyle's hat snagged on a branch of a leaf-less dead tree in the opposite corner of the field. The wind died all of a sudden and the Moon disappeared behind some now dawdling cloud. They were plunged into darkness as they tip-toed the remaining few metres to where Kyle's hat hung motionless.

It was out of his reach so Mick obliged by lifting him onto his shoulders. Then with one hand out-stretched Kyle retrieved his hat. However, the space his hat had occupied was now replaced by a giant eye as the moonlight returned with the dissipating clouds; then two eyes, four, eight, sixteen, more and more giant eyes turned towards them.

They had inadvertently stumbled across a pen holding terratons, Kolassian dinosaur-like elephants. They started to trumpet in a heavy groaning fashion, alerting their keepers and resulting in the meadow being instantly floodlit. The two intruders dived taking cover, face down beneath the ferns.

They dared not move as the commotion brought several North Polar Neridians, Kolassians, probing the undergrowth with spear-like staffs which emitted light from their tips; reminiscent of children's Halloween sparklers. As they probed the fern field, the muffled laboured breathing coming from their facial apparatus could be heard overhead by Mick and Kyle, who remained still; holding breaths waiting for the Kolassians to relinquish their position. As they passed by, the sparkling spear light caused the foliage to freeze, trapping Kyle and Mick where they lay hiding. It was possible to see the creeping frost travel from the fern tops down the stem inch by inch; as it did so their beards and eyebrows also turned white.

After what seemed like an eternity but in reality, only about ten minutes had lapsed, the Kolassians conversed amongst themselves in erratic tongues, then left the field and the two ensconced to thaw. When they felt the coast was clear, the pair stood up sending ice particles tinkling to the ground. Upon climbing over the stile at the edge of the field they were presented with a huge chasm which must have spanned nearly fifty metres across. The depth was incalculable and pitch black apart from blue tracker lights scanning its perimeter every few minutes.

They lay down on their bellies to peer over the edge. Mick procured some night-vision binoculars from his backpack and surveyed the void, considering their best access route down.

There were rigid steel ladders perfectly quartering the circumference of the sinkhole. However, as he estimated they would have to travel a depth of over three hundred metres to the rail tracks below, their presence would no doubt be discovered very quickly indeed. Then he noticed two lifts; one across the other side and one directly beneath them. As one lift travelled down the other simultaneously came upwards.

If timed correctly, they could lower themselves with only having a half metre to drop down onto the lift roof. This needed to be done one at a time because there might not be room to accommodate both of them. Also, the lift roof may not support the weight of even just one person alone landing upon it. It was decided that Kyle would go first, considering he was at least half the size of Mick.

Holding onto Mick's huge hands, Kyle was lowered backwards feet first over the edge. Mick had a clear view of the approaching lift and as soon as he finished counting down "three, two, one...," he let go of Kyle.

With a gentle thud, the lift roof flexed momentarily. Everything seemed fine and as usual as most things associated with Polar Neridians, the surface skin of the lift was ice-cold to the touch. As he descended, Kyle observed the lift on the opposite side of the chasm. It was travelling upwards and upon reaching midway when it was directly across from him, Kyle noticed another man also standing on its roof!

It dawned on him that what he was observing was somehow a reverse angled image of himself and the lift, being reflected onto a gigantic wet mirrored surface. The reflection appeared to be three dimensional and sort of holographic as it flickered every now and then. The surface was very similar to that of the craft that had tried to carry him to the sinkhole before. He wanted to call out to Mick but stayed silent for fear that either one of them would be discovered.

At the same time, Mick noticed what he thought was Kyle coming up on the roof of the lift on the opposite side of the chasm. He looked straight down, searching with his binoculars towards the roof of the lift on his side. However, as the lift disappeared from view, the only Kyle he could see was the one on the opposite side of the void now frantically waving his arms above his head. Mick, mistaking Kyle's frenzied gesturing as one of requesting help rather than a warning, ran around the circumference with the aim of helping his friend.

With one hand outstretched and the other gripping a small fissure, Mick desperately stretched for the waving arms of his accomplice. As Mick swung his left arm down he realised that it was just some sort of holographic reflection of Kyle; there was no second lift.

The swinging action had loosened his grip and he fell, first through the hologram of Kyle's anguished face and then down, silently. Kyle looked across with abject horror. Just as his lift slowed to a halt so did Mick's descent. Mick was hovering about halfway down the mirrored side when a door opened vertically. An ice net shot out, surrounding and enveloping him, Mick was taken inside. The aperture closed, leaving Kyle alone.

***

A few hundred kilometres west and a day later…

Resurfacing, Amatheia made her way to shore and gently placed Saoirse's motionless body onto the grassy bank. Saoirse had turned a pale blue colour and Amatheia tried despairingly to revive the child. After several minutes with no response, Amatheia sat by the lake's edge adding to its volume with her howling sobs.

A few metres behind her, a little four-legged friend tried with all its heart to lick life back into the face of his human sister. On seeing the utter determination of a concentrated Mister Waggles, Amatheia rushed over and continued to try and bring Saoirse back to them.

Moments later a warm colour returned to the freckled cheeks of the six-and-a-half-year-old; accompanied with a cough and then a tiny smile surfaced to float Amatheia's aching heart.

"Oh, my little one, I thought I had lost you!" cried Amatheia as she danced with joy, cradling the child in her arms.

After deciding that the drone was no longer in pursuit and that Saoirse was well recovered, they continued their journey towards the sea. Amatheia estimated it would take them the rest of the day to reach the coast where they would spend the night preparing for their ocean voyage the following morning.

As they strode through the long grass, with a dog skipping alongside, Saoirse quizzed Amatheia about her own childhood experiences on Polar Neridia.

"What age, how old are you Amatheia?" the curious child, almost over cautiously, explored.

"What age, hmmm, well I am twenty years old but I am also eighty, one hundred and sixty and there are times that I am also two hundred and forty years old," the guardian stretched her aching limbs as she pondered her own answer.

Saoirse didn't understand Amatheia's age description. Neither did Amatheia, not entirely anyway. Along with thousands of other South Polar Neridians, Amatheia was captured and enslaved by the North Polar Neridians, the Kolassians. This had happened to Amatheia at different ages of her life as she repeatedly escaped and made her way back to Neridia. Having happened many times and what with travelling at such enormous speeds back and forth on twenty-year journeys, shuffled by many hyper sleeps, the truth of the matter was that Amatheia no longer knew her true age. Although Saoirse didn't quite understand Amatheia's answer, she was not fazed by it.

"What age are you today?" she simply asked.

"Today, I am twenty!" replied Amatheia with a smile.

"Before Daddy left, we would go cycling in the park and when it was really hot we'd go swimming. Please tell, what did you do for fun when you were a little girl?" begged Saoirse.

"We did not have bicycles where I come from but I did love to ride my pet aquaton along the shore when the sea had not yet frozen over." replied Amatheia.

"What is an aquaton?" demanded Saoirse.

"Let me see, I have observed a creature on your planet called a walrus, do you know of it?" enquired Amatheia.

"Yes, yes, it's big and fat and has long tusks like an elephant but they curve the other way and it swims in icy water! I saw some of them on TV!" replied Saoirse with great enthusiasm.

"That's it, well an aquaton looks very much like a walrus except it has horns instead of tusks and is about twice the size. Back on Polar Neridia, every Oikian, *Neridians from the South Pole*, would learn to ride an aquaton as soon as they could swim! I would sit on the aquaton's back and hold onto its horns like handlebars.

"I would push down on the horns and the aquaton would dive down under the water and I would quickly have to hold my breath; with practice I could stay under for thirty minutes!" chuckled Amatheia.

The Sun was getting low in the sky and the two friends exchanged stories as they travelled onwards and upwards over the next mountain range, all the while Mister Waggles bounced along happily with his tail wagging to-and-fro.

"Mister Waggles is a very fine dog. Have you had him long?" asked Amatheia as the hound gratefully accepted an ear-rub from her massive yet gentle and kind hands.

"All my life, he's my best friend; after my sister Ellen that is. Mum and Dad love animals. My mum is always getting annoyed when she sees stories on the telly about people being mean to animals and she hates puppy farms!" explained Saoirse, also joining Amatheia in giving her pet an ear-rub.

"What? Do humans really farm puppies for food?" Amatheia had to sit down for a moment; the thought of poor Mister Waggles as a main course left her feeling more than a little nauseous.

"Well, in some parts of the world, of Earth, I think they do but not here. I heard Mum saying there are bad people who have lots of puppies for sale. The pups and mummy dogs live in horrible cages. The pups who are not very healthy are sold to anyone. Dad said we didn't buy Mister Waggles, that Mum rescued him," explained Saoirse, sitting beside Amatheia trying to comfort her.

"I think Mister Waggles has rescued me, more than we have him," finished Saoirse before they continued on.

Upon reaching the summit, the coast was now in clear view and less than half a kilometre away. They crashed rapidly downwards through the treeline, Amatheia temporarily grabbing a sapling every now and then to slow their descent. They arrived at the bottom of a hill with Amatheia a little out of breath.

Camp was set up quickly behind a sand dune with bedding provided by layering piles of beach grass. Dinner of fresh mackerel was served after only ten minutes of fishing with an improvised rod; made from a pine branch, strands from a found rope and a lure fashioned from the buckle on Mister Waggles's collar. After a hearty meal and picking a few bones from their teeth, the companions settled down for the night. From her satchel, Amatheia brought forth what looked like a wooden flute, showing it off proudly to an inquisitive Saoirse.

"This is an aulos. When we were children we would use it to summon our aquatons from the deepest waters. Look, it has only one finger hole which you cover and uncover as you blow into the mouthpiece," explained Amatheia, slowly and carefully to the child.

Saoirse took the instrument and with red cheeks unsuccessfully tried to make it play; or at least she thought she didn't get it to work. The experiment sent Mister Waggles hiding under a bush and Amatheia into fits of belly laughter.

"What! What's wrong?" inquired the young traveller.

"Nothing my child, once mastered a sad yet pleasant tone can be achieved but normally the sound can only be heard by aquatons, terratons and now it seems Earth dogs too!" laughed Amatheia.

Amatheia fell soundly asleep as Saoirse continued to practice on the aulos; convinced she could get an audible tune to reveal itself.

The following morning Amatheia woke to find Saoirse and Mister Waggles not by her side. Standing up she could see the hound by the shoreline whimpering impatiently. She walked over to the dog to find the aulos on a large flat rock beside him but Saoirse was still nowhere to be seen.

Then just as panic began to set in, an almighty splash about a hundred metres out revealed Saoirse on an aquaton's back holding tightly onto its horns. It brought her under the water and back up again like some abstract rodeo with Saoirse shouting out "Go! Go! Go!" every time they resurfaced.

Seeing Amatheia standing on the beach, Saoirse directed the aquaton to shore. She pulled up alongside Amatheia with a huge smile upon both faces. Mister Waggles was still not so sure and barked his discontent loudly at the aquaton.

"Well my child, it seems you have taken the lead and discovered our transport for the next stage of the journey! I wasn't sure but I guessed that terratons were not the only animal that the North Polar Neridians brought here to Earth," stated Amatheia in profound admiration.

Pondering the bravery of this human child, she felt a little bit less lonely in the Universe. Amatheia climbed onto the aquaton behind Saoirse and beckoned Mister Waggles to come join them.

Once all three were settled and feeling quite comfortable, Saoirse steered the great beast to the right.

They set off in a North-West direction with the Sun warming their backs as it rose into the sky and they toward the horizon.

***

Almost three hundred kilometres to the east…

Down in a sinkhole, Kyle crouches behind a carriage along the tracks trying desperately to reach Jim Kelly using his improvised communications device. One hundred and fifty metres above, a man lies on an ice-cold slab in a room devoid of any light.

There are no restraints of any kind around his wrists or ankles, yet he cannot move. He can feel a frost gradually creeping up his body; around his neck, along his ginger beard, then up around his nose until there is only a small circular opening above his right eye. It is through this hole that he can see the approaching bony hand that holds a syringe containing a sizzling liquid.

As Kyle makes his report to Jim they can both hear a blood curdling scream followed by what sounds like a grown man sobbing continuously only pausing momentarily to ask for his mother. Jim advises Kyle that perhaps it is better for him to go on alone. This doesn't sit well with Kyle and the constant pleading, percolating from behind a closed door above, drives him to ignore Jim's advice. He must rescue his friend.

Kyle clambers over to the base of the sinkhole wall and as he looks up he can just about make out the shape of the vertical door embossed into the wet mirrored surface.

Remembering the reaction of the surface of the alien craft when he had spat at it gives Kyle an idea of how he could possibly climb up to the door. He proffered up some saliva to the wall and as with the alien craft, the wet mirrored surface became liquid and rippled in concentric circles. This enabled him to push his hand into the substance. It solidified around his wrist and was able to hold his body weight when he lifted both feet off the ground. When he again spat at the surface it liquefied, releasing his hand.

Using this crude method, Kyle was able to scale the wall and gain access through the vertical door. Sitting down on the floor breathless, the small corridor he found himself in began to darken as the vertical door closed behind him. He has no means of seeing where he is going; Mick's satchel contained the night vision binoculars and goggles. He tries to stand up and begrudgingly bumps his head on the ceiling of what appears to be a narrow passage rather than a room. Finding his way along, totally blinded by the absence of any light source, he moves downwards and around a ninety-degree right turn. In doing so his ears are cruelly rewarded with yet again more cries from Mick, somewhere on the other side of this wall.

The passage then ends abruptly apart from a metal grid, from which he can feel and smell a pungent breeze passing through. Reaching down into his jeans pocket he retrieves his knife and flint. With a few sparks he garners enough light and is able to locate the edges of the grid, using the knife to gently pry it open.

It's a tight squeeze but Kyle manages to climb into the shaft with arms stretched out in front, still holding onto the knife and flint, he pushes off from behind with his feet. Careering downwards towards a now mumbling Mr Flannery, Kyle intermittently strikes the knife and flint; illuminating his path. Reaching the end of the shaft, he finds there is yet another grid to open, behind which the metallic smell of blood is stronger.

The grid is easily discarded and Kyle slithers down clumsily into the chamber. In the centre of the poorly lit room, still encased in a frost-like cocoon, Mick Flannery lies on a metre-high slab. Kyle crawls on his hands and knees closer and closer; he can now make out Mick repeatedly reciting the *"Midnight I rise..."* poem, over and over again in a monotone mantra. He strikes his knife and flint once again to bring the surroundings more into view. In doing so, one of the sparks ignites the cocoon encasing Mick. It does not burst into flames but dissipates quickly, a centimetre at a time to reveal his friend. Gradually awakening, Mick sits up and turns to see Kyle through his one good eye.

He raises his right hand to feel his bandaged eye. A blood coloured tear flows from behind the bandage and down his cheek. Its progress halted by his beard; made even more red by the ordeal he had just endured.

On hearing approaching footsteps they decided it was time to leave. To slow down the Kolassians' imminent arrival, Kyle pushed over some boxes in front of the door where the footsteps had halted and set them alight using his knife and flint. Stepping up onto another box he was able to aid Mick's access to a wider duct.

The room was now almost completely ablaze as they were followed up through the shaft by thick black smoke and the squeals of the Kolassians confronted by a wall of fire. Using a rope from his backpack, tied around Mick's waist, and with his feet pressed against the sides of the passage, Kyle lowered Mick to the sinkhole floor. Once he could hear Mick was down, he spat onto the mirror wall, again producing ripples of concentric circles, into which he thrust the other end of the rope. This then enabled him to quickly abseil down to his bandaged and bewildered friend.

Just then the last of ten carriages pulled up alongside them with its windows blacked out. A low soft hissing sound preceded an opening door to reveal a gagged Kolassian, tied up and a Glock 17 pressed squarely against the back of its head. The gun was held by a female hand with manicured, gloss-red painted nails.

A voice familiar to Kyle told them to quickly get into the dimly lit cabin. Upon entering the carriage, the Kolassian lunged towards Mick but was instantly subdued with a blow from the butt of the woman's gun.

Crystal emerged from the shadows and threw her arms around Kyle and began sobbing while she repeated their children's names over and over again.

"I tried so hard to hold onto her but I couldn't move!" she cried.

"They came while Saoirse was out playing. I called for Saoirse but she didn't answer. I tried to fight, to hold onto Ellen but there were too many of them! They shot something at me and all of a sudden, I was enclosed in some kind of net and I couldn't reach Ellen! I screamed for Saoirse and that's when they left taking our sweet little baby girl!

"After a few minutes, the net fell away to nothing. I couldn't find a pen to leave you a message so I stuck my finger into some pasta sauce and wrote on the wall before I grabbed my gun. Running outside, I saw them board a mirror coated craft and speed off in a northerly direction. This bastard on the floor was hiding at the side of our house when I came out. He pushed a weapon against my head and forced me into a smaller craft which brought us into this giant sink hole.

"In the struggle I managed to conceal my gun. As the craft came to a stop this *thing* had to momentarily unshackle me, that was when I smacked him sideways across his head with the Glock. Then I heard someone screaming, looking to where the howling was coming from... I saw you climbing up the sides of the mirror wall. This carriage provided a hiding place while I waited to see if you would return! Kyle, both of our children… gone!" finished Crystal before she fell, completely exhausted, crumpling into her husband's arms.

The carriage door closed and they proceeded to move off at high speed almost instantly. There were two bench seats facing each other. Mick was sitting on one mumbling to himself with intermittent spasms of his neck as he reached up to touch his bandaged eye. Kyle and Crystal sat opposite him consoling each other as the Kolassian lay motionless on the floor.

Time seemed to stand still even though they travelled on at incredible speeds. Crystal hugged Kyle tightly as they recounted their recent experiences, wondering when or if they would see their children again. Never could they have thought that their lives would have evolved into a situation like this. It was only a few months ago when they were carefree and happy. Of course, life provided the usual struggles; mortgage repayments, household bills, car insurance, health care, tax returns to name but a few. Ultimately, all of these things did not matter as long as they were healthy, happy and together.

Long summer days playing with the kids in the back garden; throwing a ball for Mister Waggles and how he wouldn't always let you take the ball from his mouth in a pretend tug-of-war with a comical look in his eye. Even when Kyle was tired and all he desired was to stretch out on his inflatable garden armchair, pretending to be cranky when the kids thought it hilarious to dive on him, secretly, he relished and soaked up every memory that they were creating.

More tears welled up again in Crystal's eyes. Overflowing and spilling down her right cheek, collecting in a small pool on the carriage floor next to where the Kolassian lay sweating profusely from its breathing apparatus. A drop of blood trickled and fell silently from Mick's bandaged eye.

The three elements mixed together as a result of the carriage's motion. Unknown to the occupants, a merging of blood from an alien and a human would someday prove to be life changing.

04

Rosemary's Window

How many chicks do not survive the plunge
of first flight attempts? How many final breaths
ebb from the edge of hospital beds when
the Sun is high and the days are long?

How many leaves, turning from amber to russet,
have fallen upon tear-soaked paths? How many flakes,
of thirty-five different configurations, have tumbled
from leaden skies to tickle the noses
of freckle faced children?

One hundred and fifty seasons ago, a restless woman lies confined to bed. A sweating sickness has stolen her appetite but she still possesses an unquenchable thirst. Feeling light headed and heavy limbed, she can barely move in any direction.

Rosemary's mind races to comment upon her own predicament as a provider of care, corrupted by cruelty, mocks the patient at every opportunity.

Tick... Tock... Tick... Tock... Tick... Tock..., time seems to be stagnating more and more with every breath I catch. Apart from the old grandfather clock with its heart beating ever more slowly in the corner of my bedroom and in the corner of my mind, the only other sound is a distant child crying for its mother's milk. Not my child, no longer mine, never mine. Is the child's cry in my head or outside my window? I can't tell. The sound of leather soles on tiled floors approaches, matching the slowing pace of the Waterbury's tick-tock rhythm, Rosemary's thoughts trudged on and on.

The echo of ample footsteps pauses just beyond Rosemary's locked door. A key is turned and the creaking open coincides with the pausing of the pendulum and the initiation of twelve chimes... BONG!

"Good morning Rosemary!" *insists a patronising voice but I am unable to reciprocate...* BONG!

"Tried to leave yet again? Straps need to be tightened!" *a patronising voice and leather creak...* BONG!

"Time for medicine, open wide!" *yawns a patronising voice as my swallow reverbs in my head; coughing hard trying to force two little pills down the dry sandpaper tube my throat has become...* BONG!

"Oh dear, feeling thirsty, are we?" *testifies a patronising voice as water is thrust, without care, from a jug into my face; failing to quench my thirst as the droplets roll and collect in my ear canal, flourishing like a flash flood along a dry river bed...* BONG!

"Who's been a naughty girl? Soiled yourself again!" *derisively scolds a patronising voice as an adult nappy unfurls to reveal the foul consequences of not being allowed to independently empty my bladder and bowels...* BONG!

"Now for the moment at least, all clean!" *a patronising voice rips and snaps as the fouled towelling and surgical gloves are disposed of...* BONG!

"Open wide, say 'Aahh'!" *pronounces a patronising voice as a thermometer is rammed into my mouth resulting in the undeniable dislodging sound of a dental crown rattling around my lower jaw...* BONG!

"Deep breath in!" *exhales a patronising voice as she presses too firmly near my caesarean scar...* BONG!

"Aw, there-there!" *retaliates a patronising voice in response to my death rattle effort of screaming in pain as she releases her fingers from their pressing inquisition...* BONG!

"Hmmm, have you given up on that stupid explanation yet?" *grumbles a patronising voice; flicking away through my file on her lap. Seated in a corner of the room on a hard, sterile, plastic chair which creaks under her thick legged frame every time she leans back; sighing in disgust and disbelief at my account of how I had come to have an alien pregnancy...* BONG!

"Right, I'm off shift. I will see you again in another twelve hours. Please try and stay dry, I am running low on supplies and patience!" *proclaims a patronising voice as the door handle is pulled down upon...* BONG!

"Ha, huh, ha, huh, ha, huh!" *dumbly laughs a heavy patronising voice as once again the sound of leather soles on tiles patter, fading down some distant corridor along with her laboured breathing.*

The twelfth chime signalled the end of Nurse Bates's visit. Exhausted, Rosemary fell into a deep sleep; thoughts brought dreams of a very different visitation altogether...

***

I had recently graduated from medical school and had a month or so before beginning my residency at St Michaels. The days were warm and long with the smell of lavender in the air as I strolled home through the park with a smile on my face. That evening there would be a party, organised to celebrate our graduation.

Unlocking the front door, I am greeted by my parents who are still smiling at the fact that their daughter was going to be a doctor; one who specialises in space medicine. Daddy was an aeronautical engineer at the PNSE. That was before the accident had confined him to a wheelchair and early retirement. Well, there were rumours of him seeing things the public were not allowed to know about and that the accident was meant to silence him forever.

Despite what difficulties Daddy had gone through, it never diminished his fascination - his love and wonder about the Universe - the constant question if we humans were alone in the cosmos. The fact that my passion and his could be combined, in a way made our bond even stronger. Dinner over and a party to get to, I run down the garden path looking back to wave, I shout...

"Bye Mum! Bye Dad! I'll be home around one!"

"Be home by 11.30 and make sure them Murphy brothers behave themselves!" my father had called out.

Little did I know then, that after tonight, I would never take up a residency at The Aerospace Medical Association.

Rosemary arrived a little late at The Star Baker, the gang were already there. The two Murphy brothers were evidently there very early as they were already loudly singing poor renditions of traditional Irish songs followed by even poorer versions of German drinking songs - even though it was not yet festival season!

Fionn and Finn were twins, although not identical; Fionn had blond hair and was of medium height with an athletic build. Finn was much taller, six-foot-two, a bit on the heavy side, with hair so red that it could only but confirm his Irish ancestry.

Songs were sung, stories were told and before Rosemary knew it, time was called and they had to leave. Looking at her watch she realised that Mum and Dad would already be expecting her so she decided to make a dash for home. Running over the old bridge she decided to take a short cut along the forest path which cuts through the middle of the park. Camouflaged by cloud, the Moon produced hardly any shadows. Eerie silence lay before her as she traversed along the overgrown path.

Rosemary's thoughts continue to recall that night...

My feet were killing me in these heels so I decided to walk the rest of the way barefoot. I couldn't help but feel there was someone behind me. Looking around I saw no one so I continued on and tried to suppress my anxiety.

Stubbing my big toe on a rock, I had to sit and rest for a minute. As I paused beneath a pine tree there was no movement of its branches but I could hear someone breathing heavily. Mixed in with the smell of tree resin I could detect some cheap cologne. Then, abruptly, a hand clamped over my mouth and I was dragged backwards by my hair into the forest. I tried to fight, oh how I tried but he was too heavy, too strong. I struggled against Finn with all my strength but he only laughed repeatedly telling me that I was his girl. I do not belong to anybody now, not even myself. I will not have a self any more, not after this.

Looking up at his red hair and the sweat dripping off his nose falling onto my face, mixing with my tears, I give up. I am not a person any longer. Waiting for him to finish, he is interrupted by a bright white light. All sound disappears into a vacuum and he is covered with some leafy sort of net. Shot from behind, it envelops him feet first and finishes around his mouth muffling his agonised yet futile screams of pure terror. Removed from me, I cannot see him. Within the light I can see tall figures moving about with tubes protruding from squared off masks that adorn their faces.

Suddenly I cannot breathe but strangely I do not seem to need to as neither do I suffocate. Ice crystals begin to cover my face and body. I have a sensation of weightlessness as I move upwards into some sort of vehicle hovering just above the tree tops. My tears dry up as I come to rest on a platform within this craft. Two bony hands are placed on my temples making my head spin as we move forward and up at incredible speed. Coloured lights blur in front of my eyes and I black out.

***

On waking, Rosemary is completely naked apart from an icy shroud enveloping her entire body. There is a small aperture around her eyes, nose and mouth.

An opening also appears in the covering over her stomach, above which some apparatus is being positioned and manipulated by four hairless beings.

Rosemary stays silent but her thoughts do not hide the fact she is fully aware of all that is about to happen.

They seem to silently communicate with each other, occasionally looking back at me, but I hear no sound. The machine above me pulsates concentric circles of white light over my tummy which swells to a size that makes me look newly pregnant. Bony hands are again placed upon my head. I fall into unconsciousness but not before I hear the unmistakable scream of Finn Murphy pleading for mercy; light leaves and silence descends.

Coming around slowly, Rosemary is lying on the front lawn of her parents' house. Rain falls so heavy and hard that the siren accompanied by a blur of flashing lights is barely audible. She can just about recognise her father's voice and mother's crying in the background. A medic holds her hand as she is carefully stretchered into the waiting ambulance.

***

Mum and Dad are sitting by my bedside. A month has passed since I turned up, to me from one moment to the next, I feel like it could have been only minutes or hours. Apparently, I was missing for nearly three months before I reappeared wearing the same clothes; the doctors could not explain why I was nine months pregnant. Police showed up in the days that followed asking me if I had any recollection as to the whereabouts of Finn Murphy.

Initially, I kept quiet about the rape and the abduction but eventually the events that passed that night weighed too heavily on my mind to not say anything. My first mistake was telling them about what Finn had done. I can still hear my own mother saying that Finn Murphy came from a very respectable family and with a promising career as a surgeon ahead of him, surely, he wouldn't be capable of that!

My second mistake came two days later when I was shown the ***'child'*** *which had been removed by caesarean section while I was in an induced coma. Maybe the aliens altered my impregnation by Finn, adding elements of their DNA into the mix because this child borne of rape and unearthly happenings was not, could not, be wholly human.*

I couldn't keep him, even if I wanted to, my parents refused to consider the idea, saying he was the result of evil! Upon seeing him I broke down in tears and recounted every last detail of that utterly dreadful night. I received counselling over the following days but despite their best efforts, my constant and steadfast belief that I had been abducted by aliens resulted in my parents having me committed to this place. As I was driven off towards the asylum, I caught a glimpse of a red-haired baby in another car going in the opposite direction, to where I did not know; nor did I care, Rosemary's thoughts recalled.

***

"Rosemary! Rosemary! Wake up now, come on, come on my dear, I'm here right beside you," a voice imbued with calmness and strength brings her back to the present.

A male nurse by the name of Sam wakes Rosemary from her fitful sleep and brings her back to her current reality. He kindly dims the lights a little before removing Nurse Bates's enforced blindfold.

Everything is still somewhat blurry as her medication has not yet completely receded. Sam's beautiful, brown, kind face comes into focus yet surrounded by a room devoid of any warmth of colour. The perspective of the ceiling tiles frame and mimic Sam's crow's feet; exaggerated by his broad, warm smile.

"Rosemary, how are you feeling this morning? I'm going to file a complaint against Nurse Bates, not a kind bone in her body," spat Sam with tears starting to edge slightly from the corners of his eyes.

"Don't Sam, you'll only put your position at risk. I know you need this job to help pay for your wife's care," replied Rosemary in hushed and empathic tones.

Sam poured Rosemary a glass of water; holding it up to her lips, he decided to unstrap her so she could drink it herself. Rosemary sits up and calmly finishes her drink. Turning to the right she looks past the gloomy interior and out through the window Nurse Bates keeps locked. Sam walks over and opens it. The room is filled with a rush of air gently scented from the asylum garden below. It ruffles her hair and dries her tear-soaked cheeks.

"Rosemary, you've been crying during the night. You are still sweating from some unknown infection?" Sam wonders aloud.

"The profuse sweating and same dream repeat more frequently than ever before Sam," eyes brimming over while still fixed outwards of her window.

Her gaze followed the old limestone wall running about two hundred metres from the middle of her window sill outwards, then turns right and travels about three hundred metres before it reaches a four-metre-tall iron gate, sinisterly framed within a limestone archway. The pathway leading from the iron gates to the main entrance is bordered by tall yew trees on one side, making it impossible to say how much further the grounds extend beyond. To the left of the path and directly beneath Rosemary's window is an herb garden enclosed within circular borders of stone. Radiating concentrically outwards are beds of Basil, Marigold, Lemon Balm, Peppermint, Aloe Vera, Lavender and lastly, Rosemary at the centre.

"Every time you come on shift, it is a pleasant release for me Sam. Allowing me to sit up straight and look out the window, my window; it is the only thing I have now. It releases me from the bareness of this pallid room. Looking upon the medicinal herbs below fills my heart with a little colour.

"I like to imagine the flowers of gold, yellow, green, purple and red all greeting each other in the morning as the warming Sun relieves the dew drop burden from their leaves," Rosemary's eyes lit up, reminiscent of a distant happiness they once contained.

"One morning I was still strapped down but my blindfold had slipped slightly during the night. I could just about catch a glimpse of a bird's nest precariously hanging over the edge of the roof gutter. Within it was a starling feeding her morning catch to her young; each one vying open mouthed for their mother's attention. One of them was not as eager as the other two and momentarily lost interest in the bounty of regurgitated worms. Without hesitation, the mother starling stabbed at and tossed the weaker chick from the nest.

"I understand survival of the fittest. I know nature dictates the fruit of the mother bird's labour is more wisely spent on the stronger siblings.

"It reminded me of my mother's rejection; how she sided with the perceived respectability of the Murphy brothers' family. I was cast out for demanding to be believed, to be loved!

"Another time, I noticed a boy walking his little black and white dog. They were passing by the gates when the puppy caught sight of me through the iron bars. Refusal to walk on for the boy was met with an unmerciful whack across its nose! How could that boy be so cruel? Was it my fault for catching its attention? I realised, I am no better off than that dog on a lead!" cried Rosemary.

"Tell me about this recurring dream, why does it upset you so much?" asked Sam.

"Well, it always starts with that same 'Sun/Moon' poem," replies Rosemary.

"Here, can you remember it? Try writing it down," asks Sam, handing her a pen and headed notepaper from The Filchington Institute and Asylum.

Rosemary begins slowly but then frantically scribbles onto the paper. Curiously signing her name proudly at the end...

"Midnight I rise welcomed by that blue/white guise
Are you my friend twelve hours dead?
Your colour has changed, your face rearranged
as I stare at you from my cold grey bed.

What poisons did you take?
Why am I present at my yellow star's wake?
No songs of woe do I hear,
only those below singing songs of cheer
What cheer? The writer's name? Why it's, beer!

Blanketed by watery pillows,
your head seems strangely mellow
Yet all around darkness aside
I rest upon your earthly bride

Your complexion changing, colours rearranging
Is this an old friend I see?
Warms my face, brightens this cold grey place
Time for me to re-join my own race

Another time Mr Moon, your half-brother
is strongest at twelve noon
Opposite ends of the day,
Brothers in the Universe going their separate ways"

Rosemary Flannery

She gently returns the pen and paper to Sam and returns to impart her thoughts on the poem.

"I am sitting here on the edge of my bed staring out of this window. However, instead of plain white walls and plastic utilitarian decor, I am surrounded by pine trees and the bed is positioned as the park bench was, where I sat before... *before he raped me*. I look out the window at a bright light. It might be the Moon previously shrouded in clouds imposing its presence as they clear. It could be the light from the craft when the aliens arrived.

"I keep seeing Finn Murphy's face all cold and white. I sometimes think he is visiting me from the grave or is it the shock and terror he expressed, thinking that his life might be over. I'm not sure of the significance of the number twelve. Whether twelve hours before he had raped me, he was still my friend? Maybe he was already dead twelve hours and somehow the aliens re-animated his body in such a way as to make me think he was the father, rather than the *'child'* being the result of their abduction and interference?

"The singing and laughing I guess is my dream being disturbed by the revellers leaving the pub after midnight that was just the other side of those gates, or memories of graduation celebrations. Being blanketed by watery pillows must be referring to the partial cloud cover streaming silently across the face of the full moon," continued Rosemary.

"Or maybe you are commenting on your own disturbed sleep resulting in tear-soaked pillows and the relationship between the Earth and its moon - the Moon's gravitational pull or the earthly bride could be you as a maternal figure for the aliens?" interjects Sam, excitedly putting forward his theory.

"I don't know Sam, I guess it's open to interpretation. I definitely consider you like an old friend Sam... you warm my face in this cold grey place. I feel I have known you for a long time or that we share a common bond, a connection of some sort. How come you don't disregard my story about being abducted and the uncertainties about the origins of the child I gave birth to?" Rosemary, shrugs her shoulders frustratingly.

Sam sidesteps over to the door, checks it is locked and pulls down the blind. Walking back to Rosemary he hesitates for a moment and then pulls up his shirt. Turning his back, he points to the base of his spine where five concentric circles gather together in a sort of burn mark or scar tissue.

"You are not the only one. I have been taken too, numerous times over many years. The first time, I was quite young; a high IQ allowed me to be in my third year of advanced sciences. I had taken time out from studying to practice my 400 metre hurdles. It was a heavy Thursday afternoon. The sky was pregnant with clouds so dark and foreboding; it felt like a monster storm was brewing or an apocalyptic event was about to commence.

The circuit was empty apart from myself and a caretaker putting away sports equipment before the downpour arrived. I rounded a bend with about 200 metres done and felt great but with twenty metres to go, the sky turned black as night. Lightning ripped the sky in two and within that flash of light I saw tall hairless figures surrounding me; they had what looked like boxes with tubes jutting out from their faces connecting to small tanks on their backs.

"I must have passed out because when I opened my eyes, I was somewhere entirely different. Lying face down on a table, I was naked apart from a sort of icy fabric which seemed to map every inch of me.

"I could feel a pulsating force at my lower back and then came pain. Liquid dripped from my spine. It was like they were performing an experiment without anaesthetic. I screamed for what felt like hours until I eventually passed out again. When I came to, I was still lying face down and naked. This time however, I was back on the running track. My coach found me. I recounted my story to him but he persuaded me to keep quiet as such a story might ruin my chances of graduating and a future career.

"He explained away my being missing for three days as just silly student antics involving too much partying and that I was a good student who was, literally, back on track," expresses Sam tearfully; Rosemary comforts him and he resumes his story.

"About a year later I went missing again, another abduction two years after that. These *'takings'* became less frequent over the following long years. I'm not sure if they're finished with me yet. The only evidence of any other abduction was a fresh soreness around this circular pattern at the base of my spine about five years ago. I remember pushing my son on a swing one moment in brilliant sunshine, the next moment it was night and I was standing by the swing alone. I returned home to find a police car outside my house and my distraught wife and crying child inside. I've often asked myself if they were taking some of my DNA to study us in preparation for some big invasion. I questioned if I was somehow special or different from everyone else or if I was just another one of many human lab rats for them?" ponders Sam as they both stare longingly together, out of Rosemary's window, into the distance for a few more minutes.

"I held him for only a few moments Sam!" Rosemary blurts out as she collapses back into her bed sobbing.

"I couldn't keep him after how he came about! Plus, I can't, I could never feel naturally motherly to him! I mean, he just didn't seem wholly human from the moment I laid eyes on him!" loud cries are quietened with a deep, longing, sigh.

"In what way, how did the child not seem completely human?" quizzes Sam.

"Well, for starters, he was at least twice the length of the average new-born; my caesarean scar still aches. Then, his hair was a beautiful deep Irish red but a white streak would appear and disappear if he was feeling a bit cold and shivered while he slept. There was just something eerily other worldly about him!" sobbed Rosemary, wiping tears from her cheeks.

Sam got up to leave. Following protocol, he strapped Rosemary back in bed but not as tightly as Nurse Bates would have done.

Sam decided to leave the buckle of one strap so loose that it served no purpose as a restraint. He also intentionally forgot to lock the window.

"Do you know where they might have taken the baby, Sam?" expressed Rosemary, with a raised brow.

"Ireland, one of the senior staff members in head office has connections with an orphanage in the south of the country. A place called *'The Good Herdsman Convent, Redemption Asylum'*. It takes in wayward women from the surrounding area. Women who find themselves in *'trouble'*. It is also run as an orphanage. I think your parents just wanted a solution that would remove Michael as far away as possible," Sam put on his coat as he walked towards the door.

"Michael, who named the boy Michael?" Rosemary wiped sweat from her forehead waiting for Sam's reply.

"Why, you did, in a way. During one of your restless slumbers you were talking in your sleep about not being able to start your residency at St Michaels. I guess it was as good a name as any, Michael Flannery, especially considering where his new home would be," smiled Sam, at least half-ways.

With that, Sam left disappearing silently down the hallway; he and Rosemary would meet again, but not for a very long time.

The sound of leather on tiled floors approaches Rosemary's room once again. This time there would be no receiver of these sounds, no viewer of Nurse Bates's crooked grin, no one to recoil from her ungentle touch.

"Good morning Rosemary, Rosemary?!" a sarcastic voice enquires but receives no answer.

Two beady little eyes, set into a loveless face, scan the room. A linen blind, swaying in the chilled morning air, summons Nurse Bates's gaze to the window.

The morning light creeps in, without any invitation, under the blind and claws at her, bringing forth a mundane reminder that another day had begun in this tomb of cold hopelessness.

Rosemary had gone; escaped during the night. Looking out of the window, Nurse Bates could see that an unseasonable snow shower had betrayed the direction of Rosemary's barefoot escape. The alarm was raised.

Sam, on hearing all the commotion, came into the room. Infuriated, Nurse Bates ran abruptly from the room and down the hall screaming. Although happy that Rosemary was no longer here, Sam believed that she nor he could ever be truly free. Snowflakes are persuaded to retire with a slight rise in temperature as it begins to rain. The rain pattered against the window pane washing the remaining snowflakes away and Sam could not stop crying. The more it rained, the more he cried. The window mirrored eyes that gazed upon somewhere he could not be.

***

Twelve hours previous...

Rosemary is having another night of sleep disturbed by her dreaded nightmare poem. On hearing a repeated tapping on the window, she half opens one eye, then the other; then both fully. She feels that not only is her left arm restraint loose, it is in fact not fastened at all. Slipping her arm out she manages to first undo her right arm restraint followed by freeing both leg clamps. Taking off her blindfold increases her ability to see only marginally.

The tapping on the glass continues as she reaches across to the window sill. With her right hand she feels along the roughly painted wood for the window opening.

In doing so her fingers trace along some small and hastily carved lettering.

SAM ANDERSON WAS HERE 06/07/47

Was this my kind nurse Sam? This would have been carved over twenty years ago but he would have been in Med school at that time. Maybe this was shortly after his first abduction? The passage of time doesn't fully match that within his face, he should look much older. There seems to be a twenty-year shift, in age, to where he told me he was when first abducted, thought Rosemary.

Rosemary's attention is once again drawn to the tapping on the window. However, this time the minute percussion is accompanied with a child's whispered requests of *"Let me in Mummy, let me in"*.

A cold dread moves up Rosemary's spine, out along her shoulders and arms until it reaches her right hand, now clutching the linen blind. Through which she can just about make out a red-haired boy of around five years of age. Closing her eyes shut tightly does nothing to quell the child's continuing demands.

"Please Mummy, it's cold and I'm hungry. Can I come inside for just a little while?" pleads the chilling voice, yet again, even more mournfully.

Rosemary can stand it no longer. Pulling the blinds up quickly, the moonlit face of a red-haired child with eyes completely black is presented to her.

The child is as pale as snow and poorly shielded from the cold in a much too small, grey and ragged uniform of torn linen.

The only evidence of the clothing's uniform status is a crudely sewn crest framed with the words *"The Good Herdsman Convent, Redemption Asylum"*. Now, instead of appeals to enter, the child is repeating the *Sun/Moon* poem over and over in a dogged like mantra.

"No! No! No!" Rosemary cries out as she wakes from the seemingly never-ending nightmare.

Her attention is once again harassed by a repeated drumming on the window. Again, Rosemary finds it an easy task to free herself from the bed restraints. The same as the previous instance, her fingers affirm Sam's wood engraved proclamation of presence.

This time it is not a fiendish dream. Another pulling up of the blinds reveals the authors of the rattling and crying to be spidery branch ends of a Silver Birch and a wailing ginger tom cat. Unusually for this time of year, it has started to snow.

The surrounding garden walls are already topped with three or four centimetres. Noticing the window is slightly ajar, she pushes it wide open. Almost weightless flakes tumble gently from the sky to momentarily tickle her nose. She feels as giddy as a child looking out upon the unexpected, panoramic, wintery largesse.

A moment's pause, a secondary consideration; it does not matter now, she is not staying here another second. No shoes, no coat, no hat, no scarf, no gloves - only a hospital gown - but also no restraints anymore; she has no possessions whatsoever. The other side of Rosemary's window contains no belongings, she belongs here no more but the world beyond holds the possibility of a future to be fulfilled.

Holding tightly onto the window frame, she eases herself out onto the wall crowned with soft white powdery snow. She is too excited with the prospect of escape to notice her toes already turning purple from Winter's grasp.

Walking, almost tip-toeing along, with a disregard for what the outcome of a tumble from this height could be is cruelly rewarded with a momentarily wobble, a loss of balance and then a fall. The lapse in concentration and landing face first into the flower beds below is somewhat cushioned by the deepening snow; however, not sufficiently enough to prevent Rosemary discerning the audible crunch of a nasal fracture. Arms out at ninety degrees, she pushes down upon her hands elevating her face from the almost Venetian impression left behind in the snow. Two blood-red ellipses also account for her previous position.

Sitting amongst the medicinal flower bed, feeling slightly dazed and confused, she decides to pause momentarily to gather her thoughts. Wiping a trickle of blood from her nose, she is once again captivated by the beauty of the curative blooms. Unwittingly she gathers a rudimentary bouquet and ties it together with a loose strand harvested from her shabby hospital gown.

Making her way over to the gate, egress is postponed by a much rusted but heavy-duty padlock. Looking for an alternative route she pushes partially through a gap in the row of yew trees; pausing briefly to avert being detected by the patrolling night watchman. Questioning why she had never seen the security guard before is immediately answered by unmerciful howls and screams transcending from the windows of the no longer obscured maximum security wing, beyond the yew tree border. There was a greater need for the warden's attention where the high-risk inmates were housed.

When the warden passed by her makeshift yew tree blind, Rosemary noticed a set of old, large keys hanging carelessly from his belt loop. She waited, holding her breath so it would not deliver her presence in the cold night air as the dull jangle approached.

The guard, pausing to light a cigarette, gave Rosemary the opportunity to exhale undiscovered and also the good fortune to liberate the keys. He continued puffing along the path, resembling a vintage steam engine, around the end of the yew tree hedgerow towards the gate.

There was a pause filled with silence and then broken by several profanities upon the realisation, or so he thought, of having mislaid his keys somewhere. As he ran winding back along the path towards the maximum-security wing, coughing so hard rendering him forgetful of the pain endured when he tried to do so on his wooden prosthetic, Rosemary eased herself out of hiding and made her way to the gate.

After desperately trying five keys, she had success with the second last one. Creaking open begrudgingly, the gate handed over Rosemary to a silent, snow kissed, path lit only by a flickering street lamp and haunted from above by an eager moon.

Where to now? I don't know, anywhere but here… and fast. My feet feel like they are on fire and my nose stings, at least the cold has stemmed the blood flow, Rosemary thought, somewhat gratefully.

The increasing cold also stems Rosemary's earlier child-like enthusiasm for the unexpected flurries. The road curves left and the path leads her to pause by a rural boutique. The window display has several mannequins all garbed in fashion of yester year; dressed in styles that her mother would have flaunted twenty years ago.

One mannequin above all catches her attention. Standing behind a headless naked dummy is one dressed in what looks like a carbon copy of what would be a typical *"Christmas outfit"* worn by her mother when Rosemary was about five years of age. Even more surprising, the mannequin was adorned with a blond wig fashioned into an omelette-fold, just like her mother would have styled. It had on a calf length, pleated and buttoned up at the front, red frock. The waist was fitted and finished with a large black velvet bow.

The mannequin's lips turned ruby red and eyes icy blue as it turned its head in Rosemary's direction.

"Feeling cold my dear?" enquired the mannequin.

"Yes, a little, actually quite a bit really. Hey! What? How are you talking to me?!" demanded Rosemary.

"I'll talk to you like a mother can and must dearie! If you insist going out dressed like a rag doll at this time of year... well what can you expect! Besides, such an outfit would not be acceptable at the *'Country Women's Association Annual Christmas Ball'!* Can't you wear any of the Christmas clothes I got for you?" replied the mannequin in a mocking fashion.

"This is what they made me wear when you sent me away, when you left me in that awful, God forsaken, place!" screamed Rosemary, in a low, guttural howl.

"Now little missy, you listen to me, your father and I spent good money on feeding, clothing and educating you!" the mannequin retorted.

"An education I can never use! A doctor who becomes a patient! A woman who becomes a child! A free spirit who becomes shackled and abused!" Rosemary's veins exaggerated their presence around her temples.

"Educated indeed! Obviously not smart enough to keep your legs closed! And then, to invent some cockamamie story about being abducted… by aliens! Ha!" the mannequin, laughing derisively before returning to its original pose.

Rosemary's body begins to shudder uncontrollably and snaps her out of the trance induced by going into shock from the sub-zero temperatures.

The mannequin is no longer talking to her. She realises her mother wasn't there, not now, not ever really. She must get warm and decides, even though not to her taste, the mannequin's clothes would be of better use covering her cold pale flesh than its soulless plastic torso. Rummaging around the porch of the clothing boutique she finds a key under a blue glazed plant pot containing the remains of a long dried-out pink carnation. Turning the key in the door's lock produces a click and long drawn out creak akin to that of a movie vampire's coffin.

Stepping inside, although broken, her nose is assaulted by the stench of death. Pulling the hospital gown up over her nose diminishes the foul odour somewhat and she continues blindly down a small corridor. Cobwebs loop and hang like sinister imposter Christmas chains. They seem to claw and pull at her face, attempting to persuade her to stay, to never leave and become a permanent guest in this palace of dust. After trying for the length of the hallway, they fail to ensnare her. Momentarily, her progress is halted by the unmistakable feeling of fur brushing against and clawed feet gripping, her skin.

The accompanying squeal confirmed a rat had just crawled slowly across her left foot. Rosemary pauses for a moment to calm her nerves. Then her direction is gathered and pointed towards a chink of light escaping from a doorway leading into the main shop floor and display window. Long searching beams of moonlight pierce through the dusty window and reflect off some costume jewellery adorning one of several mannequins. The same beams of light bring forth a figure out of complete darkness but still imprisoned by the shadows that inhabit the corner of the room.

Rosemary hesitatingly moves towards the shape which she thinks must be a mannequin placed in a sitting position on a rocking chair. Dread decides to visit the very core of her being and every cell in her body screams out loud... HALT! YOU MUST GO NO FURTHER!

However, just as those who suffer from acrophobia, the desire to look down can sometimes override their fear. Rosemary ignores the sweat trickling down her back, she pays no regard to the nervous twitch of her uncontrollable, flickering left eyelid and moves forward.

As she edges towards the silhouette her hospital gown falls from covering her nose. Immediately she is overcome by the volatile aroma hanging in the stale air; it breaks her concentration and causes her to stumble over the end of the curved rockers. With one hand over her mouth in an attempt to stay her gag reflex and groping outwards with the other to regain her footing, Rosemary grabs hold of the seated figure to be confronted with the fact that this is no mannequin.

Partial cloud cover outside dissipates long enough for the moonlight to garner more strength and the mistaken form is illuminated in all its gory glory! The bygone shopkeeper must have died waiting for her boutique to come back into fashion. Although mostly skeleton, there was enough meat left on those bones to make Rosemary retch at every attempted gasp. Running in the wrong direction, momentarily blinded by the sudden increase in light from the Moon and street lamp, away from the door, she bumps into her mother's plastic doppelganger sending it crashing to the floor. Hastily she undresses it and herself.

Minutes later she pauses to look at her own reflection in the window. A little loose fitting, the result of barely eating for the past few months, the outfit will suffice in keeping her warm. Back in the hallway she notices a pair of wellies; once green in colour, now a muddy grey, faded from age and neglect. They did not complement the ensemble and her mother certainly wouldn't approve.

Closing the door very gently behind her, Rosemary walks on cautiously. Pausing momentarily to look back over her shoulder, she smiles at the sight of a headless dummy no longer naked but now styled, albeit a little shabbily and blood stained, in the latest hospital fashion - courtesy of *"The Filchington Institute and Asylum"*.

Trudging up the now ascending path, Rosemary can't fight the urge to look left towards the accompanying forest edge and also rearward to the village fading behind. She simultaneously feels a presence from both directions, all the while trying to keep a steady foot in the now melting, ashen sludge.

Close behind, she anticipates the approach of something foreboding. If not evil then certainly an existence that bears her no kindness, is in attendance; to her left she senses affection. Glancing sideways, Rosemary momentarily glimpses a figure composed of flickering blue light; not evil or even scary but one with a sad yet filled with empathy, smiling face. Once again Rosemary finds herself running along a dark path trying to escape the unknown.

The friction caused by the over-sized wellies burns Rosemary's toes; forcing her to pause a while, this grants her feet some relief. A neon-blue line image of Mick Flannery is animated to her left. He walks towards her, this woman who gave birth to him unceremoniously in an asylum ward, now standing before him, is within arms-reach.

A dark shadowed figure finding difficulty in breathing follows uphill from behind. Ahead, the Kolassian can see Rosemary resting. Aiming a net gun at her, the North Polar Neridian pauses temporarily as its line of sight is disturbed by the ghostly hologram that is a time-travelling Mick Flannery.

Mick reaches out with his muscular, clumsy arm and tries in vain to gently stroke the trailing russet locks of his mother Rosemary's unkempt hair; unbrushed, unwashed, unloved yet the most beautiful thing in the Universe to him, not just at this very moment, but forever.

The time travel device is unstable and although it has brought him to where his heart desired, his outstretched arm flickers before him and cannot grasp his mother's tresses. He keeps fading in and out of her time. The Kolassian repeatedly takes aim with a net gun but its target is again obscured by the intermittent time traveller.

Then all movement ceases. Snowflakes seem to pause in mid-air, the cold easterly breeze halts its ravage of the pine trees and Rosemary drops her makeshift bouquet of flowers. Looking up, the blinding light of a small craft illuminates the forest clearing.

This causes the Kolassian to retreat and the last sight Mick has of his mother, for some time, is that of her unanimated body and face frozen in time, not unlike a string-less marionette, as she is lifted aboard the ship. This is not a capture; not even a recapture. This is a rescue. A tall twenty-six-year-old woman with fair hair and slim build gets Rosemary to lie down on a bunk. She comforts her with a drink of water and a welcoming, warm blanket.

A female Oikian is piloting the craft. Amatheia, once covered in reddish brown hair, her accumulated long years are disclosed by increasingly longer white streaks outnumbering those of cerise.

Rosemary can't help in thinking that the pilot looks familiar despite her obvious alien appearance. This nine and a half foot tall South Polar Neridian turns to smile at Rosemary, trying to ease her apprehension.

"You are not being abducted Rosemary, those years are long gone, I promise. We are here to help, we will look after you now," assured Amatheia.

"Where are you taking me? Who was following me?" asked Rosemary.

"There were two different pursuers. One pursuant was a common enemy, the other was a common relative," replied Amatheia, speaking rapidly, focussed on Rosemary's well-being.

"Who was the common enemy?" asks Rosemary.

"A North Polar Neridian, a Kolassian, trying to abduct you, until we intervened!" revealed Amatheia.

"The common relative... who... I'm almost more afraid to ask, the blue flickering image - who was that?" Rosemary demanded to know.

"Your future son, or rather, your son Michael from the future. I'm Amatheia, although he doesn't know it yet, I am his twin sister and... from some difficult to explain circumstances - your daughter," Amatheia's eyes waited patiently for Rosemary's response.

"Confusing, huh? Twenty years from now I could be twenty years younger; I currently live twenty years ahead of where I should be now.

"Some deep sleep stasis that malfunctioned - anyway, that's a story for another time," proffered the young woman sitting in the co-pilot seat.

"Where are we going?" asked Rosemary.

"South Polar Neridia, Oikia, to be precise... home.

"Today we have no need for stasis periods of two decades anymore, thanks to the wormhole located not far from here. It was engineered by my good friend and co-pilot sitting here beside us," explained Amatheia nodding towards the young woman sitting in the seat parallel to her own.

"Co-ordinates set and locked in, engaging fusion thrusters," states the co-pilot, friend of Amatheia, rescuer of Rosemary and future twenty-six-year-old daughter of Kyle and Crystal... *Saoirse.*

05

Departures

A parent reluctantly releases a child's hand without holding it; a hand not held for a long time.
Pacing up and down a bank of monitors; launch awaits countdown completion and a new journey to begin.

A last hand-held moment falls to the side as a quietened breath is followed by, perhaps, a concluding beat towards an unknown eternity.

The best part of a day had passed as ten coupled carriages continued to fly along on a cushion of electromagnetism. Suddenly, the smooth transition is interrupted by a shunt sideways and then an almost immediate stop causing the occupants to be thrown forwards into the compartment wall and then finishing up in a pile on top of each other.

A struggle ensues as the Kolassian tries to relieve Crystal of her gun. In the scuffle, a bullet is released from the Glock's chamber and it travels upwards; first entering the North Polar Neridian's chin, exiting through its frontal lobe and then embedding in the carriage roof.

The Kolassian lies motionless on the floor as Mick, Kyle and Crystal step over it while cautiously exiting through the half-jammed door. Through a burgeoning cloud of smoke and flame they make their way undiscovered to a side tunnel. Sitting down on the ground to gather their thoughts, Mick pulls off his bandage. The blood has ceased to drip from the corner of his right eye. Although the surrounding tissue is badly bruised, his vision has mostly returned to normal.

"I think this must be some sort of service tunnel that runs parallel to the main track. Maybe we can travel along it until we pass the carnage on the tracks ahead," Kyle said as he leaned forward trying to get a better view.

Mick, still a little unsteady from the trauma he suffered on the alien examination table, is helped up by Crystal and Kyle. Walking on, he recounts his ordeal.

"Of course, I've heard of abductions before but that was my first experience of one that I can remember or one that I was conscious and aware of as it happened. There has been evidence of me being abducted right throughout my life.

"The orphanage, from when I was about five years of age, would report me missing on numerous occasions. I would often be found, by a police patrol car, near the edge of a forest or even on top of the orphanage roof by the caretaker days later, blankly reciting that poem.

"When I fell through what actually turned out to be a holographic reflection of you, I thought that the floor of the sinkhole would be the last thing I would ever see.

"So, it was a surprise to say the least that I found myself floating halfway down; a greater shock to find that

I was being encased in an icy fabric and transported into that laboratory. When the syringe approached my eye, my screams were replaced with that damn poem. I must have been shocked into that trance-like mantra from sheer terror. Don't get me wrong, regardless of my vacant state, I did feel the syringe penetrate, then a slight pop just before the release of liquid and my continuing screams. I felt pain unlike any I have experienced before; I was not oblivious to the intensity of it.

"However, although I could feel numerous incisions being made, samples of tissue and fluids extracted from various apertures in the icy cocoon, the pain was not insurmountable. Gradually, my focus on the poem enabled me to keep my pain threshold relatively high. Through blurred vision I could make out three or four of the hairless North Polar Neridians. I think they were fussing over a blood sample of mine that must have caused them some serious debate because one of them pushed a cohort of his to the ground and stormed out. That's when you rescued me," recalled Mick thankfully, looking towards Kyle.

"There must be a reason why they took you rather than me," pondered Kyle.

"I'm not certain why exactly but they seemed darn interested in that vile of my blood, that's for sure!" exclaimed Mick, wide-eyed.

"Come on guys, I think I see the next doorway back into the main tunnel up ahead," interjected Crystal.

Mick, with elbows leaning down on the shoulders of both Kyle and Crystal, led the way back through and onto the tracks. The noise and carnage left behind was replaced with hours of a slow-paced passing along the dimly lit tunnel. Kyle asked Mick if he thought it would be an idea to try the time travel device in order to get nearer their destination more quickly. The three stepped into and sat down inside an alcove within the tunnel wall just out of view of any potentially unwanted trailing arrivals.

"Considering its instability, our limited knowledge and insufficient experience, I don't know if that would be such a good idea. When I first showed the device to Jim, we had only met that evening and I had experimented with it just a handful of times," cautioned Mick.

"Where did you get it from?" asked Crystal.

"About a month before I first met Jim Kelly, I, like many others had been noticing an increase in UFO or UAP sightings - especially near certain mountain ranges. That along with an escalation of very changeable weather patterns and more and more reports of massive sink holes, led me to hike and explore in the nearby hills and valleys. It was on one of these treks that I came across some wreckage near the edge of a sinkhole.

"Amongst the debris there was a dead Kolassian still firmly gripping this device. I tried to analyse it on several occasions but with no great success. After meeting Jim and realising his advanced intelligence was not wholly of human origin, I persuaded him to come work with me and we formed an alliance which ultimately led to the formation of, I suppose you could call it, a resistance of sorts," Mick carefully retrieved the shiny cylindrical contraption from his backpack and held it up to the light.

They all paused to gaze upon the swirling blue liquid and the pulsating black light contained within.

"We don't really know how to use it. What we do know is that if you hold the lower half and squeeze with one hand, time seems to move backwards but you remain in the same place unaffected by the passage of time. When you hold the top half, again unencumbered by the ravages of age, you travel forwards in time also remaining in your current location.

"However, if you grip both upper and lower sections you will be transported to another destination, either forwards or backwards in time. It seems that your emotions and where your heart's desire to be at that particular moment, is the driving force in determining the end time and destination. What happens though is you travel there in a kind of ghostly holographic form. Unable to interact or alter the events presented before you; up until now at least, we think an observer is your only capacity," described Mick.

"You say the device picks up on your emotions and it somehow uses what or where you long for as a compass to your destination, how so? I mean, I don't think the Kolassians appear to show any emotions," Crystal's interest, spiked with increased possibilities.

"Well, I somehow suspect that the device is not really of Kolassian origin; perhaps it is a technology that they stole and do not fully know how to use it either, hence me finding it in the hands of a dead Kolassian at the crash site. Maybe in time, Amatheia might be able to throw some light on this device's origins.

"You've heard of emotional intelligence? You've probably also heard of situations where a patient receives a heart transplant and that sometimes family members of the deceased have noticed traits of their departed loved one now present in the recipient of the heart donation?

"I have other theories involving muscle memory, your heart is essentially a muscular pump. Even further than that, have you ever considered the possibility of DNA memory?" theorised Mick.

"Do you mean that apart from traits passed on from our parents, it might be possible that we also pass on memories and experiences to our children?" added Kyle.

"Exactly!" enthused Mick.

"That *Sun/Moon* poem you often recite in a trance-like state, especially if you are overly stressed, in a deep sleep or even sleep walking, could that be an example of DNA memory?" asked Kyle, even more intrigued.

"Possibly, I'm not sure. Look, I think maybe I should try to use the device on my own first, just in case something goes wrong. I mean, the very nature of emotions is that they are often unstable. Also, we don't know how long this tunnel is and the end destination near Reykjavik does not have any emotional connection for us.

"So, the device might not get us there even if we clear our minds and try to only focus on that destination," explained Mick, frustrated.

With everyone agreed, Mick took the device and placed it on a ledge in the alcove. Kneeling down, he placed his left hand on the upper section and firmly gripped the lower section with his right hand.

As he suggested before, he has no bond or emotional connection with the destination they are trying to reach. He struggles to concentrate and while attempting to do so he looks at Crystal, a mother separated from her children. His concentration is disrupted and his focus turns to his own mother whom he briefly met before he was shipped off to the orphanage. He holds no hate for the woman. Perhaps if circumstances had been different she would have kept him.

He does not blame her, he can't help feeling sorry for her; he desires so much to meet her, to try and know if there is love or a shared bond. As he is filled with all sorts of emotions, Kyle and Crystal watch on as a tear-soaked Mick flickers before them, changing into a fading hologram. He fades into nothing with the background replacing the space he occupied moments ago; leaving the device unmovable, almost glued to the spot and emitting a low vibration.

***

Looking up, Mick sees he is no longer in the alcove beside Kyle and Crystal; neither is he at the underground Kolassian headquarters near Vidgelmir. Presented before him, across a snow-covered street is a tall iron gate set into the middle of an archway with a long limestone wall running for a few hundred metres left and right of it. Above the arch is a sign that reads *"The Filchington Institute and Asylum"*. The gate is slightly open and an alarm increases in volume beyond the wall.

Bare feet have left a trail down the path and continue around the curve of the road. Mick follows the footprints and notices he leaves none of his own as he looks down through his holographic self.

Proceeding along slowly, the footprints cease outside the door of a clothing boutique. Then all of a sudden, a young woman comes out walking quickly. She is dressed in 1940's style clothing and wearing a pair of mucky boots. She does not see him hiding behind a tree as she walks on up the hill. She looks over her shoulder momentarily as Mick observes a Kolassian, stealthily in pursuit of her.

Still fearing he might be seen but yet he is so curiously drawn to this woman; he decides to follow hidden in the tree line to her left.

Mick remembered an awful staff member from the orphanage once told him, with ridicule, that his mother would not be coming to take him home anytime soon as she was locked up in an asylum far from Ireland. He guesses she must have been his mother, Rosemary, at a younger age. Ahead she is resting in a clearing, nursing a sore foot. He tries to reach out but she floats up into the air towards a craft hovering above. Rosemary is taken aboard and just before it zooms off out of sight into the dark midnight blue, he catches a glimpse of a familiar alien face and an unknown woman.

The Kolassian leaves in a hurry and Mick is left alone in the forest clearing. Snowflakes begin to tumble from the sky once again. His eyes follow a giant snowflake as it flutters past some pine branches and comes to rest with its siblings on the forest floor. In doing so his attention is brought to something in the middle of the clearing that shouldn't normally be there.

Out of the deepening white, little specks of colour appear; gold, yellow, green, purple and red petals, a little bouquet of flowers. Mick recognises the flower at the centre, Rosemary.

That was it, the name of my mother was Rosemary. She must have dropped these flowers when the ship took her, thought Mick.

Mick bends down and tries but fails to pick up the bouquet; frustratingly remembering that when time travelling with the device he can only be there as an observer and usually not be able to interact.

But I know she saw me! Maybe when emotions are high it is possible to traverse and override the limitations of the device and actually participate in the time-travelled-to destination, cemented Mick in his mind.

Mick's heart swells and tears coat his face. He reaches down one more time and initially his hand passes right through the image of the flowers before him. However, as his frustration increases so does the level of emotion; another attempt in attaining purchase upon the bouquet is successful and Mick grasps the bunch of flowers with passion and tears overtaking him. As soon as he does, his holographic image flickers in both times; he then disappears from the forest clearing. He reappears back in the tunnel, beside Kyle and Crystal, still clutching Rosemary's bouquet. Sitting on the floor sobbing, repeating over and over...

"I saw her, I saw her! I saw Rosemary! I saw my beautiful... sad mother!"

"Where and when did you travel to?" asked Kyle.

"I arrived outside the gates of the asylum where my mother, Rosemary, had been forcibly kept after I had been sent to the orphanage. I know this because when I first arrived at the orphanage, the only belongings I had were a few clothes and an old bible with the inscription *'The Filchington Institute and Asylum'* on the front cover, which had been placed under my blanket by one of the nurses. Hand written on the inside cover was the name *'Rosemary Flannery'*. I guess I held on to it over the years knowing it had a connection with my past. I don't know what year exactly my time travel destination was, it might have only been shortly after her incarceration or it could have been five years later.

"I think she had somehow just escaped. I tracked her to what looked like a vintage clothes shop and on to a forest clearing where I witnessed her being taken!" explained Mick.

"Taken? Taken by who?" asked Crystal.

"It wasn't the Kolassians. I couldn't believe my eyes. I saw Amatheia! Except she was a lot older with white streaks running through her red hair. I saw someone else there too," said Mick.

"Who?!" asked Kyle loudly.

"There was a young, fair haired, woman roughly in her mid-twenties. She seemed to be helping Amatheia fly the ship!" said Mick looking directly at Kyle.

"As far as we know, Amatheia went to keep Crystal, Saoirse and Ellen safe!" said Kyle, jumping in.

"Yes, but as you know, I told you before, Saoirse was out in the back garden playing when the Kolassians took Ellen and myself off in different ships! I never met Amatheia!" frustrated Crystal cutting across them both.

"Listen, I trust Amatheia with my life. I have no doubt she made her way to your house and if Saoirse was hiding from the Kolassians or was distracted in her play and didn't see them, well Amatheia would find her. I reckon Amatheia and Saoirse are probably also making their way towards Vidgelmir near Reykjavik," appeases Mick.

"But you said you saw Amatheia flying the ship that took Rosemary!" reasoned Crystal.

"Yes, I did, but the Amatheia I saw was much older," replied Mick frowning.

"What if Amatheia's co-pilot was an older Saoirse?" wonders Kyle with tear filled eyes.

"I want my six-year-old Saoirse, I want my four-year-old Ellen! I want my family back together now!" said Crystal, with a demanding scream.

Just at that moment they could hear another string of electromagnetic carriages humming towards them from an adjoining tunnel.

They leaned back into the alcove as the train passed. The carriages halted and a group of Kolassians exited one of the carriage side doors and marched towards the earlier wreckage. As the carriages resumed their hum and proceeded to move forward slowly, a little girl about four years of age popped her head up and looked, through the carriage glass, in the direction of Kyle and Crystal. It was their youngest daughter Ellen. Crystal ran after the carriage with Kyle a few paces behind.

Upon reaching the carriage there was no easy way of gaining access to Ellen's compartment. Instinct drove Crystal to jump onto a metal frame at the lower end of the rear carriage and Kyle followed suit. By the time Mick looked up from the bouquet of flowers it was too late for him to join them; besides after his terrible ordeal in the

Kolassian's laboratory he was in no physical condition to run and jump onto a moving vehicle.

While sitting alone in the tunnel, considering what to do next, Mick pulled out a small leather-bound book from his backpack. He had kept this bible from his mother's asylum all these years; it was the only remaining connection he had to her. Opening it, he placed the small bouquet between the pages and closed the volume tightly shut; he now had one more connection to his mother, Rosemary Flannery.

Longing for more clarity and feeling a build-up of emotions he decided to take the time travel device out of his back-pack again. He felt a burning desire to learn more of his past.

***

After another flickering hologram of Mick disappeared, he once more found himself staring across the road at the austere iron gates that, normally, guarded the entrance to the *"The Filchington Institute and Asylum"*. However, this time, all that stood there now was the crumbled down archway left as a monumental reminder of the past.

The asylum was no more; a park where children played tag, flew kites and threw ball for pet dogs to fetch, took its place. Finding a park bench, Mick sits and observes a little old man approaching; carrying a shopping bag, first pausing to stretch and then sits down beside Mick. Positive the man would be unaware of his presence, Mick decides to stay put. To his astonishment, the man turns and speaks.

"Hello Mick, my name is Sam, may I speak with you for a little while?" asked the friendly stranger.

"You can see me? But I'm not here, not really!" Mick whispered in confusion.

"Where is here? Here is wherever your heart is, wherever it wants you to be," suggested Sam.

I don't know who this man Sam is but I feel I can trust him; his broad warm smile set in that wrinkled face with smiling brown eyes, he seems to exude nothing but kindness..., thought Mick.

"I looked out for your mother. She was not happy in the building that once stood here. I hope and feel she is in a happier place now," confided Sam.

"You worked here as a nurse looking after my mother?" enquired Mick.

"Not quite, I was deemed a low risk patient who had fantasies of being a nurse. I was *taken* many time during my life, just like your mother; *just like you*. After spending years in the asylum, I grew tired, almost bored, trying to convince them of my abductions. After almost resigning myself to the mundanity of my situation, I became more sedate and caused my keepers no problems; as a result, they gave me the freedom to wander the corridors and the grounds as I pleased.

"One day I heard your mother's protests; starting off with a gentle refusal to comply with any instructions but soon escalating to horrific cries of the iniquities of life which soon resulted in her being forcibly sedated.

"On another occasion I heard her having, shall we say, a very unpleasant time under the care of a nurse whose wickedness had very few boundaries. I could no longer tolerate the injustice and cruelty of the situation, so I decided to intervene. I had often posed as a nurse and passed it off as one of my multiple personalities; it would now give me the perfect opportunity to shine some light into your mother's life and perhaps disperse some darkness from the shadows surrounding her. In showing kindness, I hope that I was of some comfort to your mother. I shared my experiences of abduction with her to show she was not alone, not crazy.

"One day though, I knew she had taken more than enough abuse, she was at a very low point, so I enabled her escape. I couldn't bear to see the life in her dwindle away, little by little," recalled Sam.

"How do you know my name? How do you know who I am?" asked Mick.

"How can I see your hologram? The device you used was designed by me, while I was under a sort of Kolassian *'house arrest'*. One of my abductions lasted years, it seemed, in my mind and yet only days in Earth time. Being highly skilled in advanced scientific technologies led me to be taken far too many times; I was one of their earliest implant victims.

"Anyway, you do stand out in a crowd, I mean your size, the colour of your hair - you have your mother's eyes too by the way. It was decided that you were to be sent to an orphanage in Ireland. I knew Rosemary was distraught at losing you even if the circumstances of how you came to be were extremely devastating for her, or would be for anyone in that situation. I wanted to somehow facilitate the possibility of a future reunion between you and Rosemary," said Sam, as he moved closer.

"How?" asked Mick.

"The bible, with her signature on the inside cover," answered Sam with a thoughtful look upon his face.

"You hid the bible, wrapped in my blanket?" asked Mick, scrutinising Sam's face.

"Yes," replied Sam.

"But how come it stayed in my possession until such a time as I could read her signature; when I could understand it was a connection to my mother?" exasperated Mick, almost hyperventilating in the process.

"Admittedly, it was a slim chance but no matter where you find yourself in the world, in the Universe, sometimes there will be someone who cares; another sympathetic soul capable of empathy. There is almost always someone drawn to those in need of assistance or at the very least, a considerate eye to keep watch now and again," answered Sam.

"I do remember a kind teacher at the orphanage, a tall man with, fly-away, light brown hair. He always wore a cream coloured Aran sweater and brown brogues; his name was Mr Corcoran. How do you know I was abducted?" wondered Mick, staring down at his own size twelve shoes.

"From time to time, reports of your progress at the orphanage would be sent back to the asylum head office. This was unusual, it wasn't something that was regularly carried out. Her story couldn't be verified. It could not be determined if Rosemary was raped or whether she became pregnant as a result of alien abduction; I don't think she fully knew herself. There was no proof of rape and because of your mother's continued pleading about her abduction plus the fact the accused rapist disappeared without a trace - the authorities felt that there was more to Rosemary's story.

"While I was pretending to be a nurse wandering the corridors, I had a rare opportunity to sneak into the administration office and read some of these reports. There were several documented cases of you disappearing for days and being found miles away by the police. Sometimes the caretaker would discover you on the orphanage roof shouting out loud, at double the normal speaking speed, the same poem your mother would recall in her nightmares.

"One of the teachers transcribed a midnight recital of yours while you were in a trance-like state. This transcription found its way into one of the reports. Upon reading it, I was amazed that it matched, word for word, this poem hand written by your mother on the night before her escape," finished Sam as he carefully handed Mick an A4 sheet of paper, headed with *"The Filchington Institute and Asylum"*.

"Am I the product of rape or alien abduction?" Mick cried out, forlornly.

"I do believe the young man who disappeared, from your mother's perspective, did look like he was making drunken advances but was actually paralysed and animated by the Kolassians. They attempted to pass off an alien insemination as an act of human sexual depredation. However, they botched the abduction of Finn Murphy and nearly killed him. He had to be animated or positioned in some way as to make it seem like a case of rape," theorised Sam, forthrightly.

Mick held the sheet of paper to his nose. Smelling the paper and the ink embedded; the fragrance it imparted, he closed his eyes. He tried to imagine this was his mother's perfume. He had no way of knowing for sure if it was just that or a scent imprinted from elsewhere but it comforted him nonetheless. There was a sense of needing to protect a woman he had never met but increasingly felt he was growing to know his mother.

"You must go to the orphanage Mick. Go and observe yourself as a little five-year-old; a boy who longs for his mother. There you will discover a way to defeat them," whispered Sam as his voice began to trail away.

After a deep sigh Mick opened his eyes, shifting his weight on the cast iron bench and turned to the right to look at Sam. There was no one sitting beside him. The kind little old man had gone. At the slow pace of how his limped walk had approached Mick earlier, Sam still should have been within viewing distance.

There was no evidence to suggest he had ever sat down beside Mick apart from his mother's hand-written poem. Holding the sheet tightly in the fluttering breeze, his holographic image again began to shimmer in two different times and places.

***

Mick found himself once more in the alcove just off the main tunnel. He quickly folded the sheet of paper, containing the poem written by his mother, in half and placed it within the pages of the bible; a few leaves after where the tiny bouquet of flowers was pressed.

Peering out into the tunnel, he could see the earlier collision had been cleared from the tunnel and only silence remained in its place.

Sam said I must go and observe my five-year-old self at the orphanage. He said I would find a way to defeat them, who did he mean, the Kolassians? Mick thought, also thinking of how his friends needed each other right now.

Kyle and Crystal had chased after their youngest daughter Ellen. Amatheia, hopefully, had found Saoirse and they would all meet up somewhere near the end of this tunnel.

The communication device Jim Kelly had given them no longer worked so Jim's circumstances were unknown. He thought that perhaps the best way he could be of help was to make his departure from here and follow Sam's advice to go back in time to the orphanage; back to observe his younger self and possible answers.

***

An ocean away...

Saoirse and Amatheia had travelled almost eight hundred kilometres on the back of the aquaton. It was an ultra-clear, blue sky day. Mister Waggles yawned and stretched as he bid good morning to Saoirse.

Amatheia had taken over the steering of the aquaton during the night as the child and her dog slept soundly; curled up in the comfort of each other's warmth. Pausing to look through her binoculars, Amatheia could make out land approaching in the distance.

Initially presented with a tip of mossy green, then black lava rock broadened the horizon. It was the beginning of Hvalfjordur, the whale fjord, which was about forty kilometres north-west of Reykjavik. Night would fall before they reached the coast. This would suit her fine; Amatheia preferred to travel under the cover of darkness when close to possible danger.

A full moon, a scattering of stars and the odd random dwelling perched high every half kilometre or so, provided enough light to allow them safely navigate the inlets and submerged rocks. About two hundred metres ahead of them was a section of calm water where the shoreline seemed easily accessible. It would still be tricky enough to dismount from the aquaton though as the water was over fifty metres deep, right up to the rocky shore's edge. As they made their approach something spooked the aquaton and it refused to proceed any closer to the bank.

Air bubbles began rising to the surface all around them; a few small ones at first, then increasing rapidly in size and quantity. The aquaton let out a high-pitched groan and incessant barking from Mister Waggles ensued. Amatheia quickly grabbed Saoirse before she could fall off into the unknown depths.

The sea became more and more violent. Amatheia was losing control of the aquaton and their situation. Making a split decision, she lifts Saoirse onto her shoulders and leaps into the frigid water with Mister Waggles paddling behind. They make it close to a ledge with Amatheia treading water while Saoirse scrambles onto a craggy protuberance of sharp lava rock. Amatheia places her two mighty hands down hard to grip the jagged surface and hoists her water-logged bulk up and out of the turbulent surf. Sitting at the water's edge, Amatheia nurses the palms of her hands, bloodied by the barnacled boulders. Saoirse sits upright and her growing cries draw Amatheia's attention away from her hands and back to a more immediate problem.

A young girl's dog is desperately trying to swim in the turmoil. Drift wood, salty sea spray, churned up kelp; all contributing to the hound's struggle being emblazoned across the bay with a howling yelp. From the depths, a darkening presence is summoned. Four-metre-wide jaws break the surface, enveloping the aquaton in a bloody and unmerciful feasting. The aquaton had opportunity to draw one last breath, continuance to exhale was denied.

In their endeavours to breed certain species from Polar Neridia with those of earthly origins, the Kolassians occasionally gained unwanted results of gargantuan proportions. Presented before Amatheia and Saoirse, was one of these creations. Having finished its main course of aquaton, it was now furiously pursuing dessert in the form of a beagle hound... Mister Waggles.

The only way to describe it would be like a cross between an aquaton and a humpback whale with some features appearing to be positioned rather peculiarly. These were more evident as the monstrosity breached the surface again. The head had a pair of eyes offset to one side with a second and a third smaller and unusable mouths of fused shut baleen. At thirty metres from head to tail it must have been three times that of an average humpback whale.

The colouration was not this species of whale's usual black on the dorsal side and a mottled black and white under side; it took on the wrinkled grey textures, almost elephant like, of an aquaton.

As it raised its tail in preparation to slap downwards in the direction of Mister Waggles, it was now clear to see where the aquaton-like horns were repositioned. No longer found in a pair pointing outward from the head; a dozen or more misshapen bony probes projected out at different angles from its tail.

Seeing that Saoirse's beloved pet was almost certainly doomed, Amatheia had to act fast. Giving no regard to her already bleeding hands, she summoned all her strength with a roaring rage and plucked out a partially wedged boulder from the ledge above her. Raising her arms high above her head, she threw the boulder with all the power she could muster, towards the behemoth.

The result was a mournful and prolonged deep groan with surrounding waters turning from indigo to crimson. The brute ceased its thrashing and as it lulled nearby, motionless, a calm returned to the water as the beloved Mister Waggles eventually made it, unscathed, to shore.

Amatheia had sacrificed the skin on the palms of her hands to save the girl and her pet. In a reciprocated act of kindness, Saoirse washed the blood from Amatheia's hands. Then, as requested, placed some dried kelp she retrieved from above the shoreline, onto Amatheia's cuts. This, Amatheia told Saoirse, would help fight off any infection. Taking out her father's crumpled t-shirt from her backpack, Saoirse tore off several long strips for use as a makeshift bandage. Mister Waggles played his part too, very enthusiastically, by helping her to tear the strips of cloth; Saoirse disguising it as a game of tug-of-war.

By Amatheia's reckoning they were about ninety kilometres from Vidgelmir. There was a way to reduce their travelling time but it could potentially prove to be very dangerous.

As their walk from the beach brought them to grassy heath land, Amatheia started to notice some large footprints and animal scat that were not indigenous. There was another creature she knew the Kolassians had tried to breed, hidden in different corners of Earth. Mick and Kyle had communicated to Jim Kelly that they had stumbled upon a pen of these beasts, concealed at the edge of a fern meadow. Terratons, back on Polar Neridia, were used by Kolassians and Oikians alike. They were notoriously difficult to break but once trained they were extremely loyal.

Apart from being a trustworthy animal, they were an ideal mode of transport for trekking across rough terrain. Forests on this part of Iceland were poorly managed and suffered badly from deforestation. Some pockets of birch and larch regained a foothold after being left to recover from over-grazing but are not as plentiful here compared to the eastern side of Iceland.

However, orchard grass, spiked woodrush and several species of sedges abound; these are very similar to Neridian grasses which make up the bulk of the, herbivorous, terraton diet. The tea-leaved willow is more of a shrub but sometimes can grow to tree size and could provide plenty of cover for the Kolassians to camouflage their terraton enclosures.

As they reached the top of a knoll, Amatheia threw herself to the ground; Saoirse grabbing hold of Mister Waggles, quickly did the same. Down in the hollow below them was a lone terraton grazing on a patch of sedges. From the flattened grass it was possible for Amatheia's eye to follow the trail the terraton had left behind; it seemed to lead in the direction of a small copse of birch on the horizon to her right. Lifting a pair of binoculars up to her eyes, she could make out a small enclosure with an unclosed gate; the creature must have caught the scent of grasses wafting on the rising breeze and wandered out in search of its favourite food.

They would have to act quickly before the creature's masters discovered the open gate and one of their terratons absconded from its enclosure.

"Wait here child and do not move, I don't want the creature to be aware of our presence just yet; there is no need to worry, I will return soon," promised Amatheia, looking at the concern growing in Saoirse's face.

"Okay, but be careful Amatheia," uttered Saoirse with a burgeoning, nervous smile revealing itself from the left corner of her mouth; totally in awe and wonder at what Amatheia might attempt to do with the terraton.

Amatheia decided a wide path would be the best option; not wanting to alert any creature or Kolassian to her presence. Crouched down, she slowly made her way to the corral of terratons. She secures the gate shut so as not to disclose to any patrolling Kolassian guards, knowledge of a missing herd member.

Amatheia seizes a length of rope left hanging from a gate post and ties it to form a lasso before making her way back towards the escaped terraton. On her return she picks a handful of crowberries. Amatheia approaches the animal from its left side. Holding out an open flat hand, she hopes the freshly picked fruit will tempt the creature to follow her back towards Saoirse and to relative safety on the far side of the hill.

The terraton pauses when it notices Amatheia in the corner of its left eye. It turns and slowly approaches her, stretching out its trunk, snuffling in the scent of the berries. Amatheia bends down on one knee and fixes her gaze upon the ground; not wanting to make eye contact in case it is perceived as a threat to the animal. Suddenly the terraton charges, compelling Saoirse to warrant a whimper. Amatheia is steadfast in her position and intent. The enormous creature rapidly bears down upon her location, creating a cloud of ripped up grass which temporarily removes the terratons thundering half-metre wide feet from view.

Amatheia does not flinch, she doesn't even blink; knowing that if she did, her little companion and pet dog viewing the unfolding scene, would be left to continue the journey alone and unprotected. The fifteen-ton animal digs and ploughs its feet into the boggy terrain in an effort to halt its bulky momentum. Saoirse starts to cry and tremble, holding onto Mister Waggles tightly for comfort. She looks down upon a scene of near silence and scattered vegetation floating in the air. As the organic debris settles, the five-metre-tall beast is gradually revealed to them.

Standing only centimetres from Amatheia, it joyfully plucks the crowberries carefully one at a time from her, still outstretched, hand. Amatheia looks over her shoulder and with a downward motion of her other hand, signals Saoirse to remain where she is sitting.

Calmly yet quickly, while the terraton is preoccupied eating the berries, Amatheia throws the lasso past its trunk and over its hulking head. Pulling the rope securely around the terraton's shoulders, she begins the task of breaking the beast. With her left hand, she holds firmly the trailing edge of the rope at the side of its left shoulder. The creature attempts to steal away into a canter. Amatheia keeps pace with it but knows she will soon not be able to match its top speed and has to act fast or she will be dragged along and trampled to death.

Launching herself upwards she throws her legs sideways to the right. Now positioned horizontally with her toes gripping the armour like skin of the terraton, she pushes off. Swinging like an absurd pendulum, Amatheia gathers momentum. On the third swing she has garnered enough power to propel herself upwards and lands squarely in a seating position on the terraton's three-metre-wide back.

An hour of charging, twisting and turning around the hollow results in both Amatheia's and the terraton's near collapse from exhaustion.

After some rest and time to calm down, they are ready to resume their introductions. The beast, giving its undivided attention whether through trust or exhaustion, submits to her. Altering the lasso to now form reigns attached to the base of the terraton's enormously long tusks, Amatheia brings the beast in a trot over to the now smiling Saoirse.

"Well my child, how do you like our new mode of transport?" enquired Amatheia, wiping sweat away that was attempting to blur her vision.

"I like it lots but it's a bit scary!" declares Saoirse.

"This terraton was more scared of us little one. He is calm now and although his size is a bit scary, he will not harm you. Now we can travel the rest of our journey to Vidgelmir before sunset," beamed Amatheia.

Saoirse approached the terraton with more than a little trepidation. She reaches out her hand to pat its trunk. Emitting a low guttural sound, the terraton offers its trunk to Saoirse.

Somehow, the massive creature respected the human child's diminutiveness and adjusted its enormous bulk and strength accordingly so. Saoirse instinctively put both arms around the trunk and hugged the creature warmly as she whispered "Thank you terraton, thank you for helping us."

Gently circling its trunk under her arms, the terraton first lifts Saoirse, then a begrudging Mister Waggles, onto its back just in front of where Amatheia was sitting.

With the Sun high in the sky they set off at a good pace, leaving a pen of grazing terratons and a sleeping Kolassian guard unaware of them ever being there. Much of the day was spent travelling monotonously across wide, uninhabited, grassy plains. Occasionally the panorama being interjected with diversion by a scampering arctic fox or a soaring kittiwake whose call would temporarily disturb a child's fitful sleep. Dwindling sunlight kissed the edges of their silhouette as the little troop approached the Hallmundarhraun lava field and the awaiting caverns.

The terraton would be too big and cumbersome to take into the cave. Dismounting first, Amatheia then catches a sliding child and jumping dog; delivering both safely to the ground where grass ends and lava rock began. Leaving the terraton to happily munch on the last of the crowberries, they make their way towards an excavation in the landscape ahead. Amatheia leads them to the threshold of a large lava tube cave. They had found the cave entrance at Vidgelmir.

The entryway, as Jim Kelly had said, was blocked by an iron gate. According to his directions, they would have to gain access here as this was supposed to lead to an underground cavern, where the Kolassians based their headquarters. Amatheia beckoned the terraton back for one last task. With one end of the rope secured to the iron gate and the other tied across the beast's formidable shoulders, the opening was soon to be no longer obstructed. Amatheia then released the creature to wander back across the plains. They would need a light source to help navigate their way through the meandering tunnels ahead.

"Look! A truck! I, C, E, - E, X, P, L, O, R, E, R," spelled out Saoirse as she read the big bold lettering printed on the side of a large heavy-duty vehicle.

"You are right child, come, we may be able to get the makings of a torch!" decided Amatheia as she raced over to the all-terrain truck.

They had luckily come across an abandoned research scientists' transport vehicle. Amatheia finds some tubing in the back of the truck which she uses to syphon fuel from its tank. She ties the remainder of Saoirse's father's t-shirt around the end of a wooden stake, soaking it in some fuel. Using some matches, also found in the back of the truck, they are able to ignite the improvised torch and make their way to the lava tube entrance.

As the Sun disappears from view, Amatheia, Saoirse and Mister Waggles enter the collapsed lava tube with darkness behind and before them. The tunnel is quite narrow with a low jagged roof. This is not a problem for Saoirse and Mister Waggles but Amatheia, walking behind the little girl and her pet dog, is forced to hunch over them with her torch bearing arm extended to illuminate the path ahead.

The first section they awkwardly navigated through was all wet, grey and black stone with streaks of cold white penetrating from the outside world. As they ventured down, deeper and deeper becoming swallowed into the core, colour began to be illuminated by their makeshift torch.

Dark monotone colours were replaced with aqua-blue greens and rust golden seams. As they rounded a corner the colours increased in vibrancy and intensity as the narrow passage gave way to a wide-open cavern, flooded with light. This light was altered to turquoise as it penetrated through the ice ceiling overhead, still only centimetres from Amatheia's head. A small glacial stream trickled through the middle of the cavern, which they all tip-toe jumped across trying to avoid its icy grasp.

Darkness soon descended once more as the immense expanse narrowed and they were funnelled into a metre-wide passageway. For quite a while, the only sound filling the void was the constant dripping of water and the exhalation of their own breaths. Increasingly, other sounds entered the glacial auditorium. One consisted of a long, low groan interspersed with the odd high-pitched acknowledgement of pain; the other was a snarling, feeding frenzied cacophony.

It was difficult to determine the origin as all noise seemed to bounce and rebound off the walls; sounding both human and animalistic, the more they moved forward, the louder and more intense it became.

Suddenly, beyond the wall of ice to their side, a loud mechanical churning followed by a dull explosion stops only seconds after starting. Silence arrives and departs with all around them beginning to shake. The vibrations cause Amatheia to stumble and drop her torch. Bending down to retrieve the torch highlights a human hand and the remains of a torso scattered across the cave floor; the PNSE logo still determinable on the bloodied clothing.

Standing up and extending her torch bearing arm unveils a terrifyingly horrific scene. Locked in combat are two Kolassian, sabre toothed, snow bears. Amatheia's three metres would barely reach their shoulder height. Not wanting to witness the unfolding horror, Saoirse buries her head into Amatheia's chest. Between the two sets of enormous jaws is a, barely, still living human. He emits one last soul breaking scream as a half-metre long sabre tooth penetrates first his helmet and then his skull. Saoirse lets out a bone chilling scream, alerting the bears to their presence.

Dropping their quarry, the two bears charge towards them. Just as they begin to pounce towards the trio, more explosions ensue forcing a rift in the ceiling above.

Ice cold water floods the cavern in seconds; the weight of the water falling directly onto the heads of the bears, killing one of them instantly as the other scrambles for air. Saoirse throws her arms around Amatheia's neck in a piggy-back fashion while Amatheia grabs hold of Mister Waggles and swims towards a small metal door in the rock face.

There is a screen showing a digital image of a hand with flashing red and green lights on its surrounding frame. Leaving Saoirse clutching Mister Waggles's collar while holding onto the door and her breath, Amatheia swims back to where she first dropped the torch. She once again sees the detached human hand on the cave floor, remembering its metal bracelet too had flashing lights. Making it back as quickly as she can, Amatheia places the human hand to the screen.

A scanning light passes beneath the hand and the door opens. Thousands of gallons of water exit the cavern and carry four remaining life forms gulping for air, away from drowning. After only seconds of being washed and bashed by the surge, three find themselves clinging to a ledge, in yet another enormous cavern, looking down upon the Kolassian headquarters.

Presented below is a scene of carnage. A coupling of magnetic carriages had buckled and folded on top of each other. The front of which was embedded into what seemed to be the main Kolassian power generator which was pulsating aggressively. The generator was three storeys high and in the process of imploding; the possible plan to turn Earth into an inter-galactic cruise liner was destroyed along with it.

An incredible scene of orange and red explosions reached high into the sky, mixing with the fluorescent greens of the Aurora Borealis. Below these nightmarish fireworks, Kolassians could be seen dodging exploding containers, trying to find any functioning craft to make good their escape.

Banks of monitors flicker while several delayed countdowns overlap creating digital echoes. Beyond the chaos, Amatheia could determine what seemed to be a hanger just out of the reach of the firestorm. Amidst the mayhem, a human male and female carrying a sick child were being helped to board a craft by an injured, limping, Kolassian guard.

Holding onto a still sobbing child, Amatheia lowered themselves off the ledge and they all ran towards the hanger. As they arrived, the craft lifted off the ground, Kyle looked back out of the window with a growing despair evident on his face; the realisation that, yet again, he was leaving one of his children behind.

Saoirse did not see the departing ship's occupants and Amatheia thought it best, for now, not to tell her. There was one last remaining ship in the hanger. Amatheia was familiar with it being a long-distance craft that had stasis chambers. She had been forced to occupy these on numerous occasions as a captured slave being transported to Earth.

She lifted Mister Waggles and Saoirse up the ramp first but as she tried to make her own entry, a half metre sabre tooth pierced her ankle. She is dragged off the ramp with Saoirse crying and Mister Waggles barking furiously. The surviving Kolassian snow bear had followed them. Despite her size, the beast threw Amatheia around like a doll made of rags. With no regard for his own safety, Mister Waggles launched himself off the ramp, sinking his teeth into the bear's face. Blood pours from the bear's eyes and it is blinded. Releasing Amatheia but before it runs off in agony, one of its giant swiping paws connects with the loyal companion.

The hound howls once more before it lies motionless at the bottom of the ramp. Saoirse retrieves her friend and no sooner than the ramp is closed, Amatheia powers the ship up and away. They leave behind the inferno and smell of death to compete for dominance.

Cradling the brave little creature in her arms, Amatheia sits in floods of tears alongside Saoirse as their craft penetrates out of Earth's atmosphere. An Oikian and a human child, leaving a blue planet behind, are inconsolable. A paw slips from a six-year-old child's hand, a friendship and a life are hushed.

"Oh, Mister Waggles! Mister Waggles! Please don't go, come back to me right now!" demanded a heart-broken and tear-soaked Saoirse.

"This little creature saved my life. He is one of the bravest souls I have ever known and you are another, my child," said Amatheia, failing to comfort Saoirse.

"Well, I don't feel brave! I am tired of being brave! I don't want to be brave anymore! I want Mummy and Daddy! I want Ellen! I... I... I want Mister Waggles!" sobbed Saoirse.

Amatheia carries a tear-soaked Saoirse to a stasis chamber; the lid closes and a vacuum seals as a child dreams of running through fields behind her far away home with a four-legged companion by her side. Not knowing why she does so, as the beagle seemed bereft of life, but instinctively Amatheia takes Mister Waggles's limp body and places it in a chamber too. She does not stay long enough to notice a monitor register that a last beat was perhaps not the final one.

Amatheia squeezes into her own chamber and sets coordinates for somewhere she can keep this child safe, somewhere perhaps they could all start over again.

***

Previous to this perilous departure, other members of Saoirse's family were also in a desperate struggle...

While desperately clinging to the outside of the carriage, Kyle motions with a frantic shake of his head for Ellen to step back from the window. He swings out and drives his legs hard against the glass, which scatters the pane into a thousand pieces across the cabin floor.

Crystal follows him in and they both embrace Ellen lovingly. The child tries to warn her parents to hide because the strange man will be back soon. Before Ellen can speak another word, the Kolassian guard returns. Kyle grabs him by his face mask and swings him wildly this way and that, bashing him against the cabin interior. Blood splatters appear on the inside of the now dislodged mask. Kyle releases his grip and the Kolassian falls to the floor. Kyle raises his foot up high with the intention of stamping down hard, to finish off the Kolassian and threat to his family.

"Stop Daddy! Wait! He said he will help me!" cries Ellen with a long and wheezy cough.

"What do you mean? Are you all right Ellen?" Kyle moves quickly as he notices his youngest daughter slumping over and stumbling to the ground.

"Do you have your inhaler my love?" asks Crystal.

"No Mummy, it never really worked, it's no use," replies Ellen, feeling frustrated at having to answer questions while not feeling well.

Kyle returns to the Kolassian and removes what is left of the mask and breathing apparatus from its pale face.

"Explain what my daughter means about you promising to help her! Why doesn't her inhaler work?" demanded Kyle.

"Your child does not only have asthma, she also has… *our* illness. Please, I cannot breathe. I can tell you more but first I need a replacement facial apparatus from the locker on the wall," begs the Kolassian, gasping for air.

Kyle retrieves a mask and helps the Kolassian to a seat before replacing the one he broke in the tussle.

"Thank you, that's much better. It is not your atmosphere that causes me breathing difficulties; although the mask also reduces the temperature, making me feel more at home. It also helps to prevent me from picking up other infections, my immune system is very weak. We Kolassians are cursed with a hereditary condition that unfortunately appears to be transmittable to very young, older or ill humans. The mask essentially comforts and protects me.

"Not all Kolassians are evil, even the ones that are malevolent have children too! I am really sorry but your daughter will get progressively worse unless we can find a cure. I despise all that my superiors have done in the enslavement of the Oikians. Our numbers are small but the resistance is growing.

"However, we have as yet not been able to convene with the Oikian resistance; to try and form some sort of an alliance. My ancestors have been abducting humans for a long, long time with the sole purpose of trying to find a cure.

"After the great war, my planet was ravaged, we moved to the only habitable zones left at the north and south polar regions. Over thousands of generations we evolved into two species, the Kolassians and the Oikians. Yes, I partially admit, my people can be a brutish race and the Oikians were never the aggressors. I have seen elderly Oikians discarded as useless trash while my kind enslaved parents and their children from the South.

"They would often be transported to Earth and settled into remote regions. Have you heard of '*Bigfoot*?" queried the Kolassian guard.

"Yes, of course, but surely it's just another one of many conspiracy theories? I mean these theories spread around the globe and before you know it there are sightings of Sasquatch in Canada, Yeren in China and Yeti in the Himalayas, to name but a few," replied Kyle.

"The governments of your world have known about us for a long time but try to hide the facts, not to protect you but to profit from our advanced technologies. Our superior science brought us nothing but destruction. Unknown to us, there was a delayed fallout from mass bio-weapons which moved in a northern direction due to changing weather patterns. Massive, upper-atmospheric, cyclonic storms would normally rage for centuries.

"Due to our interference with nature, the execution and the production of these mass bio-weapons led to extremely dangerous elements, capable of corroding and altering DNA, to be discharged into the environment. These elements were held within the upper atmosphere and were ultimately deposited in northern regions due to the broken weather patterns.

"Gradually over time, a sickness became embedded in our DNA. It begins by causing breathing difficulties, hair loss and ultimately the result is the feeble body you see before you. If my blood or saliva makes internal contact with Earth children, problems soon arise. Those with compromised immune systems or the elderly, having less strength to fight infection, will develop the condition which I and my kind are plagued by.

"Your daughter Ellen may have had some benefit from using her inhaler but it is my understanding that asthma cannot be properly diagnosed before the age of five in humans," the Kolassian guard described.

"Mummy, when one of them grabbed me and took me from our house, I bit him hard on his hand. After he took his glove off, I could see my teeth marks on his skin and there was blood dripping!" cried Ellen.

"Your little girl may well have gone on to develop *Earth* asthma but I'm afraid it will be overridden by the cursed Kolassian plague," the Kolassian guard desperately tried to explain to them.

"Is there no cure? You said you were going to help her, there must be a way!" Kyle was becoming impatient.

"Yes, I want to try. I believe if we can help Ellen we may also be able to help Kolassian children too. Who knows, it may also lead to a reconciliation between the people of Polar Neridia, both southern and northern," hoped the Kolassian.

"You just used the name *'Polar Neridia'* but an Oikian friend of ours said there was no name for your planet, just Oikia in the south and Kolassia to the north. It was another friend, Jim Kelly who came up with the name. How do you know the words he came up with, *'Polar Nerida'*?" asked Kyle.

"We must have had a name for our planet at some point in the past; whatever it was, became long forgotten after the war-desolated populations migrated to the poles. I think as it stands, *'Polar Neridia'*, seems an apt name for my planet.

"We are sometimes able to listen in, to monitor those previously abducted who show promise. I believe and hope your friend Jim Kelly may be able to help in finding a cure. He has the concentric circular mark on his neck and apart from acquired super intelligence, a tracking and monitoring device were implanted. This method was and remains to be, the way how some humans are abducted many, many times over. I was part of a squadron responsible for the abduction and implantation of devices in chosen humans.

"I did not like having to do it but when you are led to believe that this research has the potential to help save your own children, certain moralities are really very easily discarded," the Kolassian admonished, without any true apology implied.

"But why us? After becoming aware that you are not alone in the Universe, I would guess we might not be your only choice of guinea pigs!" shouted Kyle.

"Indeed, you would be forgiven for thinking that. However, you must believe me, in all of our explorations so far, Earth is the only planet apart from our own that we have studied hominid civilisations. We, like you, are predisposed to searching for alien life that walks on two legs, has a reasoning mind and communicative abilities. There may well be non-hominid life right under our noses. We have observed another potentially habitable planet. A place that has plenty of liquid water and possibly a breathable atmosphere; your scientists have called it Kepler 186-f. Life could be possible there but if you were super-human, even super-neridian, your powers would be nullified by the overly red light from its sun," suggests the Kolassian guard, proud at his impartation of such knowledge.

"Okay, let's say we believe you, what's next, where do we go from here?" asks Kyle impatiently.

"As I said previously, I no longer want to participate in the enslavement of Oikians or human abduction. Nor do I want anything to do with the harvesting and sublimation of Earth. Originally it was thought we could move Earth closer to Polar Neridia for it to become, if you will, a Polar Neridia II. The axis of your planet was altered in preparation.

"The theory was that the sublimation of your planet at its northern pole would produce enough thrust. This theory was only that, a theory, and one which was borne out of desperation.

"A by-product of our investigations was that we could create a super light metal for use in our space craft. We did this by putting hydrogen under immense pressure, similar to when you place great pressure on carbon, diamonds can be produced.

"The generator ahead is used to power that operation. I think we must try and crash this high-force magno-transport into the generator. It would be the best way to, perhaps not stop, but at least delay operations here. We must then go to your friend Jim Kelly in order to progress the seeking of a cure for all our children, be they Kolassian, Oikian or Human!" exclaimed the Kolassian.

"Agreed, but before we go any further I would like to shake your hand. I am sorry for attacking you and thank you for wanting to help my child. What is your name, friend?" asks Kyle, apologetically.

"I am called Tereo. Thank you for your apology but it is not necessary. I have the same love for my children. Now, you must all sit on the floor and tie yourselves to something. I am going to override the autonomous controls of this magno-transport," cautioned Tereo.

Using the straps from their backpacks, Kyle and Crystal secured themselves, with Ellen cradled between them, to the base of the pod's seats. After accessing a panel in an overhead compartment, Tereo quickly joined them on the floor.

A muffled whirring was the only indication of an increase in speed. The magno-transport, made up of a group of ten pods suddenly deviated from its intended course and careered with increasing terror in the direction of the base's power generator.

First, slow motion silence, then, high speed clamour seemed to be repeated again and again while their carriage was shunted this way and that for the next few moments. Explosions rained all around while the four of them safely vacated the concertinaed mess, out into the green tinged glow that proliferated and swelled about them.

During the pandemonium, a strip of metal had ripped into Tereo's right leg, causing him to limp intermittently.

"Due to the base's imminent demise, we need to find transport out of here and as quickly as possible. There is a hanger beyond the edge of this grid. We must hurry, come now!" implored Tereo.

Undeterred by his injury, he quickly got them safely to the hanger and into a craft. They hovered a few metres off the ground before Tereo turned the craft to point in the direction of the coordinates given by Kyle...

53° 15′ 6.7″ N, 6° 19′ 49.24″ W

Before they accelerated off, Kyle took the opportunity to have one last look through the back window at the devastation they were leaving behind. He was presented with a heart breaking but also heart-warming scene.

Amatheia, Saoirse and Mister Waggles were boarding a craft too. Saoirse did not see him but Amatheia gestured to show they were okay. Curiously, a shadowed figure covered in sweat and out of breath was also making his escape below them.

"I just saw Saoirse! She's alive! She is with Amatheia, and Mister Waggles too!" Kyle tells Crystal excitedly, searching her face for belief and acknowledgement.

Crystal and Ellen rush to the window but their craft was already penetrating through the clouds which blanketed a view they longed to behold.

"You must remain seated, we will reach close to the point of contact for Jim Kelly in ten minutes," instructed Tereo as he concentrated on the craft's readings.

The coordinates brought them to land at the edge of a large forest. The last to exit the craft, Tereo, pressed his hand against a panel and the craft became perfectly camouflaged from detection.

After they hiked a short distance along a pine needle carpeted trail, a trap door is opened by a man breathing heavily. Sweat drips from his matted hair and onto the barrel of the gun he is pointing directly towards the face of the Kolassian standing before him.

"Leave them be, you son of a bitch!" roars Jim Kelly.

"Hold on! He's with us! Don't shoot!" pleads Kyle.

Ellen runs to Tereo's side and takes hold of his hand.

"Ellen? Where's Saoirse and Amatheia?" asks Jim.

"Saoirse and Mister Waggles are with Amatheia! They were getting into another spaceship, maybe they will come here too," replies Ellen hopefully.

"They are not coming to this place; I think they might have had alternative coordinates. Amatheia must have possessed a desire for a different destination.

"Our ship's monitors did not show them to be close behind us. I am not sure why, I did not know if I should tell you, but my scanners determined that they were possibly headed towards Polar Neridia," said Tereo, turning his head away, unable to witness the child's sorrow and disappointment.

The Kolassian was feeling somewhat responsible for contributing to the dismantling of this family. His revelation caused quiet to descend over them all. Silence was broken, once again, when words tumbled awkwardly from Jim's mouth.

"Well, fair enough, best come inside."

They submerged beneath the forest floor and then through the same rooms Kyle had previously visited; warmed by turf fires and alcoves lit by slumped and deformed candles. After relaying their recent escapades to Jim, he had only one utterance to project upon those who might listen.

"I do not want this damn implant in my neck a second longer!" roared Jim, like a wounded animal!

The venom and velocity with which the words left Jim's angry mouth only served for their deliverance to crash around the ears of Tereo. The Kolassian shrank back into his seat upon receipt of such an undiluted and targeted onslaught.

"With a local anaesthetic and some basic equipment, I could perform this task. However, all knowledge you have gained be it learned or acquired as a result of the implant, could be lost or at the very least shuffled around and faded beyond recovery.

"Furthermore, we need your advanced intellect and knowledge to help Ellen. Indeed, finding a cure could benefit us all," offered Tereo shyly.

Crystal, tired of the arguing, walked to a corner of the room and poured herself a large brandy from a decanter that stood on a shelf in a little alcove. Looking, transfixed upon the multiple facets that in unison shared her name, she caught a glimpse of herself and turned her back to everyone as she drained the last drop from her glass.

"You reach a certain point in your life; a moment's reflection of your face displays lines that leave a track not always traceable. A path unable to lead away from a life unfulfilled. When you reach this juncture, you tire of waiting for absent answers.

"You momentarily hesitate until that potential full stop morphs from a comma into a prolonged daydream. A moment ensnared in the present, imprisons you once again," proffers Crystal as she sits down angrily on a tufted brown leather armchair.

She leaves her glass on a side-table as her arms are repurposed to give comfort to a tired child in much need of such distraction.

"Jim, I need you to retain your implant until such a time that I have my children back safe where they belong, back home with their Mum and Dad," finished Crystal as she closed her eyes, hugging Ellen closely.

"Okay, for the sake of your children and to honour our friendship, the implant can remain for now. However, when our search is over, I want peace from this monotonous existence. I too, am weary," responded Jim upon receipt of Crystal's commanding tone.

"What do we need?" Jim eagerly asks, still perspiring heavily, as he turns to face towards Tereo.

"From our studies, we have ascertained that two separate DNA samples are required for the formula. Firstly, from a sick Kolassian adult in the final stages of the disease and secondly, from a human child in the early stages of the disease.

"We will also be needing a donor-matched extraction of human bone marrow from a healthy sibling. Plus, we need gold and a space laboratory; microgravity will give our science project a distinct advantage. We will be better equipped to examine and understand what mechanisms control the actions of the disease; there is a facility that can simulate these conditions," states Tereo.

"If you need gold, come with me," indicated Jim.

The group followed Jim down a winding staircase, hewn out of the rock. They approached a curious steel door framed within part of the mountain which protruded into the subterranean dwelling. Opening the door slowly evolved all of their jaws dropping in amazement. An exposed seam of gold ran the entire width of the room with a few nuggets scattered on the floor beside some basic mining equipment and a couple of glass jars filled with gold dust.

"I do recall once, a long time ago, you claimed that there was *'gold in them thar hills'*, my man," Kyle patted Jim's shoulder firmly who bizarrely shrank from the friendly gesture.

"Why the need for gold?" asked Jim, turning to Tereo.

"Gold, in different forms, is very useful for a number of medical applications.

"Apart from using diluted solutions in the treatment of rheumatoid arthritis, it can have an effect on gene expression. Fallout from use of bio-weapons, brought about corroding of our DNA. It had become increasingly difficult to regulate the expression of our genes. I know this may be difficult to comprehend but I trust you can understand it Jim?" suggested Tereo, hesitantly.

"As far as I can interpret, genes cannot be used by an organism. They need to be transformed into a gene product. Gene expression is the action whereby data within a gene turns into a usable product," replied Jim rather confidently.

"Correct. Now, aside from the sinkhole having a direct link to our headquarters, you can see why we chose here, gold does not exist on Polar Neridia," Tereo pointed to the seam nearby.

"When Mick and I first decided to set up base here, the discovery of this gold seam was pure chance. To hide it from intruders, we built a room around it. We could easily extricate gold from beneath the rock surface. It provides us a means of sustaining ourselves. We can pursue our mission and fund our basic necessities," explained Jim.

"Ellen and I fulfil two of the formula requirements, but we need the donor match from a healthy sibling," suggests Tereo.

"Saoirse has an O-negative blood type just like Ellen," interjects Crystal.

"Well, it seems we must now leave for the facility on Polar Neridia and find your other daughter," Tereo calmly states.

Provisions are quickly gathered before the trap door is covered one last time with fallen leaves and pine needles. After a short hike they make their return to the camouflaged craft. Kyle notices Jim's shirt is saturated with sweat and remembers his friend heavily perspiring and short of breath when he had, albeit angrily, greeted them at the trap door earlier.

"Are you okay Jim?" explored Kyle.

"I am fine, I'm just finding it a little warm today," explained Jim hurriedly as he pushed past to get into the craft before the other passengers and crew.

As he did, Tereo noticed the soles of Jim's boots were coated in a pale blue colour and nudged this observation to Sam's attention.

"I wonder... it looks to me as if someone has been walking through puddles of rocket fuel," whispered Sam, but here was no time at present to explore any reasons for this, they had to get on with the task at hand.

Everyone quickly settles into their hibernation pods in hurried anticipation of what was to come. All lay silent, wondering what Polar Neridia might have in store for them; their craft breaks through Earth's atmosphere and they make their departure.

06

Arrivals

A parent reluctantly reaches for a child's hand without gaining hold of it; a hand not held for a long time.

Pacing up and down a bank of monitors, waiting tentatively for the healing to complete and a new journey to begin. A last hand-held moment restored after a quietened breath returns and introduces a beat towards an uncertain future.

Once more an image of Mick oscillates in the alcove and back through the decades. Holding onto the device this time, he arrives at a dark, rain sodden path looking up at yet another gate. A worn and faded sign reads *"The Good Herdsman Convent, Redemption Asylum"*.

Beyond the entrance, a huge red brick fortress, with limestone plinths sprouts from a rocky, granite strewn field. Winged statues still stand guard, looking mockingly towards him with vacant eyes.

The lower walls look to be increasingly ridiculed by unkempt bramble and gorse. Mick walks towards the structure, up a steep embankment, via a central stepped walkway. The main building consists of five large bays; standing three storeys high. Looming up ahead are a foreboding pair of timber panelled doors. As he mounts the last step, a door creaks open. A ginger-haired boy is dragged out by the ear.

"This is the last time you will dare to disobey me, Michael Flannery!" shouts an angry, belligerent woman dressed in a sombre uniform and apron.

The door slams shut and so does across the yard, almost simultaneously, the door of an outbuilding as the matron and a young Mick Flannery withdraw inside.

Feeling an outpouring of sympathy and rage, Mick decides to investigate further. Aware that he may be visible in moments of extreme emotion, he composes himself and treads very carefully. A narrow cobblestone path winds its way around barren flower beds which punctuate a muddy courtyard. The curved valleys between each cobble began to turn white before Mick's feet as an obnoxious easterly wind delivered fresh flurries and a stinging nip to his face.

The chevron pattern created by the interaction of stone and snow reminded him of the long thin curtains which once adorned the great sash window next to his dormitory bed; useless in their function of keeping out neither the cold of night nor the early morning light.

Standing by the rotting outbuilding door, he decides to peer through a window rather than entering the hovel. A fracture in a corner glass pane allows the time traveller's aural witnessing of a small child being viciously berated to accompany the visual castigation.

The outbuilding was used as stables comprising of five stalls which housed only four horses. The fifth stall was often used as over-night accommodation for disciplined children once they had completed their punishment. Mick was painfully witnessing the retribution he had received as a young child whenever he sleep-walked on Miss Walsh's shift. He distinctly remembers on this occasion being found naked on the roof just above the open sash window of his dormitory.

After an hour of being frantically coaxed and prodded with a broom, he perilously swung back through the window with a slippery clench of moss laden guttering.

Miss Walsh had dragged his naked, five-year-old self, by the ear across the snow dusted courtyard; all the while his increasingly purple toes finding it progressively difficult to gain purchase on the frozen cobbles.

"I told you time and time again Michael Flannery! You will not cause me any more trouble! You know what to do, here is a bucket. When you're finished, sleep down there and you will be collected in the morning, you little brat!" spewed Miss Walsh with all the bile and spit she could furiously muster.

The child could not stop trembling as his body battled the cold and the rebuke he had just received. Miss Walsh, holding her skirt out of reach of the fouling on the floor, scuttled back across the cobbles which were now almost hidden by the deepening snow.

Provided with no shovel; a bucket and his bare hands were the only tools he had at his disposal to clear horse manure. Even though he heaved at the smell, heat from the dung warming his frozen hands was of some solace.

After he had filled and emptied three buckets worth, young Mick moved to the second last stall. This was the only provision of happiness during the whole ordeal. Strider was his favourite horse; a Connemara pony, white in colour with a mottled grey pattern fading from his chest to flank and partially down his rear legs. He was the only living thing apart from Mr Corcoran, his teacher, that showed him any kindness in this loveless place.

On sight of young Mick, Strider sauntered over to his favourite human and nestled his nose into the crook of Mick's neck, snorting gently. It tickled the boy and caused him to relinquish a seldom heard giggle. The filling of a fourth bucket was not required. Perhaps Strider decided young Mick had suffered enough and the horse's internal motions could be best saved to provide an unpleasant surprise for Miss Walsh's next visit. Tired, mucky and cold, young Mick lay down in hay that had been set into a pile in the farthest corner of the last stall.

Falling asleep, a tear spilled from the corner of his left eye and was absorbed by his trailing red locks. Viewing this tragedy, Mick Flannery's hologram shuddered as he fought to hold back a tear of his own. He fails to do so and a single drop leaves a little indentation in the snow as he departs to visit yet another distressing scene endured by his five-year-old self.

Even in 1970s rural Ireland, candle or gas light were not very common; most places had electricity. However, not *"The Good Herdsman Convent, Redemption Asylum"*, it was built about a hundred years previous and had never been completely updated to the modern age. Walking down a corridor, in the dead of night, with paint peeled walls bathed in dimmed gas light, you could be forgiven for mistaking what century you occupied. This was occasionally underlined by a fleeting glimpse of a solitary staff member, darting across from one dormitory to another, wearing the same style of uniform as was worn when the institute first opened its doors in 1872.

Mick found himself standing at the end of this long corridor. It was usual for the silence in the dark hours to be randomly broken by a misbehaving child being scolded, or groans from an orphan's disturbed sleep. As he moved further down the hall, the calm was becoming more and more abbreviated by an increasing discord. Then half a dozen staff briefly split the corridor in two as they stormed to the left of Mick's line of sight, into the boys' dormitory. As Mick breached the threshold of the dormitory he was presented with a scene encompassed by tears torn from trauma. A local police officer, Sergeant O'Malley, had a barely clad young Mick by the wrist in a vice-like grip.

The boy was soaked to the skin after being found at the edge of the River Leap, cowering behind some trees that lined the water's edge. Missing for three days, his bed had been found not slept in. The sash window was wide open; cold February morning air entered as a casual dance partner to the thin linen curtains.

"After the boy was reported missing, we searched all the usual places but he was nowhere to be found. Then this morning we got a call from a guy while out walking his dog; he said there was a kid, with eyes all black - no whites showing, spouting some gibberish about the Sun and Moon.

"When I got to him, he was soaked from head to toe. There were no tracks or any other evidence to suggest he had been in the river and it hadn't rained in over a week!" said Sergeant O'Malley, feeling bemused.

Mr Corcoran, young Michael Flannery's teacher, entered the crowded room.

"Thank you, Sergeant, I'll look after the boy," stated Mr Corcoran, over-flowing with cautious respect.

With a quick nod and a look, Mr Corcoran ushered everyone out of the room and the other boys being tired of all the commotion, went back to sleep. After fetching the boy some dry clothes, Mr Corcoran quizzed young Mick on his whereabouts for the past three days.

All the child could remember was, as he returned from the bathroom he paused at the foot of his bed, seeing a bright light penetrating the curtains made him feel dizzy. He thought that he had fallen asleep or fainted onto his bed. A couple were out walking their dog; he was awoken by barking and the feeling of being rather cold.

Then the police arrived and brought him back to the forever waiting orphanage. To him, it felt like the whole episode happened only last night and that he had no idea where the other two days had gone.

Mr Corcoran had taken note of the boy's continuing disappearances over the years but also kept an eye out for him and tried as much as he could to deflect the evil doings of certain staff members away from the child.

When Mick turned eighteen he would leave this place; leave the screams in the night, leave the punishments, leave the cold damp walls to fall into ruin. Mr Corcoran would himself leave before the institute closed for good.

Returning to his passion for writing poetry, Mr Corcoran would retire to the coast; his first publication containing a dedication to a lost child and a final verse referencing young Mick's *"Sun and Moon"* entranced recitals.

***

Mick Flannery's hologram fluctuated in and out of time again. He now found himself in an open field at the back of the building. Snow turned to rain and the ground beneath his feet to mud. In search of shelter, he made his way to a small copse of trees which denoted the back of the field. The leafy covering gave him some respite from the downpour and time to gather his thoughts.

The emotion-based time travel devise has brought me to a number of places within these grounds but where is, what is, Sam's prophesied discovery that will help us to defeat them? Mick puzzled to himself.

Piercing through the hanging branches and almost horizontal rain, a diffused and glowing light meekly announced its presence. A break in the deluge entices Mick forward to explore further. A small limestone building, inoffensive in outward appearance and covered completely in ivy, began to emerge from the gloom.

The light source was penetrating through a tiny rain streaked window. The movement of water across its pane had caused the light to recede and rise like that of a lantern on a fishing boat being swallowed by the troughs and peaks of stormy seas. The view within was distorted by a second pane of frosted glass. A figure seemed to be swaying back and forth on a rocking chair whilst singing, in a bizarrely distorted voice, what could be described as a bastardised, nightmarish lullaby. The muffled words protruding through the walls seemed familiar and felt like each ascent of intonation was akin to a piercing blade from a resentful soul.

Mick wanted, he needed, to know who or what was inside. With escalating emotion, he took firm hold of the round, Victorian, brass door knob. A partial turn of the handle was all that was required to gain entry. An oil lantern hung untidily on a heavily rusted butcher's hook, just above the window. A picture positioned above the fireplace was composed of a figure running across a field towards a bright light; the luminescence permeating the cloud cover did not seem to volunteer any warmth at all. The dying flames of a fire would have licked tentatively at the edges of the grate.

However, the temperature in the room was sub-zero and blocks of ice cut into briquettes occupied the position normally taken by wood, peat or coal. A rocking chair curled back and forth, creaking the century aged wooden floor boards. The form which drove the chair's motion had its back to Mick. As he approached, the poor light gave way and an uneasiness began to crawl over his skin.

The chair's occupant was singing oddly, in a lullaby fashion, the *'Dr Sun, Mr Moon'* poem which he had often unwillingly recited over the years; as had, according to Sam, his mother Rosemary. The terrifying chanteuse was partially silhouetted by the lantern light. There were tubes protruding from a backpack, they curved and folded towards the sides of the figure's head; from which an icy fog and death rattle were being exhaled.

Stepping closer with fear beginning to conquer him, the lullaby performance halted. Mick could now hear a ravenous suckling sound following, what sounded like, the cry from a hungry infant. The occupant of the chair sensed that her solitude had been interrupted and turned towards Mick's direction. She could not see Mick but he was now made fully cognizant of the terrible innocence contained within this scant and abhorrent outbuilding.

Mick felt faint and his head began to spin. His hologram started to vibrate wildly, tears streamed down his face and he had the distinct sensation of losing control of not only his bodily functions but also that of his mentality. Exposed in the rocking chair was a female Kolassian. She looked not much different from a male other than the dreaded duty it was currently preoccupied with. It was breast feeding what appeared to be a small, weak and malnourished, Oikian youngling. The child had the same red fur as Amatheia and although it appeared to be feeble and underweight, it seemed far too old to be breast fed.

The scene was grotesque in the utmost way possible. Mick's emotions overpowered him and the reverberation of his hologram intensified. The Kolassian wet nurse stopped what she was doing and stood up to approach the now partially visible Mick Flannery.

The small child released its mouth from the frigid bosom belonging to the leather clad governess, who had undone her bodice and parted a mass of tubing and wires to reveal her squalid breast; providing some sustenance for the ailing five-year-old Oikian. The child paused and turned its head towards the emerging presence.

The meeting of the young Oikian's eye with that of Mick's was more than his soul, more than his very core could handle. In that moment there seemed to be an exchange, an awareness of an unknown bond.

This sent Mick screaming outdoors. As he ran through the wet grass he was aware of a burning sensation in his hands. The time travel device was overloading, it was being overfed with emotion. The black light at its centre was now pulsating immeasurably fast. Mick pauses in mid-stride and freezes as if he were about to experience a heart attack. He retreats from this time, leaving only a muddy footprint discontinued in the middle of a field and a Kolassian nursing an Oikian child who had a brief sense of a link to a sibling.

Mick also fades from another time at the alcove in the lava tunnel. He goes screaming across galaxies; the time travel device, in its last action before it implodes, delivers him to a time which all his siblings and friends would occupy. No longer a hologram, he awakens lying on his back. Mick opens his hand, the scorched and broken time travel device trundles along the ground as he looks up at an alien sky.

***

From another point in time, three others accomplish their arrival…

Nineteen years, eleven months and thirty days had now passed; Amatheia and Saoirse's spacecraft pauses in orbit around Polar Neridia.

The cushioned hush of a glass screen slides open and Amatheia emerges from her stasis chamber as planned; albeit feeling nauseous and quite dehydrated. She has a pounding headache. Before attending to the others, she goes to the bathroom to find some medication to alleviate her thumping affliction.

Looking in the mirror, Amatheia can tell something has gone wrong. She has aged uncharacteristically during hyper-sleep. Nausea was not uncommon, she had become accustomed to it. Headaches were a nuisance, but usually easily dealt with.

Having experienced abduction by Kolassians and transportation back and forth between Polar Neridia and Earth, almost her entire life, the side effects of travelling through deep space were nothing new to her. She would not normally show any distinct signs of physical ageing. However, there were now long white and grey streaks running through her red fur, accompanied by additional wrinkles around her eyes and neck.

Amatheia runs to Saoirse's chamber and quickly types in the end destination code. As the screen withdraws to reveal Saoirse, Amatheia opens her mouth wide but is unable to speak; she is taken aback by Saoirse's metamorphosis. Trying to hide her initial shock, she helps Saoirse to her feet.

"Are we there yet?" asks Saoirse quietly.

"We are, my... child," replies Amatheia cautiously.

"Amatheia, you look older, there's white in your fur and you're shorter - what's happened!" asks an increasingly worried Saoirse as she looks upon the darkening of Amatheia's furrowed countenance.

Saoirse raises her left hand and traces her own profile with her fingertips, then looking down at both hands she sees they are no longer those belonging to a six-year-old. She screams and asks for a mirror. Amatheia leads her slowly to the bathroom.

"I have not gotten shorter, it is you who has grown taller," states Amatheia.

"No! No! No! This is not me! I am not me! I want my Mummy and Daddy!" howled Saoirse.

Standing beside Amatheia, a bewildered six-year-old child in the body of a twenty-six-year-old woman is beyond consolation. Both Saoirse's and Amatheia's stasis chambers must have malfunctioned at the beginning of their journey. Mentally they had stayed the same but their bodies had aged twenty years.

This should not be an insurmountable concept for Amatheia, an already mature adult, but the sight of a grown woman speaking with the vocabulary of a little girl, crying for her parents, was not.

During the voyage, their bodies were nurtured and maintained but the circuits pertaining to keeping them in a state of equilibrium had been disconnected; perhaps due to damage sustained to the craft while fleeing the base at Vidgelmir or by someone, intentionally. Amatheia left Saoirse in silent contemplation, in front of the mirror, trying to come to terms with her transformation.

Looking across at her reflection, it was difficult in the extreme to come to terms with how she now appeared. Long gone were her blond curls, now replaced with straighter, light coloured hair. No more the skinny, androgynous frame of a child; she now occupied the body of a grown woman with curves that she had not been given the time to grow into.

Saoirse looked like a younger version of her mother; remembering photos she had seen in an album of her parents' honeymoon trip. There was one more stasis chamber to check. Walking across the cabin, Amatheia was both amused and bemused; seeing a tail wagging and gently drumming against the glass screen of the third pod.

This chamber also possessed a medical diagnostic application. Mister Waggles was alive, he had survived! The pod had repaired his injuries and in doing so, somehow, bypassed the stasis malfunction suffered by both Amatheia and Saoirse. Mister Waggles remained the same age that he was when they had first departed Earth. The hound had not quite woken up yet. He seemed to be dreaming of going on walks and playing with his beloved owner; evident by his paw movements and excited, half muted yelps.

Having calmed down and wiped away her tears, Saoirse joined Amatheia by the sleeping beagle's side. With a caring arm around Saoirse's shoulder, Amatheia promised she would continue to help and protect her.

Amatheia also told Saoirse that while, unfortunately, she did not know if there was a way to reverse the ageing process, she did think there might be a solution to get her mind to catch up with her older body. A smile returned to Saoirse's face as Mister Waggles waking up, undeterred by the changes in her appearance, seemed to recognise her and tried frantically to lick her face through the glass screen. Amatheia typed in a code, releasing the beagle into Saoirse's arms.

After lots of cuddles with her dog and much soul searching, Saoirse turned to Amatheia.

"Okay Amatheia, what do we have to do, to fix me?" asked Saoirse, with an inkling of determination and leadership beginning to emerge.

"Well, I seem to remember a facility, a large building, hidden amongst the trees of the Stygian Forest. As children, we were told stories of abducted humans and Oikians being taken to this strange place.

"If we misbehaved we would be scolded and it would be said that the bad Kolassians might take us there to be punished. Some believed the tales, others thought they were just made up to frighten disruptive children into being good. However, one time when I was about to be transported back to Earth again, I escaped.

"I was recaptured within a day but that evening and night I spent in the Stygian Forest made me realise that the stories were true. I know the place exists and I think we may find a way to help you, there," replied Amatheia.

"Tell me about the night you spent in... in the Stygian Forest," asks Saoirse timidly with a whisper.

"We have to prepare to break orbit and try to land undetected," said Amatheia.

"Please Amatheia, if I know what the place looks like I won't be as scared when we get there," asks Saoirse.

"I cannot, I will not. I must warn you, nothing can prepare you for how scary the forest is, even if I play it down a little, the appearance and the feeling the Stygian Forest casts over you cannot be candy-coated. To this day, I often have recurring nightmares about the place. When we arrive there, I want to be in and out as quickly as possible! Trust me, you will probably spend most of the journey clinging to me with your eyes shut tight," said Amatheia, now looking directly at Saoirse.

"Well, okay Amatheia, whatever you say. Can we go now? urged Saoirse.

"Sit back and fasten your harness, I have prepared our final approach. It is night time over the Stygian Forest. The ship's monitors have detected a structure contained within overgrown vegetation, it must be the place. I can land in a small clearing a few kilometres from the facility but we will have to walk the rest of the way. So, are you ready for our next adventure?" asked Amatheia.

"Yep, ready and able... so is brave Mister Waggles!" replied the brave, still a child for now.

Having successfully broken through the atmosphere, bizarrely, all the instruments went haywire as they approached the Stygian Forest; one moment the screen gave an altitude reading of fifty metres, then three hundred metres and then two kilometres. Ignoring the dials and flying by eye alone, Amatheia piloted the craft down through thirty-metre-tall fern-like plants; the clearing wasn't exactly a clearing, just less menacing than the surrounding area.

The liquid metal coating of the ship mirrored its surroundings providing automatic camouflage. Further on, the densely wooded forest would provide barely enough room for themselves to manoeuvre through let alone land a space craft. Although no less dense, at least here, the vegetation was soft enough to yield a cushioned landing and also provide cover for the craft while they set about the daunting task ahead of them.

As they left their craft hidden behind them, the tall fern-like plants gave way to hundreds if not thousands of thin, tall and twisted trees. They were only about ten centimetres in diameter but being so densely planted, Amatheia and Saoirse spent an hour of the trek moving their shoulders sideways past the black, heavily knotted wood. The trees would generally be rough to the touch but soon their progress increased as the wood thinned out a little, the next tree's bark was sticky and malleable in Saoirse's hand. As she pushed forward, it gave way and collapsed to the side.

Mister Waggles began sniffing the air and growling in a deep guttural tone they had never heard before now. The hound had a sense that something awful was approaching. This followed with a deafening, banshee sounding, wail to surround and disorientate them completely. The ringing in their ears got louder and they both felt light headed while Mister Waggles began to howl. There was a change in the orientation of the stars above. The position of the trees before their eyes also appeared to shift from left to right repeatedly.

"Quickly, wipe that stuff off your hand and put this scarf over your mouth," instructed Amatheia to Saoirse.

"There are stories of giant owl or bat like creatures that would fly through the forest at night in search of flesh and blood to feed upon, the elders called them *'Stryckons'* and they only lived in the Stygian Forest. They leave a sticky residue on trees when resting or observing their prey. They were responsible for that haunting sound you heard. The mucous they secrete can make you feel dizzy and possibly black out," continued Amatheia.

"What is their prey? What are they hunting? What are they trying to eat?" asked a curious Saoirse.

"Anything warm blooded that walks through this forest," replied Amatheia.

Saoirse went pale and looked off into the distance.

"I'm really sorry my child, my descriptions are too frightening for a six-year-old! I forget you are still a child despite your adult appearance," cried Amatheia.

Saoirse did not respond and continued to look past Amatheia with a vacant stare. There was an approaching sound of a whipping wind and a dark shadow was cast over all three of them. A piercing scream accompanied as black talons, as long as the fingers they protruded from, were suddenly embedded into Amatheia's shoulders. She was lifted off the ground and disappeared into the darkness; her trailing feet brushing past Saoirse's hair who was still standing gaping into the nocturnal emptiness where Amatheia had stood moments ago.

Amatheia didn't make any sound as she was carried off by the Stryckon. Saoirse blinked and shuddered back into the present. The forest became silent again and she felt completely alone as the erratic foliage seemed to surround her. Saoirse retreated with her still barking pet into a hollow and pulled giant ferns around them to keep warm and hidden from new terrifying sounds, now emerging from the bowels of the forest.

Taking refuge in the hollow and unable to see past the tip of her nose due to the complete darkness, heightened her other senses. As Saoirse sat awkwardly on a moss-covered log, the heavy odour of compacted undergrowth greedily took her sense of smell hostage. A light breeze brought some relief but also caused the spore laden shelter to tickle against her face and deliver a drop of rainwater onto her forehead. It flowed downwards, tracing her profile until it departed from the tip of her nose. Splashing onto a flat rock between her feet, it seemed to echo with unusual loudness in the sombre silence. After staring blindly into its direction for several minutes without moving, not even blinking, her isolation is disturbed by an approaching luminescence.

Mister Waggles moves around to the front of Saoirse, putting his body between impending danger and his loving master. The light flits hither and thither, highlighting the veins and spines of her leafy abode. Saoirse ponders if she should investigate the disturbance or remain hidden.

Peering out beyond the fronds, every now and then Saoirse would see a passing orb of pale-yellow light, seemingly in search of something as it moved whimsically from tree to tree. Mister Waggles tried to snap at it but Saoirse pulled him back; the dog obeyed her command to stay silent. It appeared innocuous enough but on one occasion the orb moved towards her and within that flavescent glow she witnessed a semblance of a pure and lonely terror.

The meeting of petrified eyes sent the orb screaming off to be devoured by the darkness of the Stygian Forest. Saoirse's, breath consuming, panicked convulsions sent her head spinning and she fainted, rolling softly back into her moss carpeted hideaway.

From a few hundred metres away, large feet came bounding and thundering through the undergrowth, ploughing through flowerless plants and leafless trees. A dark shadow stood before Saoirse's improvised lair and dropped a carcass to the ground beside her.

"Are you alright my child?" asked, a barely audible, almost out of breath voice.

"Amatheia? Is that you? I thought you were gone! I thought you might be... dead?" puzzled a timid child's voice, not yet ready to be an adult.

"Dead?! Not I child! I thought it best to allow the Stryckon take me, I had to keep you safe. Once far enough away, I dispatched of it easily; although if it were not for the thick vegetation below my mid-air battle, I fear the thirty-metre landing would have been a differently unpleasant one," explained Amatheia.

"But your shoulders are bleeding, let me help you!" said Saoirse as she reached for her backpack.

"What have you got there?" asked Amatheia as she attempted to carefully force her enormous bulk into Saoirse's makeshift refuge.

"Dried seaweed, I kept some from when you hurt your hands saving us from the sea monster," explained Saoirse as Mister Waggles enthusiastically licked both their faces.

After Saoirse finished nursing Amatheia's wounds, her attention was drawn to the bloodied carcass lying next to Amatheia's feet.

"Is it dead? Why did you bring it with you?" asked Saoirse, repulsed at what laid before her eyes.

"Saoirse, it is, I had heard stories about brave hunters venturing into the Stygian Forest in pursuit of such game. Apparently, it is supposed to taste like Neridian chicken!" said Amatheia with a cheeky smile on her face.

Saoirse didn't question Amatheia again. Her tummy rolled and groaned with hunger; drooling longingly as Amatheia made a fire and prepared their evening meal.

Sitting by their campfire with full bellies, conversation turned to the strange light Saoirse had witnessed.

"Other beings, or rather, more a reflection or the remaining spirit of a being, are said to move among this forest in search of their former self. The elders, when telling their old tales, referred to them as *'Eidolons',*" explained Amatheia.

"Is that what I saw, an *Eidolon*?" asked Saoirse.

"Perhaps it was, but do not dwell on it my child. We need a good night's sleep, for tomorrow we shall attempt to make your brain catch up with your body! The facility, by my calculations, should be past the line of trees over there, beyond that ridge," said Amatheia as she pointed northwards with a Stryckon wing bone.

With the remaining embers safely extinguished and the welcoming safety of daylight, they set off in the direction of the facility. It had snowed during the night but their progress was only mildly inhibited due to the fine powdery nature of the dark hours' precipitation.

It didn't take them long to clear the ridge and they took some respite at the tree line's highest point. Looking down into the valley before them, it was possible to just about make out a long cuboid structure announcing its presence through the surrounding foliage; courtesy of a surface glint conveyed by the emerging sunlight.

The structure was almost entirely covered in the same mirrored material as the Kolassian craft and it appeared to have no visible entrance or outward activity.

"The Kolassians who operate that facility are the same ones responsible for shipping my kind back and forth over all those long years. In fact, the landscape here is similar to parts of Earth where I had spent some of my childhood, albeit on a larger scale," explained Amatheia.

"I thought you once told me of happy times when you would call for your aquaton with an aulos and ride amongst the waves in Oikia?" asked Saoirse.

"Indeed, yes, there were some happy occasions. Part of my youth was spent on the shores of Oikia. Long before those days, a distant memory often resurfaces of some Earth people along with a female Kolassian bringing me to a dark, rain soaked, place.

"I have no recollection of being hurt by them but neither do I remember much love given. I hold a buried feeling that it was just a matter of sorting practicalities, that I was somehow evidence of an experiment gone wrong. All my life I have felt different to other Oikians, especially as a child. I was little more than five years of age when brought to my first adoptive family on southern Polar Neridia," explained Amatheia.

"Different how?" asked Saoirse.

"Well, I was always smaller than the other Oikian children. Also, my red fur was never as thick and sparsely covered my body until I became a teenager. In the early years I struggled to thrive but through perseverance I eventually came into my own, plus I eventually grew to the full Oikian size. I was taken from my first adoptive parents at a young age.

"The second family, while never showing any great affection, did not project any unkindness onto me either.

Seemingly they were only carrying out orders from their Kolassian masters," answered Amatheia.

"Their Kolassian masters? The Kolassians had them as slaves? You were a slave?" asked Saoirse, confounded.

"Yes, my child, my adoptive family were slaves. I was told, during an angry outburst by one of my adoptive brothers, that I wasn't a real Oikian. This left me feeling confused and lonely but during the many years I spent on Earth, his statement to me started to feel, not untrue," said Amatheia.

"What do you mean? That he was right in saying you weren't a real Oikian?" asked Saoirse.

"I would often try to escape from the colonies I had been placed amongst on Earth. Many enslaved Oikians were often transported to Earth and forced to live within hidden settlements, it was the only other liveable planet that the Kolassians had discovered. Polar Neridia was starting to die and Earth became a solution. I was one of very few who tried to escape. This would, on occasion, bring myself and other Oikians into contact with humans; thus, leading to so-called 'Bigfoot' sightings! When hunters or people out hiking accidentally came into contact with us they would report seeing giant apes or monsters, the Kolassians for fear of their plans being discovered would transport us back to Polar Neridia or to another remote part of Earth," explained Amatheia.

"Well, I don't think you look like a monster! I know you are kind and gentle, I love you Amatheia," Saoirse warmly hugged Amatheia.

"I love you too child, come we must make our way to the facility while those that live here in the Stygian Forest are quietly resting and will not cause us any harm," replied Amatheia, gratefully accepting Saoirse's affection.

The trek down to the facility was much easier than their previous hike; the foliage, although dense and sprawling, still allowed light to penetrate through and banished thoughts of vengeful dwellers. Dappled light fawning in the morning along a revisited path reveals leaves like a young child's newly trimmed fringe; clipped and lifted by a gentle breeze.

Amatheia and Saoirse are on a journey again; a sojourn to reconnect, to match a child's mind to her adult form. Saoirse approaches, with child-like exuberance, to grab hold of Amatheia's hand. She pulls her to the edge of the trail to show her the pretty patterns projected by the Neridian sun. Its rays penetrate a cluster of leaves; one of the few things of beauty, suggests Amatheia, contained within this haunted place.

"It is said that the tree to which these leaves belong, an organon tree, possess the power to be an instrument of understanding or wisdom. Let us take some with us," Amatheia paused in reflection before plucking a handful.

Mister Waggles jumps up and then runs off in an attempt to entice them to play chase. Saoirse giggles and tries to persuade Amatheia to join in the fun.

"Come now, I'm afraid it's time for children's games to stop. I, we, you need for your mind to catch up with your body. Let us put my plan into action," disciplined Amatheia with some regret.

They reached the mirror coated building to find pools of concentric circles rippling at various points on its surface. Without hesitation, Amatheia plunged her fist into the nearest undulation. An aperture appeared and, using both hands, she widened the opening just enough to allow them room to crawl inside. They passed through a two-metre-thick wall and were presented with a tunnel that travelled downwards at a gradient which forced them to sit and slide rather than walk.

Upon reaching the bottom of the passage it was evident, from the dripping water and pungent humid smell, that they were deep underground. They were in a long dusty corridor with walls that had been roughly hewn out of solid rock. Every three metres or so, the hall was perforated by thick steel doors which concealed individual cells; they had arrived at a dungeon in the bowels of the facility.

Heavy footsteps and heavier breathing approached from the end of the corridor. Amatheia looked around and with nowhere to hide, dragged Saoirse behind her enormous frame for protection. Their impending discovery caused every muscle in Amatheia's body to tense up in preparation for potential combat. Just as a Kolassian boot appeared from around the corner, one of the steel cell doors promptly opened behind them.

"Quickly, come this way," ushered a faceless voice.

With not many other options available to them, Amatheia picked up Mister Waggles and taking Saoirse by the hand, they entered the light devoid room.

"Close the door gently and do not say a word before the Kolassian guard passes by," hurriedly announced a voice shrouded in shadows.

Footfall slows and then pauses momentarily in the corridor. The door is pulled firmly shut and locked from the outside; in her haste, Amatheia had not fully followed instructions from the voice. The Kolassian guard grunts in disbelief at one of his colleague's ineptitude; resuming his duty, he disappears quickly around the next corner.

A match is struck and a soft glow forces the darkness to relinquish its grip, revealing the voice's source in the corner furthest to their left.

"Interesting isn't it? Something all dominant species have in common, the spark of life! In its innocence it gives power to create, propels us forward. However, with indiscretion, it also has the potential to destroy everything it touches," suggests the voice as its owner stands up and moves carefully to transfer the flame to a candle waiting on a nearby window ledge.

Illumination increases and they are beckoned to come forward and sit on the cell's only bed. A dark-skinned man, wearing time-worn clothes, sits with a shopping bag beside his feet. Saoirse looks down and observes that the bag contains cylindrical objects. She also notices that although his clothes are threadbare, his brown leather brogues are immaculately polished. The man's eyes follow those of Saoirse and upon recognising their direction he instinctively places his right foot in front of the bag to guard its contents. Amatheia moves forward and Saoirse follows behind. Mister Waggles senses no harm is intended and bounds over to lick the man's hand.

"Let me introduce myself, my name is Sam. What is your name young fellow?" asked Sam, revelling in the attention given to him as he petted the dog.

Saoirse looks to Amatheia for approval; the Oikian nods her head slowly and smiles in agreement.

"He is called Mister Waggles, this is Amatheia and my name is Saoirse, I am six years old," replies Saoirse, with caution but still exuding enthusiasm.

"Only six? My oh my, you are very, very tall for your age. Is he your dog?" asked Sam kindly.

"Yes, well he is mine and my sister Ellen's dog too. Mummy says I am tall but she has not seen me really big like this, I am six but I am also twenty-six, I think?" replied Saoirse, unsure if she was revealing too much or something she should have kept secret to herself.

Amatheia explains to Sam the reason for Saoirse's appearance and her aspiration that she can bring the girl's mental age into alignment with that of her physical maturity. She hopes an answer to the predicament can be found within the facility.

"It is indeed unfortunate, the malfunctioning of the hyper-sleep modules, but I can possibly help you achieve the balance you desire. Would you be so kind, in return, to assist me in helping others achieve their freedom and some sense of calm in their lives?" asked Sam.

"Others, what others?" asked Amatheia.

"Inside this facility there are over a hundred abducted humans, many failed experiments, captured Oikians and Kolassian defectors; all incarcerated while the Kolassians decide what to do with them.

"Some will be reunited with their families back on Earth, confused and unaware of why or how long they have been missing. Others will re-join adoptive slave families living on Oikia or hidden in colonies on Earth. Lamentably, some Kolassian defectors, of which there are many more than you might initially think, will spend what little time they have remaining, confined within these walls," explained Sam.

"We will help, won't we Mister Waggles?!" declared Saoirse as her beloved pet gave his paw in agreement. Sam and Amatheia look admiringly at Saoirse and exchange a lingering half-smile.

"Amatheia, come closer, let me have a look at you," requests Sam as he takes her hand in his and moves the candlelight nearer to reveal her face in more detail.

"You have your mother's eyes. The same sad, yet kind, eyes I once looked upon," croaks Sam, steadying himself as he continued.

"You knew my mother? Does she still live on Oikia?" asked Amatheia excitedly.

"You misunderstand, I do not refer to your adoptive slave mother. Your biological mother is human. You are part human, born on Earth," explained Sam patiently.

"What? How? Why?!" demanded Amatheia, trying to contain her emotions and not alert the Kolassian guards to their presence.

"There is so much to explain and perhaps when you know the truth, it will set you free as it often does for anyone in search of difficult answers. Your mother's name is Rosemary and you have a twin brother. Well, when I say *'twin'*, he appears more human," said Sam.

"What is his name? Is he alive? Is my mother alive? Where are they?" asked Amatheia desperately.

"They are both alive, well I trust Rosemary is okay. I hope she escaped. I did all I could, at that time, for her. Your brother's name is Mick Flannery and...," said Sam unable to finish as Amatheia interjected.

"Mick Flannery is my brother and an Earth female, by the name of Rosemary, is our mother?" asked Amatheia, sitting back down quickly as she felt dizzy upon hearing the life changing revelations.

"Listen to me, I know of a laboratory on the top floor. It will have the equipment required for Saoirse's transformation. I helped to design most of it while I was detained here; being abducted many times over the years. After we readjust Saoirse's mind there will be a right time to tell you of your beginnings. I would be opposed to speak of it now as that conversation would not be for young ears," whispered Sam as he drew closer.

Sam suggested they rest until the Kolassian guard finished his shift and then it would be safer to make their way to the laboratory. Amatheia lay on the floor wondering what Sam might reveal about her origins. Saoirse and her loyal pet were now curled up together, fast asleep on the hard bed while Sam tried to get comfortable on what little space was left at the end of the lumpy mattress.

Saoirse was awoken softly a few hours later by a large Oikian hand gently stroking her face.

"It is time my child, we must go to the laboratory now while the Kolassian guard sleeps," whispered Amatheia.

Without speaking, Saoirse stood up to join an already waiting Sam and Mister Waggles. Amatheia, after several attempts, forced the steel door open with her shoulder, they then proceeded to walk softly down the dungeon's torch lit corridor. The guard's boots could be seen protruding out of a small side alley as he lay slumped, sleeping in an uncomfortable looking metal chair.

They tip-toed past the snoring Kolassian; Mister Waggles taking the opportunity to sniff his boots in the process. As they rounded the next bend their presence was acknowledged by the facility's other inhabitants.

Groans, cries and insane laughter combined with relived, rehearsed or revisited conversations shouted mockingly at ghosts or past memories - all beckoned Sam, Amatheia and Saoirse as they approached each door along the hallway; bringing with it, tremendous anxiety in anticipation of what might peer out of each cell door shutter. The first revealed a human adult businessman dressed in a navy pin-striped suit. He was holding a brown leather briefcase in his left hand and paced back and forth holding out his right hand to shake that of invisible clients.

Another cell had a female Kolassian adult rocking back and forth on the edge of her camp bed while she desperately clutched onto a human child's baby doll. However, the most unsettling sight revealed through one of the cell door shutters was that of an Oikian child. Upon seeing Amatheia walking past, it called out longingly as the child mistook Amatheia for its mother. Amatheia attempted to open the door and upon failing to open the lock, she proceeded to pull at the hinges with all her strength. The door did indeed shift within its frame but with a gentle hand from Sam she was persuaded to wait until they had completed their task of transforming Saoirse's young mind.

As the disturbing sounds faded, they reached a set of steel steps that wound upwards to the next floor. Blinding light greeted them as they entered the second level.

Metre thick glass simultaneously formed the ceiling above them and the floor of a landing pad. Covering the entirety of the room's walls were ten-centimetre-wide, oscillating circular mirrors; each one angled slightly differently than the next.

The resulting effect gave the illusion of being alone, even though it was possible to hear the voices of those who walked alongside. Amatheia, Saoirse, Sam and Mister Waggles continued onwards, enduring the bizarre feeling that they were being accompanied by spirits, bodiless voices whose reflections were banished to where they knew not.

The mirrored walls eventually ceased, to be replaced with bare, polished concrete and to the relief of everyone, their bodies became visible again. Towards the end of the room there were rows upon rows of machines with random lights and soft whirring noises busily keeping the facility running smoothly.

"The Kolassian guard sleeping below us is the only keeper of this place. The whole building is fully automated. It is only visited once a week by his superiors to deposit or extract some poor unfortunates, very much like the ones we witnessed a few minutes ago," deepening furrows belied his calm tone.

"Where do we go now Sam?" asked Amatheia.

"The laboratory is one more floor up, near the launch-pad, we can access it by a delivery elevator at the far end of this room," replied Sam confidently.

As the lift moved upwards a narrow window running the height of the building afforded them a glimpse over the tree line outside.

"Look! I think I can see something way over there!" Saoirse pointed outwards; charcoal smoke was rising high above the treetops.

"It appears to be coming from a craft that has crash landed. I can see part of it hanging from the tree branches. Our sensors did identify a craft following a similar route from Earth, about two days behind us," said Amatheia.

"I wonder who it could be? Do you think you were followed?" asked Sam.

"It's impossible to know at this stage. The craft may have gotten into difficulty, if it were over-loaded, delivering abducted humans or transferred Oikians. Right now, let's focus on Saoirse," replied Amatheia.

The lift doors opened with an ominous silence and delivered them into a room full of equipment none of them, apart from Sam, had ever seen before.

A dozen or so pods were aligned along the entire left-hand side of the room; the right was occupied by a similar number of medical tables and incubators.

"This, Amatheia, is where you were brought for a period of time to ensure your survival, shortly after you were born on Earth. I will tell you more when time is a little less pressing.

"So, Saoirse, shall we begin?" Sam took the adult child gently by the hand.

Saoirse tentatively allowed Sam to lead her across to one of the incubators. The pressing of several keys in sequence resulted in the incubator extending its length to accommodate Saoirse's, newly attained, increased height. The touching of another button opened the glass cover with a hushed gliding motion.

Still holding her hand, Sam helped Saoirse to sit into and slowly lie down inside the incubator. He proceeded to place a number of electrodes around Saoirse's head and one above her heart.

"Now, just close your eyes and think happy thoughts. It will take no more than an hour to complete the pairing of mind and body," explained Sam.

The glass cover moved gently back and clicked with a cushioned thud, forming a vacuumed seal. A pale blue gas fills the pod sending Saoirse to dreams of home and temporarily obscuring her from view.

"Now what?" asked Amatheia.

"Now we wait," answered Sam.

Sam stays by the incubator, monitoring the progress of the procedure. Amatheia sits back on a reclining chair, stroking Mister Waggles as he curls up on her lap. The hound keeps one eye closed and the other fixed upon the incubator containing his best friend.

An hour has passed and as the incubator's digital timer counts silently to zero, a soft hiss signals its glass door opening. A slightly dizzy Saoirse, yet with a distinctly different look in her eyes, emerges from the pale blue gas. Without speaking and with outstretched arms, she welcomes Mister Waggles's affection. Then turning to hold Sam's hands, without speaking and with a warm smile she silently thanks him before moving to hug Amatheia tightly.

"How do you feel my child?" asks Amatheia, sitting back down again in anticipation of Saoirse's reply.

"Not like a little girl anymore. Even though I am sad at the loss of my childhood, for now I am happy to have the calmness the procedure has brought into my mind," answered Saoirse with a lingering half-smile.

"Saoirse, there is one final task to be performed in order to complete your transformation," interjects Sam.

"Okay, what should I do?" asked Saoirse.

"Lie down on this medical table please. I need to place a circular chip into the base of your neck, close to the brain stem. It will stabilize the results of the procedure," explained Sam.

"Will it hurt?" asked Saoirse as she lay down.

"You will feel a slight pinch and some nausea is common. A beneficial side effect will be dramatically increased intellect. This will be somewhat disconcerting to begin with but, believe me, the advantages might make some people desire a trip in a malfunctioning hyper-sleep pod," assured Sam.

Moments after the implant had been completed, it was as if a light went on behind Saoirse's eyes. She began rambling on at speed about quantum theories, time travel and ideas on how to get back home to Earth more quickly and without the need of hyper-sleeping for two decades. Then she paused and silence filled the air, only to be replaced by her retching and vomiting. Sam feared the process may have been too much for Saoirse to handle and held her tightly until her body relaxed.

When Saoirse had composed herself again and Amatheia had helped clean her up, they decided to make their way back down to the dungeon level.

It was time to fulfil Sam's request of also bringing some serenity to the paused and anguished lives of the facility's forced inhabitants.

As they approached the corridor where the Kolassian guard had been sleeping, there was an absence of snoring and there were no boots protruding out from the side alley. With everyone holding their breath, they pushed open the guard's office door. As it was devoid of any Kolassian presence, Sam thought it would be an opportune moment to search for the keys to unlock and free the cells' occupants. As Sam rifled through the office, there was a scream from behind him. The Kolassian guard had returned and was wrestling a fearsome Amatheia on the ground just outside the office. Saoirse was screaming with tears running down her face; she could clearly see the Kolassian guard pointing a weapon at Amatheia. Using all of her strength, Amatheia head butted the guard and threw him casually to one side.

"Come now! We must leave!" roared the Oikian.

They ran as fast as they could, feeling terrible as they left the sound of pleading inmates trailing behind. Amatheia led the way, punching and stretching an opening in the liquid metal, outer wall. As they made their way out, Amatheia turned to see the Kolassian guard unleash his weapon. He fired multiple shots and a blast glanced off Sam's left leg.

"Saoirse! Help Sam!" screamed Amatheia as she picked up Mister Waggles and continued to run.

Saoirse put Sam's left arm over her shoulder and chased after Amatheia with the Kolassian guard gaining ground behind them. Saoirse began to feel dizzy but nonetheless held on tightly to Sam. She could see that Amatheia was moving further away from her as she herself began slowing down. At the same time she was very aware that the Kolassian guard was closing in on them; almost feeling his breath upon the back of her neck.

***

Meanwhile, another arrival was imminent…

Two days after Amatheia and Saoirse had first arrived in orbit around Polar Neridia, another ship was desperately struggling to stabilize its trajectory above the same troubled planet.

Where am I? With all this condensation I can't see past my assisted breathing visor. I feel terrible. I am soaked through with perspiration. I hope this pod has followed the set destination and timing; if I could summon enough strength I would force it open. I think I might be close to death, thought Tereo.

Tereo raises a gloved hand to his breathing apparatus; upon its opening, he is able to wipe away some of the condensation. He catches a glimpse of his reflection in the pod's glass cover above; staring at his colourless face, he knows it is only a matter of time before he is finished.

Struggling out of the hyper-sleep chamber, he falls to the floor. The other four pods had all opened as planned, simultaneously upon arrival.

Although still a little groggy, Kyle rushes over to Tereo's aid. Upon seeing Tereo's devastating appearance, Ellen cries and turns in fright to bury her head into her mother's chest. Crystal takes hold of Ellen and stares blankly at the dying Kolassian, allowing a single tear to trace a line on the curve of her cheek.

Jim runs over and helps Kyle to lift Tereo onto a nearby medical table. Kyle holds Tereo's hand while the Kolassian desperately tries to tell him something. As he attempts to form words, he continues to sweat profusely and groan in agony.

Fragments of the metal strip which had become embedded in his leg during their escape from the exploding base, where never fully removed. The injury had not healed during hyper-sleep and his disease was now advancing rather rapidly.

"You must act quickly! Take a sample of my blood, before I die!" whispered Tereo breathlessly.

"You're not going to die, you can't! We need to create the antidote and vaccine so we can save my daughter and Kolassian children too, just like you said!" shouted Kyle in frustration.

"Listen to me, I know I am not long for this world or for any other! Jim, you will be able to continue without me. Take this data, along with a blood sample, find Kyle's other daughter and complete our mission," said Tereo handing Jim the downloaded data as he fought against increasing pain and shortness of breath.

Jim did as Tereo instructed and extracted the blood sample. He decided to put the data into his chest pocket for safe keeping. Moments after Jim finished the task, Tereo's hand slid from Kyle's grip as his final breath rattled and echoed throughout the craft.

An alarm sounds announcing a serious problem with their transport ship. The floundering craft attempts to bank, then lilts dramatically to one side and Jim decides to jump into the pilot seat.

"In reality, I have never flown one of these ships, only in a theoretical scenario, comfortably seated in safety at my desk!

"I have studied Kolassian plans for various propulsion systems but never actually piloted one of their craft!" shouted Jim in growing desperation, over the deafening engine noise.

Crystal quickly straps herself and Ellen into their seats while Kyle buckles himself into the co-pilot's chair beside Jim. The craft vibrates violently as they break through the atmosphere, unbeknownst to them, at the wrong angle. The turbulence increases as everyone is bathed in a fiery orange light. The flames outside the cockpit dance in the reflection of Ellen's tear-filled eyes and are mirrored across the cabin in the dead Kolassian's vacant stare.

Speed increases and the ship roars in contempt at their efforts to direct it to a safe conclusion. Deafening noise followed by silence surrounds them all.

A snowflake melting on the tip of his nose encourages Kyle to open his eyes. He is in a horizontal position on the side of a mountain. Liquid metal carnage is strewn across his view from where he now finds himself.

Now sitting upright he feels uninjured apart from the fact that although Crystal is mouthing screams in his direction from ten metres away, he can hear nothing.

A loud ringing sound comes and goes as it echoes inside his head. It seems to exit via his left ear, preceding the opening of a floodgate of pandemonium to enter abruptly into his right.

"I can't find Ellen, I can't see her or Jim anywhere!" screamed Crystal as she limped towards Kyle.

Kyle Picks himself up and both he and Crystal search desperately through the wreckage.

"Up here! We're up here!" shouted an exasperated voice from behind a line of giant black bark trees.

The voice belonged to Jim Kelly and was then accompanied by that of a child calling out for her mother and father. Kyle and Crystal pushed hard through the undergrowth that had tangled its way around the base of the dark tree line. Suspended about five metres up was a dissection of their shattered craft.

The ship's starboard side had been abandoned to hang precariously in the branches after the craft was sliced from nose to tail down the centre during the crash landing. Jim and Ellen had previously been seated to the right of Kyle and Crystal respectively.

The port side of the craft was scattered and smashed in pieces along the hillside. Nobody had died in the crash. The only casualty being Tereo who had succumbed to a combination of his disease and infected leg injury while they floundered precariously in orbit only a few short minutes ago.

After several nail-biting moments of the craft shifting in the branches and gasps from everyone, Kyle and Crystal successfully helped the rest of their makeshift crew safely to the ground. Checking that he still possessed the vile containing Tereo's blood sample and that the data had remained safely in his pocket, Jim suggested they make their way above the ridge to get a better view. He wanted to estimate if they had at least landed near the same coordinates Amatheia and Saoirse's ship had taken.

"Hold on a second Jim," said Kyle.

Before they headed off, Kyle searches and finds Tereo's body amongst the wreckage. Carrying the corpse of their Kolassian friend to a small clearing, they bury him under a pile of rocks; with no shovel and frozen ground, it is the best they can do. Jim and Kyle then continue, side by side, up the hill.

"Many a time we spent walking up the Wicklow hills over the years; I'd never have thought we would be doing something similar on another planet!" said Jim as he pulled his hood up against the biting cold.

"Me neither my friend, I wonder if we'll ever get the chance to cycle along the trails around Silver Mountain reservoir again, or for you to play your harmonica under the reservoir bridge?" responded Kyle wistfully as he too pulled up his coat hood, fending off the wintery grasp around his neck.

With no flowers to place, Crystal softly knelt down at Tereo's grave to whisper words of thanks to honour him for helping to save her daughter. Hugging Ellen closely, she then followed on behind the two friends.

Upon reaching the top of the ridge, Kyle takes out a pair of binoculars from his backpack and surveys the distance from left to right.

"I can't see anything apart from tightly packed forest and the odd patch of snow-covered ground," said a deflated Kyle.

"Let me have a look," Jim said, taking the binoculars from Kyle.

As his eyes diligently scanned the horizon, a Neridian sun emerged momentarily from behind ominous, snow burdened, clouds.

"I see something! There is a corner of what might be a building, glimmering just behind that area of giant ferns to your right Kyle!" exclaims Jim.

They all decide it would be their best option to move downhill towards the reflective structure. Jim and Kyle lead the way through the towering foliage with Crystal following close behind, cradling a now sleeping Ellen.

Just as the trees and ferns thinned out a little, their progress was soon halted by the sound of weapon fire and shouting ahead of them. Jim and Kyle pushed back some of the vegetation in order to get a better view of the source of the pandemonium. In doing so, they witnessed a terrifying scene unfolding before their very eyes. Kyle could see a tragedy about to happen unless someone intervened very quickly.

About fifty metres ahead, an older looking Amatheia could be seen carrying Mister Waggles as she ran from the facility. Trailing behind her was a man limping, dragging his left leg, being helped by a tall fair-haired woman in her mid-twenties. They were being chased and fired upon by a Kolassian guard.

"Get down!" ordered Crystal.

Jim and Kyle dived for cover when they turned and saw Crystal with Ellen on her hip and pointing her Glock 17 in their direction. A single bullet whistled through the air; ending its short existence and the life of the Kolassian guard as it passed through his skull. Amatheia, Sam and Saoirse stopped running when the only guard that had been policing the facility now lay horizontal and silent.

Mister Waggles ran in circles being overjoyed to be reunited with his family. Amatheia and Sam moved to greet Jim while Saoirse paused to stare at a still sleeping sister, a smiling father and a weeping mother.

"Mum? Dad? You're here!" cried Saoirse.

"Saoirse? Can it, really be you? Where is my child? What happened to my beautiful little girl?" sobbed Crystal as she ran to embrace her daughter.

After a brief reunion of the Parsons family, Sam and Jim approached and gathered everyone.

"Jim has informed me of the plight of little Ellen here. I suggest we waste no more time and make use of the facility's laboratory. With the blood sample from the Kolassian named 'Tereo', the data on this file coupled with three advanced intellects among us and a blood type match from Saoirse, I believe we can accomplish a cure!" explained Sam.

"I must stress that time is of the utmost essence! The dungeons below are full and I would imagine it won't be too long before the deceased guard's colleagues return!" Sam fidgeted becoming restless thinking of priorities.

Once again, Saoirse found herself lying on a medical table inside the facility's laboratory. This time she was accompanied by her younger sister on a table parallel to her own. She placed her right hand on the back of her hip, over the bandaged site where liquid marrow from her pelvic bone had been extracted; her left hand remained held tightly in the right of her sister's.

After many complicated calculations and much heated debate, Jim and Sam were now prepared to administer a serum into Ellen's bloodstream. There was nothing left to do but wait and allow the two sisters time to sleep and hopefully recover.

Darkness drew around them and despite Sam's growing anxiety about the inevitable return of other Kolassians, they all decided to settle down where they could to try and get a good night's sleep.

Morning arrived and with it the gentle smile and giggle of a child no longer struggling to catch her breath.

Crystal and Kyle had slept, rather uncomfortably but content, on the floor underneath the medical tables which both of their children occupied. The parents cried and smiled upon hearing the happy exchanges between their two daughters above them.

"We have both of our little girls back with us again," said Crystal to Kyle.

"Yes, we do, although one is not so little anymore. If only I had not abandoned you. Why did I go on that stupid mission, following co-ordinates by bicycle? I should never have thought of leaving my family alone when we all knew the world was a very changed place, with *'them'* abducting and experimenting on anyone, even innocent children!" stressed Kyle.

"Shush now, you abandoned no one, do I look like someone who's defenceless; besides, look at everything that has happened since! We have two healthy children, yes, I know one has lost her childhood but they are alive!

"Who knows, with all the advanced technology we have observed, maybe one day Saoirse can retrieve her childhood that was taken away," suggested Crystal.

"Well, a bright new day and a fresh new beginning!" stated Amatheia, eager to get going.

"Well, Ellen's antidote has worked, we must not delay! Let's free the guests below and get out of here!" said Sam.

They return to the dungeons and using the skeleton key, Amatheia procured from the dead Kolassian guard, it is not long before one hundred and fifty lost souls get to see and feel sunlight again. Amatheia walks out in front, leading the entourage away from the forest towards the coast; holding the hand of an orphaned Oikian girl. Saoirse leaves her mother's side and catches up with Amatheia and the young Oikian.

"What is your name my child?" asked Saoirse in a gentle tone; the phrasing of the question brings a smile to Amatheia's face, reminding her of how she would often address Saoirse.

"My name is Elpida," replied the little Oikian, with a smile beginning to appear from the corner of her mouth.

Amatheia, also smiling, turned to Saoirse.

"The meaning of her name translates as... *hope*."

07

Origins & Beginnings by Firelight

An ember once thought to be long extinguished,
sparks into life again.

Future and past, both attainable
for those who dare to dream.
Trying to right many a wrong
in hopeful receipt of forgiveness;
constantly moving back and forth
searching for what was once loved
and now lost.

The little troop were followed noisily, but thankfully, by those once lost and unfortunate. They came to a halt on the cold eastern shore of Kolassi, North Polar Neridia. Beyond, spread out before them, was a horizon filled with a near frozen ocean; dotted with icebergs as far as the eye could see. A rising Neridian sun occupied the centre of the lower sky; still permitting a fading Neridian moon to let its presence be known for a while longer.

"Saoirse, do you still have the aulos I gave you?" said Amatheia, standing up.

"Yes, it's here somewhere," Saoirse searched the bottom of her little pink rucksack; it looked slightly amusing, now that she was a grown woman in both mind and body.

"Ah, you have it! You know what to do but you must continue playing until I say stop, we will need far more than one aquaton this time!" Amatheia gestured towards the sea.

Saoirse moved away from everyone and finding herself a place to sit, hunkered down by the breaking waves, she put the aulos to her lips and began to play; now having mastered the instrument, unheard even by Amatheia's ears, she extracts beautiful sounds. The crowd that stood behind her fell into silence, mesmerised by the beauty of the music's simplicity and profound sorrow.

One by one they rose from the depths. A small wet nose and whiskers would emerge first, similar in appearance to Mister Waggles. Then with a little trepidation, the aquatons' enormous bulk broke the surface revealing their handlebar horns. As Saoirse continued to harness anguished tones from her aulos, the amount of aquatons coming to the surface increased dramatically. They now came forth without hesitation, in both speed and number.

"And... STOP!" bellowed Amatheia.

Saoirse gradually removed the aulos from her lips and Amatheia's voice echoed off into the far distance to be replaced by the lapping of water against the shore, the mewling of about fifty aquatons and the murmuring of the beach populous. In an orderly fashion, as directed by Amatheia and Saoirse, each aquaton accepted three or four passengers onto its back. Once everyone was accommodated and seated comfortably, Saoirse, who was sitting on one of the lead aquatons alongside Amatheia's ride, blew a single hopeful tone on her aulos signalling the convoy's immediate embarkation.

"Amatheia, I fear that some of these we have rescued are not fit to travel far, how long will this journey take?" the task ahead filled Saoirse with uncertainty.

"It should not take us more than one day. Normally the distance would require about a week to navigate but approximately two kilometres out we will encounter the *'Grigora Stream'*; a fast current that is strongest at this time of year. I estimate it will increase our speed at least sevenfold," suggested Amatheia.

As they entered the current, Amatheia alerted everyone to hold on tight. Each aquaton instinctively manoeuvred into single file. As the convoy's pace increased rapidly there were several alarmed yelps expelled to the waves; the exclamations were short lived in both supply and volume as the pilgrims became accustomed to the motion.

Ellen sat cradled in front of her father with her mother seated just behind the aquaton's metre wide head; its horns jutting out a further metre to either side. Turquoise contrasted against indigo and cobalt as the child gazed in awe at the colour difference between the stream that carried them and the surrounding waters. Ellen looked down with wonder at small turtle like creatures swimming alongside in pursuit of a shoal of red fish that swam just beneath the aquaton's jaws, hoping they might be in receipt of a free breakfast. She dipped her hand into the water and was immediately surprised at the difference in temperature between the two bodies of water; the turquoise stream was almost tropical in comparison to the near freezing chill of the parallel dark blue ocean. As Ellen leaned over to get a closer look at the submerged activities, the aquaton turned its enormous head and drove its right horn beneath the surface. Crystal who had been mesmerised by the strangely echoing song of a large gull like bird passing overhead was wrenched out of her trance by her youngest daughter's sudden squawk. Ellen let out a squeal and she would have fallen in for sure if it were not for her father's steadying hand. The aquaton had snagged one of the red fish and as the beast tossed its impromptu snack into its mouth, Ellen's shriek was replaced with a gasp at first and then a giggle.

Time passed quickly and the icebergs diminished. The harsh freezing conditions gave way to, albeit far from tropical weather, only the odd snow flurry. It was at least a far more comfortable position and warmly appreciated by all. The current's speed dissipated. Rounding a jutting headland, into view came a sheltered bay; painted with small rounded pebbles, obsidian and polished glass of bounteous colours, signalling their journey's end.

"Welcome to Oikia, my child," whispered Amatheia softly to Saoirse.

"Welcome to Oikia! Your new home!" announced Amatheia, in a raised voice, to everyone else assembled.

The aquatons docked abreast a sand bar allowing their passengers to disembark. With a few minor grunts and grumbles coming from some having to get their feet wet, little by little, they gradually dismounted and waded the last one hundred metres to shore.

"There are cave-like dwellings about a half day trek further up the coast. They were dug out by my ancestors a very long time ago. After most Oikians had been enslaved or transported to Earth, the caves were abandoned soon after; the Kolassians had over-fished and over-hunted the region. I did hear tell though, that over recent years there has been a resurgence of wildlife, perhaps we could make it a new home for all of us. I do not think the Kolassians have any interest in the area now," said Amatheia, moving quickly on, eager to reach their expedition's end.

With the aulos once again pressed to her lips, Saoirse released yet another wistful tone to drift off into the sea air and send the aquatons on their own journey home.

Everyone moved further along the beach, haphazardly placing one foot in front of the other; glass rounded and smoothed by the waves would at times make for unsure footing. Amatheia knew they were all a bit weary from the journey and so she instructed everyone to rest for a short while.

"Look Mum, lots and lots of beach jewellery!" Ellen sang out with joy.

The youngest Parsons child had made a full recovery and was enjoying beach combing as they travelled along the shoreline. Saoirse, having decided to join in the fun, ran over to stroll alongside her mother and sister. She took a piece of fishing line from her pink backpack; carefully accepting the coloured gems from her sister as they sat down. Saoirse fastened the glass fragments, one by one, until she had fashioned a wonderful necklace of many colours. Indigo, crimson and emerald hues; each transparent piece momentarily stealing the sunlight upon its wind caressed rotation.

After a short time had passed, everyone stood up to recommence their journey towards the caves. Amatheia, holding Elpida's hand, paused to admire the beach jewellery necklace that Saoirse and Ellen had made.

"It is beautiful, you have made something from nothing, you are all very dear to me," Amatheia cherished each glass piece meandering through her fingers.

Amatheia handed the necklace back to Ellen. When Ellen saw Elpida's fascination with how the rounded glass fragments projected colours to dance upon their faces, she decided to gift the necklace to the Oikian child. Seeing her sister's kindness brought joy to Saoirse and she decided her pink backpack more fitting for her younger sibling. Saoirse placed the bag upon her sister's shoulders once she had transferred her own belongings to another rucksack received gladly from her mother. Then with Ellen taking Elpida by the hand, the two children of similar age but from many light years apart ran together giggling with joy at the coloured projections that chased their little feet.

"What are we?... Who are we now?" Saoirse pressed upon Amatheia as they stood looking at the children playing without a care or a worry to trouble them.

"We are those who are departed - emigrants, exiles, evacuees. Fugitives of fear, outcast from whence we came and now refugees and travellers of the Universe left to wander in uncertainty. Many labels could be attached to each and every last one of us. Perhaps we are all aliens living in an alien world. However, similar to the glass necklace you fashioned, we are all of different colours, shapes and sizes. Yet if we coexist together in harmony, something of beauty that will stand the test of time can be made from nothing but allowing a little time, effort and understanding," answered Amatheia, putting her arm around Saoirse's shoulder.

Even with snow and ice abound, the midday sun that cast its rays over Polar Neridia was redder in colour than the one that shone in the Milky Way and had the potential to burn skin if exposed for a lengthy period of time. It was now beating down upon them as the caves came into sight; everyone was happy for the shaded retreat the caverns provided. The caves were divided into small rooms that could each accommodate up to ten souls comfortably. Most of the group didn't know each other but there were some family members happy to be reunited, including a father and son who eagerly approached the lead group of Kyle, Crystal and their family and friends.

"Hi, eh, this is all a bit surreal. My name is Jacob and this is my son Ethan. You seem to be a few of the only competent humans here, we are grateful for your assistance. I suppose we all have questions that need answers but for now I would like to help get things organised before nightfall," offered Jacob.

Jacob was a tall, slim, balding man in his mid-fifties. His torn clothes hung limply on his bony frame as if he was the survivor of some catastrophe.

He had a moustache that drooped over his top lip which gave the impression he was constantly chewing when he spoke. His son, Ethan, was about thirty years younger but mirrored almost a carbon copy of his father nonetheless; same drooping moustache but without a greying or balding head. He wore a similar style of outdoor clothing, also torn and hanging loosely on a near emaciated body.

"Hi Jacob, my name is Kyle, this is my wife Crystal and our two children, Saoirse and Ellen," forwarded Kyle with a welcoming nod.

"Jacob, I'm Amatheia, how would you like to help?" asked the smiling Oikian, towering above him.

"Well, back home I ran summer camps for youth groups, teaching survival skills and such in the wilderness. As a side hobby, my son and I were interested in trying to shoot *'Bigfoot'*, I don't mean to capture or kill with a gun, but trying to photograph them, no offense," Jacob, looked rather uneasy as he communicated with Amatheia who clearly resembled his former prey of sorts.

"That's fine, I understand. I am not really a *'Bigfoot'*, well yes, I kind of am but more to the point, what you call *'Bigfoot'* does not exist so to speak. What you were trying to photograph would almost certainly have been members of my kind in colonies of enslaved Oikians, transported from here by the Kolassians. If you witnessed an Oikian on their own or in a small group, they were probably desperately trying to escape from one of these colonies," explained Amatheia.

"Okay, some of this is starting to make sense to me but all I can mostly think of, for now, is the rapidly approaching darkness. I am pretty good at making camp though. I reckon we need bedding for the caves, firewood and a reliable source of clean drinking water for a start," continued Jacob eagerly.

"Agreed, that sounds like a plan. Perhaps Jacob, you could make a fire. Saoirse, will you and Ethan check for a good water source; I seem to remember a freshwater stream once flowed from about a few hundred metres up behind these caves. I will take Mister Waggles as a hunting companion and search for our evening meal. Kyle, Crystal, if you would be so kind as to make sure the rest of the group have bedding for themselves within the caves. Sam, could you and Jim see if anyone needs medical attention," directed Amatheia.

Amatheia and Mister Waggles provided a meal from a bounty of small flightless birds, similar to Ptarmigans found in North America, and an almost endless supply of fresh wild berries one could ever desire.

Firelight flickered and bounced off the cave walls as everyone was settling down for the night while a small group sat around the campfire, just outside the cave entrance, looking up at the stars clustered above.

"I don't know what happened to my wife. We were on a camping trip not too far from where we live, from where we once lived I guess," mused Jacob.

"Where did you live, Jacob," asked Crystal.

"Hudson, a small town about thirty-five miles west of Quebec in Canada. Ethan and myself heard noises that we thought could possibly be made by a Bigfoot. My wife was asleep, we thought it was a good opportunity to take photos. The Moon was hidden by cloud and we were afraid to use torches in case we alerted any Bigfoot to our presence. A fallen Giant Redwood, was partially hidden by overgrown brambles and ivy. I could detect that the distinctive sounds were coming from inside the felled, decaying tree.

As we approached I heard some strange weapon fire, it momentarily lit up our surroundings. In the fleeting light, through a tree hollow, I could see two adult and one infant Bigfoot, or as you Amatheia would rightly say... Oikians. The sheer terror and distress upon their faces will remain with me for the rest of my days," Jacob turned away, filled with regret.

"We did try to help them, to entice them out of their refuge and to come with us; but fear had them trapped inside that tree and I don't think us humans appeared to be a welcoming rescue party," offered Ethan.

"Before we could do anything more, we became ensnared in a type of net that was fired over us by one of the Kolassians. We were hoisted up above the trees and as we were being taken aboard a space craft I could hear my wife screaming below. Everything went dark and silent.

"When we woke up, we found ourselves strapped onto metal slab tables in a cell, within that facility you rescued us from," a solemn Jacob continued.

"I could hear my Mom pleading for her life while we were being taken onto the space ship. I was powerless to help her!" cried Ethan. Unable to dwell on the subject any longer, he left the campfire and conversation to turn in for the night.

"One time, maybe a few months back before you all arrived, I did think I heard my wife's voice cry out from an adjacent cell. Even through the thick walls, I could make out that it was definitely a female voice and most certainly human. When you liberated us, I searched the cells next to ours. In one of them, I found a blood-stained nightdress on a steel table; I knew from its scent that it must have belonged to my wife, Esther. Positioned beside the table, were monitors and equipment still turned on. One of the screens had a still image that looked similar to an ultrasound scan; I remember seeing one when Esther was expecting Ethan. At that time, even though I was made fun of by my work mates for doing so, I didn't care, I would have been one of the few fathers to accompany their wife to all the scans, doctor visits and whatnot," sniffled Jacob.

Jacob also decided it was time to try and get a good night's rest and as he walked off, Sam and Amatheia exchanged a knowing look.

"I do not want to add to that man's distress but I fear his wife may have shared a similar ordeal to what Amatheia's mother, Rosemary, endured," stated Sam, gaining the attention of everyone huddled by the fire.

"Sam has already informed me that I am part human and that Mick Flannery is my twin brother; both of us being born to a mother who was incarcerated in a mental asylum on Earth. Please Sam, you said you would tell me more of my origins," pleaded Amatheia.

"Amatheia, are you sure you wouldn't prefer to have this conversation in private?" asked Sam.

"I am tired of all the secrets. Unfortunately, I suspect it was my mother's need to reveal the truth about her pregnancy that more than likely was what caused her to be committed. That said, I still believe everyone deserves to know the facts. If we are going to try to forge a new life here, together, I think it best to know where we are starting from," answered Amatheia trying to catch her breath in anticipation of Sam's explanation.

"Very well, but firstly, you may wonder how I came to have all this information. I too have been abducted, I have been for most of my adult life. With my IQ, education and knowledge, I proved to be a valuable asset for the Kolassians. I helped, it must be stressed, under duress and threat of torture, to create a lot of the equipment in the facility.

"I also invented, without their permission and for a while without their knowledge, an *'emotional time travel device'*. Amatheia, your twin brother Mick has used one to witness past events in his life. At times, if you will, I have been able to witness him witnessing those episodes.

"I was hoping and praying that perhaps the device might deliver him here, but that remains as yet to be seen. This object allowed me to observe many of the events you all have endured. Even though I was forced to assist in an indirect way to unintentionally aid the Kolassians in your abductions, I still felt somewhat guilty. So, I tried to be a guardian angel of sorts, where and when time allowed me to be," Sam raised his hand, showing an emotional time travel device to those gathered by the campfire; all on the edge of their seats in a collective gasp of wonder.

"You mean to tell us, you invented this time travel tool that feeds off emotions, that somehow it is able to get an individual to a time or place that they most desire? Why?" demanded Kyle.

"Despite what you may think, I am someone who cares and worries about all living souls. Regardless of how successful or not or how happy you may or may not find yourself, at the end of it all, the most precious thing we have, is our life.

"I felt I owed it to you all, a chance to regain the lives you had before they were taken away from you. Plus, I needed to devise a way to find... well let's just leave it at that," Sam's voice was fading slowly as his head and mood gradually lowered towards his chest.

"A way to find what Sam, are you alright?" Crystal was becoming increasingly concerned.

"I too have experienced the tragic loss of a loved one, someone I am desperately searching for, I have a son; he was about the same age as Ellen is now when I last saw him. That was more than twenty years ago.

"He was taken hostage while I worked in the facility. I was told, every single time, that once I had completed an assignment he would be returned to me. However, there always seemed to be another project. Ultimately, they denied any knowledge of his whereabouts; coldly informing me that my child may have gotten lost while in transit back to Earth! When they had no further use for my talents, I too became an inmate of the facility. I fear my son is no longer living because in all my travels, the device has not once brought me to visit upon him.

"Even when I reached the darkest depths of sadness and feeling completely lost, with my emotions utterly consuming, the device would often bring me to places I once knew; but never destinations associated with my child. The running track I raced upon whilst in college, for example, why there I do not know. The track was where I was first abducted, long before I ever became a father; a place with no connection to my son.

"The device would always keep bringing me back, again and again to my cell in the facility; it's as though, subliminally, it recognises that I have an emotional tie to the site. It is the last location in which I ever saw my son's beautiful face or heard his wonderful, cheerful voice. Maybe now that I have somewhat fulfilled my oath to help restore your lives, I might have a better chance of being reunited with my son.

"Before Jake was born and after my wife became ill, we had moved away. I needed to find answers about her illness and my abductions. I had read in a local gazette about a young woman, a daughter of a distinguished PNSE engineer who, years before, had suffered a terrible car crash, losing the use of his legs. The article told the story of how his daughter, with a promising career in space medicine, had fallen pregnant and had delusions of alien abduction.

"I did not succeed in securing a job as a nurse in the asylum. However, when I tried to convince the doctors of myself being abducted, it was not long before I got to meet Rosemary," Sam informed Crystal, reluctantly.

Saoirse rises from her cross-legged position, massaging her temples and wincing a little in discomfort.

"I need to lie down for a while, the headaches are back again. I can't explain it, they have been there on and off ever since the hyper-sleep malfunction. The procedure did nothing to eradicate them. It has altered the regularity of my headaches to occur only once or twice every few days but increased the intensity. Every night since then, I've been dreaming of finding a way of never having to get into one of those damn chambers ever again. I never got the chance to be a teenager, a childhood of playing with my sister and my pet dog, stolen from me. Years of love from my parents never permitted to be showered upon their eldest daughter. Despite the headaches, I am driven to find a solution. When I wake up from these dreams, I have an incredible urge to divulge, to write down theories and ideas. Sam, do not wait for me, I think Amatheia has held on long enough to hear what you must tell her. I just need to rest for a while and I'll be back out later," insisted Saoirse anxiously.

"Saoirse's merging of mind with her new physical self has worked, but her IQ has increased rather more dramatically than I had anticipated. That coupled with her fear of maybe one day having to use a hyper-sleep chamber again is over-loading her brain at times, it must be very exhausting for her," Sam considered Saoirse's emerging intellect as she retired for the evening.

"I would like to discuss Saoirse's theories with her, another time perhaps, sorry for interrupting Sam, please continue," Jim Kelly apologised.

"Right then, Amatheia, as I previously said, you are indeed part human. Your mother, my friend Rosemary, was abducted and inseminated by the Kolassians. Shortly before her abduction she thought, mistakenly, that she had been raped by one of her college class mates; a young man by the name of Finn Murphy.

"He and Rosemary had become friends in the local amateur dramatic society. Being tall and clumsy with bright red hair often precluded his interaction with the opposite sex. Finn's parents encouraged him to mix with girls by attending drama classes. His blond-haired twin brother, Fionn, was an athlete who garnered female attention without endeavour.

"After graduating, Rosemary and Finn had both gone to attend the celebrations. Afterwards, she took a short cut home through a poorly lit park, where the mock rape would take place; it was an opportune moment for the Kolassians who had been monitoring her movements very closely for some time.

"Rosemary assumed that Finn was responsible for her pregnancy, but in actual fact he was in an induced paralysis and was remotely animated by the Kolassians from a nearby craft. He himself had left the party slightly earlier than Rosemary but never made it home either. He had been abducted, then prepared for his starring role; oblivious to the pain and humiliation Rosemary would receive. Only nonhuman seed would enter your poor young mother on that fateful night," Sam's phrasing and unintentional lack of tact led Amatheia to becoming visibly upset.

Crystal moved to sit beside her, placing a hand on her shoulder in an attempt to comfort the Oikian.

"My sincere apologies Amatheia, sometimes when I am divulging facts, I can be too clinical. You would think my emotional intelligence should be more evident; often those in possession of a very high IQ inadvertently allow the head to disregard the heart," Sam placed a reassuring hand upon the Oikian's shoulder in an effort to assure his intent was not to offend.

"It's fine Sam, I understand. I know you are a good human, please continue," Amatheia clasped Sam's hand, welcoming his good intentions.

"Why did they choose Rosemary? What I mean is, one could understand picking Finn, a shy boy with little or no social skills, he should have been an obvious target?" interrupted Jim.

"Rosemary's father was once an aeronautical engineer, worked for PNSE, Probe National Space Exploration where he had the misfortune to fall out of favour with a corrupt colleague. He discovered, by chance, that his fellow engineer was operating as a spy for the Kolassians. It seems that making sure her father would never walk again was not enough revenge for being discovered by his co-worker and so his colleague decided to bring Rosemary to the attention of the Kolassian High Command as a possible host for their experiments. You see, the disease that Ellen is now cured of is one that pervaded Kolassian society for generations.

"They were trying to create a hybrid that might be immune to the condition and unfortunately, Rosemary was one of many subjected to their harrowing trials. I would like to be able to attempt the cure for Rosemary, if I ever get to see her again. She became very ill in the asylum, whatever Kolassian seed they used, the supplier whether unknown or not, was himself suffering from the Kolassian sickness.

"Some female humans were impregnated with seed from Oikian slaves and others from a select few Kolassian guards, who were unique in that they themselves were part Oikian. They may have volunteered or might have been forced to participate against their will, I do not know for certain. So Amatheia, in truth, while you are part human but more Oikian in appearance, in actual fact it would be more correct to say you are also part Kolassian as you possess Kolassian DNA, inherited from your father," informed Sam.

"This is incredible, go on, don't stop!" pleaded Jim.

"Yes, indeed Jim. Kolassians and Oikians had both evolved from one original species living in central Neridia; evolving and separating into two distinct groups over time. The Kolassians migrating north and the Oikians to the south after their great war destroyed most of the planet. As the Oikians did not suffer from the Kolassian illness, it was thought that exploiting them would be the safest route to develop a cure. However, an antidote could not be wholly achieved in this way. They needed sample DNA from another being with no possible connection to the Kolassian disease; humans were the first and only viable option discovered.

"If you remember, I told you that Rosemary was very ill in the asylum. Well, when the Kolassians orchestrated the mock rape and consequently abducted Rosemary, they took her to the facility where she was inseminated with seed from a Kolassian guard. I observed that guard, from a window in my laboratory, being forced against his will to participate in their trials. As Rosemary lay there, she was oblivious to the foul act and to the unwilling guard's protestations.

"They knew he possessed Oikian DNA because he had previously fathered a child who also exhibited Oikian characteristics; that child did not survive past infancy.

"However, unknown to the guard's superiors at the time, he did not show any signs of having the disease himself. The Oikian DNA he possessed, somehow temporarily masked the presence of the condition or delayed its development.

"They would have been unable to ascertain the cause of death of his previous child, due to his refusal to disclose the whereabouts of the boy's burial; not wanting the infant's body to be used for their research was one last element of control in his possession," Sam theorised.

"My poor mother, Sam I would like to find her if I can and bring her here so that you and Jim may cure her. I would love to give Rosemary the happy life she deserves, to explain all these things you speak of. I want to tell her that she was not raped by her friend Finn Murphy and that the unfortunate guard was an unwilling participant; perhaps my father was a good Kolassian," Amatheia began weeping.

"I too would like to see your mother again someday, she became a close friend and it would bring me joy to see Rosemary eventually live a contented life. There is more that I must tell you, some of which I know has been revealed to your brother, your twin, Mick. A period of time had passed after Rosemary's insemination, I was in the middle of yet another project when I witnessed the arrival of an infant. The young child was weak and while predominantly Oikian in appearance, she exhibited some mild human characteristics.

"The Kolassians wanted, they needed, this child to survive. They seemed to recognise some value in the use of twins for their research. Yes Amatheia, that child was indeed you; because of your twin connection, they ideally wanted to keep you within easy reach of Mick. You would not meet him then, it would have to be in an environment under their control. As long as you remained frail and weak they would require your twin to be near, to be close at hand. Then, if an emergency arose, Mick would be a ready-made donor match.

"You were nursed by a female Kolassian in a secluded outbuilding within the grounds of the orphanage that housed Mick, amongst other children. It was possible to keep him there because, despite his rapid growth rate, as he grew he appeared to be wholly human in appearance; granted, a gargantuan one at that.

"When you were strong enough, the Kolassians made the decision to insert you into an adoptive family here on Polar Neridia. As you well know, that childhood proved to be quite nomadic, what with being transported to and from various colonies of *'Sasquatch'*. These were based in remote parts or sparsely populated areas of Earth, all the while allowing the Kolassians to observe your progress," finished Sam as he paused to take a sip of water.

Stretching his arms above his head, Sam felt the urge to roll and crack his neck. This brought some relief and he shrugged his shoulders as he made himself more comfortable by moving closer to the campfire. He had felt quite wooden from being seated in the same position for a while as he disclosed to them, all the details that he was able to recall.

"I can sort of remember parts of my childhood from when I was at least five years old. However, I do recall once while I was being cradled and fed, the overwhelming feeling of another presence; a connection that has stayed with me my whole life. Through blurred vision my eyes met those of someone with sheer terror upon his face. That brief encounter scared me in equal measure.

"I am not quite sure if the nurse could tell for sure, but she paused my feed as she stood up to turn around and look. Something else had interrupted her task and demanded her attention. A noticeable fluctuation in the room's temperature, the sound of a creaking door or some significance caused her to discontinue my sustenance. Could it have been Mick?" Amatheia looked to Sam's face for confirmation.

"More than likely, it may well have been Mick who was transported back in time as he searched for answers of his own," replied Sam.

"Why did my mother not keep Mick? Why did she not want me either?" pondered Amatheia.

"It wasn't exactly a case of not wanting to keep you or your brother. In the beginning, Mick did not look like an average human baby. He was extremely big even back then and his appearance frightened Rosemary terribly. That in addition to the fact she thought he was the result of her being raped, was far more than she could cope with either physically or mentally. The poor woman was left drained of all her faculties," Sam turned away cautiously.

"And me, was I an abhorrence too?" asked Amatheia.

"I would imagine your appearance, at that time, might well have perturbed Rosemary. However, she was simply unaware of your existence, you were removed while she was incapable of knowing what was happening," said Sam as he returned his eyes to look directly into Amatheia's.

"But you became friends with her in the asylum, why would you not have told her about my existence?" said Amatheia, scratching her head.

"You must understand, Rosemary was in no condition to process that kind of information. When you were born, you could never have been passed off as human. The trauma your mother endured during Mick's birth resulted in her having to be placed into an induced coma before you were carefully extracted. She would have been oblivious to the fact that Mick was not the only child she had been carrying.

"Some of the doctors, hospital staff and government officials must have been collaborating directly with the Kolassian High Command in aiding the abduction and insemination of Rosemary and perhaps many others.

"She became infected with the Kolassian illness during insemination, but somehow the condition was not transferred to either yourself or Mick. If ever there was a way to rescue her, we might be able to make her well again," hoped Sam.

"There is something familiar about your face Sam, have we ever met while on Earth, when I was no longer a sickly infant maybe? Perhaps somewhere other than the orphanage or the facility?" Amatheia crouched down, taking a closer look at Sam's face.

"Somewhere else other than the outbuilding on the grounds of the orphanage, the place where Mick had spent his childhood, '*The Good Herdsman Convent, Redemption Asylum*'... and not at the facility either? It is a possibility that during my investigations I might have had the opportunity to observe the '*Sasquatch*' or as some might say *'Bigfoot'* colonies. It was during one of those adventures when I was captured by the Kolassians.

"They confiscated one of my time travel devices, not knowing how to use it and unaware I had more in my possession, meant I was compelled to stay no more than one night in the colony. Again, the search for my son was proving fruitless and as usual, the device transported me back to my cell in the facility," recalled Sam.

"Ah, now I recall that time. On one of my insertions into a Bigfoot colony, a human was put into a cell along with myself and a few others. Sam, you looked many years younger than you do now but I am certain it was you who...," Amatheia paused as Sam interposed.

"Yes, it was I who gave you water and left the cell door unlocked before I travelled on again," affirmed Sam.

"That was, coincidentally, a place called Twin Lakes, near Colorado. I made my escape that following morning and stowed away aboard a cargo ship that happened to be bound for Europe. Whilst in hiding, I overheard a conversation between two of the crew. One of them was telling the other how there had been sightings of large walrus like creatures in the Atlantic Ocean, just off the south west coast of Ireland. He described seeing their large handlebar shaped horns, but his shipmate didn't believe him.

"However, I knew that it must have been an aquaton that provided the topic of their conversation. As the ship passed a few kilometres out from the coast, I jumped overboard. Treading water for a short while, waiting in anticipation for the *'Horizon Seeker'* to disappear from view, I retrieved my aulos from my backpack.

"Sure enough, the ship worker's tale was true and I was able to summon one of the great beasts from below. The aquaton rose up beneath my feet, lifting me up onto its back and out of the water. I soon found myself cruising towards the south coast of Ireland," recalled Amatheia.

"When were you in Ireland?" asked Crystal.

"I think that must have been a few months before we met for the first time," Jim Kelly thought aloud, trying in vain to hide a frown.

"Yes, indeed it was Jim. When I got ashore, the Sun had just dipped below the skyline and so I made my way northwards under the cover of darkness. I wasn't too sure what I was going to do or where I was travelling to. I thought maybe it might be an idea to try and seek out a colony of imprisoned Oikians and once I had set them free, perhaps we might have been able to find a way of returning to Oikia. Unfortunately, that intention was short lived. I travelled along the east coast and was making my way up a mountain range, through a heavily forested area, when I was captured. The poor creatures in that compound were so institutionalised that they would never leave. It was a greater kindness to leave them there. At least they would be fed and could live out the remainder of their lives in the company of other Oikians, albeit far from their home.

"On the third day, when a guard mistakenly stood too close to the cage as he fumbled with his keys, I was able to subdue him with a single blow to the side of his head. I ran and ran until my lungs were burning and my legs felt like they were turning to jelly. Collapsing to the side of a firebreak in the forest, I fell asleep.

"I was awoken by the sharp sound of twigs snapping underfoot. Two figures approached, silhouetted by the morning light. I was far too exhausted to move even an inch so I thought to myself, if my first real meeting with humans is to be my last, well so be it, I had grown tired of running," Amatheia sat down; even the thought of her ordeal was tiresome.

"It was not long after, that you soon had the desire to fight for what you wanted from life again," grumbled Jim.

"Thanks to you and Mick, my brother. At that moment I didn't know he was my sibling, but I felt a connection," Amatheia shrank in response to Jim's tone.

"Yes, I remember, when we first met Amatheia, myself and Mick were doing some reconnaissance along the Wicklow Way. I had convinced Mick to accompany me in trying to locate one of the giant sinkholes. By then I had thought that they might have been used as an entry point for the Kolassians.

"We were trekking through Crone Forest when we exited out onto a fire break. Up ahead we saw a stumbling figure, much taller than any human yet not scrawny like the Kolassians. As we approached, Amatheia, you looked to Mick and then proceeded to keel over. We made a makeshift stretcher and brought you back to our hideout. After that, well we had some interesting conversations to say the least. She told us of the Oikians' plight; her and Mick soon became good friends. It would have been a few months later when Amatheia first greeted you Kyle," recalled Jim Kelly.

"Yeah, from time to time, I still ache a little from that hug Amatheia," grumbled Kyle, rubbing his shoulders.

"Apologies my friend," Amatheia clumsily tried yet failed to hide a slightly embarrassed smile.

A hollow groaning and ill whining announced the agitated twists and turns of a troubled mind, unable to release itself from a disturbed sleep. It began as a low echo frantically searching for an exit out of the cave just behind the campfire gathering.

Saoirse's dream encapsulated someone being trapped in an achingly desperate search, climaxing with her sweat soaked soul spitting out towards the stars and the entire Universe beyond her horizon.

"I've got it! I think I've found a way to get back to Earth! No more twenty-year journeys!" screamed Saoirse, waking herself and making those encircled about the campfire, jump from where they sat.

Pulling a blanket tightly around her shoulders, Saoirse hurriedly scampered out of the cave to quickly re-join the expectant faces illuminated in front of her.

"Ever since the procedure at the facility, I have been going over and over in my dreams about trying to figure out a way to travel across the great empty void, without the need for hyper-sleep. I think I've found a way!

"The theories you all had about the Kolassians trying to transform Earth into a sort of galactic cruise ship were misplaced. Yes, the abductions were part of searching for an antidote but have you ever asked yourself why they were based near Earth's northern pole? I mean, some of us have had encounters with them in warmer climates. Therefore, it could not just be because they wanted to settle somewhere that had parallel weather systems to North Polar Neridia!

"There must have been another reason why they were attracted to that location in the first place. Jim, let me ask you this, if an alien ship was approaching Earth, what would be one of the first things its occupants would see? What would catch their eye? What would spark their interest?" Saoirse paused to rub her temples.

"Well, they may be pleased to find it is a blue, water based, oxygen-rich planet?" suggested Jim.

"Perhaps so but what do you think would stand out to an interstellar visitor?" Saoirse's eyes began to widen.

"The Northern Lights! Plus, I do remember Mick recalling an article he had read about the Inuit elders reporting to PNSE that the Earth's axis had tilted to the north!" exclaimed Jim, strangely faking his enthusiasm.

"Exactly! I think they must have been trying to harness the Aurora Borealis. They somehow changed the angle of the Earth's axis in order to direct the untapped energy somewhere!" beamed Saoirse.

"How? Why would they?" said Kyle scratching his head methodically.

"Sam, there are massive black holes in existence that would crush everything in their wake, correct?" Sam nodded in return to Saoirse's question.

"Jim, where in our own Solar System would be the science community's current favourite location for life to exist, outside of Earth?" asked Saoirse.

"I would say the optimum choice would be Europa, Jupiter's ice-covered moon," Jim nodded in approval of his own answer.

"What if a minor black hole existed nearby in our solar system, positioned right under our noses. Perhaps Europa could be, somehow, masking its existence. Imagine if the Kolassians were not as interested in Earth as much as we first thought, that it was not their primary focus.

"I think they could have been trying to direct plasma energy from the Northern Lights towards that minor black hole; as a way of creating a means of transport, a direct link from Polar Neridia to Europa.

"I think one of the Kolassians' main objectives was the construction of a wormhole!" expelled Saoirse with a feeling of triumph.

"You may well be correct Saoirse. There have been documented theories regarding the drawing of usable power from the Northern Lights. I remember seeing facility monitors displaying beautiful colour images of the Aurora Borealis; over which, graphs and diagrams were carefully superimposed.

"The Kolassians had built a base on Polar Neridia's red moon; occasionally, the red tinge would lessen to be replaced with a greyish, blue/white, colour. Beyond it, is an asteroid belt that seems to be moving towards empty space. If they were creating a worm hole that was capable of having an end point near Jupiter's Europa, well there would need to be an entry point this end," explained Sam.

"Those images you had seen of the Northern Lights, perhaps they weren't only visuals of Earth's aurora. As we arrived in orbit around Polar Neridia, its moon stood out to me as it was turning a vibrant red and it seemed to be projecting many spectacular colours far out into space," remembered Kyle.

"Yes, the Kolassian moon does have an atmosphere capable of giving displays of its aurora but still remains not conducive to habitation. I think their plans to direct the aurora power from this end may well have been interrupted by your activities at their polar base on Earth," suggested Sam, looking towards Kyle.

"Perhaps our interference distracted them, especially with the explosions and carnage we left behind, but if we could complete the harnessing of the aurora from here, would it then be possible for the wormhole to open up?" asked Kyle.

"The huge wall of mirrors that we saw in the facility! Do you remember them Sam?" shouted an excited and impulsive Saoirse.

"Yes, indeed I do. I think the outer wall of the facility is retractable. With some calculations I think we could re-calibrate the wall of mirrors to direct the aurora towards that peculiarly flowing asteroid belt. I believe that to be the position of another minor black hole and the entry point of your wormhole Saoirse!" Sam's voice quickened to match his growing enthusiasm.

"I think once the aurora's power is captured we can direct it in short bursts towards the black hole. The Kolassians must have already started the process behind Jupiter's moon, Europa.

"If we can successfully start the process from here, both ends of the wormhole will, I think, naturally join up themselves. It's akin to skipping stones, the bursts of plasma energy from the aurora. Each burst of energy is like a stone making contact with the surface of calm water; you don't see that it is there until the splash, the contact, is made. The plasma charge coats the inner tube of the black hole.

"A craft travelling through is therefore protected from the immense crushing force by that very force expelling it at immeasurable speeds far away from the tumultuous congestion. In my dreams I almost see it like a signal travelling along a fibre optic cable. The whole idea seems crazy yet entirely plausible, we must try it Sam!" Saoirse, stopped smiling in awe of her own understanding to reflect upon her divulged deposition.

08

Familiar Families
& Founding Fathers

Neither stone nor ice maketh a home, only the love from and for the souls contained within can bond a family.

Blood is thicker than water,
but both can turn to ice if left out in the cold.
A father once unknown but no longer unowned.
Celestial siblings casting shadows over biological twins.

Morning arrived cold and early as a coastal party on the backs of three aquatons made its return to the facility. Saoirse, Sam and Amatheia made the journey leaving the rest of the group and the one hundred plus they had rescued, to rest in the safety of the caves.

There was no longer a *"Grigora Stream"* to speed them along but the seven days passed relatively quickly with their minds focussed solely on the task ahead. It was dusk on the seventh day when they dismounted from their aquatons. Darkness quickly descended like the velvety cloak of a night raven's wing deftly sweeping across them;

proclaiming daylight had decided to depart. Saoirse and Amatheia, led by Sam, found themselves standing in anticipation at the rear of the large facility. The dead Kolassian's body had been removed. While there was no sight of any replacement guard, a craft with its engines idling was docked at a landing pad directly on top of the transparent roof.

Once again, Amatheia punched an entry hole into the liquid mirror wall, gaining entry to the facility. They tip-toed and held their breath in an attempt to refrain from unnecessarily announcing their presence. The three went up the winding stair and into the almost unbearably bright mirror room. Sam sat at a nearby workstation and began. An hour or so passed when he finally stood up, stretching momentarily before pressing one last button and urgently directed them towards the roof.

As they huddled in a corner of the landing bay, they noticed the craft was no longer unoccupied. A lone Kolassian guard appeared to be readying the ship for launch. His progress was then halted by a sudden jolting motion; the result of Sam's endeavours. The whole facility began rotating forty-five degrees. The Kolassian pilot ceased his preparations and exited the craft; disappearing inside the facility to investigate the reason for the building's unplanned rotation. An outer barricade lowered beneath their feet to reveal the wall of oscillating circular mirrors. After a few moments of mirrors numbered in their thousands, rotating to predetermined angles and doing so with a simplicity akin to the turning on of a flashlight, the harnessing of the Polar Neridian Moon's aurora began in earnest.

The aurora's energy is redirected towards the asteroid belt and finds the minor black hole. This results in a blue tinged glow threading its way, twenty light years, out into the Cosmos. A distant popping sound and almost neon tinged illumination, focussed their gaze on the emerging wormhole's entry point. A long stream of various sized boulders from the asteroid belt momentarily paused their course, became captured, then circulated like remnants of an emptying sink and disappeared from view.

"Quickly Saoirse, you and Amatheia must take this, it is an updated emotional time travel device. I have set it to minus twenty years. Amatheia, because of your increased emotional bond resulting from your desire to help your mother, I believe it will bring you to her. Once you are at the other end of the wormhole and while the ship is still in forward motion, grasp the device with both hands just as you exit. Saoirse, you must also hold onto the device. There is perhaps an unknown, but certainly limited, amount of time that the device will allow you to remain at minus twenty years. If you are successful in rescuing Rosemary, I must warn you, do not delay in returning through the wormhole. I will travel back to the caves. Now, you two must commandeer that ship as fast as you can, perhaps this will be your first of many missions, a rescue mission at that!" directed Sam.

"We can help Rosemary now! We must go find your mother and perhaps we might be able to find Mick too," Saoirse stood up, ready to make a move.

Leaving Sam with the aulos to call an aquaton and make his own way back to camp, Saoirse and Amatheia proceeded towards the ship. They were showered in all the colours of the rainbow as they traversed the roof above the high wall of circular mirrors, which were steadily continuing to refract and redirect the red moon's aurora.

Tip-toeing, they arrived at the craft with its engines humming lowly. Amatheia took the pilot's seat and once Saoirse was strapped in, she manoeuvred the craft slowly upwards. Rising a few metres above the roof, Amatheia turned the ship in the direction of the wormhole.

As the engines released a volatile mix of fire and turbulence, the Kolassian pilot returned. Protesting with flailing arms and muffled fury, he was reduced to a pile of crumbling ash as the ship's pulsating engines increased in ferocity to leave an inferno in their wake.

"Okay my child, we are here, it is now or never!" Amatheia adjusted the craft's controls to hover a few hundred metres from the edge of the wormhole.

"Just do it!" screamed Saoirse, desperately fighting to be heard above the deafening bluster of the engines as Amatheia pushed all levers forward.

Sam, gripping the aulos tightly, paused to look over his shoulder towards the stars before starting his return journey. The nose of Amatheia and Saoirse's ship wavered then appeared to stretch into the wormhole, slowly at first before the remainder of it was inhaled in a millisecond.

Silence...
Snippet of a scream...
Look outwards...
Stars expand, unravel and die...
Several Amatheias in several pilot chairs, one fading behind the other in decreasing percentages of opacity.

Chaos...
Glimmer of stillness...
Look inwards...
Stars compress, form and are reborn...
Several Saoirses in several co-pilot chairs, one strengthening in front of the other in increasing percentages of opacity.

Time races and crawls, then blackout...
Nothingness.

"Saoirse! Saoirse! Saoirse! Wake up!" roared Amatheia, seemingly in a whisper at first and then increasing in such volume as to compel Saoirse in the placing of hands over ears as her eyes fluttered open.

Amatheia and Saoirse were unceremoniously ejected from the wormhole, delivering them to the dark side of Europa. Their heads felt foggy as if awakening from a sleep that had held them ransom for far too long. Shaking off their torpor and composing themselves, both pilot and co-pilot stared intently into each other's widened eyeballs as they hastily grabbed hold of Sam's new and improved emotional time travel device.

While the ship still edged forwards with residual momentum, the device engaged. Their ship once again increased its velocity, now towards Earth and as it did so, a small display on the side of the device showed a digital count down from minus twenty to minus fifteen, minus ten, minus five and then, zero.

The brilliant light of their craft easily illuminated a forest clearing below; already sparkling with moonlight reflecting off the frozen, snow covered ground. With all their senses firing, they still managed to focus and kept the ship hovering steadily at a height of about twenty-five metres. Beneath them, a woman dressed in a 1940's style red dress adorned with a big black bow and strangely completing the outfit with muddied green wellies, stood frozen with terror exuding from her pallid countenance.

"Quickly Saoirse, position yourself beside the floor hatch. There is a control panel beside it, from which you can operate the capture beam. I can see a Kolassian aiming a net gun at that woman. My heart tells me it must be my mother, Rosemary! Quickly Saoirse, get ready!" shouted Amatheia.

Nothing moves outside. The howling wind halts and the snowflakes suspend their tumble from leaden skies. Rosemary floats upwards, arms limply aloft mimicking a suspended puppet. She is brought safely into the craft with her mouth still agape while Saoirse wraps a warm blanket around her.

As the Kolassian flees and before they set coordinates back to the wormhole, both Saoirse and Amatheia see a holographic Mick with an arm reaching for something no longer present. He flickers in and out of time as he bends down, trying to retrieve a small bunch of flowers from the cold, hard ground.

His hologram begins to materialise into reality as it increases in intensity, powered by heightened emotion; finally allowing the fragile giant of a man to gain purchase on the bouquet dropped there by his mother. She has left at the speed of light towards Europa in a craft piloted by his twin sister.

The digital minus twenty on the side of the device begins to flash and ultimately fades to nothing just as their ship is pulled into the wormhole. Time and space distort and unravel once more as a small craft carrying three souls is thrust through the wormhole.

Arriving safely in one piece at the Polar Neridian end, they pause for a moment to refresh coordinates and occupants alike. Amatheia washes dried blood stains from Rosemary's face and gently tends to her broken nose. Red moonlight flickers upon the outer hull of their craft as the rescue party exit the wormhole. Rosemary, who remains not much older than she was when she gave birth to her twins, asks with growing trepidation of her son Mick's whereabouts and is embraced by Amatheia.

"You said my son was out there, you also said that he is your twin brother? I don't remember much about giving birth to either of you but I wonder if I will ever get to see him again?" hope attempted to introduce colour upon Rosemary's complexion.

"Mother, at this very moment in time, I do not know. There is much to tell you but for now please take some solace in the fact that you were not raped by your friend, Finn Murphy. Sam would be the best person to explain it all to you. Right now, the best thing for us three to do, is fly to the caves and attempt the administering of your cure, we need to try to make you well again," Amatheia's lip trembled as she forlornly looked down upon a pale and shivering Rosemary.

"Sam? A cure? Sam, my friend Sam? He was the only soul to show me any kindness in that horrible place; I reckon he enabled my escape.

My father was not well and didn't have much influence over my mother; she abandoned me to the *'care'* of that sadistic nurse! My wonderful Sam, is he here? How?" muttered Rosemary as she passed out.

***

Rosemary's son was much nearer than she could have ever expected...

Still in silent shock from what he witnessed in one of the orphanage's outbuildings, the sight of an Oikian child being breast fed by a Kolassian nurse, Mick lies still and quiet in the long grass as he collects scattered thoughts. His diaphragm expands and contracts violently. Cupping a hand over his nose and mouth, he tries to stop himself from hyperventilating.

He barely recalls running from that absurd scene and being subsequently catapulted across the stars. Opening his other hand, the burnt and buckled device trundles from his grip and comes to rest by his feet, exhausted of any further use.

Mick's view of a red tinged moon, shadowed by a strangely moving rock field, is suddenly interrupted when a dog proceeds to lick his face in uncontrolled excitement. Mister Waggles is soon joined by two others who had come to investigate a blabbering and screaming voice that seemed to fall from the sky a few kilometres beyond their campfire; the sound travelling on the wind.

"Come on boy! That's enough now Mister Waggles, leave him be," ordered Kyle, holding the hound's collar.

They could not believe what was presented before their very eyes. Their friend whom they had last seen disappear from view as they chased after the underground carriage with Ellen inside, now lay here on Polar Neridia at their feet; struggling to speak as he gasped for air. They had no choice other than to leave him behind in that tunnel back then, while they desperately clung onto the outside of the carriage as it sped towards the Kolassians' Earth headquarters.

Crystal lifted Mick's head and held a canister of water to his lips, sobbing as she tried to express how sorry she was for leaving him alone in that tunnel.

"Please, do not apologise for trying to save a loved one, I would have done the exact same thing! Besides, I was in no condition to run after you," Mick was now sitting up and feeling a little more relaxed.

Slowly, Mick stood up and with the support of his two friends; they began their trek back towards the caves.

***

Mick's mother was also much nearer than he could have ever expected…

Amatheia and Saoirse land the craft on frozen ground, adjacent to the caves. They carefully carry Rosemary on a stretcher towards the campfire. Announcing their arrival, they call out for Jim and Sam. Finding that Sam has not yet returned, they ask Jim to assist treating Rosemary with the cure. Curiously, he seems somewhat reluctant as he mumbles to himself.

"Tereo was your unwilling father! I have seen more than you all could imagine!" spat Jim with venom as he stood up from where he had been sitting by the campfire.

"You shall explain yourself later but for now you will help Rosemary!" roared Amatheia, Jim quickly complied.

By the time they have made Rosemary comfortable in a makeshift bed, positioned at the farthest corner of the caves, daylight has departed.

"She needs rest Amatheia, let the medication do its work, we will see what morning brings," advised Saoirse.

As they bedded down for the night by the warmth of the campfire, Jim Kelly decided to move his bedding; preferring to sleep away from everyone else.

The first rays of morning sunlight eagerly peered over the treeline above the back of the caves as three figures ambled towards the camp.

As they came closer, a dog could be seen circling them whilst running back and forth; Kyle, Crystal and Mister Waggles had returned, with Mick!

Kyle and Crystal had not yet told Mick about his newfound twin sister, so it was a surprise to say the least when a nine and a half foot Oikian ran towards him with arms outstretched shouting *"brother!"*

Gladly accepting her embrace, Mick sat down beside Amatheia as she relayed to him all that Sam had told her. He in turn recounted his experiences with the time travel device. All talk paused and silence befell everyone once she told Mick that their mother, Rosemary, was here.

"I want to see her now! Let me go! For the first time in my life, I am no longer alone, no longer abandoned! Please, I need to tell my mother that everything is okay, that it wasn't her fault. I don't blame her for not wanting me, back then, the choice was taken away from her!" howled Mick as he broke free of Amatheia's grip and ran into the labyrinth of caves.

Dust and the moans that escape disturbed dreams float about Mick's face and his eyes dart furiously left and right as he clumsily bumbles through winding corridors, hollows and dead ends. The first woman he sees is lying on a bed of cut pine branches with her back to him, she screams as he pulls at her blanket, trying to find the face of his mother.

It wasn't Rosemary, just some other unfortunate, cruelly woken from dreaming of tending to hens on her long-lost farm somewhere in America's Mid-West; he leaves the woman to gradually return to her sleep filled with desperate longing.

Long right turn, sharp immediate left, straight on, then a child's hungry cry distracts him momentarily, causing him to cast his thoughts back to a much younger Amatheia. The memory of her being breast fed by the Kolassian wet nurse sends an evil chill coursing through his entire body.

Shaking his head, he refocuses as another groan pulls him onwards. His ears are flooded with the chastising scowls, barking coughs, spit and discontent of the weary souls gathered within this maze.

All of these unfortunates were huddled and cuddled in dusty stone corners; some lying on creaky rotten beds of tired and abandoned wood. They clung onto threadbare blankets trying to banish the cold and memories of their past lives from haunting them.

As the groans fade, he hears a sweet voice gently reciting familiar poetry. The fourth verse of the *"Dr Sun, Mr Moon"* poem draws him to the end of a passageway. A woman lies on sweat soaked sheets but still with a smile upon her face. She looks towards the man approaching and knows it is her son; she continues,

"Your complexion changing, colours rearranging
Is this an old friend I see?
Warms my face, brightens this cold grey place
Time for me to re-join my own race"

Kneeling beside her, Mick takes her hand in his and without thought or hesitation recites the final lines,

"Another time Mr Moon, your half-brother
is strongest at twelve noon
Opposite ends of the day
Brothers in the Universe going their separate ways"

Smiling eyes are reciprocated, safe in the knowledge of finally being home.

"I was always curious about the origins of that poem. I wrote it, or so I thought, while I was kept from sleep one night, a very long time ago, in my college dormitory. Raucous sounds of drunken students falling out of bars after closing time granted me no rest," recalled Rosemary.

"Those last two verses were not penned by your hand, nor mine. They had been implanted by the Kolassians as another sort of marker; a way for them to identify their chosen abductees.

"Those verses were originally a lullaby the Kolassians sang to their children who found it difficult to fall asleep as their planet's dramatic changes rained upon their homes. On my travels, I witnessed a Kolassian nurse singing the lullaby to Amatheia, my sister, your daughter. The other parts of the poem, I guess, you did indeed write yourself. Perhaps through DNA memory, the poem was passed onto me," Mick reasoned aloud.

"My son, please forgive me, I feel better, now I just want...," whispered Rosemary... the cure had worked.

"Hush now mother, save your energy. How about I bring you outside to cast your eyes upon a new day," said Mick as he bent down to gently lift his tiny mother into his caring arms.

Mother and son leave the darkness and move towards the welcoming light of a new beginning.

09

The Wildered;
Reunited, Reborn & Returned

Many of those who wander confused through life
finally find answers, but not all are at peace
with the conclusions to their questions.

A child lost once before is lost once more.
A man never born begins his journey towards
the boundary of life and sanity.

Others live out a sanitised existence,
awaiting a cure for the ravages of time.

A son carries his mother in arms made strong from a life of struggle. They emerge to be greeted by a silhouette displaying a nervous quiver which turns to whimpering tears and then to chest heaving sorrow, mixed with hope; followed with a sigh of recognition that a family is finally together; a circle may have been unbroken, for now.

Amatheia guides Mick gently by his left elbow as he exits the cave, carrying their mother. Once her eyes adjust to the brightness, Rosemary sees Amatheia and bids her son to let his mother stand so that she may properly introduce herself.

"Hello, my name is Rosemary… I believe I am your mother," offered Rosemary as she ambled cautiously forwards; the words tumbled, one by one, awkwardly from her lips as she gazed upwards.

"Hello, my name is Amatheia, I believe I am your daughter," replied Amatheia as she knelt down to match her mother's height.

"Hello! I am Tereo, your dead father!" sneered Jim Kelly, mockingly, as he lay across from the campfire.

Mick, with a furrowed brow, was bewildered by Jim's outburst and turned to get up. Amatheia restrained Mick with a hand on his shoulder; deciding to confront Jim's venomous tongue herself.

"You! You are going to explain yourself, now get up!" bellowed Amatheia as she grabbed Jim by the back of his coat and carried him unceremoniously over to where her mother and brother sat astounded at this development.

Composing himself, Jim had no option but to do as Amatheia commanded; her considerable strength was overpowering and prevented him from escaping.

"Tereo was a Kolassian guard whose seed, along with others, was forcibly taken. Under the direct orders of his superiors, he was an unwilling participant in the Kolassian insemination programme; of which, Rosemary was one of many victims. The result of which stands either side of you Rosemary. Tereo was a Kolassian who defected and wanted to help all Polar Neridians, North and South. He died of complications from the breathing disease, never knowing who his children were nor their mother," finished Jim as he scowled towards Rosemary and her newly found family.

"Why are you so angry, so hateful?" begged Rosemary.

"Even after all the torment, the obstacles endured, you still get to play happy families! I always played by the rules, did what I was told and never had the love of a family like you lot and then there's Kyle!" screamed Jim.

"What about my father, what are you trying to say?" demanded Saoirse, nearly spilling her tea.

"Never mind, just leave me be!" spat Jim, returning to the other side of the campfire as Amatheia released him.

There was a pause, then a collective sigh accompanied by tears from more than one pair of eyes. Tears flowed and dried and then flowed again as mother, daughter and son hugged and embraced each other.

Mick left his mother and sister to comfort each other while he went to fetch something from his satchel. As he walked past the campfire he glanced at Jim Kelly looking on, again mumbling to himself; the smouldering image of his sulking demeanour shimmered just beyond the embers of the dying fire.

Mick retrieved the bible from the orphanage he had kept safe and returned to where Rosemary and Amatheia were seated.

"Mother, I have something for you," announced Mick as he moved closer to sit beside Rosemary.

Upon opening the cover, Rosemary's eyes lit up as she gazed down at the tiny bouquet she had left behind in a previous existence; slightly flattened yet surprisingly had remained bounteous with colour and exuded life.

"Oh look, all the little flowers are still alive! I had carefully picked them and kept their roots intact. Lavender, Peppermint, Basil, Marigold, Lemon Balm, Aloe Vera and...," Rosemary paused as her words faded to a whisper.

"...Rosemary," finished Amatheia with a smile.

Saoirse sat a few feet away sipping on a mug of pine needle tea, watching the family of three gathered together. It was strange to see a mother who appeared to be not much older than her son, stranger still to see that mother's daughter with grey streaks running through her fur while Rosemary herself had not even one peppery strand, thought Saoirse; co-pilot pensively observing pilot who looked older than her years in the unforgiving red-hued morning sunlight.

Rosemary jumped up from where she had been sitting and surveyed the line of cave entrances. To the right, at the very end, was a small unoccupied cave. It had a narrow doorway but possessed a large window opening, carved out of the exposed rock. She walked over and was pleased to find that in front of the cave, the soil appeared to have been cultivated at some point in the past. It was once a garden of some description; cared for by some long gone resident.

Kneeling down in the soil, Rosemary began to plant each flower from her bouquet; gladly accepting a bucket of water carried by Ellen and Elpida, she completed the task. Rosemary gave no concern to the interior of the cave, so long as she had a pretty view from her window. Mick and Amatheia followed and helped Rosemary settle into what would be her new home on Polar Neridia.

***

After Sam witnessed his friends and their craft disappear into the worm hole, he turned to make his way back to the beach with Amatheia's aulos firmly in his hand. Wanting to get back as quickly as possible, he decided a shortcut just inside the outer fringes of the Stygian Forest should not bring him to any harm; besides, it would be a long enough walk to the beach and if he kept close to the forest perimeter he could reduce his journey time. Normally an astute man, rarely making rash decisions, this was unfortunately not one of Sam's wisest choices.

Upon entering the darkness, Sam immediately lost all sense of direction. He did not want to use his flashlight for fear of drawing attention to himself, luckily, even with what little light there was available, he could make out a path just ahead. The overgrown and winding path led him deeper into the forest.

He travelled the path for what felt like an eternity as there was little distinction between night and day with light not seeming to penetrate this far into the thick plexus of vines and branches. Sam survived by eating tubers he dug up with his bare hands and grubs retrieved from rotten tree bark. He drank from pools of rainwater and the days passed relatively uneventful apart from hiding whenever an unearthly sound approached. Upon discovering familiar landmarks, he realised the trail he had been following had kept him going around in circles for days if not weeks; it was near impossible to judge the passing of time. Sam knew he had to put away his fear and leave the trail.

No sooner than he had stepped off the path and into the wood, all birdsong disappeared, not a leaf stirred in the vacant breeze and the temperature seemed to fall by more than several degrees. Putting the aulos into his top pocket, he pulled his jacket tighter around his chest with one hand to fight off the cold and decided to take out the flashlight from his backpack with the other.

Ghoulish screeching echoed in the distance and would occasionally increase in volume as the sound swirled about his head. The nauseating mastication of some poor creature being fed upon by another meagre beast seemed to be only an outstretched arm's distance away from Sam as he trudged onwards. He thought a break in his flashlight's beam was evidence of someone or something crossing ahead of him but he could hear no movement. The ground now squelched underfoot and as he paused to free a water-logged boot from the boggy terrain, a foreboding dread began to envelop his soul, paralysing him with fear.

Before he could try to free his foot, a flapping sound approached and talons sank into his shoulders, leaving one boot lodged in the mud below as he was lifted upwards. Being physically frail, Sam could not defend himself against the Stryckon. Accepting his fate, Sam has no energy to scream. Even if he had the strength to call out, surely it would be an exercise in futility with no one nearby to help.

As Sam is carried off, he drops his flashlight which is joined by the aulos falling from his torn pocket. Both of the items tumble silently towards the forest floor; waiting patiently below in the dark to receive them.

The bare feet of an adult human stand confidently, half submerged, in the marshy ground. A male figure bends to retrieve the aulos and flashlight; the torch still switched on, its light flickers and illuminates a silver identity bracelet, linked around the right wrist of a man in his mid to late twenties.

First walking, then running, the young man bounds through the darkness in pursuit of the creature that carried Sam away. The Stryckon rises higher and higher into the darkness, enormous bat-like wings cease flapping as the beast glides on thermals towards its lair. Dropping its prey into the circle of twisted and entwined branches, the Stryckon leaves to continue its nightly hunt.

A wildering childe, first lost to his father two decades previous, knows the forest too well. Scrambling up a scree laden cliff face, he reaches the edge of the Stryckon's lair. Satisfied that the creature is absent, he swings his left leg over the top of the nest and falls in beside Sam.

Looking upon the man, he can't help but feel a long-lost connection rise within him. There is no time to waste and nowhere to hide as he hears the Stryckon returning. He can hear the Stryckon's giant wings folding as it comes to perch at the lair's edge. He thinks quickly and temporarily blinds the beast with the flashlight; in its confusion, it is quickly and methodically dispatched by a discerning stab from the young man's blade.

Sam mumbles in shock induced sleep as he is lowered, a vine tied around his waist and under his armpits, to the forest floor. Carried over a shoulder, Sam is brought to the safety of the shore where his wounds are attended to and a weave of giant leaves provide him with warmth.

The young man places his hand kindly on Sam's face, pausing to look upon the time engraved lines encircling his eyes; leaving a few items in Sam's pocket, he then makes his departure.

Crashing waves and increasing light cause a tired old man's eyes to flutter open and welcome the morning. Wondering if it was all a dream, he sits up to rub his face and feels a newly grown beard, indicating to him more than one night had passed. He has wounds on his shoulders and his arms are covered in scratches. He hurts all over and upon rubbing his leg in an attempt to soothe away pain, he feels several objects, crammed tightly into his pocket.

He pulls out the flashlight and the aulos but there is a third item. Reaching back into his pocket, he feels something cold and metallic. Sam holds the trinket up for closer inspection; glinting in the sunlight he can see lettering that spells out the name of his disappeared son. 'J.A.K.E.' is engraved on the silver identity bracelet, cradled in the palm of Sam's right hand.

You were only five years old when I gave this to you as a birthday gift, my son, was it you that saved me last night? Did you want to let me know that you are alive and well? Why did you not speak? Why did you not stay? Do you blame me for not being able to protect you? Did you know it was your father's pocket you placed the bracelet in or was it an attempt to signal for help while helping a lost stranger?

The Kolassians told me you were missing; did you survive all those years in that wretched forest alone? Perhaps out of some warped form of respect for me or just my technological contributions, they let you live untouched by their research?

Where do I go now? I would not survive another hour in that place. My beautiful son, thought Sam, remembering his lost child.

Emotions begin to get the better of Sam and although tear filled eyes obscure the engraved name from his eyes, he traces the lettering with his right thumb; looking out to sea, his anguished voice casts beyond the waves with a deep sigh, the name of his wildering childe, Jake.

Sam's attention is drawn back to another of his pocket's contents. Hardly a note loud enough to be heard above the waves crashing on the shore drifts from the aulos; released with a weakened breath from the distraught father. Even so, an aquaton surfaces nearby and with his last remaining strength, Sam climbs onto the docile beast before drifting off.

He sleeps for most of the seven-day journey, waking occasionally to drink from his flask but eats nothing. When he next awakens, he is lying upon the coloured glass shore. The aquaton has gone and the aulos is in his back-pack alongside his flask and flashlight. Opening his right hand, he is relieved to find he had not lost his son's identity bracelet. He clasps the bracelet around his own wrist before struggling to his feet, beginning his trek towards the caves.

A month had passed since Rosemary moved into her new home. Rudimentary but practical, it served its purpose of giving her shelter and somewhere to lay her head at night. It is Rosemary's new window that gives her the most pleasure. She was uncertain whether her new-found happiness and joy for life was the result of her present situation.

Her contentment may have emerged from the view of her beautiful garden in full bloom or the fact that she could now come and go as she pleased; without the scolding of an unloving mother or the torturous practices of a cruel nurse. Either way it no longer mattered because she was indeed happy. Gazing out upon her garden, Rosemary's smile grew broader as an approaching figure added to the inviting panorama.

Sam had left the shore and was surprised to see a beautifully manicured garden in front of the first cave. As he hobbled down its meandering path, he was stopped in his tracks by what he thought was a vision from the past. The woman looking out from her window was smiling broadly and that smile widened as she recognised him. Smiles disappeared momentarily as she mouthed his name and he hers. They exchanged a lingering half-smile before Rosemary ran out and threw her arms around Sam. She could feel her friend collapsing within her embrace and called for the others to help carry him inside; it was Rosemary's turn to nurse her friend.

Everyone, except Jim Kelly, stood inside Rosemary's cave and gathered around Sam as he sat up in bed; feeling much better after his three-day sleep.

"I know why Jim is not here, I feared this would happen. Time has taken its toll on all of us, some more than others. I gained and lost a son again during my bewildered state. You all still have family, I do too albeit removed from me for now.

"Jim belongs to no one and no one belongs to him. He arrived into existence, not by the love of a mother and father but as the result of another Kolassian experiment.

"He deeply resents you all, even the poor unfortunates who ramble on incoherently to themselves next door. Perhaps time and patience are all that can be prescribed for time patients," theorised Sam as he fell asleep again to the sound of Jim Kelly ranting.

10

Views Framed in Stone,
Reflected in Water,
Encircled by Time

Loyalty and disgrace. Skipping stones and leaping lives;
flying so high and sinking so low.

A parent's perpetual love tested.
A man almost dead but who was never truly born
is now dying for attention with murderous intentions.

A kiss and a flower surrendered.

Sam is woken by the agitated vocals of a tortured soul, continuing outside Rosemary's window. Looking around his borrowed bedroom, Sam can see empty picture frames hung upon the walls; no family history, no achievements recognised or recorded, no evidence of Rosemary or her children's existence. Above the fireplace, which frames an unlit fire, hangs a beach jewellery necklace; made by Saoirse and Ellen, who gifted it to Elpida, who then in turn, gave it to Rosemary as a house warming gift.

Some are washed up on the shore together, some alone; those that share similarities will gather in harmony, thought Sam to himself as he lay there trying to block out the din penetrating from beyond his broken slumber.

The ongoing commotion outside drags him from his thoughts and his bed to stumble from the cave entrance into the overwhelming daylight. He is presented with the bludgeoning tirade of an unstable, imbalanced and deeply wounded individual. Stood before him is a lost soul whose mind is a raging sea, in constant turmoil but with an empty heart; desolate as a windswept beach where a solitary piece of colourless glass has gathered alone.

***

Another restless mind tries to make sense of things…

Kyle cannot sleep and rises before the dawn, taking a solo stroll in an attempt to clear his head. Mister Waggles opens one eye and decides to seize the opportunity of an early walk along the beach with his master. The hound nudges Kyle's hand, inviting his owner to throw a ball for him to fetch.

"Sorry boy, we never brought a ball from Earth," said Kyle as he gently rubbed the dog's cheek.

Sitting on a log, gazing out to sea, Kyle welcomed the hound's companionship as the dog leaned against him.

I wish I had never read that note, I wish I had never taken that bike, I want my calm life returned to me with all its normal chaos! How I wish I had my little girl back again, thought Kyle, entranced by the mirror-like still water.

"Hi Dad!" uttered Saoirse, promptly bringing her father back to the present as she sat down beside him; Mister Waggles, as usual, lived up to his name and sent his tail into a wagging motion while he narrowed his eyes in a smiling contentment at his human sister's arrival.

"Can't sleep either?" asked Kyle.

"Dad, my mind is constantly racing, full of thoughts, imagining ways of returning to Earth as a child again. While Sam has been recuperating, I've had discussions with him about combining the capabilities of the newer version of his emotional time travel device with a hyper-sleep pod," announced Saoirse with hope pouring from her eyes.

"I'm sorry Saoirse but that would be a little more than too advanced for me," offered Kyle as he looked upon the concentric circular mark on his daughter.

Saoirse picks up a flat stone and walks closer to the shore's edge. The pebble hops about twenty times when with a flick of her wrist she sends it skipping across the water's surface, allowing her father to smile again.

"That must be a record! Remember how we would have a competition to see who could get their stone to skip the most?" asked Kyle.

"I sure do! Come on, it's your turn!" beamed Saoirse.

"Ah, I won't beat that! I could never get as many as you, but okay, here goes nothing," Kyle picked up a pebble of his own and drew his arm back.

With one awkward throw, Kyle sent his, not so flat, stone hurling through the air; starting with one skip and ending with a clumsy splash! They both laughed and Mister Waggles barked enthusiastically in agreement.

Saoirse paused and by resting one hand on her father's shoulder, she curbed his laughter before pointing out to where his awkwardly thrown rock had disappeared from view courtesy of his butterfingered lob.

"Look at that," whispered Saoirse, her mind racing.

The splash gave birth to ripples radiating outwards in concentric circles.

"See, I am still as clumsy as ever! If only I could reverse the ripples and retrieve my stone back to try again; if only I could relive this experience with you as a child again," pondered Kyle.

An idea explodes in Saoirse's head, she thinks she has confirmed her artificial ageing reversal theory. The rapid advancement of their physical ages, cruelly inflicted upon her and Amatheia when, during transit, their hyper-sleep pods malfunctioned.

"That's it! I must tell Sam!" shouted Saoirse, running back fast towards the caves with her father and pet dog following behind.

Upon their return, they arrive into the middle of Jim Kelly's ranting. Saoirse, too excited to notice, runs straight to Sam as he emerges from the cave entrance.

"Sam! Sam! I know how to fix me, how to return to my original age, who I should be!" announced Saoirse excitedly, falling to her knees at Sam's feet.

"Tell me your thoughts," instructed Sam, taking her by the hand as Jim Kelly paused his vitriol, also intrigued.

"I have already set up a pod onto a launch system; built from the wreckage of the craft that brought my Mum, Dad, Ellen, Tereo and Jim to Polar Neridia. Secretly, I have been experimenting with one of your emotional time travel devices. I focused my emotions, my desires, my needs - so intensely that it was possible to transport myself back to the crash site and retrieve the necessary components. Don't get me wrong, I still have reservations but the idea became clearer to me when Dad and I were skipping stones across the surface of the sea. Dad was a little clumsy and his stone made a splash instead of skipping. The concentric circles it produced, reaffirmed my idea should be possible.

"My theory is, if I were to get into one of the hyper-sleep pods, holding onto a circle of linked emotional time travel devices, your updated ones set to minus twenty years, then be fired into the artificially created wormhole, while focussing on my desire to return to my original age - I just know it could work! As a child, when we were on a road trip, my Dad would often say that he could think more clearly when driving; something about forward motion that allowed your mind to travel in any direction. What if you could allow your heart to travel in any direction - back home to my life as a six-year-old on Earth! It might be a solution to reverse the effects of my malfunctioning hyper-sleep!" described Saoirse speedily, trying to catch her breath.

"It never malfunctioned, you poor fools! It was me!" laughed Jim Kelly with a malicious vengeance.

Everyone cowered and ducked as Jim Kelly strutted, circling about the campfire, spitting verbal bile while he swung a fiery branch in their faces.

"It was I who sabotaged Amatheia and Saoirse's hyper-sleep chambers! I wanted to stop the cure from ever being created; without Saoirse's matching blood type, the cure could never be achieved! Remember how I never joined any of you on your missions. Did you not wonder as to why I was covered in sweat and out of breath when you returned from the Kolassians' Earth Headquarters to collect me? I had a secret tunnel containing a hyper-loop carriage that could take me directly to their base. I observed the craft that Amatheia and Saoirse were heading towards and I managed to disable some of the pod's functions and get back just before Kyle, Crystal and Tereo returned with poor, little Ellen!" screamed Jim, his face red and contorted in anger.

"Jim, you have been my friend since we were kids, why would you want to deprive us of the cure?" asked a shocked and saddened Kyle.

"I didn't want the Kolassians to get their hands on a cure, but eventually the inevitable would come to pass. They would either forcibly take it from you or it might be used as a peace offering, or a bargaining tool. You seriously thought the Kolassians would allow you all to continue living out your little lives here without their interference? After what they did to me, well, I only wish an early death for them all!" roared Jim Kelly.

"But that's not all, is it Jim?" prodded Sam.

"No, it's not! I'm sure you are aware of how I came to be, how I originated - please enlighten our friends!" Jim's anger heightened as he continued to pace up and down, scowling at everyone who had gathered to listen.

"Kyle, Mick, as you both know, Jim was always fascinated with Kolassian technology. He never married, nor ever desired to have children of his own. Standing here before us is a man who has an 'A' type personality, determined and precise in his ways, but always socially awkward and is of an asexual disposition.

"He has never seen value in the progeny of offspring, other than a cumbersome and time-consuming process of furthering the human race or any other species for that matter. To him, a child is nothing that can't be replaced," offered Sam.

"A child is nothing more than a distraction! I was indeed just that to my foster family; something to be fed and clothed until adulthood when it was time to be tossed aside, out of the nest, to repeat the process! howled Jim, interrupting Sam.

"Kyle, I was present when the Kolassians created Jim. He never occupied a mother's belly for nine months; he was rapidly grown in a laboratory with samples taken from... your mother and father, Kyle," continued Sam.

"So, is he my brother?" asked Kyle.

"No, technically he could not be called your brother. The best way to describe the process that resulted in the creation of Jim, would be a merging of DNA from two clones. As strange as it may sound, it would be more accurate to identify him as both your mother and your father," explained Sam.

"So, I am just the result of a process, am I? Hey Kyle, let's see how you process this!" squawked Jim Kelly.

Lunging forward, Jim hooked his right arm around Saoirse's neck, under her chin and dragged her away; fending off her would-be saviours by waving a fiery branch in their faces. He forced Saoirse to direct him towards the launch site's location. They made their way up the hill with Kyle and Amatheia leading those who followed behind; Sam made up the rear, somehow instinctively bringing his bag of devices along.

Jim, despite Saoirse's protestations, forces her into the hyper-sleep pod. He has no intention of letting her launch. Once she is inside and the pod sealed, he sets the surrounding scrubland alight. The flames had already started to creep closer, towards the pod, by the time the others arrived.

Amatheia knew she had to act fast as there was little time to spare. Looking around she noticed there was a nearby conifer with branches weighed down by a recent heavy snowfall. Using considerable strength, with fury, Amatheia pushed forward at the base of the tree trunk, sending the wet snow flying towards the growing flames. The blaze was quenched in an instant.

Despite Amatheia's best efforts, danger had not yet subsided for Saoirse. Jim Kelly was now head-first and half-way into the pod; his rage echoing in the chamber.

"Let's see how your father deals with the result of this process!" roared Jim Kelly, with his arms aloft he began raining blows down upon Saoirse.

Kyle reached up and gained purchase of Jim Kelly's dangling legs. He yanked his erstwhile friend out and away from his daughter. As he did so, Jim Kelly's forehead connected with a protruding piece of steel. Kyle released his grip and Jim Kelly's body continued to spasm where it had fallen in the mud; the sludge quickly turning red as the life force drained from Saoirse's attacker.

Kyle finds it impossible to contain his primal instinct and decides he is not yet finished with Jim Kelly. He struggles, trying to crawl forward on his hands and knees, slipping and sliding in the muck as base rage sours his tongue; spitting sin upon the coward lying beneath him.

Sitting upon Jim Kelly's chest, Kyle raises up a rock with both hands. However, before he can bring an end to Jim Kelly's gurgling and his pitiful existence, a gentle hand and bright smile draw Kyle's attention and intentions away from the physical and mental mire. The lightness of his daughter's smile and the gentleness of her caring hand lifts Kyle from the debasement into which he was falling.

Silence and calm, perforated with the thankful cries of a father and mother for their daughter, are short lived.

"Dad, it is time for me to go," announced Saoirse, pointing to Sam, standing beside the pod with a ring comprised of three, emotional time travel devices.

Sam had already directed Amatheia into the chamber as he beckoned Saoirse to come forward. Holding her hand, Kyle reluctantly helped his daughter back into the hyper pod. As she sat beside Amatheia, the two of them held tightly onto the emotional time travel ring.

"We need a third," stated Sam.

"A third?" questioned Kyle.

"Yes, I have thought long and hard about Saoirse's theory and I believe it to be correct. Both Saoirse and Amatheia deserve to live and experience time that was denied them; to retrieve their missing years. However, in order for it to work, we need a third person. Three is the number of non-collinear points needed to determine a plane and a circle; the minimum number of points or elements required to complete the circle, is three," explained Sam.

Kyle thought he had killed him but he realised that Jim was still breathing, turning to hear him muttering incoherently into a puddle of his own blood.

Kyle stepped back to sit Jim up, baffled to hear him pouring out sorrowful pleas and promises of atonement; he looks back to Sam who nods in agreement.

"If he is truly sorry, perhaps he deserves another chance at life. Jim did not choose how he entered into existence; created in a laboratory only to be abducted to further the Kolassians' cause.

"He was aware of this; informed by them about the true nature of his manifestation and subsequent sterility. Jim's despising of those who are lucky enough to have the capability of family, has grown over the years.

"It wasn't a difficult leap to commit the dreadful deeds and betrayals - but attempted murder of his life-long friend's child, shows how much he is truly lost. If he seeks redemption, as the necessary third in our equation - he may fulfil that proclamation," proffered Sam.

Kyle hauled Jim up over his shoulder and into the waiting pod. Unsure of his repentance, he tied Jim to the ring of devices, beside Amatheia and Saoirse.

Giving their eldest daughter one last kiss, Kyle and Crystal then moved away to stand nearby, holding Ellen between them. Rosemary steps forward tentatively, hand in hand with Mick. She pauses at the base of the pod before throwing a flower, that shares her name, to her daughter, Amatheia.

Looking out through the glass screen at all of the faces simultaneously filled with sadness and happiness, Saoirse bids everyone to stand clear.

As the launch commences, she sits back contemplating the fate of herself, her family, friends and everyone else...

What are we when we turn to dust?
What remains?
What do we leave behind?
What continues on?

In the blink of an eye, she is gone as the pod skips across the atmosphere and splashes into the wormhole.

10+1

Recycled Circles

A natural number divides by three
but when a family is dispersed or separated
by time and distance, the circle is broken; motion,
regardless of direction, will come to stand still.

Perhaps circles need to be broken
in order to grab hold of second chances
and have wrongs righted.

Time and distance become irrelevant
when you travel within your own heart and mind.

In the initial days that followed, Sam observed the others continuing on with their lives, at least they endeavoured to do so as best they could. The simple chores of everyday life occupied most of their time. Boiling a pot of water to make some tea, chopping wood or tending to the young ones, were all welcome distractions. There was still time to pause and reflect though; always too many endless hours available to dwell on loved ones not present.

It was difficult to carry on, not knowing if their eldest daughter had found what her heart desired, or whether she even still lived. Kyle was all too aware of his eldest daughter's internal struggles and although it broke his heart to let her go, it was because he loved her that he did just that.

He went to join the remainder of his family and sat down by a freshwater stream beside Crystal, Ellen and Mister Waggles. As he washed the face of his youngest child, he glanced from her ice blue eyes to those of his wife, filling up while they shared a lingering half-smile.

He thought to himself that he had shared many short-lived smiles throughout his life and was damned if they were going to continue as the kind only ever to endure a little while. Kyle was determined that from now on, their smiles would always be full-faced, beaming, heart filling expressions of utter joy; he was going to try find a way to have Saoirse returned, for his family to be complete again.

Sam left his observations and returned to Rosemary's cave where he found her and Mick sitting in her makeshift kitchen; basic at its most sophisticated but nonetheless, it served Rosemary's needs. She had a little cupboard to store utensils; lovingly handmade from soft pine wood. A sink with no running water but a freshwater stream was mere minutes away.

However, the amenity she was most proud of, was her little oven. Mick had lovingly fashioned the stove's main compartment from an old storage container. Positioned beneath the oven was a metal grid set over an open fire. Protruding above it and out of the cave roof, was a flue constructed from piping, salvaged from the crash site.

From this marvellous contraption, Rosemary happily brought forth a loaf of her home-made bread. It was the aroma of which that filled Sam's nostrils and his senses as he bid them good morning when he passed merrily over the threshold.

"That smells wonderful!" Sam was ready to satisfy his appetite as Mick eagerly pulled up a chair for him.

"As usual, you are right on time! Fill your boots my dear friend," Rosemary smiled as she placed more freshly baked bread on the table.

"I would never miss an opportunity to taste some home baking, I can't think of a better way to start the day. Although I must admit, I suspect my physique will not forgive me," Sam laughed heartily as he patted his hands on his blossoming belly.

As the bread quickly disappeared from the plate, their conversation was replaced with the sound of Rosemary pouring more coffee and then silence permeated the air for several minutes.

"To lose a child once is a tragedy, to lose that child a second time is more than I can...," overwhelmed by her utterance, Rosemary was unable to continue the facade.

"I know my friend, something we unfortunately both have in common," agreed Sam solemnly.

"Come on now you two, they had to take their only opportunity of reliving, regaining their lost years. Perhaps their hearts' journeys will lead to life both relived and lived for the first time. There's us three maudlin in here while those three out there spend every waking minute, pining for Saoirse," Mick then pointed to Kyle, Crystal and Ellen as they approached along the garden path.

"Hello you three," Crystal released her youngest child from her arms as they crossed the threshold; Ellen ran in first to give Rosemary a hug.

The two groups of three sat around reminiscing about Amatheia, Rosemary and forgivingly, Jim too. The conversation began to fade from Sam's consciousness and his eyes glazed over as he became separated by thought.

"I've got it! I think I might know how to reach them!" interrupted Sam.

"It's impossible, how could we ever join them? The launch device was destroyed after one use and besides, we have no more hyper-sleep pods," declared Crystal.

"They were three, you are three, we are three! I have more devices - enough to make two emotional time travel rings. We don't need to travel into the wormhole in order to join them, we need to allow our hearts and minds to travel emotionally! Mick, you mentioned *'every waking minute'* but what about sleeping minutes, more precisely - dreaming minutes! I believe that when we dream, we have the ability to travel anywhere that our hearts and minds desire. I would like to propose that both groups of three gathered here, go to sleep tonight whilst holding onto a ring of the emotional time travel devices," suggested Sam and with nothing to lose, everyone agreed to try his proposition.

The following morning, the party of six reconvened in Rosemary's kitchen. As they all sat down for coffee and bread, wild goat's milk for Ellen, a smile grew broadly on each of their faces; the experiment had surprised them all with its success. They shared stories of their travels which although indiscernible if they were experiences based in reality or lucid dreams, it mattered not, the end result felt real; they had been reunited with their loved ones.

Days rolled along calmly without incident and the two groups of three continued their morning ritual of coffee, home-made bread and long tales of starlight transit. Kyle recounted how he had once again skipped stones along a shore with Saoirse, not as a child, nor as an adult, but with his teenage daughter for the first time.

Crystal was in tears of joy while telling of how she had experienced brushing and styling Saoirse's hair when she helped get her ready for prom night. Another occasion, cheerfully recalled by little Ellen, was one whereby as teenagers she and her sister went on their first camping trip together as Girl Guides.

One morning, everyone gathered around Rosemary's kitchen table as usual, but she was not present. There was recently baked bread, still warm on the table and freshly brewed coffee on the stove, but no Rosemary. When everyone had eaten and drank their fill, they left to carry on with their daily duties; assuming that their mother and friend had urgent chores to attend to and that they would more than likely see Rosemary later.

The following morning arrived, still with no sign of Rosemary. The group of five sat and drank hot coffee, without any of Rosemary's delicious bread for breakfast. Their evolving conversation was interrupted abruptly when Rosemary arrived back through the entrance, out of breath and her face as pale as the flower she loosely held in her hand. Fearing his mother was going to faint, Mick jumped up and ran to support her; ushering Rosemary to sit in a nearby chair.

After taking a long slow sip of her coffee, she returned her cup to the table and began to speak.

"I met Tereo last night," Rosemary announced.

"Met him? But he died, how?" wondered Kyle.

"I don't know for sure, I wasn't trying to contact or dream of him. One moment it was a happy experience with Amatheia showing me how she could skilfully command an... *'aquaton'*, I believe it's called, to take her amongst the waves. Next, things became overcast and I found myself watching Mick as he quietly sat alone in an orphanage while the other children played without him. My dream grew darker still, I witnessed Tereo's death, seconds after he had given instructions for the cure. I saw his final resting place. While I kneeled at his grave side, he visited and begged my forgiveness. I told him that was not necessary, with the cure he had saved not just Ellen's, but my life also.

"Tereo asked if we would journey to the Kolassian Palace and present them with the cure, he felt it might bring peace to his former homeland. He then made one last request before he left; for me to place flowers, from my garden, upon his grave. Whilst still in my dream, I did as he requested and put flowers upon his burial site.

"Two mornings ago, I woke from that dream and left Sam and Mick still holding onto the ring of devices. Once breakfast was prepared, I stepped outside into my garden. I soon noticed that the same flowers which I had placed upon Tereo's grave, in my dream journey, were missing from the garden outside this window. Not fully aware of my intentions, I found myself walking towards the glass beach. There was an aquaton waiting off shore.

"I did not summon the creature but it was there all the same, so I instinctively waded out and climbed onto its back. The beast took me near to your crash site and somehow, I managed to find where Tereo was buried. I saw those same flowers, laid upon the rocks of his grave, just as I had left them in my dream. Look, this is one of them I am holding in plain sight - not in a dream! The dreams are becoming stronger and are starting to manifest into reality!" described Rosemary.

"I believe you are more than correct Rosemary. I had a conversation with my lost son, Jake, last night. We did not skip stones or go camping but I saw his face and he was smiling. He told me that one particular Kolassian guard had taken pity upon him. He said the guard told him that his superiors would eventually kill him once they had no further use of his father's talents, my skills," recalled Sam.

"I'm guessing, I have a feeling, that guard could have been Tereo, but Sam, why did he not tell you of your son Jake?" asked Rosemary.

"Perhaps he had lost contact with Jake, felt somewhat responsible and did not want to get my hopes up. Jake told me how from the age of five, the guard set him free into the Stygian Forest where he educated him; not just in academics but in how to feed and fend for himself.

"Jake told me that the guard had at one time pointed to his identity bracelet, telling him that it was his last connection to me, his father.

"Before he left my dream, Jake informed me that he will be with me again but for now he had something to do, somewhere to go; what or where, he would not say," said Sam, then slowly raised his arm up, holding his child's identity bracelet aloft for everyone to see.

"I had a vivid encounter last night too, with Jim. He seemed in good health but still displayed a prominent scar on his forehead, the result of our struggle when I had dragged him away from Saoirse. He could not apologise enough and told me how he wanted to make amends.

"He told of how Amatheia and Saoirse had fulfilled their missing twenty years; retrieving many of the life experiences those years should have originally provided.

"Jim had been near death when they left here and that although he had not previously lost two decades of his life, he was somehow able to live and enjoy a life filled with experiences he never had the privilege of enjoying the first-time round. Jim had theorised that the years they had been away from us, would only equate to the same number in days, at our end of the wormhole and that they had nearly completed a solution of how to return back here," Kyle stood up and smiled while he stretched, happy that his experience was a shared one.

"They've been gone for fourteen days, perhaps they will return before the end of the week, if twenty years parallel twenty days?" wondered Rosemary aloud.

"Even so, I fear that all our lives are under threat if we stay on this planet, I include the lives of all Kolassians and Oikians in that comment. Eventually, all of us will have to find another star to shine upon our faces if we are to survive; this planet's days are numbered.

"In order to successfully achieve that objective, I think it will need to be a combined effort. Earth is showing the early signs of this planet's fate so determining a new destination entirely, may be necessary. The problem is, how do we convince the Kolassians?" pondered Sam.

"Tereo's request, the cure," replied Rosemary.

"They have their main headquarters in the Kolassian Palace, a northerly aquaton ride from here. Perhaps we could get there and back before Amatheia, Saoirse and Jim return?" announced Sam.

Everyone sat together in that kitchen agreed with Sam and Rosemary's plan. Preparations were made for the journey. However, little did they know that events ahead of them could dictate that it would be a very long time before they shared breakfast again; one with freshly brewed coffee and home-made bread, sat around the table in Rosemary's kitchen.

Morning arrived and with it, a noticeable change in the weather. It was decided three would go and three would stay; in the event that Saoirse, Amatheia and Jim returned early, they would not be greeted by absence. Mick volunteered to swap places with Kyle; thinking he would be better equipped, physically, to protect against any intruders or a possibly unreformed Jim Kelly. As Kyle, Sam and Rosemary left by the garden path, the petals of the flowers were beginning to hide under a layer of newly fallen snow. They pulled their coats tightly around them in an attempt to fend off the rapidly dropping temperature. Mick, Crystal and Ellen retreated back inside from the wintry flurries; with the iron click of the front door's closing, three left and three stayed.

By the time they reached the shore, their feet had already begun to disappear under an increasing depth of powder and slush. Sam, who had retained the aulos, beckoned three aquatons for the perilous journey ahead. The *"Grigora Stream"*, to their advantage, was flowing in the opposite direction which presumably would enable a faster convoy towards the Kolassian Palace. This became partially impeded by the formation of large chunks of ice, momentarily and without warning, careering into the fast-paced stream; resulting in anxious aquatons and bruising of passengers' legs.

The journey took them past the Stygian Forest by several days where they found themselves presented with a foreboding structure looming up ahead. The Kolassian Palace both clung to the edge of a sheer cliff face and plunged beneath the shoreline to join with submerged ice caverns. They dismounted, sending the aquatons off towards the horizon.

As they approached the wall they could see it was made of basalt merged with steel and coated with a thick layer of clear ice. The base of the enormous structure was surrounded with black, jagged glass-like rock which prevented them from reaching the wall. They could see no discernible entrance to the fortress and no obvious security presence.

However, as soon as Sam placed a hand upon the obsidian barrier, a prehistoric horn-like sound caused them all to pause in fear. In the ensuing aural assault, a five by five metre section of the outer surface transformed into the same mirror-like substance that composed the chromed facility's walls. Upon the welcomed cessation of the turbulent sound, the giant wall panel fluidly morphed outwards over the scabrous obsidian, forming a solid and foreboding draw-bridge.

The three looked around at each other during the silence that followed. The lull was acidly broken when a loudspeaker cut through the dead air.

"Welcome back Sam! Come forth and bring your friends with you," announced an artificial, metallic voice.

"Well Sam, we're here, this is what we intended, shall we go in?" asked Kyle.

Sam said nothing but merely nodded and motioned for Kyle and Rosemary to follow behind him.

As they passed over the threshold, the panel seemed to accompany them into an internal courtyard. Once inside, the entrance disappeared and the mirror panel morphed once more. This time, it rapidly changed into a barrier that surrounded them; continuing to move, growing upwards and over their heads to form a holding cell. Light still permeated through the enclosure and they could see someone approaching, flanked by two Kolassian guards.

The figure in the middle was difficult to comprehend. It appeared to be a Kolassian from the head to the waist but from there on down, it was mechanical. Upon its head sat a crown made of obsidian shards, encrusted with no precious stones but hideously decorated with the deformed skulls of failed Kolassian experiments.

"Do you not recognise me Sam? Granted, my lower half is a vision you will not be accustomed to but are the face and voice not the same?" laughed the figure with a tormented wheezing cough, echoing inside its mask.

"Kol? Is that really you? But, I...," Sam's mind struggled for a moment.

"What, are you really surprised to see me alive Sam? When you pushed me from the edge of the facility roof,

I should have been killed. We allowed you to think so, after all, you thought you were finishing off an evil Kolassian colleague. One who suggested the use of your son in our experiments; a way of testing your loyalty to the High Kolassian, namely me!" declared Kol, his breath continuing to rattle and whistle.

"So, the King of Kolassi, disguised as a lab assistant, thought by seeking my allegiance, my confidence, that I would agree to surrender my son to your quest of finding a cure? That enforces your delusion! I would rather die than give up my child!" roared Sam.

"That could yet be arranged Sam, but I am curious, what has brought you three here," asked Kol.

Before Sam could respond with more pent up anger, Rosemary nudged him with her elbow, urging him to calm down and remember why they had come here in the first place.

"Ah Rosemary, it seems you are to be the voice of reason! How are the twins?" cackled the High Kolassian.

"The well-being of my children is no concern of yours but this may be of interest to you and indeed all Kolassians alike. Sam, along with others not present, has developed a cure for the Kolassian breathing ailment. There is no further need of abductions or enslavement," announced Rosemary as she held up a vile containing a curious liquid.

"Nonsense! We have been in search of such an elixir for countless years. We've taken so many of your kind and others to participate in failed attempts of warding off this dreaded affliction!" spat the High Kolassian with growing rage.

"My daughter is now cured of the illness, the antidote works!" interjected Kyle.

"Where is the child? Why did you not bring her here? We could have performed tests to verify your bold claim! But it is just a fabrication, an attempt to eradicate every last Kolassian from this planet!" shouted Kol.

"I am cured of the same disease too, you can test me!" offers Rosemary, stepping forward.

"Not acceptable! I require proof that the cure is also applicable for children! Rosemary, you are no longer of interest to us!" stated Kol, as he nodded to the Kolassian guards standing either side of him.

Both of the guards pointed their weapons towards the enclosed truce party. A few short blasts and the liquid-mirror cell dissolved and disappeared beneath their feet. In the struggle that followed, the vile containing the cure, fell from Rosemary's grasp and smashed, leaving the life-saving potion to drain away through the cracks in the courtyard floor. They are abruptly taken to subterranean cells, discarded from the world above, to be forgotten.

As night falls, Sam is lying on his bunk gazing out upon another courtyard, one formed by the outer walls of ice caverns beneath the cliff face. The bases of the ice walls are stained red by blood from discarded bodies dropped from above; adding to a growing pile of corpses in the centre of the courtyard.

Momentarily, Sam shakes his head, thinking his eyes are deceiving him, for outside the small window he sees a young man approach.

"Father I am here, it is I, your son Jake," whispered a strong young, yet hesitant voice.

Filled with emotion, Sam began to wail and splutter but ceased when Jake raised his forefinger to his lips.

"Hush now Father, do not draw the guards' attention. There is someone else who requires my assistance more urgently," Jake turned slowly around and pointed to the nearby corpse pile.

Within the mound of bone and rotting flesh, a lone survivor struggled in vain to free himself. Aided by Jake's persistence, the one remaining life buried deep beneath the towering assortment of bloody cadavers, is eventually set free. Diligently scraping ice from the ground, Jake presses it between the palms of his hands. He uses the resulting melt-water to quench the thirst and wash the dried blood from the recipient of his kindness.

The two return to Sam's window as another corpse is unceremoniously dropped from above, adding to the blood splatter on the walls and the height of the pile.

"Who are you, young man, another of the abducted no doubt?" asked Sam of the rescued soul.

"Finn, Finn Murphy! Where am I? My parents will think terrible things of me back home. It must be such a long time since I was taken away.

"I didn't hurt her, it was not my doing, I promise! These bastards have frozen and defrosted me over and over again, each time they wake me it is to perform a new, sick and twisted procedure while I am fully conscious!" cried Finn.

"Finn, is that you?" asked Rosemary, hurriedly joining Sam by the window.

"Rosemary, oh Rosemary, it wasn't me, I tried but I couldn't stop them!" sobbed Finn.

"I know Finn, I am fine now but we need to escape before we join that pile behind you," Rosemary stretched her hand out through the window bars, gently pushing Finn's hair out of his eyes.

"I will try to free you all if I can," Jake stood tall, ready to take action.

"No, I'll figure something out for us but there is more important work that you must do. We have to prove the cure for the Kolassian sickness has worked for children, we must provide evidence to the Kolassian King. I need you to travel to the glass beach beyond the Stygian Forest, nearby you will find a cave dwelling, fronted by a garden filled with flowers not of this world. Inside, you will find our friend Mick, Kyle's wife Crystal and their youngest daughter Ellen. They stayed waiting for three others to return from Earth - Amatheia, Saoirse and Jim Kelly. The young child, Ellen, is the proof we need to end all this madness - now go quickly!" ordered Sam.

Agreeing with an accepting nod to his father, Jake struggled on through frozen tunnels with Finn over his shoulder to emerge outside into the frozen landscape of a diseased planet.

Kyle, Rosemary and Sam returned to their cold bunks. They held onto an emotional ring device and as the sound of ice water dripped like the count of a metronome, they drifted off to sleep.

Sam dreamt of a young man dragging another on a roughly made stretcher, with care along a frozen shore. The deepening winter had caused the sea to freeze over and so rendered the call for an aquaton pointless; Jake's aulos, given to him by Sam, remained in his pocket.

***

Somewhere far away, far beyond a star scattered sky...

A relived and relieved Saoirse, Amatheia and Jim Kelly travel through the wormhole once again and make their way to arrive outside Rosemary's cave. The flowers could barely keep their heads above the sea of snow now drifting up the sides of the dwelling and hiding half of the front door. Amatheia, using her shoulder, forces the door inward enough to gain admittance. Saoirse and Jim follow her inside to discover Winter had also gained entry long before them.

"Let me check for a pulse, Mum! Ellen!" screamed Saoirse, falling to her knees beside her mother and sister.

Huddled by the frozen stove, Crystal had cradled Ellen in her arms while Mick had wrapped his around them both in a desperate attempt to shield them from the encroaching cold. The three figures, partially frozen, resembled a scene akin to that of an ice age Pompeii; their faces blue, staring vacantly towards the window.

***

Back in the Kolassian cell, Rosemary travels...

While Rosemary slept, her heart brought her back to look upon her wheelchair-bound father. He gazed out of his nursing home window, thinking of the daughter he had lost long ago and his wife now buried six feet below the frozen ground.

***

Kyle finds himself journeying along a path he has travelled many times before…

Cycling along the reservoir path, in his dream, Kyle is revisiting a familiar situation. Similar to once before, it is about seven in the morning as he rises out of the saddle to peddle up a short steep incline, at the top of which he is presented with the upper lake. Normally, there would be a green metal frame bridge leading out to a small stone tower. Again, oddly as before, the bridge is missing and although there is a stiff breeze picking up, the water is completely calm.

He dismounts and leans his bike against the perimeter wall. Walking over to the waters-edge, he once again discovers that although the air temperature must be reaching well above ninety degrees, when he bends down to touch the surface of the water - it freezes solid!

A light suddenly goes on in the tower and as a pulsating alarm radiates across the valley, something different happens within his dream. This time however, no concentric circular rings of light emerge from deep within the centre of the reservoir. On this occasion, the top half of a small door opens on the side of the tower; leaning out of it, is Sam.

With one hand he waves to Kyle and with the other he points towards the now darkening sky. By the time Kyle looks from Sam to where he is pointing, the sky has turned from the height of morning to the depth of night. At the same time, a swirling rip in the expanse above gradually becomes evident. Snow begins to fall, covering the valley in Winter's deep embrace. During all the time that had passed, while they were on Polar Neridia, the Earth's axis had continued to shift. Sam and Rosemary wake from their dream to find Kyle nowhere to be seen.

Light years away, Kyle falls backwards in shock to sit upon a gravel shore. Snowflakes settle and melt on his face as he stares up at the now fully visible wormhole; the colours of which reflect on the surface of the reservoir and the vacant stare of his disbelieving eyes, he had fallen from his dream into a new reality.

***

Time passed... too much time... not enough time... never enough time... a pair of shoes, waiting to be filled at the bottom of the stairs, gather dust...

I have not been with them in ten years, plus one… one decade. I stole twenty years from you all; a wife without a husband's love, two daughters without a father's care, friends without a companion's benevolence. Now I will repay you all, with dust… my dust, thought Kyle to himself.

Ten years ago, plus ten more, Kyle sat at the water's edge staring up at a vengeful sky. He firmly believed time was repeating itself; that he was reliving occurrences from a previous experience. He thought that, on this occasion, Sam's devices had delivered a rather more vivid dream travelling experience than usual. However, he was not dreaming, he had been physically catapulted to where his heart and mind figured he needed to be.

The dream voyage, which was made reality by the ring of emotional time travel devices had become all too real; he had physically left everyone behind.

Sam, sensing something was not quite right, had tried to warn him by merging into Kyle's dream. However, he had inadvertently increased all emotion exponentially; resulting in the separation of Kyle from everyone and everything he knew.

He needed to reach the tower that Sam beckoned from but he could not move. It was not snow that fell on him that day. Whatever it was had the appearance of snow; it tumbled from the sky in snow's usual benign guise, giving no immediate indication whether its presence would be the type short lived or that which would cause disruption to many. Thirty-five different configurations did indeed present themselves but they did not tickle the noses of freckle-faced children, nor did they fall from a leaden sky.

Beneath an angry rip in the emerging expanse above, a Kolassian craft hovered and directed the snow-like substance to surround and cocoon Kyle. He was taken within the confines of the tower, where he hung floating at the top of a winding staircase. While the cocoon finished enclosing him, the last sounds he heard were those of Sam screaming his name as shoes fell from his feet, pattering solemnly onto the stone-slabbed floor beneath; gathering dust at the bottom of the stairs as he began a twenty-year slumber.

Sam's presence resulted in Kyle not being present for one decade and one more, he had been paused; his life suspended while his family and friends continued on living and not living on Polar Neridia without their husband, father and friend.

He remembers the struggle. The weight of the *'snow'* increasingly heavy with every effort to move until it was impossible to bear the burden anymore and upon giving in to the process, he involuntarily slept.

Now, two decades had passed and upon his waking, he found himself looking down upon a winding stone staircase, at a pair of dust covered shoes… his shoes.

Dust… What are we when we are no longer here; when our bodies cease to be a practical vehicle for our souls? Time is a friend to dust when the original host has ticked its last tock; crumbling away to powder the soil or merge with the ether, travelling on and settling elsewhere… waiting for a return. A return to what? A re-emergence to nothingness, a reveal of emptiness or an assembling of all which appears unfamiliar, thought Kyle as he pondered his past, present and future.

***

Twenty years ago, back in a miserable Kolassian cell on Polar Neridia…

A sweat covered Sam awakens to see Rosemary twist and turn as she cries out from a mournful sleep.

"No! No! No! Daddy, speak to me, we have so much to say! Come back to me, please!" sobbed Rosemary as she woke to view Sam's saddened face in front of her own.

"Kyle has gone, back to Earth, I tried to warn him but it was too late, he was taken. My dream was diverted to merge with his and in doing so, emotions quickly became heightened and overloaded. I beckoned to him from a reservoir tower, he sat frozen on the shore as his body became cocooned and transported towards the very tower I called to him from. I turned my head towards your cries and my eyes flickered while the scene before me changed; as Kyle's fantasy became reality, I was then cast out… expelled from his dream. I was no longer able to see Kyle, but looking over your shoulder, I witnessed what you saw in your dream as you entered your father's room in his nursing home." explained Sam.

"If you saw what I witnessed well then, your eyes too would have rested upon a man reduced to a fragile shell, one who can see his wife's resting place from his window; unable to visit or tend her grave, only counting down the days before he can join my mother beneath the earth!

"Why could I not I engage with him? Why were my emotions not strong enough to cross the barrier between illusion and reality?" asked an exasperated Rosemary.

"That was my fault, so to speak. Our dreams would inevitably be connected via the joined ring devices and there was always the possibility for our dreams to overlap. However, because Kyle's experience was becoming so intense, I was drawn into it and as I felt his need for help rapidly increase, I involuntarily drained emotions from your sleep travelling, rendering you powerless to interact; unable to cross that barrier.

"There may well be another time to connect with your father but right now I suggest we escape to catch up with Jake and Finn. We know not yet the fate of the others," proclaimed Sam.

Sam hurriedly connected several emotional time travel devices around the cell's window bars. He and Rosemary held onto them tightly and both tried to recall their most emotive thoughts. As emotions began to build, so did the temperature and energy that was emitted by the devices. Becoming too hot to hold, Sam and Rosemary released their grip and dived for cover as the overloaded devices exploded. When the noise and dust had dissipated there was a gaping hole where the window had previously been. Wailing sirens announced an approaching menace. Sam and Rosemary wasted no time in climbing out of the tunnels, following footprints along the way; Jake's still clearly visible in the hardened snow but Finn's were the muddied and dragged kind belonging to someone who had difficulty staying upright.

Weather conditions improved enough allowing Sam to summon an aquaton and he and Rosemary made swift their progress thanks to the Grigora Stream. Almost a day had passed when they spotted what they at first thought was a lone figure trailing along the shoreline.

On closer inspection, after commanding the aquaton to move nearer to the beach, they could see Jake pulling a roughly made stretcher behind him; upon it appeared to be a very pale Finn Murphy, almost all life drained from his countenance. Calling out seemed fruitless as the wind was blowing away from Jake, who wore a thick hand-made coat of bear hide with the hood pulled tightly around his face.

The aquaton brought them close to the shore but a slippery dismount into the frigid waters encouraged them to wade quickly onto land. Jake didn't notice Sam and

Rosemary at first; he continued his steady, focussed and blinkered march forwards. Fifty metres ahead, he paused before gently relinquishing the arms of the stretcher to about-turn and accept the embrace and support of those belonging to his father.

"I did hear you call out father, but thought my mind, due to tiredness, was playing tricks on me," whispered Jake as he clutched longingly to Sam.

Over Sam's shoulder, Jake looked towards Rosemary cautiously approaching. Moving his father gently to one side, Jake dropped to his knees with his eyes trying to avoid Rosemary's gaze, he began to apologise repeatedly.

"He could not hold onto any warmth and his weight was too much for me to bear. This stretcher was the best I could do, he kept slipping in and out of consciousness. I'm not sure when he passed exactly but his voice trailed off into a ghostly whisper earlier this morning and then nothingness… I'm sorry Rosemary," Jake apologised.

Sam felt for a pulse that had long disappeared and knelt beside his mournful son. After a last look and stroke of the face of her one-time school friend, Rosemary fell to her knees and with arms wrapped around father and son, the three hugged tightly in silence.

Breaking waves upon the shore asked them to consider what was to be done with Finn's body. Deciding that the ground was too hard to dig, they released his corpse to the waiting sea and stood in silence as the achromatic figure floated momentarily before gradually exchanging surface for submergence. The three of them decided to continue on towards Rosemary's cave house; three, there always seemed to be three.

Although Kyle being absent, a group still numbering three trudges up Rosemary's garden path to a door half closed and the sobbing of three converged around another three, huddled together... frozen in time.

The door is pushed open; Saoirse, Amatheia and Jim turn to see Rosemary and Sam enter. Saoirse's eager anticipation of seeing her father again is short lived as the third to arrive is not Kyle but Sam's son, Jake. Fearful that she may be the last of her family, Saoirse returns to the statuesque trio. Placing her index and middle fingers to Ellen's neck, she feels a pulse; repeating the process with Crystal and Mick, Sam announces loudly...

"They're alive!"

The inanimate three are quickly wrapped in blankets by Sam and Saoirse while the others busy themselves by getting a fire lit, shovelling any remaining snow out through the door, now firmly closed banishing the icy gale increasing in ferocity outside. As the evening progressed, warmth gradually filled the house and the life-force of all enclosed within the little dwelling surrounded by a formidable winter also gained in strength.

"Ellen, where is Mister Waggles?" asked Saoirse.

"He was right here beside me, cuddling for warmth and then I... I fell asleep and when I woke up... you had returned," replied a baffled Ellen.

Just then, a faint but repeated scratching beyond the front door caught Amatheia's attention. Upon opening the door, in bounded Mister Waggles promptly dropping a freshly caught Ptarmigan-like bird beside the stove. The bounty provided small sustenance to all enclosed but was a welcome addition to their evening meal.

Snow continued to fall heavily throughout the night until morning arrived unannounced; the windows could not allow any admittance to light, due to the unrelenting nocturnal wintery accumulations.

Once again, the aroma of home-baked bread and freshly brewed coffee permeated the air. All nine, plus one happy-to-be-home hound, gathered around the warm stove to eat and drink their fill; including a smiling Crystal, chuckling Mick and a very chatty Ellen. The morning meal was happily consumed while everyone recounted their experiences; conversation drew to a close and fell silent upon Saoirse's utterance...

"Where is Dad, where has my father disappeared to?"

Pushing his chair under the table, Sam moved to open the door; light and a gentle flurry entered temporarily before the door was quickly shut again.

"Winter is easing and a new plan is emerging from my overnight thoughts.... I think it pointless to return to the Kolassian Palace with Ellen to allow Kol experiment upon and test her; there must be another way for the cure to be administered freely and not under the control of Kol and his corrupt command.

"We must return to the facility. I think I can release the cure into the atmosphere. I need to use the laboratory there to manufacture enough of the cure in liquid form which can then be converted into a gaseous state and released into the air from the facility roof. On the roof there are cannons once used to combat any intruders. I can fire explosive cylinders into the lower atmosphere; once detonated, the wind currents circumventing the planet should complete the task," informed Sam.

"Who will go and who will stay?" asked Mick.

"All nine of us should go. Once our task is complete I think we should leave this planet for good and rescue Kyle. Earth's axis continues to alter but I think it will correct itself once the nexus between Earth and Polar Neridia is broken. The continued alteration of Earth's axis might release it from this planet's grasp.

"The Kolassian's Earth-based headquarters hid its interference by being based deep beneath the North Pole. This connection was inadvertently increased by our artificial wormhole; once we rescue Kyle, we must destroy it thus severing the link and breaking the circle forever," declared Sam.

"What about all of the people we rescued from the facility?" asked Crystal.

"There has been very little movement since the snow storm intensified. I last saw Jacob and Ethan tending to some of the injured shortly before I cradled you and Ellen from the cold, before we fell into a frozen slumber," recalled Mick.

Mick, Sam and Jake decided to venture outside to check on the occupants of the other cave houses. One by one, they discovered the dwellings were bereft of life until they made their way to the end of the row and turned the corner; they were presented with a frail figure bent down sobbing as he supported the limp body of another in the arms of his own raw-boned frame.

As they drew closer, the figure turned to reveal it was unmistakably Jacob; his scant countenance still adorned with a drooping moustache. Regrettably, the body of his son was no longer occupied by a soul; confirmed by his pallid expression and the placing of Sam's fingers on his throat, searching for an absent rhythm.

"There, that is all that is left of us," muttered Jacob as he pointed towards the nearby stream, behind the caves.

"Most of us had perished from the cold and hunger. I looked for you lot but you had disappeared off on your little adventures while we stayed and tried to live. I checked in on Rosemary's dwelling and found you Mick, the lady and one of her daughters frozen… I thought you were dead.

"That evening a raiding party under orders from someone by the name of Kol arrived to finish off those of us who remained! The Kolassian soldiers announced that by order of Kol, our lives were to cease! Ethan, my poor boy Ethan… he tried to intervene and they made an example of him; slowly draining the life from him and turning that stream crimson in the process.

"They then started to execute, methodically and without emotion or change of expression, every last one of us. Except for me, I was told that only one would be spared to inform you, if you returned, that the same fate would await you unless you left permanently!" cried Jacob as he released the body of his son to the frozen ground.

Then disregarding any attempt at comfort given by and choosing to ignore the presence of Mick, Sam or Jake, the heart-broken father quickly covered his son's body with rocks scattered nearby and wedged a makeshift wooden cross at the head of the pile. Rising up and stumbling off towards the shore and then, unknown to Sam and the others, in the direction of the Kolassian palace and hopeful vengeance. A steadying hand upon

Micks shoulder halted his instinctive attempt to pursue the grieving father.

"Let him be, whatever fate lies before him may be the only cure for his heartache; that poor soul will not have enough time left to heal. We however must return to the facility. Our parting gift to the wretched populations must be the cure released into the air before we too take flight and rescue our friend from the reservoir tower," Sam, with a purposeful look in his eye expressed in a tone of voice that came, lovingly from the heart.

Tired feet plough coarsely through miniature peaks and troughs of quartzite, slate and pumice until they are cleansed by the welcome saltwater rushing between and over the toes and feet of a detached and benumbed man.

Jacob who often took comfort in the words he found in his bible had but one purpose, a single objective, to fulfil before his life was completed. Without his wife or son to share existence with, his only focus, his last task... was the seeking of an eye for an eye.

Jacob had seen Amatheia and Saoirse both call for an aquaton using an aulos. Being a skilled woodsman, he had spent many a campfire vigil carving toys and trinkets for the children of the caves out of pine with his pocket-knife. He had easily hewn an aulos for himself one night, thinking it may come in handy one day; little then did he realise it would be his ticket towards retribution.

Placing the instrument to his pursed lips, with a gentle blow, he evoked a familiar mournful tone that while summoning an aquaton close-by it also released a wailing sorrow; travelling out beyond the lonely crests and swells. Before scrambling onto the beast, he returned the aulos to his shirt pocket accompanied by a small glass pipette. Jacob spent the next few days drifting in and out of consciousness allowing the aquaton, with minor and infrequent corrections, to follow the Grigora stream and deliver him to his dreadful destination.

Sliding from the aquaton's back, Jacob boldly set forth single-mindedly to shore. Standing before him, reaching out aggressively towards the spiteful sky were pointed and snagged, black glass shards which were several metres in length; preventing any attempt in gaining entry to the Kolassian palace. Jacob then decided to meander a little further on, pursuing an alternative entrance; an icy side passage presented itself.

As he travelled along he noticed the erratically struggled footprints which, unknown to him, had been laid in a desperate escape by Jake and Finn. Light retreated behind him as his sense of smell was assaulted upon venturing further into the subterranean void.

To his left were the remains of a cell window lying amongst scorch-marked rubble. To his right, the origin of his nasal onslaught teetered precariously towards the roof and a blood-spattered hatch. Without any other discernible way forward, Jacob began the delicate task of climbing the corpse pile. Every subsequent hand-hold brought revulsion to his fingertips; blood stained skin and rotting flesh were not the easiest of surfaces to gain safe purchase upon. After dislodging several cadavers and a momentary falter, Jacob reached the top.

As he paused to catch his breath, the hatch opened once again to add to the height of the putrid elevation. The addition landed briefly beside Jacob, exchanging a bewildered glance momentarily before groaning and then descending unwillingly to the cavern floor.

By the time Jacob turned his head away from the murderous vista, the hatch had begun to close; a quick scramble gained him entry above and sent the towering mass crashing beneath. Very little effort seemed necessary to pull himself up beyond the hatch until Jacob realised a pair of Kolassian hands clenching tightly onto both of his shoulders had assisted in his ascension.

"Welcome…, who might you be?" inquired a hideous malformation of a Kolassian, slumped forward from its mechanical lower half.

The hatch door closed firmly beneath Jacob's feet with a begrudging thud as the two Kolassian guards dropped Jacob to the floor in front of a much-weakened High Commander, Kol.

"I am the last of my family, your murdering pawns spared me to inform others of their potential fate, should they return but nobody came back. I left the cave houses to be consumed by snow and ice… deserted," lied Jacob.

"If that is true then you have served your purpose and it is no longer necessary for you to breathe. I might as well dispose of you now; my future too is limited and I do not possess the energy required to continue our conversation.

"This wretched shape before you, all withered and warped, can no longer retain the want nor the will to meet a new day; it is all but wiped out," croaked Kol, his torn voice trailing off to a whisper as he feebly motioned to his guards with a weakened wave of a scrawny limb.

As Jacob was hauled upwards over the once again opened hatch he reached into his shirt pocket; retrieving a small glass object containing an intriguing liquid which he held aloft for Kol to observe.

"What is that in your grasp? Do you possess the same *cure* once brought here by your companions? Is that the answer to my ailing and fractured existence?" quizzed Kol, with a rasping purchase of air.

"Perhaps, but you shall never attain it," replied Jacob deceivingly as he pulled away from the guards' clutches.

Incredulous to what was within his reach, Kol lunged forwards causing his mechanical base to tip over, the subsequent fall separating his upper torso from his metallic lower half; the detached body turning a pale shade of grey while careering forwards pawing at Jacob with futility. This motion sent both Kol and Jacob crashing against the hatch door as they fell through the opening towards the cavern floor and an awaiting cold and crimson conclusion.

***

Back at the caves, a concerted group is about to set forth with determination…

"If twenty days here still correlates to twenty years back on Earth, my father may be a senior citizen by now," ushered Saoirse worryingly.

Unbeknownst to Saoirse, her cocooned father was very much preserved within an organic material that not only sustained him physically but also paused any normal advancement towards old age. Using a calm reassuring voice, Crystal suggested Saoirse gather her things and to assist her other daughter in preparation for the trip ahead. Two rucksacks, a large one made of tired old leather and the other formed from a light synthetic material was small in size and pink in colour, sat slumped in the corner of the room waiting patiently to take shape.

Jumbled cotton t-shirts stacked upon layers of leggings and hand-me-down jeans occupied the floorspace of Ellen's half of their cave bedroom... and almost all of Saoirse's headspace.

The occupation ebbed away with a gentle nudge from a loving sister, pulling her attention from reminisces and back to the task at hand. Rummaging through clothes, that once adorned her six-year-old self, saddened Saoirse as they now only existed as second-hand shirts and shoes for her sister or framed fragments of memories hung on walls of an abandoned house twenty light years beyond the horizon. As the pile shrank, so did her sorrow; wiping an escaped tear with a paper tissue plucked hurriedly from her chest pocket, Saoirse moved momentarily to the doorway, allowing her sister to finish packing without the hindrance of an emotional older sister.

The desire to return to a life filled with mundane everyday tasks back on Earth, awakened by just a simple chore, spurred the elder sibling onwards to hope for a better day.

Saoirse, on quick completion of her mother's bidding, persuaded her younger sister to join in soaking up one last view of their alien home before the next journey began. The hill before them inclined to draw heavy breaths from silent mouths and beads of perspiration from furrowed brows. Brushed and caressed by whispering, knee-high rye grass perforated with the amber and alabaster beauty of wild daises; willing effort was duly rewarded and the occasional stumble forgiven.

A much greater remuneration was soon captured upon summitting the hilltop. To the left, icebergs dotted the horizon, temporarily obscuring the view of the Kolassian Palace. Once the strong Grigora stream had assisted in discontinuing the icebergs blocking the view any longer, a plume of smoke could be seen darkening the sky above the former high commander's residence.

Turning her gaze to the right, Saoirse could see the cave houses, empty and cold. Beyond the dwellings, a warm smile and a gentle hand waving, beckoned Crystal's children to come join her; it was time to leave. The two sisters heeded their mother's request but while the elder sibling moved downhill at a cautious pace, the younger child ran and jumped without any foresight for self-preservation. Saoirse watched Ellen falter at first, then after momentarily correcting her oversight, a stumble became a tumble.

Laughter mixed with screams, indiscernible whether the result of fear or joy, rolled down the hillside. The squeals decreasing in volume along with Ellen's increase in distance from Saoirse, now sitting alone perched on an overhang as she watched her younger sister come to a gentle thud against a peaty mound.

***

Another tumble nearing completion further along the coast, would not end with a soft landing…

As Jacob tumbled through the air his hand released a pipette containing not a cure but only saltwater, collected from the sea on his journey from the caves. Both Kol, Jacob and the glass cylinder smashed into the ground. The terminal view beheld by the Kolassian High Commander's eyes would be that of a dying smile of a heartbroken husband and father; happy to finally join his wife and son. As Jacob drew his final breath, his nostrils filled with acrid smoke as deserting and fleeing guards set the compound alight.

Saoirse rose from where she sat and walking slowly down the rest of the hill, wisdom and resilience of age merged with the exuberance and recklessness of youth in a comforting embrace; before the two daughters of Kyle and Crystal joined the rest of the group on their next journey, towards the facility.

The route took them close to where Kol once ruled from his dastardly lair. The stench of smoke seen earlier billowing above the skyline by Saoirse and the leaving party is all that remains of the palace; gone are the wooden ramparts and the surrounding courtyard formed from ice and snow, now disfigured by the intense heat of flame, fuelled by oil and hate. As the party cruise past the dying conflagration, the skeletal remains of the corpse pile slump forward to darken the icy waters which surround them.

Pushing onwards, leaving the destruction and stench of death behind, the group eventually arrived and dismounted near the edge of the Stygian forest. Deciding to take the longer trek around the woodland perimeter, Sam and Ametheia led the way; preferring an albeit longer but light-filled hike rather than an unplanned sojourn filled with unknown shadows and evoked disquiet.

Eventually, the shimmering of the facility's mirrored surface grabbed their attention on the horizon. To their dismay, the Kolassian Palace was not the only structure to be abandoned in flames. Due to the intense heat, it was not possible to gain entry in through the liquid mirror surface at the base of the building. An alternative method of access would involve the last remaining spacecraft, parked some thirty metres to the side.

Both Amatheia and Saoirse instinctively sat in the pilot and co-pilot positions; with everyone else seated, the craft lifted upwards above the facility roof. Deciding time was of the essence, as flames began to lick higher and higher, only Sam descended to the roof below while the remaining party hovered above him. He moved quickly towards an entrance, leaving several layers of his shoe soles sticking to the roof as he traversed the scorched platform. He sneaked through the silent facility; quiet apart from the dull electrical hum of monitors and other abandoned machinery.

The Kolassians had departed the laboratories and cell blocks after the demise of Kol. It was not just the downfall of their gruesome leader that instigated a hasty departure. Increasingly, the planet was becoming unstable; tremors and falling debris every few minutes caused Sam's hands to shake and brow to perspire as he struggled to complete the manufacturing process.

Finally, with the roof canons containing the cure in a gaseous form directed towards the upper atmosphere, Sam made his way quickly back to the waiting craft. As they lifted upwards towards the dwindling wormhole, the canisters swiftly flew over and past them; the proceeding explosions sent buffeting shockwaves against the side of their ship. They corrected their position and hovered a while watching a purple tinged gas descend upon the remaining populations below and beyond.

Many Kolassians and Oikians alike were scrambling onto waiting spacecraft, aided by reformed Kolassian guards, to leave the dying planet; unknowing that this curious vapor that fell upon and within them was a cure gifted by a small circle of family and friends.

The shrinking wormhole was directly linked to the continual turning of Earth's axis and weakening of the nexus between the two worlds. Such a sight steeled the purpose of the crew to return to Kyle's aid.

After several elongated minutes of mental and physical distortion, endured within absurd momentum, they pass safely through the other side; the wormhole all the while weakening and threatening to dissipate into nothingness.

They made their way towards Earth, passing unaware populations, busy dealing with how Earth's altered state was impacting upon their own lives. A father was focused on strapping his two-year-old boy into a car child seat, too busy to notice the craft streaking by, pausing only momentarily to look up, too late, towards where his child was enthusiastically urging his father's attention.

They continued towards the tower at the edge of a reservoir in a little corner of Ireland which encapsulated and interned a father, husband and friend.

The roaring of engines outside his cocoon, past the quaking walls and beyond his trembling consciousness, failed to distract Kyle Parsons, even momentarily, from his internal discourse...

Life carries on, it continues to exist outside of this imprisonment. Not all has turned to dust, not yet. I cannot see now... my eyes were not fully covered by the cocoon but my eyelids have become stuck down from sleep and dried tears. I sense light permeating through to rest upon my face.

My suspension feels threatened, my tether loosened but my mind has ceased to unravel. With some effort, I can open my eyes. Although my vision is blurred I am able to roughly make out something below, a silhouette of my dust covered shoes perhaps? They seem to have moved, by who, by what? I can feel a draught of air upon the sole of my left foot; it itches and burns a little where some of the cocoon has become undone. Have twenty years come and gone?

Who or what came and went? Something is changing within me, I can feel it. My physicality and mentality are somehow emboldened. I am no longer afraid of what has happened or of events that are yet to pass; an increasing energy inside me is dispelling any doubtful thoughts... everything is becoming clearer.

The trembling of the walls surrounding Kyle was not responsible for a shaken displacement of his footwear, something or someone else had removed his shoes. As the wormhole continued to attenuate and weaken above, other forces increased within the tower. A deep humming vibrated within and around its walls, sending g-forces to pull and push upon Kyle's physical and mental presence. A silent pause halted everything momentarily.

A mother starling about to deposit her morning catch into the throat of her hatchling, hesitated for a second.

Snow falls from a tree branch but a fraction of time passes before allowing it to hit the ground beneath.

A fox, furiously trying to catch breakfast, turns its head when it is interrupted from digging at a rabbit hole.

An unoiled reservoir gate ceases its wind aided groan as an easterly breeze begins to slow.

The rapid explosion and expulsion of the surrounding brickwork revealed the humanoid shaped chrysalis to the occupants of the craft lingering nearby. Kyle, encased inside, was held aloft in mid-air for those within the hovering craft to gape and gasp upon as a transformation continued to transpire.

When a caterpillar has gorged itself and is satiated beyond fullness, a metamorphosis ensues. A period of time consuming all that is desired comes to an end when rest and preparation are required for the next stage of life. Stillness, waiting and allowing time and space for change, to transform into something better, but perhaps at a cost.

What price does the caterpillar pay for attaining the beauty of a butterfly? As it flutters by, instilling awe and wonder at nature's artistry in all its passing observants, the clock is counting down precious time into a matter of days if not hours left to live. Is this transfiguration worth diminishing time? If that shortened time is spent benefiting others, calculation is perhaps immeasurable.

Kyle's cocoon started to spin at first and then began unravelling around him at an ever-increasing pace. As it separated from his body an intense and blinding light projected out from him, accompanied by an ear-piercing scream which sent shockwaves to buffet the craft idling close-by. There was a pause and silence took over for a moment until Kyle fell towards the void where the tower once stood.

As he fell, fear departed Kyle; replaced with a new confidence. A growing strength both inner and outer, radiated from him; an invisible shield protecting him from the flying debris and forces that abounded as he descended downwards out of view from his apprehensive family and friends, waiting in the adjacent spacecraft. Like a caterpillar into a butterfly, he too had changed; a parting gift perhaps bestowed by a thankful race, who once were misanthropic but now grateful for a cure given by those who needed not to be altruistic but chose to be so, regardless of hardships endured. Kyle falls further but the swirling waters that surround him are kept at bay by the force which pulses outwards from him; a shaft of space and time comparable in dimension to the departed tower protects him from drowning as he descends.

His descent is paused every so often, like an elevator stopping at the next floor. At each sudden declination, he is presented with an insight to his family and friends, be they human, part-human or a different species entirely.

The observation, or wisdom he is able to discern from each revelation is not always earth-shattering but just as valuable to him nonetheless.

At one pausing, the unmistakeable silhouette of Amatheia showed itself through the swirling waters. The lengths at which Amatheia was prepared to go and had gone in order to protect his daughter, Saoirse, on their journeys were revealed to him.

At another level down, his pausing was to witness the watery shadow of his wife Crystal. He noticed, using her thumb and forefinger, she was rotating her wedding ring around several times. Immediately, without her speaking, it was simply explained to him that every year on their anniversary, she had always rotated her wedding ring the corresponding number of years they had been married. There was no great revelation other than it was a personal tradition of hers that she wanted to share with him.

Kyle's children and also his other friends, made their expositions to him as his lowering further downwards was briefly paused; some were unexpected while others were warmly envisaged.

Saoirse hoped to skip stones along a calm shore again someday when they could leave these stormy seas behind.

Ellen, who never complained and always got on with life despite what it may throw at her was, surprisingly angry with her father. It seems she was fed up with living in her sister's shadow and wanted him to recognise, that she was an emerging powerful young woman.

Kyle's travelling below the depths was halted one last time to meet an unrecognisable form, a tall figure not to remain half hidden, like the others, by a watery curtain.

"Break the circle! You must break the circle!" shouted the figure as it emerged to hover alongside him.

"I can see you now. Who are you? I must break the circle?" asked Kyle.

"My name is Tom, Rosemary's father. I am no longer confined to a wheelchair, not when my mind has a comparable ingenuity to that of your friend Sam. The tower was circular inside, it was an ancient tower, squared off on the outside to disguise it. Even though the bricks and mortar have disappeared, the tower continues to surround you. Use your new ability to stop this circular motion and finally end this!" the older man, being right beside Kyle now, no longer needed to raise his voice above the swirling waters.

"But why, how are you here?" Kyle reached out to discover that Tom was present visually and audibly but not physically as his hand moved through Rosemary's holographic father.

"Do you feel any different now that you are free of the chrysalis? From erectus to neanderthalensis to sapiens, your transformation may be comparable to the next level of hominid. It is an opinion shared by Sam. We're not sure if it is a permanent change but time will tell," stated Tom with uncertainty.

"Sam? What has Sam got to do with my new abilities? I thought you implied that my new-found state was a parting gift from the cured and fleeing Polar Neridians?" Kyle's glow that surrounded him intensified and its colour changed rapidly with his increased anger and confusion, similar to the dramatic movement of the aurora borealis.

"Indeed, that is still our belief. I must tell you that under orders while we, Sam and I that is, were working with PNSE … we engineered and developed a lot of their technology. I am relaying our conversation in real-time to Sam, your other friends and family aboard a craft in the sky just above us. They are now fully aware of my presence, this situation and are in preparation to follow you," explained Tom.

The ferocious swirl of water surrounding Kyle moved faster in a clockwise direction. Instinctively, with arms outstretched wide he began to rotate anticlockwise. As his rotation increased in speed, the swirling vortex of water equally decreased its velocity. When a point of balance between forward and backward circular momentum was reached, the whirlpool ceased. The waiting family and friends, from the craft above, viewed the surrounding waters move to fill in the void; they took Kyle for drowned. However, moments later, still protected by the energy emitting from his core, Kyle was expelled up and out of the depths towards the wormhole which was now beginning to dwindle.

Amatheia powered up the engines, aided by her co-pilot, Kyle's daughter; they then raced in pursuit of the glowing humanoid figure leaving this planet for another.

Upon arriving at his destination, Kyle found where once there was, albeit a plunged into turmoil yet still functioning and spherical Polar Neridia, a segment of planet was all that remained. He landed upon it and immediately found himself losing his new-found strength and confidence. It all seemed to dwindle away as quickly as his brilliant outer glow dissipated and the remaining atmosphere leaked oxygen; the deprivation of which caused his mind to meander...

Hard to think straight. Head feels woozy. Arms, legs, all barely possess the energy to support their own weight; best sit down and rest awhile... try to think, try to breathe...

"It's the government's fault, you can't breathe for all the taxes and rules and regulations!"

...That's what Dad used to say. A brief phone call to tell him about a good deal on a nearly new car would follow with an inquisition on service costs, insurance, motor tax and invariably lead to...

"The government want us all to drive one litre electric dinky little excuses for a car; gone are the days when an engine was an engine and had more power than a goddamn useless hairdryer!"

...That's what Dad used to say, then his play on words...

"When is that career of yours ever gonna start bringing you in some real money? What's the purpose of all this? You've got no purpose, only poor pose!"

I suppose I didn't help matters with my replies to such barbed accusations...

"But Dad what would I do with a porpoise? I'm not planning to open a sea-world or replace Fungi!" said in my best New York accent, followed by both of us slamming several doors in our respective houses at opposite ends of the city, to what purpose, poor pose or porpoise even? I do not know as the door slamming was preceded by both of us hanging up and grunting our incredulities at life!

I miss my dad, I miss my mam, I miss my family, I miss my dog. I guess, I miss everyone... Harder to think now... harder to breathe too...

What's that speck of light? It seems to be growing or coming closer? Dad, is that you? I shouldn't have hung up, I'm sorry but... you're dead and I'm dying and why am I starting to feel weightless?

Kyle's body and mind began to gradually fade as the approaching light became stronger.

"Sam's theory, he shares with Rosemary's father Tom, of the emergence of a new hominid species gifted by the Polar Neridians was in reality nothing more than short-lived conjectures of hopeful scientific minds.

"I think someone's aim was indeed to gift Kyle a certain power, thus enabling his safe deliverance to what remained of Polar Neridia, but to what end? What purpose has your father yet to fulfil?" quizzed Jim Kelly of Saoirse, from the back seat of their craft.

"I can't say for sure exactly but what I do know is if we don't get there in time, there won't be much of the planet left for my father to sit upon, look!" screamed Saoirse as she pointed to a tiny figure in the distance, barely protected by a weakening atmosphere.

With all remaining inhabitants long gone from the almost non-existent planet, the crew endeavoured to rescue the last Polar Neridian.

Amatheia and Saoirse carefully positioned the craft twenty metres above Kyle. Before they attempt to lock onto him, Sam scans Kyle's weakened figure for any possible hidden booby-traps or an unwelcome stow-away.

"Saoirse, there seems to be a foreign body embedded within your father. I can't determine whether or not it could be a threat to us. It may not be safe to retrieve him," announced Sam.

"We can't wait very much longer Sam, the collapsing atmosphere surrounding Kyle is about to surrender him to nothingness if we don't act fast!" bellowed a growingly impatient and impassioned Amatheia.

Without any further hesitation or permission from the others aboard, Saoirse securely locked onto and captured her father; putting him into a medical stasis chamber just a few moments before the remainder of Polar Neridia imploded. The shockwave sent them spinning rudderless, out towards an unknown destination. All control was very quickly lost when a sudden and prolonged momentum, imposed upon them by the fragments of a dead planet, lasted for several days before the ship's navigational systems came back online.

While Kyle remained in an imposed deep slumber, Sam gathered everyone to gather beside him as he had something to show and discuss with them.

"Saoirse, there was a diagonal scar along the sole of your father's left foot, from which I retrieved the foreign body that the scan had picked up, take a look at this," Sam placed in the centre of the table, a small blood-stained scroll.

Saoirse carefully rolled it open. Ellen came forward and pulled something out of her pocket; from a long-gone colourful shore. She placed a glass bead upon either end to prevent the scroll from curling back up and hiding the curious diagram scratched upon its surface.

"The exodus from Polar Neridia... it seems someone belonging to that evacuation wanted us to follow them. Maybe this is a star-chart with exact directions to their destination… if we choose to go it will require, yet again, the unwelcome usage of stasis chambers," said Sam who looked to Ellen's sister, waiting nervously for a response.

Before Saoirse could respond, Ellen burst forward.

"Look! Look! There is some writing and a name signed at the bottom!" Ellen, catching a glimpse of her older sister's stern countenance, sat back down as quickly as she had stood up.

"It reads... *a gift from a twenty-year older Elpida...* Elpida must have had her own experiences with time travel. Even though she may have given us what her name translates as... *hope*... I will not endure those machines and the uncertainty of an unknown state of being. I choose to go, yes... but I also choose to age," Saoirse rose from the table with a determination and an acceptance in her eyes as she began to prepare a stasis chamber for everyone assembled, apart from herself.

"Nor I child, the two of us will safely deliver this crew to that little scroll's coordinates and together we shall share the next twenty years growing older... together!" Amatheia had joined Saoirse and placing an arm around her shoulder, she pointed to the reverse side of the scroll and whispered some additional information into her ear.

Saoirse hastily picked up the scroll to look at the back of it and in doing so, scattered several glass beads onto the floor. Bending down to retrieve the colourful stones, she left the scroll to curl up on the table; revealing that the star chart and coordinates had in actual fact been written on the reverse side of paper headed with *'Probe National Space Exploration'*.

Unseen by all family, friends and crew present, apart from Amatheia and now Saoirse, was that curiously,

'Probe National Space Exploration' had been crossed out and written beneath it were the words... *'Polar Neridia Second Earth'*.

In agreement with her co-pilot and with the remainder of the crew safely tucked in, they set coordinates for yet again another decade long, plus one more set of ten years, journey towards *hope*.

***

Nineteen years, three hundred and sixty-four days had passed by in a prolonged whisper. Saoirse who now possessed a few grey strands and a white-streaked Amatheia, both shared a pot of coffee while discussing what was about to unfold. They had much to do before waking everyone and preparing them for their destination which was looming, only a day away.

They sat at the same table which still displayed a little scroll, held in place by a few glass beads carefully placed by Saoirse nearly twenty years ago. Curiously, the beads would often appear to have been moved overnight. Saoirse was unsure if it was her imagination but this repositioning was often accompanied by bumps in the night and crumbs of food left on the floor. She wondered had they mice, a visitor or even a stowaway. Saoirse drained the last of her coffee and looked across to Kyle's stasis chamber.

"My father was, still is, about the same age as I am now when all this sorry mess, this journey, began. He lies before me, encapsulated in time, perhaps dreaming of his family and friends from twenty years before now.

"It breaks my heart to wake him but we are near our journey's end and upset him I undoubtedly will, I must," Saoirse stepped back awaiting her dad's reaction to a daughter now similar in age to her father.

Slowly awakening, a father communicates with a smile and then a tear. Amatheia feels she is intruding in a moment that should only be shared by a father and daughter; calmly removing herself from their presence, she busies herself with releasing those still held inside their stasis chambers.

Kyle cannot speak yet, whether as a result of recovery from his ordeal or sadness at what befalls his eyes is uncertain but his hand reaches for a pen resting upon the table beside the scroll. Saoirse hands the pen along with a notepad to her father. He scrawls frantically for a minute or so before emotion and exhaustion cause him to cease and the pen to fall to the floor.

As Saoirse bends down to retrieve it, Kyle stretches upwards trying to pull himself up onto something... something which is not really there, not visible to anyone else but him; an object or substance within his grasp but seemingly out of reach. Lying back down his focus shifts and returns to Saoirse.

"Daughter, you are still my child regardless of age, time or place in the Universe. Please hand me the pen, I must finish writing everything down before they take me again," croaked Kyle fighting back tears with nothing but love pouring from his reddened eyes.

He continues scribbling and finishes his desperation fuelled scrawl a few short moments before an incredible force envelopes the craft. Everything and everyone not tied down is first lifted up to the ceiling before being slammed into the floor.

Darkness invades and silence accompanies while all motion ceases. Starlight penetrates a porthole window, an unbroken circle, to highlight scribblings on a notepad lying on the floor; resting a short distance from where the memorandum's now absent author once lay.

Kyle's worst fears had come true. His scribblings were a confused and desperate warning to those that he loved. He had been taken again. Saoirse picked up the notepad and realised that they all must allow themselves to, once more, be taken.

Kyle had been reaching for a ledge to pull himself up, perhaps this time he would succeed and not fall, perhaps none of his family and friends would fall again. Elpida knew that in order for all the souls connected to Kyle to return home, they must first travel farthest from it. In doing so they would best arm themselves by obtaining enough emotional power to restore their original place in time. She had encouraged them to journey to a place that would increase risk of capture, of heightened danger and thus higher emotion and greater power to emotionally time travel; improving the chances of their preferred destination and an opportunity to make things right.

A father's memorandum to his family and friends was a series of muddled thoughts; written down in an abstract thought process as though he were trying to make sense of them. Methodically penned, almost in the format of an equational poem; they were speculations of a person whose mind and emotions had been dragged out to the back of beyond and then some more for good measure.

The end of the message was very clear to a daughter who wanted nothing more than to be held in her daddy's arms and to laugh... and to cry, once again... but also forever.

10 + 1 = 20
1 = 10
10 = 1
1 = one

one life
one journey
one conclusion
+1?
for infinity…
infinity +1...

one plus all must go back,
interrupt the equation,
halt the cycle,
listen to your heart and break the circle at the beginning!

Saoirse and Amatheia, beaten and bruised by the force of being thrown about when the Kolassian mothership had locked on, knew that they only had a few moments before the occupants of the ship that had consumed their own craft would arrive to take them. They quickly handed an emotional time travel device to everyone aboard with instructions to travel back to their own personally desired beginning... and ultimately break the circle.

For some, it would be the last time they would see each other; heartfelt goodbyes were exchanged as sounds of heavy-booted footsteps and laboured, rattled breathing approached from beyond the outer door. After several blasts of weapon fire, the Kolassian soldiers gained entry.

Amatheia's thoughts were racing back to a point in her past when she was separated from her parents and was about to be taken away in stasis to Earth for the first time.

Upon quickly passing through the charred and twisted entrance, the first two soldiers found themselves being dive-bombed by a furious and screaming Oikian who, anticipating their imminent arrival, had perched herself up high on an upper-deck bridge.

Rosemary and Sam looked on in awe at the sight of Amatheia and her soldiers turned captive, beginning to dimly fade from this existence. At the same time, every last member of the crew, family and friends alike, with emotions building to extreme levels aided by the devices held tightly in their collective grasps, were also a blur of bright blue contrails.

Some simultaneously, others slightly before or after, individually were becoming transparent and departing in an attempt to correct or change a moment in their history; to render the circle broken.

Amatheia, with an emotional time travel device held tightly between both hands and two Kolassian soldiers, both head-locked under each of her crushing arms, began to oscillate in a neon-blue, furious flurry.

They disappear right before Sam and Rosemary's eyes, arriving roughly in a kaleidoscopic tumble as thousands of colourful glass stones are scattered; propelled skyward in the melee. Amatheia and her two captives had arrived back at an Oikian beach, upon which there silently stood three recognizable figures; detained by a dishevelled mob of Kolassian guards.

Amatheia relinquished the two, tightly ensnared in her bulking arms, to the ground; dazed and confused they ran and stumbled in the opposite direction. Upon seeing this unfolding disturbance, the troop ran towards Amatheia's location. She was bemused and also amused as they ran through and past her holographic presence. Leaving them to continue in the direction of her recent releases, she wandered softly over to the three figures standing near the lapping waves.

Five years of age, a young Oikian child has her hands held by both parents standing guardedly either side of her as she looks up at an older, holographic, version of herself. At first, only she can see the hologram, only she can feel the presence of confident kindness surrounding her. All fear has left the child and the new-found peace permeates through her hands to those she holds tightly and dear to her heart; her first adoptive parents were about to become her only and forever there after guardians.

The older Amatheia walks forward and about turns so that her holographic presence occupies the same time and space as her younger self. Strangely, she feels something sitting upon her head. She reaches up to feel for what rests there; finding a white floppy hat, she holds and looks at it with love.

As emotions build and surge again, her holographic self transcends the physical barrier and she places the hat upon the head of her younger self. As she begins to fade from existence she drops the spent emotional time travel device to the ground. Curiously, it is sent rolling up and down humps and hollows until it finally comes to rest against a small pile of colourful glass beads, seemingly arranged in a small collection; perhaps left by another Oikian child.

The younger Amatheia's parents gaze at this curiosity for a moment before turning their attention towards the shore and their daughter who stood commandingly as she placed an aulos to her lips. Almost silent, mournful tones are cast out upon the waves; soon beckoning an aquaton that gracefully accepts passengers of an Oikian child and her parents.

As they head towards a rising sun and a new life, a young Amatheia, a soon-to-be the only Amatheia, turns to take one last look at the pretty Oikian shore. A few seconds away from fading into nothingness, holographic Amatheia is standing on the shore, looking out at herself and her parents departing to forge a new life. The two Amatheias exchange a lingering half-smile and the hologram disappears shortly after; the circle holding Amatheia has broken as she leaves for home.

A luminous image of Saoirse holding onto Mister Waggles fluctuates sporadically before exiting the craft, just as the remaining Kolassian soldiers halt frozen where they stood; their eyes a wide-open exclamation at the sudden disappearance of their two colleagues along with the raging Oikian.

Saoirse returns to a familiar place where her physical and mental self both share the same six-year-old child's form once more; spinning round and round over and over again and again as she arrives. In doing so, she lets go of the shiny thing that feels hot and was hurting her hand;

an emotional time travel device, devoid of life, falls to become lodged between the compacted and intertwined stalks of wheat. She falls over giddy from excitement with Mister Waggles frantically licking her face and barking for her to resume their game as she looks up at a big blue Earth sky. The only sound she can hear is that of a tender wind whispering along the ears of wheat that envelop and cushion the young girl.

She finds her balance and remembers that Mummy told her to be back home in ten minutes. Not having a watch and only able to tell the time from looking at a digital clock, like the one in their kitchen and after all she is doing brilliantly at learning to tell the time, according to Daddy; she guesses her ten minutes of play must be nearly up. Saoirse turns to go back home to her mum but realises she had lost her floppy hat while running and spinning around.

A flicker of white dancing along the top of the wheat field reveals the whereabouts of the lost hat; it stops to get caught on a blackberry bush at the end of a hedgerow. About to run and retrieve the hat, she turns around when her mother's voice calls out beckoning her loudly from beyond the hedges.

Before Saoirse passes through a gap in the hedging, a rustling behind the trees and blackberry bush where her hat now no longer hung, causes her to pause and look back at where the disturbance materialised. A very large creature, bear-sized but ape-like in features, smiles and waves at her. Saoirse didn't feel afraid, only happiness and kindness exuded from the presence. Looking at the beast wearing her white floppy hat made Saoirse giggle and they shared a lingering half-smile. Momentarily distracted by her mother calling again, Saoirse looked back to wave at the friendly giant but Amatheia was no longer there. Saoirse ran, with Mister Waggles trailing behind, to her mother's outstretched arms; her circle was broken as she finally returned back home.

Ellen clings to her teddy for comfort as the shouting and screaming intensifies outside her stasis chamber. Looking up from where she lays, blue lights flash all around and reflect, inches above her face, on the surface of the stasis chamber's glass screen. Cradled against her chest is her teddy and within her tightly clenched hands, a device pulsates and flashes as the blue lights now seem to enter the chamber and whirl around the small girl's shrieking face. The stasis chamber is suddenly laid silent and empty as Ellen's emotions carry her to somewhere her heart longingly desires.

Ginger-nut biscuits tumble from a now empty packet Ellen holds upside down as she stares at her dad chasing after Saoirse; her sister had just disappeared from view over the edge of a grassy mound and he had thought she had fallen down injured.

Standing behind Ellen is a newly arrived version of herself. The two Ellen's exchange a lingering half-smile as one Ellen gives the other her teddy. They share a few whispers before the departing Ellen hands over a little scroll and promptly fades away into the background.

Crystal looks to Ellen and is momentarily stunned by something that is different about her youngest daughter's demeanour; an almost electric blue hue behind her child seemed to frame her pretty, day-dreaming, face. A trail of neon disappeared into the scenery behind the child as her consciousness snapped back to the present.

Fifteen broken biscuits lay scattered on the picnic blanket alongside a battered and worn metal object. Ellen wandered over to see what the rest of her family were staring at. As they gazed in silence, Ellen felt the warmth from her former self's hand still present on the scroll she held tightly in her grip. Rolling open the small scroll of paper, with writing and diagrams a four-year-old couldn't understand scratched onto its surface, she broke the silence when she raised up her little arm and handed it to her dad saying,

"This is Elpida's, I think she might need it. We should give it back to her when she is older!" suggested Ellen, smiling interruptedly.

Kyle and Crystal looked at each other dumbfoundedly as they gathered up the tartan picnic blanket. A scorched cylindrical device fell with the remainder of the ginger-nut biscuits; rolling to the edge and tumbling down to be swallowed by the thick gorse and wet peaty soil.

The family got back into the car to drive home. As Kyle and Crystal clicked in their children's seatbelts, Ellen looked out of her window. Far off into the valley below, she noticed the large cylindrical holes that had begun to appear in the distant landscape, were now shrinking away before disappearing altogether. Ellen's circle was broken and she sat back in her seat with a knowing contentment evident across her face as Dad drove them back home.

Sam released Rosemary's hand as flashes of bright blue intensified amid the chaos; rendering her face no more visible than an unfinished and hurried pencil sketch.

His emotions too began to surge but his heart's desires were also increasingly conflicted. On the one hand he longed to return to a time before he was first taken by the Kolassians. On the other, his love for his son Jake was causing the neon blue contrails to fluctuate until Sam seemed to divide into two images of himself.

Both manifestations of Sam began fading from view, looking back towards Rosemary's gaze. Their faces were simultaneously displaying a serene and profound look of understanding as Sam's two forms gradually merged into one; mouthing goodbye to Rosemary before disappearing from her sight.

Moments before Sam left, his son was flickering in and out of this present. The only destination Jake's heart desired was wherever his family was, where his father Sam ultimately chose to be. Jake's indecisive figure followed in the direction of Sam's momentarily faltering and dividing image; in desperate pursuit of happiness, his own and that of his father.

Crouched down between two white lines, looking at a familiar red ochre surface, Sam realises he is in a starting position on a running track. Already soaked to the skin with sweat from his emotionally time-travelled ordeal, he instinctively begins to run.

The sky looked ominous and foreboding, about to give birth to a monster of a storm or the precedence to a cataclysmic event. The track was devoid of other runners apart from Sam and a caretaker busy tidying up race blocks and discarded batons before the deluge would begin its onslaught. Making good time, Sam cornered deftly as he passed the 200-metre mark. Feeling like he might achieve his best time yet, he strode onwards with the automatic track lights coming on as the sky darkened to almost night.

However, with twenty metres to go, lightning tore the sky in half and within that electrostatic discharge Sam saw several Kolassians appear before him. In the ensuing struggle he beat them off with the hurdle he had just leapt over. They abandoned their kidnapping, leaving Sam breathless and lying on his back staring at a sky beginning to brighten.

In his mind, the caretaker counted the twenty steps it took him to move across the track as he wandered over and helped Sam to his feet. Without looking directly at his face, Sam instinctively began helping him to gather up the remainder of the scattered sports equipment. It seemed the caretaker had finished retrieving the last few items when Sam noticed what he thought was one remaining baton, lying to the side of the running track.

Bending down, Sam could see it was not like any baton he had ever held before, it had a curious liquid pulsating inside its glass body and was very hot to the touch. The caretaker was now by his side, standing tall above Sam with his arm extended, waiting for the last baton to be placed into his waiting hand. Sam stood up and automatically turned to deliver the object into the caretaker's grasp.

As the two men stood looking at each other, both holding onto either end of the familiar emotional time travel device, a mutual recognition was shared and they exchanged a lingering half-smile before the caretaker spoke... "Dad? Sam? Is that you?"

Overfilled with joy, Sam hugged Jake warmly. Before they left, Sam switched off the device and placed it into a shopping bag filled with many others. Their circle was broken and they left together for home.

Crystal, cocooned in a blaze of dancing blue light, sobbed inconsolably not knowing if she would ever see her husband and children again as she was the last of her family left on the craft. Surrounded by more Kolassian soldiers entering the craft, her emotion fuelled device carried her away from danger to where her heart yearned.

Feeling light-headed from her crossing of space and time, Crystal grabs hold of the edge of her kitchen counter-top; she had landed at home on Earth. Her vision gradually clears and focuses on a digital display; five, ten, fifteen, twenty... twenty-five grams of parmesan weighed. Crystal's mind begins to drift off to times past... or future, when a countdown eked out the final moments before a craft would take them somewhere alien.

She gazes at her image caught in the polished splash-back and as the remnants of neon blue light fade, she exchanges a lingering half-smile with her own reflection. Crystal's attention returns to her current present and to a pot of boiling water on the hob behind her. She reaches over to her right and picks up what she thinks is a large spoon to stir the almost ready pasta. It is not an item of cutlery but a depleted time travel device that has become too hot to hold and Crystal immediately drops it from her grasp, into the waiting boiling water.

Stepping back, Crystal sees Ellen is happily playing on the living room floor. So she then decides to take the pot containing a mix of water, overcooked pasta and a now broken emotional time travel device, outside to be safely discarded. As Crystal steps through the kitchen back door she is confronted by a Kolassian, towering above her with a weapon pointed at her face. The being takes hold of Crystal by the neck and lifts her upwards above its head as a craft descends with cargo doors open; preparing to gather up the two struggling below.

Without any hesitation, Crystal quickly empties the contents of the pot out and down upon the Kolassian. The would-be abductor released Crystal from his grip and a scream from his scalded face; now partially merged with a melted mask. The Kolassian's howling rendered all the birds in the surrounding trees silent and motionless.

The waiting craft, along with the assailants inside, left hurriedly to perhaps never return again. Crystal recovered herself and went, with Ellen, calling out to Saoirse in the back garden. Her eldest daughter ran and jumped into her open arms. With both of her children now returned, cradled in her embrace, her circle was broken. She fell back laughing, with joyous enthusiasm, into the long wheat grass behind their family home.

Jim Kelly was next to leave his stasis chamber amidst a riotous swirl of neon and weapon fire. He arrived back at base in the Wicklow mountains on Earth, beneath a pine needle covered underground hideout, with a violent slumping into his office chair. The seat was gradually becoming saturated with sweat, dripping from the angry back pressed against it.

Jim Kelly had not possessed a happy thought, nor a heart-filled memory of a loved one to cling to while he was being catapulted past stars in seconds. Being barren of all emotion, other than anger, he gave the device no direction so it dumped him in the last known place that had brought him at least a little satisfaction.

He sat, staring blankly, in front of his office wall. A space that displayed the only achievements he had attained in life; thirty framed certificates, diplomas, and degrees that outlined his accomplishments but encased and imprisoned his mind. Jim Kelly stood up and the, starved of emotion, time travel device fell from his hand to the floor and rolled under his desk. Getting down on his knees, he reaches under to retrieve the device and notices a gun he had previously taped to the underside of a desk drawer.

Retrieving both the device and gun, he walks closer to the array of accreditations. Catching a glimpse of his face in one of the framed awards, he exchanges a lingering half-smile with himself before the remaining neon falls away to nothing.

He proceeds, using the nearly dead device, to smash and obliterate all of his awards from the wall and into a thousand pieces, strewn across the floor. Rage began to coarse through his veins; anger and sadness building ever more increasingly from within Jim Kelly's core, the device sparked into life once more and exploded before finally falling, lifeless to the floor.

Jim Kelly fell to the ground beside it and as he did so, the gun released the only remaining bullet from its chamber into the femoral artery at the top of his leg. An accidental man meets an accidental end; Jim Kelly's circle was broken but so too were any aspirations of ever finding a place to call home.

Mick Flannery, anxious and weary, had more than a little previous experience of using the emotional time travel devices. He had thought long and hard about where he wanted the device and his emotions to take him now. His sole focus was on his mother Rosemary and to halt her suffering from continuing any further.

A cocktail of anger, love and vengeance raced through every fibre of the former bartender; a volatile mix that he, or the stasis chamber, could no longer contain. Exploding in neon fury, Mick's outstretched legs burst through the end of the stasis chamber. It began rapidly collapsing and dismantling around the space his gargantuan frame had formerly occupied before he left, to right a long overdue wrong... Mick Flannery's circle was a wider one to break.

***

A tall ginger-bearded man stands alone in darkness, in the middle of a lonely country road. The last few contrails of emotion fuelled neon dissipate from his outline while an overnight storm emptied the contents of the sky down upon him. A flicker of light edges over the rise from the north, as does another source of illumination, peering up from the south. Two cars, thirty-five seconds away, approach from opposite directions; their headlights temporarily blinding the driver of the opposing vehicle as the beams pick out the silhouette of a monumental figure blocking their way.

The car travelling from the north is driven by an aging man, wearing a nurse's uniform; a North Polar Neridian sits cramped and uncomfortable in the back. The alien has an infant Mick Flannery cradled in one arm and the other holds a weapon pressed firmly against the back of the driver's head.

The car coming from the south is also driven by a *caregiver*, a younger female nurse that maintains no care for her passenger. She possesses two beady little eyes, set into her loveless face; sweat dripping profusely as she momentarily looks into the rear-view mirror at her patient sitting in the back. Rosemary had been drugged to a state of near unconsciousness after her alien children had been removed from her.

The medication's power was diminishing and the car lights ahead were gaining her attention while accelerating the process of Rosemary's returning awareness. This was causing Nurse Bates to perspire excessively at the thought of a passenger potentially becoming a troublesome one.

As the cars approached from both directions, Mick was steadfast in his resolve. Engines roared in his left and right ears but he did not flinch. The car containing an infant form of himself screeched to a halt; its chrome front bumper stopping just a few inches from Mick's left leg. To his right, the car that held his mother and driven by Nurse Bates, went into a spin.

Mick could see two beady little eyes peering out from behind the clawing hands of his hysterical mother. The car continued to rotate with tyres screeching and metal moaning regretfully at being forced to move irregularly. The vehicle careered along the road until it came to a stop, pointing away from Mick. Both car engines idled with no movement from the silent occupants within. Several seconds of silence ceased when a creaking car door was suddenly flung wide open. The driver, a male nurse, absconded into the darkness with a shopping bag in hand; before doing so, he quickly locked the Kolassian holding the infant inside and tossed the car keys to Mick.

Large boots stomped heavily towards the back of the other car. Mick first opened the passenger door and bid his mother to release her grip of the driver and to relax momentarily. Nurse Bates recoiled in terror, into her seat, as a large hand entered the driver's window of the car and proceeded to drag her, by the neck, abruptly out through the broken-glass-framed aperture. Mick effortlessly threw her screaming and kicking over his shoulder and calmly walked back towards the car containing the North Polar Neridian and his infant self.

Still holding the car key previously thrown to him, he opened the boot and dumped the howling nurse inside before securely locking it. The Kolassian fired twice through the back window but narrowly missed as Mick ran to the side and pulled the door open. Another attempt at halting Mick's progress didn't work when the weapon jammed and failed to discharge. Still holding onto the firearm, Mick dragged the Kolassian out by holding onto the gun's opposite end. Pulling the weapon from its grasp, he pointed it directly at the cowering alien.

The Kolassian was soon rendered lifeless and Mick deposited the body into the car's boot, muffling nurse Bate's cries for help, before rescuing the now bawling child. About to walk back to the other car, Mick paused as thoughts of all the hardship, both he and his mother had endured, filled his head and heart. Emotions began overloading him and also the time travel device he had retrieved from his back pocket. Opening the petrol flap, he inserted one end of the device into it while continued to hold on tightly, allowing his emotions to build. Mick released his grip just before sparks began to fly about the gas tank.

Mick placed the infant incarnation of himself into his mother's arms and they quickly drove off. As they reached the next bend a small ball of fire, visible in the rear-view mirror, exploded to light up the entire cabin as if it were daytime for a few seconds. The sound of the explosion was replaced with the dying screams of Nurse Bates as she fought in vein to escape the burning wreckage and the dead Kolassian lying on top of her. The cries and flames were ceased by distance. The car that now contained Mick Flannery, his mother and the infant form of himself disappeared over the rise; the lonely road was once more returned to darkness.

Mick drove on through the night. As the Sun was rising and the Moon still visible in the cold blue sky, he pulled up outside a *'cash for gold'* business. Leaving Rosemary cradling the infant as she and the child continued to sleep, Mick stepped out of the car. Pausing to look upon the Sun and Moon, the bell chime of an opening and quickly closing door prevented him from slipping into a trance. The door was locked but Mick could see that the owner was inside sitting down to consume a hastily bought breakfast at his desk.

"Come back at nine, I don't open shop for another few hours," grumbled the elderly gent, spitting out pastry crumbs and spilling his coffee, as he vented his frustration at the early morning disturbance.

"Please sir, I don't have much time, I'd be very grateful if you would accommodate me just this once," Mick had his towering bulk pressed up against the glass.

Mick wasn't sure whether it was the ominous presence his large shadow cast over the diminutive shopkeeper or the large gold nugget he held up to the light that finally gained him admittance. Nonetheless, he got a fair price and left the little man closing up shop early after his unexpected windfall.

Rosemary and the baby continued sleeping as Mick stopped the car to complete yet another transaction. He was less than ten minutes gone when the sound of a truck passing by broke Rosemary's sleep. She looked around, confused and worried to be alone but then a smile erupted across her face as a baby hiccupping in its slumber quickly reminded Rosemary of its presence.

Mick returned shortly after and before he could turn the ignition, Rosemary placed a hand on his shoulder. She needed confirmation of what she thought had, what was and what would be taking place.

"You, who have rescued me from the clutches of that nurse and from an insanity I thought inescapable... who are you? You, who should but does not frighten me, what connection binds us? Is it the child I hold in my arms?" releasing his shoulder, Rosemary sat back as Mick turned to face her.

"That child and I are one and the same, separated by time and circumstance. I can tell you all of what has been and what will now not be, because of my actions. But, I must drive now and you must listen," informed Mick as the engine roared into life.

The road began to rise ahead of them in twists and turns as did Rosemary's emotions while Mick provided her with the answers she needed. Every bend in the road, every new insight to a life she had lived in another space and time, gracefully revealed a more beautiful view than the previous. Their destination ahead beckoned them as they turned one last corner.

A small stone cottage, nestled shyly amongst conifers, welcomed the travel weary wanderers. Upon entering the dwelling, the sight of a stove where she could bake fresh bread brought a smile to Rosemary's face. As she explored further, a rocking chair, positioned to take advantage of the views through an almost panoramic window, invited her attention. Sitting comfortably and having finished feeding the baby, Rosemary turns to Mick who is waiting for her to take two keys sitting in the open palm of his huge right hand.

"Mother, one key is for the car outside and the other is for this house, your new home. There is a university hospital, only twenty kilometres south of here; perhaps not as near as I would have liked but it's a far cry from twenty light years. I know they are hiring and have creche facilities, so perhaps you can make a life for yourself and the child. Now I must go and I must stay," explained Mick who had already begun to fade.

Rosemary didn't think things were fully right in her timeline, they were not completely corrected yet. She knew from what Mick had told her in the car journey here that surely her other self must be in a neon blur of blue on a spacecraft, about to try and right another wrong. Rosemary knew that she was meant to be here and that her other self was compelled to assist in this outcome. Unsure of what to do, she simply sat and waited for her other self to catch up with her present... to merge with her current reality.

She understood and yet it still broke her heart to say goodbye to this kind man who was, would be, her son. She handed the infant form of Mick to the adult version and watched on with love as they shared a moment, an acknowledgement that spanned light years. One held the other while he faded even further. Sitting in the rocking chair with the baby cradled in his lap, he looked across at Rosemary and whispered...

"It's time," Mick looked upon the child's perfect face for a moment before returning his attention to Rosemary.

Rosemary and Mick exchanged a lingering half-smile and leaving his infant self in the arms of their mother, the elder Mick disappeared into the ether, content that his circle was broken and he had delivered them home.

***

Back on the craft amid a neon-blue tinged chaos…

As Sam released Rosemary's hand and exited their space and time, she too thought of where she wanted, where she needed to be. Rosemary had just seen her dear friend Sam and then her son disappear to wherever their hearts had desired. To her right, although the din and an exploding light almost obliterated her sight and hearing, she could just about confirm that she was the last one still onboard. That was apart from Kyle Parsons who, for some reason unknown to her, had returned. After being taken he had come back; wanting to make sure of everyone's escape. He was busy beating off several Kolassians attempting to cross the ship's threshold in the process.

Determined to catch up with her son, Rosemary thought intensely of a moment in time when perhaps she could alter events; memories of when Nurse Bates had come to take her to the asylum, not long after she had life removed so calculatedly and coldly from her body.

Once again, emotions overloaded a time-travelling device and the person holding onto it. Rosemary had departed the ship's cabin for that of another vehicle. She journeyed far, beyond dying stars, passing seasons in seconds, to arrive in the back seat of a car that was being driven erratically and at speed down a dark country road.

The steering wheel was held tightly by two grubby little hands as the corpulent arms they were attached to, pulled violently this way and that in a poor attempt at commanding the vehicle. This was further impeded by another form of Rosemary, sitting beside her and directly behind the driver.

Her other self who had, just moments before, awoken from a state of semi-consciousness by approaching car lights that flooded all their eyes, was in the process of trying to gouge out those of Nurse Bates.

When the squealing of tyres and steelwork's lament had finally ceased mourning, the car came out of a spin to a grinding and abrupt stop; pointing in the opposite direction from whence they came. The last few sparks of neon flickered out of existence and caused both versions of Rosemary to gaze upon each other.

The Rosemary who continued to cling to the driver's eyes remained silent while the newly arrived Rosemary began to speak.

"In about forty seconds, those approaching footsteps belonging to our son Michael will stop just outside your door. He will take you and his infant self away from here, far from strife and worry... he has come to take you home," explained the recently alighted Rosemary.

Just before the car door was opened by a tall ginger-bearded man, who would compel his mother to release the driver from her grasp and to be calm, the two women shuffled sideways along the bench seat to move closer to each other.

They happily exchanged a lingering half-smile before the visiting Rosemary who first became transparent, then almost invisible before she finally... disappeared.

***

Ten years plus one decade passed by in the blinking of an eye...

Rosemary, now retired, had completed her internship and had gone on to be a well thought of surgeon. Mick had grown into a fine young man.

He too made plans to enter the medical profession; working as a bar tender during college mid-term breaks helped contribute to the hefty fees involved. Although, unbeknownst to Mick Flannery, Rosemary had banked a considerable sum of money many years ago, this made possible by cashing in a large bag of gold that her son had, with the kindness of his heart, handed to her along with the keys to a car and their new home.

Mick had just finished his shift at the local bar and returned home to his mother's cottage in the mountains to study for final exams. Rosemary was sitting in the same rocking chair that had warmly received her so many years ago, as she welcomed her son with a smile, beckoning him to come join her by the panoramic view.

"All these years later, after my former self had rescued us and left me here to grow... to live a life, I could not have expected to be sitting here, gazing upon this view with you and... considering I was an infant at that time, strangely, I do remember him," the son commented, without turning away from looking out into the beyond.

"Perhaps you and he are one and the same. Maybe I and the former Rosemary also share existences; all members of that crew had, not so much as a parallel life but a consciousness that decided to rewrite the past so that our futures connected and merged into a happier place. We were... we are, ten plus one; ten souls with one more chance at life," mused Rosemary, also refraining from looking away from the view.

Mother and son sat and enjoyed the night sky from Rosemary's window. The Sun had departed and the Moon shone its light upon their smiling faces. They enjoyed the spectacle of a meteor shower and as they paused to exchange a lingering half-smile, a knowing look in each other's eyes confirmed in their hearts that their circle was broken, that they truly were home.

***

A scroll through time…

All nine members of the crew were initially oblivious to the presence of a tenth passenger. A hopeful child had not only left a message to guide them but was intrinsic in assuring their safe arrival. She had ensured that they would be discovered.

That discovery would enable them all to achieve a life fulfilled by having a second chance, a life plus one more; a more settled, content and happy one. She too would also attain a second chance at happiness; together they were ten plus one. Initially, Elpida had warmed to Amatheia what with them sharing similar childhoods but she also had a fondness for Sam. He had seen a keen intellect in the Oikian child and enjoyed imparting his knowledge and life experiences to her. When the rest of the crew had first left Polar Neridia, Elpida had decided she wanted to explore a different life, she wanted to find out about her origins.

A question buried deep within her needed to be answered and so although she had continued being tutored by Sam, she drifted, bit by bit, away from the others. When the exodus left the dying planet, some ventured on in the hope of a new life on Earth while others took their chances of stasis-hopping deeper into space with the hope of finding a new home elsewhere. Elpida had eagerly boarded one of the convoys with nothing more than a backpack containing a parting gift from Sam... an emotional time travel device.

Elpida had hatched a plan to deliver Amatheia, Sam and all of her new friends into the hands of the Kolassians. This was not to betray her rescuers but to place them at the nearest point from Polar Neridia that would facilitate the greatest source of emotion; enabling their travelling to each plus one scenario.

Her choice of destination was a Kolassian outpost where some of the Kolassian High Command based themselves. It seemed inevitable that Kol would only lead them to a negative outcome, he had become too much of a loose cannon and they needed a back-up plan. They had also chosen to build the station as it was now becoming increasingly evident that their planet's demise was going to become inescapable. Also, it was no coincidence that *Probe National Space Exploration* shared the same initials as Rosemary's father's project. *Polar Neridia Second Earth* was something he had conceptualised and although it had originally been conceived with good intentions, Tom's bosses had other plans.

Earth's days also seemed potentially numbered with the rapid degeneration of climate but the truth was that Polar Neridia was in worse shape. Tom's superiors had decided to exploit the natives of southern Polar Neridia with the assistance of the northern inhabitants, known as Kolassians, in exchange for a sharing of Earth's resources. It was an unfortunate series of events that led Tom being one of the first humans to set eyes upon a Polar Neridian. Two in fact, a male and female, both Oikians from the southern pole. They were taken while their daughter, Elpida, had been left behind to be imprisoned in a facility at the edge of the Stygian Forest.

Elpida's parents were to be the very first Oikians the Kolassians had surrendered for experimentation and analysis; after several days of torturous examination, they were to be disposed of and the appalling task was forced upon Rosemary's father. It was a shameful secret that weighed heavily upon the former PNSE engineer, but Tom's only choice was either to press the button that would finish Elpida's parents or have the threat made against his own family carried out in front of his eyes. Through kind conversations with Sam, many years later, Elpida had learned of her mother's and father's fate.

The moment before her parents' passing would be her emotional-time-travel destination. Being stowed away on the craft was necessary because she feared knowledge of her presence would alert Sam to her plan and Sam didn't often see eye-to-eye with Elpida's point of view.

Sam, although a far from inexperienced time traveller, was protective of the young Oikian and worried that such journeying would take its toll on the child and that she may end up injured or worse in any attempt at rescuing her parents.

Elpida had become adept at stealthily following and observing her friends. She knew that she must provide them with directions to her chosen destination. She was also aware that the bond they shared would mean never leaving anyone behind. On one of her explorations she had obtained some headed paper from Probe National Space Exploration. It was onto which, she scratched out a map and co-ordinates before waterproofing the scroll. Where, when and who to trust the scroll with was freely facilitated by Kyle's predicament.

Arriving in the tower, Elpida recognised Kyle's shoes gathering dust beneath his cocooned figure. She had to place the scroll somewhere not easily detected by the Kolassians and not left behind by Kyle's family and friends. She managed to tear away a small section of the cocoon at the sole of Kyle's left foot. A small incision allowed Elpida to plant the scroll before leaving for her planned stowing away.

Moments before the reservoir tower exploded and extruded out above the water, Elpida had held tightly onto her time travel device and willed herself onto the hovering craft nearby. She would stay hidden within the cargo bay, only emerging to feed at night and to keep a watchful eye on progress. Ensuring her friends would discover the implanted directions, she would then keep them on course to the little scroll's co-ordinates and towards their collective happiness.

Even though mayhem played out above her stowed away position, Elpida was confident that her friends would find their way to their hearts' desires. It was also time for her own plus one, her chance of rectifying and redirecting her own path in life. She squeezed the device with all her might and returned to a point in time where she would have the chance of choosing a much happier direction. It would be a moment in time belonging to someone else she would have to gate crash. Elpida was an orphan who, because of too big an emotional disconnect from parents she never really knew, could not focus on a moment where she would be able to intervene in the fate of her birth parents. Her longing heart had to decide upon another family.

***

Elpida finds herself landing softly upon a glass bead shore. Remembering fondly when she once made a necklace from the colourful stones, her hologram strengthened and then her emotions cast it away along with the spent device. Crouching down, she paused a while to form a little mound of stones, comprising of many colours; counting each one in turn as they increased the height of the pile. Elpida had counted up to forty-five when her concentration was interrupted; she saw Amatheia walk towards three figures further along the beach. As older Amatheia's hologram was fading away and her younger version had accepted the parting gift of a white floppy hat, Elpida made her presence known.

Both young Amatheia and Elpida now shared a similar age and a lingering half-smile with the older Amatheia as she disappeared. Elpida had broken her circle and left, with her soon to be adoptive family, towards a new future and home.

***

Kyle had fought off the Kolassians long enough for his family and friends to depart the craft. Unfortunately, his stamina had waned as the number of guards piling on top of him increased. Content in the fact that everyone had escaped, Kyle decided to bide his time and conserve his energy. Relinquishing control of his destiny, for now, he surrendered his body to the Kolassian guards and they carted him off easily without any further strife or strain.

Somewhere between leaving his own craft and entering the lower decks of the colossus hovering above, Kyle lost all consciousness.

When he comes around, Kyle finds himself stretched out on a lab table and covered in an icy shroud. Beneath the frosted cloak he can see the pulsating lights of the emotional time travel device which he had refused to give up and the Kolassians could not withdraw from his right hand's steadfast grip. He managed to free his left hand and as he was attempting to hold the device with both hands in order to leave for his plus one, a waterfall of bony hands descended upon his body.

For what seemed like endless minutes, they scratched and clawed about his face as the device and his emotions began to thaw the ice covering. His intended departure had been interrupted and he found himself in a struggle for his life yet again. Managing to first loosen, then free himself, from the grip of one Kolassian and head-butting another, Kyle ran to the lift.

He made his way back down onto the bridge of his ship where he set the propulsion controls so the engines roared into overdrive. Still coupled with the Kolassians' leviathan craft above, this set in motion the destruction of both vessels. Everything and everyone aboard would soon expire into the vacuum of space, apart from Kyle whose holographic blur vacated moments before the torrent of fire. A series of loud booms preceded the end of both crafts and the Kolassian High Command aboard.

Kyle was catapulted mega distances in moments. However, the sensation of rapid motion did not cease upon arrival at his destination.

He found himself descending speedily and upon landing on the top of a rocky outcrop, he viewed another version of himself clinging onto a mossy ledge below.

Is this version of me falling yet again? Will he reach his next birthday... counting down... no, racing towards the big five-O. I must help myself return to my family... I will not allow the same series of events to unfold again..., thought Kyle, reassuring himself.

Something compelled Kyle to not give up, an inner determination to go full circle, yet maybe break that circle in the process, had brought his spirit to the surface. His predicament was halted when a hand reached down to pull him up to safety.

Looking straight ahead, Kyle realises he is staring at another version of himself in holographic form; gradually strengthening into physicality before him.

Kyle's doppelganger points to something black and red, partially hidden by thick gorse bushes nearby; his mountain bike was scratched and scuffed but still fully functional. The two Kyles exchange a lingering half-smile as the newly arrived Kyle hands the bike to the other before beginning to fade from this existence. As the last trace of one Kyle dissipates, the other can distinctly hear his own voice resonate, as it trails away, telling him to...

"Turn around Kyle, go home!"

Kyle throws his leg over the saddle and makes his way, not towards the co-ordinates previously taped to the bike, but in the direction of the reservoir. This time he pauses at the upper lake's rear gate. Dismounting and then sitting on an old stone wall, he looks across at the bridge under which his once-upon-a-time friend's harmonica would often echo blues filled maladies. A passing reservoir gamekeeper, bearing an uncanny resemblance to his deceased friend, tips his hat as he bids him good morning.

The brief interaction breaks Kyle's nostalgic trance and he continues onwards. This time he decides not to go through the reservoir grounds but instead peddles hard up the steep incline of *'Long Tall Sally'*.

After reaching the summit, he pauses again briefly to enjoy the view before freewheeling back down towards being reunited with his family. Just before the twists and turns of the road remove him from sight, a cylindrical object, still in his possession, peaks out from the top of his back pocket.

Kyle stopped at the end of the street, deciding to walk the last short stretch towards his house. Arriving at the driveway, he could hear the heart-warming sound of his children laughing and playing joyfully behind the wall. Leaving his bike at the side of the family home, he opened a gate which led into the back garden.

Crystal stood and cried and stood and laughed, then cried and laughed a little more; the release of emotion being the result of knowing that they were finally back together as a family. After a long group hug, Saoirse and Ellen peeled away from their parents embrace; ecstatic to be reunited in play with their loving pet, Mister Waggles.

Feeling the need for contemplation, Kyle removed himself from the frolics and sat in a corner of the garden; enjoying from a distance, the view of his family being safe and happy together again. He sat there, in the same spot, amongst the scent of lavender and rosemary, beneath the consoling arms of a weeping willow for the rest of the day.

A sadness had descended over him and while it did not overly concern him, he was confused as to why this emotion was beginning to override that of the happiness he should be feeling. Perhaps the essence of missed friends was brought to the fore; memories were triggered by and thoughts caught up in the garden's bouquet, which had overwhelmed him slightly.

The Sun had set as birdsong quietened and Crystal brought a weary Ellen to bed. Saoirse wandered over and sat down beside her father. They sat in silence for a while, staring upwards past the tips of conifers brushing the edge of a sky turning gradually from indigo to charcoal.

Kyle's gaze was drawn momentarily to look upon Saoirse as she was lost in fascination at shooting stars skipping across the Milky Way. It was curious to Kyle that even though his eldest daughter had returned to her original age, after all the transformations and transitions, there was something new; a different look, a knowing, evident in her eyes.

"Dad, you know the way some people say a shooting star is a star that has just died... but you told me before that it's a meteor and not a star at all? What about when a star does... die? You once said that a star may already be dead but we can still see its light in the sky. How can something so pretty be gone but not gone?

"I do not want Mum, Ellen, Mister Waggles or you to ever be gone. What if we travelled far away and I got lost again? What if I die in one part of the Universe and you in another?" Saoirse's brow and mind gradually became more furrowed and heavy with worry as she contemplated their existence.

"Do not dwell on such things, time and place will be of no importance and distance will not matter. When we leave this life, we will not need the help of emotional time travel devices to journey where our hearts feel they want to be; we will already be there. Just by thinking it, it will be... we will be... home," assured Kyle, bidding his eldest daughter good night as she disappeared into the house.

He calmly sat and pondered the sky for a while longer. Just where it appeared its darkest, an area almost devoid of stars, Kyle thought he saw a neon spiral beginning to emerge and beckon for his attention. He pulled the still working time travel mechanism out of his back pocket. Looking from the device to the sky and back again, he began to contemplate... for a moment... if he had another journey in him. Paused in speculation, he was drawn to yet dismissed any further thoughts of starlight travel.

Reaching for a nearby rock, he raised it high above the device with the intention of rendering it broken forever. Then deciding against an act of destruction, in case his circle ever needed to be unbroken, he dropped the rock to the ground and carefully put the contraption back into his pocket before also disappearing inside.

The last Polar Neridian drifted off to sleep and perhaps dream of travels to the beyond of beyond, far from home.

ABOUT THE AUTHOR

Clive Parkinson lives in Dublin, Ireland. Becoming an author has been his main focus in recent times, while still retaining a passion for graphic design and visual communication.

You will probably find him at his desk writing, or working on his latest design project. If not, he will more than likely be found hiking up the side of a mountain; *allowing his mind to travel in any direction* in preparation for his next book.

A Broken Circle is his first novel.

Printed in Great Britain
by Amazon

45193074R00202